AETERNUM

VINCULA REALM BOOK II

JAMIE APPLEGATE HUNTER

MG PUBLISHING LLC

COPYRIGHT

Cover design: BooksandMoods.com

Aeternum
Vincula Realm Book II

A Realms of the Aether novel
Copyright © 2023 MG PUBLISHING LLC

DEDICATION

To Jimmy Allison
For teaching me how to hustle college boys out of their
dollar bills with a few dice and a box.
I'll meet you in the aether one day.

WORLD GUIDE

<u>Realms:</u>

Erdikoa
- The light realm
- Ruled by the Lux King
- Consists of a sprawling city and The Capital
- The Capital contains the Lux Palace and other Crown sanctioned facilities
- The Capital was enchanted by the *Seraphim* so that any mystic other than the royals would lose their memory upon leaving; once they return, their memory of their time in The Capital is returned for the duration of their stay
- Normal days and nights
- Powered by the essence, or magical power that gives mystics their abilities, of the inmates in Vincula

Vincula
- The dark realm (or prison realm)
- Ruled by the Umbra King

- Has no essence other than the *Royal* quarters, powered by the Umbra King's essence
- When inmates arrive, they lose their abilities, as their essence is used to power Erdikoa
- Inmates are immortal and unchanging while in Vincula
- A large town with normal things imported from Erdikoa
- Inmates not residing in the palace live in a large apartment building with their own apartments
- Vincula's "days" are equivalent to dusk in Erdikoa
- During Vincula's night, there is no moon and no stars —Once a month on the Plenilune (the full moon in Erdikoa) they can see the moon and stars
- Enchanted by the *Seraphim* so that when inmates leave, they lose all memories of their time spent in the prison realm

Aether
- Where the *Seraphim* live, and where good souls go when they die

Hell
- Created by different *Seraphim*
- Open to all realms regardless of who created them
- Ruled by the *Seraph*, Orcus
- Where wicked souls go when they die

...

<u>Mystics:</u>

Mystic type and abilities are not hereditary.
For example:
The heroine is a *Fey*, her sister is a *Shifter*, her mother is a
Sibyl, and her father is a *Sylph*.
All mystics have an identifying mark behind their ear.

Aatxe

- Gentle souls
  - Big in stature with small, bull-like horns on top of their heads
  - The only mystics allowed to be enforcers, due to their pure nature

...

Aeternum

(They have the mark of whatever mystic they were born as)
- a *Royal's* eternal mate
- They are born with grey-scale sight and will meet their

Royal mate by the time they are twenty-five years old

● Once they have skin-to-skin contact with their *Royal* mate, their grey-scale sight lifts

● When the mates sleep together, their bond is solidified, and once they marry, the *Aeternum* becomes immortal

● When both mates are of age, they share a soulscape (dream) when they are asleep at the same time, but until they solidify their bond, they will not remember the soulscape

● When one mate is in danger, the other has a vision through their eyes

● Once married, they share a mark on their right palm

...

Alchemists

● The only mystics able to create potions and perform spells

...

Angels

(No Mystic Mark)

- Wings
- Can shapeshift between several forms
- Originate from the Aether, and their exact powers are unknown

...

Eidolons

- Also known as phantoms
- Can walk through any non-living object except iron

...

Fey

- Have regular-sized ears with a slight point
- Stronger and faster than other mystics
- Graceful and light on their feet
- Can see the souls of others through skin-to-skin contact

...

Merrow

- Soul stealers
- They capture the dead's souls in a jar
- They absorb the souls to heal injuries or prolong their lives
- All merrows must take a potion monthly to bind their abilities
- The potion lasts two months, but they are required to take it every month in the event they try to skip, giving enforcers time to find them

...

...

...

Munin

- Can manipulate memories
- Anti-social and do not like to spend time with other mystics other than fellow *Munin*
- Most live in a compound on the outskirts of the city (by choice)

...

Royal
(No mystic mark)

- Rulers of the realms
- *The Lux King/Queen* – rules Erdikoa and controls light
- *The Umbra King/Queen* – rules Vincula and controls darkness/shadows
- *The Scales of Justice* – the final judge. Possesses the ability to see the souls of lesser mystics and the accused. When the Scales of Justice looks upon a criminal, they know the perfect punishment for their crime
- Have ears with a slight point like those of a Fey

...

Seraphim *(singular: **Seraph**)*
(No mystic mark)

- Creators of the realms
- Reside in the aether
- Celestial beings with three sets of wings: a large set on their back, a small set on their face, revealing only their eyes and mouths, and a set covering their legs

...

Shifter

- Every shifter can shift into one specific animal
- They do not have any animalistic qualities, even when shifted, other than their physical body when it shifts
- Shifts are fast, and when they shift back to their mystic form, they still have their clothes

...

...

Sibyl

- Oracles
- Once their abilities manifest, they see every potential future
- Their abilities begin to manifest in their 40s, and by 60, they take over fully

...

Sylph

- Can manipulate air

...

Visitant

- Control the moods through skin-to-skin contact

<u>Key Terms</u>

- enforcer – *police officer*
- essence – *magical power that gives mystics their abilities. It is the "essence" of their abilities*
- essenet – *internet*
- ES/essence screen - *television*
- legion – *the law enforcement of Vincula, made up of enforcers and two Angels*
- netsite – *website*
- soulscape — *a dream a Royal shares with their Aeternum when they are asleep at the same time. Before the Aeternum bond is solidified, they have no recollection of their dreams. After their bond is solidified, they only meet in the soulscape when separated, and when they wake up, they remember everything*

PRONUNCIATION GUIDE

REALMS

ERDIKOA
ER- DI-KO-UH
VINCULA
VING-KŌO-LUH
AETHER
Ā-THUR

MYSTICS

AATXE
(SOUNDS LIKE ATTIX)
ALCHEMIST
'ALKƏMƏST
EIDOLON
EE-DUH-LON
FEY
FĀ
MERROW
M-EH-R-OH
MUNIN
MOO-NIN
SIBYL
SIB-UHL
SERAPHIM (PLURAL)
SEH·RUH·FM
SHIFTER
'SHIFTƏR
SYLPH
SILF
VISITANT
VIZƏDƏNT

NAMES

AURORA (RORY)
AH-ROR-UH (ROR-EE)
DUME
DŌOM
KORDELIA (KORDIE)
KOR-DILL-YAH (KOR-DEE)
LENORA
LEH-NOOR-AH
CORA
KOR-UH
CAIUS
KAI-US
GEDEON
gID-EE-UHN
ATARAH
AET-AH-RAH
ADILA
AH-DEE-UH
TALLENT
TALƏNT
SAMYAZA
SAM-YAH-ZUH
ANASTASIA (STASSI)
AN-UH-STAH-SEE-UH (STAH-SEE)
JOPHIEL
JAH-FEEL
SERA
SEHR-UH
AEMAS
EE-MUS
LORA
LOR-UH

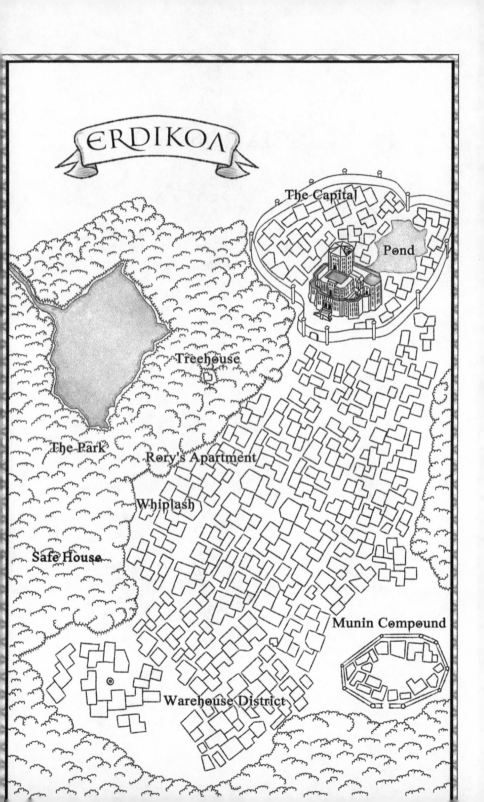

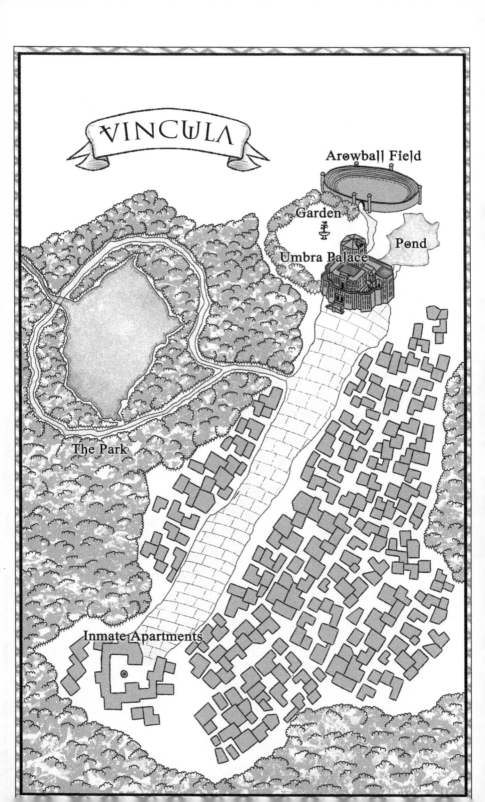

NOTE

Content warnings can be found on the last page.

CHAPTER 1

ERDIKOA

No one reconsiders their life choices until it's too late and the consequences are staring back at them with taunting smiles.

Rory wished she'd reconsidered her actions before they ruined her life, but she didn't. Now, here she was, on her hands and knees, as the cold from the concrete floor seeped into the hand holding her up.

She looked around the tiny room, trying to figure out where she was. The last thing she remembered was the Scales of Justice sentencing her to five-hundred years in Vincula, and then everything went black.

Was she in a holding cell in the prison realm?

In one of her hands, she clutched a book for dear life, and, upon further inspection, she was surprised to see it was one of Cora's favorites from when they were kids. She didn't remember bringing this with her to The Capital.

Sitting back on her heels, she surveyed the small room and covered her mouth to muffle a scream. Everything was in color. Plush red chairs lined one wall, and a brown wooden table sat between them.

The door to the room flew open, and Rory scrambled to her feet. A woman with white-streaked hair stepped inside and looked at Rory with a tinge of sadness.

"Hello, Aurora Raven. Welcome back to Erdikoa."

"Welcome back?" Rory squeaked. "It's been five-hundred years?"

The woman shook her head. "Somehow, your sentence ended early. It's been three months."

Rory's jaw dropped to the ground, elated to be home but terrified to see her friends and family again. Would they hate her? Either way, it was a miracle.

Rory stared at the woman with her mouth still open. She heard what was said, but understanding the information was proving to be difficult. "What?"

"Your sentence is over," the woman said slowly, as if talking to a child. "We will process your release and take you home."

Rory trembled as her brain tried to process not only her early release but the colors bursting around her.

"I can see color," she blurted, not caring if she sounded insane.

The woman's face softened with something akin to sadness. *Strange.* "Yes," she confirmed. "Your grey-scale sight lifted during your time in Vincula."

With the exception of souls, she'd only ever seen in shades of black, grey, and white, and now her realm was overwhelmingly bright. Her soul whispered the names of colors she'd never seen before, and it was too much to take in at once.

The book in her hand dropped to the floor when she

pressed her fists to her eyes. "What is happening?" Her voice was edging on hysterical, but she didn't care.

A gentle hand landed on her shoulder, and Rory cracked open an eye.

"I know this is a lot, Rory, but we need to get you processed and out of The Capital as quickly as possible."

Rory's brow furrowed. How did this woman know her nickname? "Who are you?"

The woman's eyebrow arched as a smirk played on her lips. "Lauren. I'm having clothes brought in for you to wear home," she added, motioning to the pajamas Rory wore. "And you'll need to drink a shapeshifting potion. No one, other than myself and another guard, is aware of your return, and we need to keep it that way."

Rory stiffened. "Was I released illegally?" Something itched at the back of her mind, telling her she was missing something.

Lauren snorted. "No, but the early release of The Butcher will not be well received."

It wouldn't. She'd have to face her parents and friends *if they agreed to see her.* The thought of their disgust and rejection ripped her wide open, and she covered her mouth to swallow a sob.

Lauren glanced at her over her shoulder and hardened her gaze. "You are not a weak little lamb being led to slaughter. Stop crying."

Rory's mind had the same itching feeling. Lauren's words felt familiar, but she couldn't place why. She eyed the woman again, wondering if they'd met before she was arrested.

There was one hard knock on the door before it busted

open, and the largest man she'd ever seen walked inside. *What did they feed this guy?*

The man had severe features and light blonde shoulder-length hair. She was sure the t-shirt he wore was seconds away from ripping as it stretched across his enormous chest.

She hadn't realized she was gawking until he said, "Close your mouth and put these on."

Her eyes ticked from his face to his outstretched hand, and she tentatively took the bundle of clothes. "You don't have to be so rude about it," she mumbled under her breath.

"I was not rude," he stated, and her head snapped up. *Did he have supermystic hearing?* "Drink this." He held out a bottle, and Rory shuddered.

"Who will it turn me into?" she asked, staring at the bottle.

When he didn't answer, she begrudgingly accepted it and took it like a shot. *Don't gag. Don't gag. Don't gag.*

She gagged.

After handing it back to him, he didn't leave.

"Are you going to watch me change?" She looked at him, trying not to laugh, when he narrowed his eyes and left. "Who was that?" she asked Lauren.

"That," Lauren said, her face alight with amusement, "was Sam, and yes, he's always blunt. You get used to it."

Why would she get used to it? Rory straightened. "Am I going to be monitored?"

"Yes," Lauren replied. "Sam and I will rotate." Seeing Rory's disbelieving expression, she added, "It's for your safety. As I said earlier, the public will not take kindly to your release. We're hoping to prevent them from finding out at all costs."

"Why?" Rory's suspicion peaked. "Why don't you hate me, too?"

Lauren pointed to the clothes still clutched in Rory's hands. "Get dressed. You would not have been spared from hell and released early if you were the villain they've made you out to be, but if you want me to be a bitch, I will happily oblige."

Rory grumbled under her breath as she ripped the pajamas from her body and pulled on the jeans, t-shirt, and black cap. She expected the clothes to sag on her straight frame, but they didn't. "They fit perfectly."

"All of your information was documented during your stay in Vincula," Lauren replied and stepped into the hall to grab something. "Here."

Rory took the socks and sneakers from Lauren's outstretched hand and pulled them on. Her mind was reeling as she tried to process what was happening.

She was missing three months of memories.

They released her early from Vincula.

She would be followed by a scary woman or an ornery giant for an undisclosed amount of time.

Nothing stressful about that at all.

"Won't you two being with me every second of the day look suspicious?" She looked up to find Lauren examining her nails as though babysitting a serial killer was just another day on the job.

Maybe it was.

"Why would people not think we were friends or dating?" Lauren countered.

"Point taken." Rory chortled. "But my apartment is small, and there are no extra bedrooms." The thought of seeing her mother, Lenora, made her chest ache.

When she glanced at Lauren, the woman looked at her with pity, and Rory was immediately suspicious. Before she could ask what was wrong, Sam opened the door with a frown.

"What is taking so long?" he demanded and stomped into the room. "Do you not remember how to get dressed on your own?"

Rory bristled and motioned to her body. "I dressed myself just fine."

"We need to leave," he said, more to Lauren than Rory. "It is not yet daybreak, and the streets are empty, save for a few workers."

"The potion hasn't shifted me yet," Rory pointed out, gesturing to her unchanged body, but when they looked at her, something on their faces told her to find a mirror. "What do I look like?"

They ignored her and discussed leaving, and as Rory continued to look around, her gaze snagged on the book lying on the floor. It bothered her that she didn't remember taking it to Vincula, but she pushed the mystery aside and picked it up. Returning her attention to the two guards, she sighed and followed them into the hall, wondering what awaited her on the outside.

～

They ushered her into the dark night toward a black SUV with tinted windows. If they wanted it to look inconspicuous, they failed.

Once they piled into the vehicle and drove to The Capital gates, Rory held her breath. Usually, they made everyone get out, hand over their mystic cards, and take a truth potion to ensure nothing was being snuck out, but when Sam jumped out and spoke with one of the *Aatxe* working the gates, the guard nodded and stepped back.

Sam climbed back behind the wheel and waited. "Who are you?" Rory demanded as he drove through, but before he answered, the magic surrounding The Capital perimeter washed over her.

She jerked in her seat, looking around frantically. *Where was Dume, and why wasn't she in the transfer van?*

She grappled for an explanation, but the bursting colors around her made her gasp and cover her mouth. Two people sat in the front seat, and the woman with white-streaked hair turned around.

"Shit," she cursed when she saw Rory's frightened state.

"Am I being taken to the Scales of Justice for judgment?" Rory choked out.

The man's gaze caught hers in the rearview mirror. "I forget the gates erase their memories," he said to his companion, looking at Rory again. "Listen closely because you have already been told once."

Rory looked behind her. The Capital gates grew smaller as they drove away. "What is going on? Who are you two?"

The woman sighed. "I'm Lauren. This is Sam, and you have been released from Vincula early. It's been three months. The last you remember is being transported to The Capital, correct?" Rory nodded dumbly, and Lauren continued. "Because of the magic surrounding The Capital, you don't remember, but you were sentenced to five-hundred years in Vincula, released early after three months, and now we are taking you to your new home."

The magic surrounding The Capital made it so that when you left, you forgot everything that happened there, as did the magic in Vincula, but when you returned, you remembered everything. It irked her she'd lost her memory twice.

Wait. Sentenced to five-hundred years and released early? "What did you say?"

Sam glowered at her through the mirror. "Are you having trouble understanding or hearing?"

Rory narrowed her eyes at him. "Excuse me if I'm having a hard time grasping the fact that I have somehow come back from Vincula four-hundred and ninety-nine years early." She motioned wildly to her surroundings. "Or that everything is in color."

Her chest heaved as she fumbled with the safety belt pinning her to the seat. It was too tight, and the vehicle was too small. She needed out.

"She's taking this worse than she did the first time," Lauren remarked. "Calm down, Rory. Yes, your sentence ended early, and yes, your grey-scale sight lifted when you were in Vincula." Lauren spoke as though she was explaining the weather forecast for the week.

"What the fuck?" Rory breathed, unable to form a sentence more complex than that.

Lauren undid her safety belt and twisted all the way around. "We're driving you to a safe house. You need to keep yourself hidden."

"If this is supposed to clarify things, it isn't working," Rory grumbled.

"You used to be smarter than this," Sam grumbled, shaking his head. "No one other than us and your next of kin knows you have been released."

Rory's shoulders tightened at his sharp tone, and Lauren noticed, silencing him with a scathing look. "What he means is that it would be in your best interest if the citizens of Erdikoa didn't know you've been released. Believe it or not, not everyone is a fan of mystics being slaughtered like cattle."

Rory's cheeks heated, but something Lauren said caught her attention. "You told my parents?"

Lauren turned back around. "Yes."

The leather seat creaked beneath Rory as she slumped down. "No one will be there waiting for me, but I need to ensure my mother is taken care of." When she moved, a book slid off her lap and onto the floorboard. Why did she have a book? She leaned forward to see what it was, but Lauren's words stopped her.

"Don't be so sure they won't come."

Would her parents be there? Would her friends?

She blew out a long breath. *Doubtful.*

The look on Dume's face when he arrested her was seared into her brain.

No, she would spend her days alone, and with no loved ones to disappoint, she would hide from the masses and resume her search for Bane. The *Seraphim* gave her another chance to avenge her sister, and she wouldn't waste it.

CHAPTER 2

After what felt like the longest drive of her life, Sam pulled into a long driveway lined with trees. "What part of Erdikoa are we in?"

Sam parked in front of a house, and he and Lauren exited the car without answering. Rory fumbled with the door handle before scrambling out after them. When her feet were on solid ground, she craned her neck to look at the large log cabin nestled amongst the trees, secluded from everything nearby.

The greenery jumped out at her, and when she spotted bright yellow flowers at the base of the porch, her mouth parted in awe. She'd been so caught up in what happened that she hadn't taken time to admire the vivid colors of the realm.

Her eyes ate up the scenery, from the deep-orangish hue of the logs to the blue of the sky. "Wow."

The front door banged open, and a figure she'd recognize anywhere stepped out. Dume's eyes met hers, and Rory almost fell to her knees. *He came.*

A look of confusion crossed his face, and he turned to her guards angrily. *No,* she almost cried. His face made it clear he didn't know about her arrival.

"Who is this?" he demanded. Only a few times in her life had she seen him this mad, and it made her stomach drop.

"It's Rory," Lauren replied. "We gave her a shapeshifting potion to conceal her face. It will wear off in another half hour."

Rory ran to look in the side mirror of the SUV. A face that wasn't her own stared back at her, and she ran her hands over the unfamiliar features.

When she turned back to the others, Dume pounded down the stairs. His muscular arms banded around her, almost knocking her over, and her emotions toggled between relief and guilt. She'd put them through hell.

His blinding soul engulfed her, and she had never been happier to temporarily lose her eyesight in all her life.

He pulled back. "I missed you."

Sniffling, she looked at him, confused, before realization hit her. *Was she supposed to say it back?* To her, they saw each other only an hour or two ago, but to him, it'd been three months.

"I need to see my little girl," a familiar voice said from behind them, making Rory's breath hitch.

Dume stepped aside, and there stood the man she'd known longer than anyone else. Grey streaks peppered his dark hair, and his grey eyes had dulled with age. The golden hue of his skin was beautiful against his green shirt, and Rory couldn't get to him fast enough.

Her father, Patrick, was a tall man, but she threw her arms around his neck anyway, needing the comfort only he could give. His emerald soul surrounded her as he rubbed a hand over her hair like her mother used to do.

When she pulled back and looked around, her heart dropped. "Mom didn't come."

"You didn't tell her?" Dume boomed, making Rory jump, and when she spun around, he was glaring daggers at Sam and Lauren.

"Tell me what?" she demanded.

Sam crossed his arms and stared at Dume without shame, while Lauren had the decency to look remorseful.

"We thought it would be better if she heard it from one of you," Lauren explained. "She doesn't know us."

Dume looked furious. "You said you were close—"

"We had to explain her early release to her *twice*," Sam said, cutting Dume off. "Once when she arrived, and again when we left The Capital gates. You know better than anyone how the memory magic works."

"Someone tell me what the fuck is going on!" Rory shouted, her emotions so out of sorts that she wasn't sure if she was angry or scared.

Her father's hand landed on her upper back as he walked around to face her. "Your mother saw something," he began, and Rory's chest tightened. She didn't need to ask what he meant. *The prophecy.* "Once you were arrested, she chanted more than usual on her bad days, but on her good days—" His weary eyes slid to Dume.

Panic clawed its way across Rory's skin, leaving tiny pinpricks in its wake. "On her good days, she what?"

"She became obsessed with getting to you," Dume answered ruefully.

"What does that mean?" Rory tried to make sense of what they were saying, but too much information was thrown at her in the last hour. "Trying to get to me? I was in Vincula. She would understand that during her good days."

Her father sighed. "She tried to get herself arrested."

Rory covered her mouth to muffle a strangled cry.

"Whichever of us was with her always stopped her," her father continued. "But she had more and more good days."

Her abilities were retreating? How was that possible?

"Keith stayed with her one night, and in the early morning hours before he woke, she snuck out." Dume looked apologetic, as if it was any of their faults. "She'd never woken earlier than any of us before, and we didn't think to put any safeguards to alert us if she tried to leave."

Rory needed to hear the rest, no matter how painful. This was her fault. "Then what happened?"

Dume and Patrick shared a loaded look. "She waited until one of the local banks opened and tried to rob it."

"What?" Rory asked and staggered back a step. "And she was arrested," she concluded, earning a single nod from Dume. "This is all my fault." Her voice broke.

"No, sport, it's not," her father said, wrapping an arm around her shoulders. "Your mother is a grown woman. By stopping her, we only prolonged the inevitable."

She pushed him away. "She wouldn't be in Vincula if it weren't for me," she cried, jabbing a finger into her own chest. "I killed by my own free will, and I am every bit the monster they say I am." She ripped the cap from her head and threw it. "She predicted this. '*Darkness is poison,*'" Rory recited. "She tried to warn me, but I wouldn't stop."

She sank to her knees with her head in her hands as sobs racked her body.

"*His* darkness," Sam's deep voice said from the porch.

Rory lifted her head. "What?"

"You said, '*Darkness is poison*,' but the prophecy states, '*his* darkness is poison.' It could not have been you to which she was referring." He looked bored, and she wished she'd thrown her hat at him instead of the ground.

"How do you know about the prophecy?" she asked.

Lauren jumped off the porch, careened around Dume toward Rory, and hauled her up. "Your mother's incarceration is not your fault. She made her own choices."

Rory's pain morphed into anger. "What the fuck is wrong with everyone here?" she shouted as she looked from her father to Dume. "Why are you even here? You know the fucked up, horrible shit I've done. At least Keith and Kordie had the good sense to stay away." She'd tried to ignore their absence because she understood. It still hurt.

"We wouldn't let them come," Dume said instead of answering her.

Rory swiped at her face. "What?"

Dume rubbed the hair between his tiny horns. "What can I say to make you understand that we all love you? None of your victims were innocent." *How would they know?* "People have been coming forward," he continued, seeing the unasked question in her eyes. "Nine people said you saved them from a person you killed."

Rory's breath caught in her throat. "It doesn't matter. My actions were horrendous."

"It does matter," Sam said, surprising everyone. Rory couldn't bring herself to meet their gazes as shame settled heavy in her gut. "You sent dangerous people to hell. They would have ended up there, eventually." He paused. "Or they would have hurt more people."

What would they think of her if they knew she enjoyed it? It's true; she would never kill an innocent, but hearing her victims beg for their lives was music to her ears, and seeing their black souls dissolve made her feel lighter than anything she'd ever experienced. Sure, guilt pricked her soul momentarily afterward, but the act of killing the wicked was euphoric.

Her friends wouldn't understand. No one would.

"Your mother wouldn't have cared if your soul was black," her father said, and Rory scoffed. "You could have the blackest soul in the realm, and she still would have found her way to you."

Her father meant well, but his words made her guilt worse.

"Vincula is not the hell hole you think it is," Lauren said, earning her a death glare from Sam.

"What?" Rory and Dume asked in unison.

Lauren ignored Sam. "Vincula is not what they taught you in school. The scary tales of the prison realm are for deterrence. It's a functioning town, and the inmates are assigned their own apartments to live in. There are no barred cells." She paused when Sam said something to her under his breath. "I could go on." She jerked her head toward Sam. "But this guy will kill me if I continue. I assure you, she will want for nothing."

Other than Sam dragging Lauren away and whispering angrily, no one said a word. Rory watched the two guards exchange words, and judging by Sam's reaction, not only did Lauren tell the truth, but she also told highly classified information.

Lauren bitched Sam out, pointing from his hand to her arm, and Rory suppressed a smile. If he grabbed Lauren's arm again, he might lose a hand.

Sam stalked back to the porch. "We will show you your

new living quarters before I take my leave." Much to Rory's surprise, his face held no hostility when he spoke to her.

Lauren signaled for Rory to go first and then followed her up the stairs. "He's not normally like this," she whispered. "Blunt, yes, but never intentionally rude. He's upset and taking it out on everyone else."

"What is he upset about?" Rory asked against her better judgment. She shouldn't care.

Lauren sighed and shook her head. "Nothing I can discuss with you, but just know it cut him deeply, and I'm afraid he will never forgive the friend who wielded the knife."

Rory watched Sam's large back as he barked out information about the house, and her heart ached for him.

He turned to her with a scowl, his earlier expression gone. "Are you listening?"

And just like that, Sam could fuck off.

CHAPTER 3

The cabin was two levels and unnecessarily huge. The expansive main floor housed a formal dining area, large kitchen, living room, office, and powder room. The upstairs had four bedrooms, each with its own en suite.

Were they hiding a small army? The house looked homey, like someone lived there. "Who lives here?" Rory asked Sam, who was still brooding as he tromped through the house.

"It is a safe house. Why do you keep asking questions we have already answered?" The sharp tone he used was unnecessary.

She halted and grabbed him by the arm, forcing him to face her. "If you think I'm so vile, then reassign yourself. It's clear you have the power."

His shoulders slumped a fraction, and the uncharacteristic action startled her. "I do not think you are vile." He scrubbed a large hand over his face. "I apologize for taking my anger out on you."

She tried not to laugh at the pained expression on his face. You'd think he had never apologized in his entire life. "Forgiven."

His lips lifted into an almost smile before he turned and led her to the main level. Dume, her father, and Lauren sat around the large dining room table, arguing in a hushed whisper, but when Rory and Sam appeared in the doorway, they stopped abruptly.

"What's going on?" she asked, holding her breath. Another surprise might do her in.

"We're discussing living arrangements," Lauren replied and motioned between herself and Sam. "One of us must stay with you at all times."

"I thought I was free." She looked between the two strangers. "I understand following me during the day, but why do I need guards living with me?"

They traded a look that made her uneasy. "If people hear of your release, it will not be received well," Sam replied. "It is for your protection."

Rory popped a brow. "I killed fourteen people. I think I can handle myself."

Dume and Patrick blanched, but Lauren's mouth curled into a feline smile.

"The charges were for thirteen," Dume said with obvious unease.

Rory shifted uncomfortably. No one knew about the first victim she'd left dead in an alley. "That's what I meant."

Their silence cut her to the bone. They could say it didn't bother them all they wanted, but it did.

Sam's voice cut through the quiet. "Your protection is the most important thing. It is not up for debate. Lauren and I will take turns. There are plenty of bedrooms."

He left no room for argument, and she bit her tongue, deciding to pick her battles.

"We're staying here, too," Dume said, crossing his arms across his wide chest.

She whirled around to him and her father. "You can't do that. You both have jobs in the city."

The area was secluded enough that she knew the city wasn't within walking distance, and neither Dume nor her father had a vehicle.

Dume shrugged. "Patrick bought a truck, and we've agreed to switch out using it."

Her father was quiet, and Rory resisted the urge to glance his way. *Did he really want to stay?* As if reading her thoughts, he said, "I work the night shift now. I'll stay with you during the day, though I will sleep most of it."

The night shift? Her father was a vet, and veterinarians didn't have night shifts. She didn't want them altering their lives for her. "No."

They stared at her as she shook her head. "My return will not disrupt your lives. I have these two to protect me." She tipped her head to the two guards. "Besides, no one will know I've returned, remember?"

Dume opened his mouth to argue, but she held up a hand. "This is not up for debate. I'll still meet the group for drinks," she promised. "But we should probably choose a new spot."

Her father looked up with a stern expression. "Aurora Raven, I am staying here, and that's final."

Rory bit back a smile. Turning to Dume, she said, "I'd like to see Kordie and Keith soon." *If they really wanted to see her.* "Can you three pick a new spot? Preferably one where no one will recognize me."

"Many people lobbied for your release," Dume said. "Not everyone is afraid of you."

"What does that mean?" she asked cautiously. *Lobbied for her release?*

"Sera organizes protests," he said, smiling to himself. "And the other people you saved speak to anyone who will listen."

Rory licked her suddenly dry lips as she processed the information. Her eyes burned at the thought. "Who is Sera?"

"A person you saved," Sam said, making her jump a foot in the air. *How did someone that large move around that quietly?*

"Can you not yell?" she snipped over her shoulder. "Your voice sounds like a megaphone." He scowled at her. "You know this Sera person?"

"Sam showed up at Whiplash a couple of months back," Dume interjected. "Sera found us there, too, and demanded our help to clear your name."

Rory studied the behemoth beside her. "Why would you find my friends?"

His eyes flicked to Lauren before returning to her. "That is none of your concern."

"Bullshit," she bit out. "Tell me, or I will cut your hair in your sleep." Was the threat immature? *Yes.* Would she still do it? *Also, yes.*

Sam's jaw hardened. "I would like to see you try."

"Stop fighting, you two." Lauren butted in and then muttered, "Some things never change." She directed her next statement at Dume. "You need to keep holding the protests."

Rory turned to her. "Why? I'm free."

"No one can know you've been released," the guard reminded her. "If the protests stop, people will wonder why."

Rory threw her hands up. "I can't stay here twenty-four seven. I'll go crazy."

"We know," Lauren said, looking bored. "One of us will go with you."

Rory waved her hand over her face. "I'm pretty sure people will recognize me, and I refuse to take shapeshifting potions every time I leave the house. I can take care of myself, and if I can't, you two will be there."

"Wear a hat," Sam said flatly. "Everyone thinks The Butcher is in Vincula. Say you are a cousin."

Dume nodded. "He's right. Your sentence has been all anyone can talk about."

She blew out a long breath. "Fine."

"I'm hungry," Lauren said out of nowhere and pulled her phone from her pocket. "I'm ordering food."

"I can go pick it up," Patrick offered, standing.

Rory eyed Sam's large body. "Dume, you should go too. I think it'll take two grown men to carry it all."

Everyone sat around the table eating and catching Rory up on everything she'd missed over the past three months, but she barely heard them. Her mind raced, wondering why she was released early and obsessing over her missing memories.

Lauren insisted Vincula was not the horrid place everyone believed it to be. *Had Rory been happy there? Did she make friends, or was she ostracized?*

The black hole in her memory was unsettling and bothered her more than she wanted to admit to the others.

Lauren sat beside her, quieter than the other three, and after glancing at Rory, pushed her chair back and stood. "It's time for you to leave," she said to Dume. "Rory had a long day and needs to rest."

Rory looked at Lauren, silently thanking her. It was strange. She'd been gone for three months, but she didn't miss her friends. In her mind, she had seen them earlier that day, not three months ago, and it only added to her distress.

She was relieved they didn't hate her, but she needed space. Guilt nibbled at the edge of her mind. Her memory might be flawed, but theirs weren't. They dealt with her absence and the fallout of her crimes. *Were they mistreated for associating with her?*

Dume didn't argue, and he approached her with a big hug and whispered, "I'm glad you're home."

Home. She didn't feel at home. "Me too," she lied, hugging him back.

Her father patted her on the shoulder. "I'm headed to work. I figure you could use some time for yourself."

Rory hugged him. "Thank you for still loving me," she murmured.

"Your mother isn't the only one who loves you, no matter what." He kissed the top of her head and left.

"Can I speak with Rory privately?" Dume asked the two guards, who nodded and stepped outside.

Rory fought the urge to fidget. "Dume, I—"

"Don't," he cut in. "I don't need your apologies, but I owe you mine."

She swallowed past the lump in her throat, wondering what he had to apologize for.

"I should have known." His voice was pained, and she hated it. "I've known you almost my entire life, and I should have questioned your motives from the beginning. I couldn't believe you'd do something like that, and I kept telling myself it wasn't true."

Humiliation colored her cheeks because it *was* true.

"I know you, Rory, and I know you wouldn't kill someone without reason," he asserted. "That you actually had a reason never occurred to me until Sera."

"I never expected you to second guess my crimes," she replied. "No one looks at a serial killer and thinks they have rational thoughts, and even though I believe I did the realm a favor, it doesn't make my actions any less heinous."

"But I should have," he argued. "I should have known. I'm sorry."

She reached forward and placed a hand on his arm. "Don't; it will only make me feel worse."

"Keith thinks you're a supermystic, you know." Dume rolled his eyes, but his mouth curled into a half-smile.

Rory busted out laughing, and her chest warmed at the thought of her friend. "Keith is an idiot."

Dume's smile spread across his face. "That we can agree on. I'm going to let you rest, but I'll talk to you tomorrow."

Rory gave him one last hug and watched him leave. The moment he stepped through the door, Lauren and Sam filed back inside.

She sighed and forced a smile. "Take me to my cell, please. I'm beat."

Sam was closest to her, and his hand moved like he wanted to reach out. "I must leave, but I will return in a few days." He nodded briefly, not waiting for a reply, and left without a word.

Rory blinked, impressed with how fast he moved. "You'll get used to it," Lauren said, breaking her trance. "Come on. I'll show you your room."

CHAPTER 4

VINCULA

Lenora sat across from Caius, looking devastated. "Why did you do it?" she asked him. He'd expected more yelling or crying, but what he didn't expect was the poised calm she exuded.

It was on the tip of his tongue to blame her and her outbursts. If not for Lenora's actions, Rory wouldn't have felt the bone-deep guilt that crushed Caius as if it were his own.

But deep down, he knew it wasn't her fault. Had he been in her position, he would have done the same because Rory was worth fighting for. He would do whatever it took to bring her home, even if he had to rip the realms apart to do it.

Her last words pounded into him on a loop. *'I will find my way back to you.'*

"I asked you a question, young man," Lenora clipped, bringing him back to the present.

He chuckled. "Lenora, I have been around much longer than you."

"Don't take that tone with me," she scolded him. "Answer my question. Why did you send my daughter back to Erdikoa?"

The hurt in her eyes nearly killed him, and he knew he wouldn't tell her the truth. He wished he had never allowed Sam to tell Rory of her mother's behavior, and while he couldn't go back in time, he could protect Lenora from the same guilt.

"She missed her friends and family, and I couldn't bear to see her in pain." It was a half-truth.

Lenora studied him. "You love her?"

He nodded, not trusting himself to talk.

"And she loves you," Lenora stated with finality. "We have to get her back," she said sternly, switching from a grieving mother to a commander of a legion.

Caius' brows rose, and despite the hole in his chest, he smiled sadly. "She's a lot like you."

Lenora harrumphed and smoothed a wrinkle from her pants. "Of course, she is. Her father is a big puppy dog."

A laugh burst from Caius. "A gentle puppy dog she is not, but from what she's told me, Cora was."

Lenora nodded. "My girls were opposites on the surface, but not here," she said, patting her chest, just over her heart. "Despite what Rory believes, she is good."

"I know, and I told her as much, but—" He stopped to clear the emotion from his throat. "She won't remember the confidence she gained in herself while here, but maybe her soul will."

"When I first saw you and your brother, it was difficult

to tell you two apart," she confessed as she regarded him with keen eyes.

"I am nothing like Gedeon."

Lenora leaned forward and grabbed Caius' hand. "I know, honey." She gave his hand a pat and sat back. "Once my visions were clearer, it was obvious. That is why we must bring her home."

Caius studied the woman closely. *Bring her home.* Did she mean Rory's home here with him or in Erdikoa with her old friends and family?

He leaned back in his chair. "You didn't see how we do that in one of your visions, did you?" As a *Sibyl*, Lenora saw every potential future. In Erdikoa, her mind was muddled most of the time, but she didn't have her abilities in Vincula, allowing her clarity.

Lenora's eyes glassed over. "I must have, but when my mind is clear, the memories of my visions are patchy at best."

Caius' jaw tensed. "What do you remember? Your prophecy was vague, other than the part about us being identical twins."

The prophecy she'd had about Rory ran through his head on a loop. *Two were one, and one is yours. Do not let him fool you. His darkness is poison. Only the golden child can save you.*

Lenora rubbed her temple before sighing. "I don't remember much, but your brother will find her, and when he does, he will scar her for life. Or kill her."

Caius hadn't realized his hands gripped the arms of his chair until the wood splintered. "Over my dead fucking body."

Her head turned slowly toward him. "It will be."

The silence stretched between them as Caius used all his

self-restraint to tame the shadows threatening to destroy his office.

The door slammed open, and Sam stepped over the threshold with a menacing glare.

"Were you raised in the woods, boy? Don't slam doors," Lenora chided. Normally Caius would laugh, but he didn't feel like it today, or maybe ever again.

Caius could tell Sam was fond of the woman, and his submission was a sight to behold.

"Yes, Ms. Raven," Sam mumbled as he closed the door softly.

"Call me Lenora," she replied before turning back to Caius.

Sam stood next to the desk with a sour look on his face. "She is settled in the safe house. No one knows she is there, not even Adila."

"How did you manage that?" Caius mused.

"No other inmates were scheduled to arrive, and the bunker was empty. We gave her a shapeshifting potion to alter her face in the event anyone saw her leave," Sam replied. The thought of someone changing her beautiful face made Caius frown. "There will be speculation of why you have not made an appearance."

The same thought occurred to Caius. "Perhaps you should start a rumor among The Capital that I am refusing to leave Vincula." He tried to rub the tension from his forehead. "We need to keep her hidden until I can bring her back."

"How is she?" Lenora asked Sam.

The *Angel's* lips pressed into a thin line. "She remembers nothing." Caius deflated. He'd held on to hope that *Aeternums* were immune to the memory loss magic.

Sam turned to Lenora and looked... *nervous*. Whatever he had to say would devastate her. "She did not take the news of your incarceration well." His eyes tightened when they slid to Caius. "She feels guilty."

In trying to help her, Caius traded one hurt for another. He hated himself.

Lenora stared silently at the commander. "You tell her not to worry about me. I am better than I've been in years, and the only thing I want is her safety."

Sam gave a small nod and walked to his bench to take a seat. "Lauren told her Vincula was nice, and that eased her worry a fraction." He pulled an orange from his pocket and peeled it angrily. "We need to tell her everything."

"No," Caius snapped, his fury rising. "I am your king, and I'm telling you to not open your fucking mouth. The same goes for Lauren."

Lenora swatted his hand. "Watch your language." He yanked it back with an indignant look. She was a tough old bird.

"Give me one good reason we cannot tell her." Sam ripped into the orange like a wild beast. "Because not telling her is what put her in this position to begin with."

Caius wanted to flip his desk. "If you tell her and she believes you, nothing will stop her from going after Gedeon. *Nothing.*" He lost his battle with the shadows, and they swirled in the air.

Lenora looked around the room at the books and pictures falling to the ground. "Calm down." Her voice was stern, demanding his obedience. Closing his eyes, he concentrated on reigning in his outward emotions. He could do nothing about his inner turmoil, but he could control his reactions.

She leaned forward and patted his hand again. The gesture was motherly, and his eyes flicked to hers. If they met under different circumstances, would she like him? Would she approve of his marriage to Rory?

"Caius is right." She sighed. "Rory would have tried to avenge her sister, no matter the cost. Telling her should be a last resort unless we want her to be the one alerting Gedeon of her existence."

"You knew," Sam guessed.

Caius looked between the two. "Knew what?"

His friend smiled sadly at Rory's mother. "Do you want me to tell her?" Caius opened his mouth to protest, but Sam stopped him. "I will not tell her about Vincula, but I will tell her this."

"Tell her *what*?" Caius asked as his irritation grew.

Sam stayed silent, and Lenora sighed. "I was aware of her *hobby*." She lifted her chin defiantly, the action so much like Rory that the aching inside of Caius intensified. "I saw it, but I also knew she wouldn't stop, no matter what I said. And thank you, Sam, but I'll tell her myself."

Caius blinked. *What?* "She thinks you hate her," he whispered. "Why didn't you tell her? If only so that she knew you wouldn't think she was a monster."

Lenora's face transformed to one of fury, and he sat back. "Do you have any idea what it is like to wake up and a month has passed? I only had one day to spend with my family, and there wasn't a chance in the seven rings of hell I would waste it by telling my daughter I knew she was a murderer."

Caius and Sam wisely stayed quiet. If he only had a short time with his mate, he would also do whatever he could to make her happy, not upset her.

"I still do not understand why you did not marry her," Sam said, changing the subject. "She would have been immortal and able to switch between the realms once free."

He looked at Sam incredulously. "If Gedeon finds out about her and I am not there to protect her, he *will* kill her, if for no other reason than to hurt me."

Lenora shook her head. "How would he find out? You could have kept it between the two of you, and no one would have been the wiser."

Caius pinched the bridge of his nose, not wanting to dive into a history lesson when they had more pressing issues to address, but he owed her an explanation.

Had he married Rory, Gedeon and Adila would have known instantly. "When a *Royal* marries, there is something called the nova creatura, or *awareness*, for lack of a better word, that runs through the others." Lenora looked at Sam for confirmation, and he nodded.

"It happens when the Lux heirs take their thrones, but only the reigning *Royals* experience it," Caius explained. His parents encouraged him and his siblings to read history books on the *Royals*, and he could recite them by heart. His siblings never cared much for it, but he'd always enjoyed reading and devoured them all. "I didn't feel the nova creatura when Atarah took the throne because I was not yet the Umbra King, but I felt it when Adila became the Scales of Justice. When Atarah died, Adila and I both felt her power transfer to Gedeon."

He searched Lenora's eyes and implored her to understand. "It wasn't something I could risk. Had we married, Gedeon would have known another *Royal* was blessed, and nothing would have stopped him from tracking her down." Caius massaged his forehead, attempting to erase this nightmare of his own creation. "And if he knew she was important to me, he would try to take her from me."

"She could have stayed here," Lenora objected. "If she could pass between realms as a *Royal*, she could have stayed here with you until your new contract was fulfilled."

"And when she went to visit you?" he challenged. Nothing would have kept Rory from seeing her mother. "Or how about the fact that Gedeon can pass between realms, too? Vincula is the first place he would look. My power is not at its full potential while I'm locked away. I am powerful, but the magic keeping me here blocks my ability to tap into the shadow power of Erdikoa. Without it, Gedeon is stronger than I am."

Lenora huffed. "There is no light in Vincula, meaning your brother only has access to one realm. How is he more powerful than you?"

"There is light," Sam corrected her. Caius was thankful for his friend. He understood Lenora needed answers, but he wasn't in the right head space to give them. "You cannot have dusk without sunlight. Though you can barely see the Vincula sun's light through the shadows, it is still here." Sam nodded at Caius. "Gedeon has access to both realms, and Caius does not. He is weak."

Caius shot daggers at his friend. He wasn't *weak*, just weak*er* than usual.

"You really thought this through," Lenora remarked, and when Caius nodded, she ran a hand through her grey hair. "Why does your brother hate you so much?"

"He has since my power manifested." Caius thought back to the pure hatred he saw on Gedeon's face every day of their lives growing up. "He felt jilted that the shadow power skipped him. He thinks I stole it from him." Gedeon was the older twin, and the *Royal* powers always went to the same child.

The light power went to the oldest Lux heir, making them the Lux ruler; the shadow power went to the second oldest, making them the Umbra ruler, and the power of justice went to the youngest, making them the Scales of Justice.

There had only ever been three Lux children until he and his siblings. Identical twins were technically one child split into two in the womb. It was assumed there would be no more children after the twins were born, and when their mother became pregnant with Adila, it shocked everyone.

Their parents assumed Atarah would be the Lux Queen, Gedeon the Umbra King, and Caius the Scales of Justice since they were the three oldest. Every *Royal* child inherited their power at six years old, and when the twins turned six and Caius inherited the shadow power while Gedeon inherited nothing, it stunned everyone.

Lenora spoke, pulling Caius from his memories. "I know you only want to protect my daughter, but make no mistake, Gedeon *will* find out about her, and when he does, it's up to you to save her." The weight of her words crushed him. "I don't know why he killed my little girl all those years ago, but I know he has already scarred Rory once. Please, don't let him do it again."

Sam adjusted his stance awkwardly. Neither of them wanted to tell her their suspicions. "We think we know why he killed Cora," Caius said grimly.

She clasped her hands tightly in her lap. "Why?"

Caius couldn't get the words out because he knew they would wreck her.

"Cora was Gedeon's *Aeternum*," Sam answered for him.

"We believe he killed her and kept her soul so that he couldn't have children with her. If he doesn't have children to pass the three Royal positions on to, he will rule forever."

Lenora's wrinkled hand shook as she covered her mouth. The men stayed quiet while she collected herself, and when she lowered her hand, her features hardened. "Why couldn't he just stay away from her? She was a child!"

"We don't know," Caius admitted. "These are just theories, but my guess is that Gedeon already felt the pull toward her and didn't want to chance giving in to the bond."

Lenora stood abruptly, almost knocking over her chair. "I would like to be taken to my room, please." Caius wished he could snatch his words back and tell her he didn't know why his brother killed her daughter.

Sam walked into the hall and returned with a maid. "Gracie, please take Lenora to her chambers."

Caius put Rory's mother in the finest guest room they had instead of the apartments. It was the least he could do.

"Yes, Your Grace," the older maid said and waited for Lenora to follow her.

Once they left, Sam's large wings flared slightly. "We must tell Rory at some point," he said.

Caius ignored him, tired of this discussion. "How is she?"

The *Angel's* face fell. "She is not our Rory, at least not yet. What little light she had in her left when she learned of Lenora's incarceration."

The words made Caius clench his fists as he fought for control again.

How had things gotten this fucked? She was supposed to return to Erdikoa and live a full life with her friends and family. Now, her mother was here, informing him Gedeon would eventually find Rory.

His attempt to control his frustration was futile.

"*Fuck!*" Everything flew off his desk with a violent swing of his arm, and the shadows exploded around them. Bits of wood from the furniture and bookshelves flew around the room.

Sam batted the shrapnel away from his face and glowered at Caius. "I know you are upset, but losing your temper will not help. Lauren and I will protect her with our lives."

Caius said nothing as he tried to push his anger down. It took everything in him to force a semblance of calm, pat Sam on the shoulder, and slip through the passage leading to his and Rory's room. His only solace now was the soulscape.

Caius walked through a field of wildflowers that covered the floor of his throne room. He craned his head back to inspect the ceiling. Everything was the same, yet different. He couldn't put his finger on why.

"Who are you?"

He'd know that voice anywhere, and the recognition made his heart lurch. They were in the soulscape.

When he turned, the air left his lungs at the sight of the most stunning woman he'd ever seen.

And she was only wearing a pair of panties and a bra.
Fuck.

It felt like roots held him in place as he restrained himself from pulling her into his arms. He didn't want to scare her away, but as soon as she saw his face, he realized he'd forgotten one very important detail.

"Bane." Her eyes flashed between shock and hate, the same hate she displayed when she appeared in his throne room.

The memory made his mouth pull into a smile. Sam was wrong; she was still his Rory, deep down.

She looked around, and when she saw the elegant room covered in flowers, her brows knit together as she mumbled something to herself.

"Hello, Miss Raven," he purred. She thought he killed Cora, but he'd won her over once, and he would do it again.

"Fuck you," she sneered. Looking around again, she feigned turning her back to him and then charged, kicking out her leg.

He expected the attack and sidestepped her easily. "Usually, women try to get in my pants a different way," he taunted. "Kicking them off is a method I've not seen yet."

His words did nothing to deter her as she came at him again. And again. And again. She said nothing, only grunted as she attacked with impressive skill, and it made him proud. Even if she didn't remember their lessons, her body did.

Finally, he grabbed her and pulled her back to his chest, pinning her arms to her sides as she thrashed against his hold.

"I am going to fucking kill you," she swore like an oath.

"Mmm," he hummed. "How will you do that, Miss Raven? You seem to be in a bit of a bind."

His words ruffled the hair above her ear, and small bumps peppered her flesh. He smiled. "If I let you go, will you be a good girl?"

Her head almost split his lip when she threw it back, but he dodged just in time. "Now, now," he crooned. "You're being very naughty."

She stopped struggling, and her chest heaved from exhaustion and anger.

"Let me go," she demanded through gritted teeth.

He wished he could kiss her neck and tell her he loved her, but she wouldn't understand. Instead, he lightly squeezed before releasing her.

She stepped forward and spun around to face him. "Where the hell are we?"

He smirked. "You are stunning when you're mad."

If looks could kill, his head would be on a spike. He motioned around them. "It appears to be a throne room."

Rory stared at the ground. Caius saw her eyes widen, followed by her shoulders relaxing. "Figures."

He watched her closely and chanced a step forward. "Is something wrong?"

"Fuck you," she snapped. "I can't even enjoy sleeping." She glared at him, and he smiled widely.

"It's not unusual for me to be the star of someone's dreams." Advancing forward, he glanced at her lips. "But it's usually more fun than this."

She tried to push him back, but he stood firm. "I wouldn't touch you with a ten-foot pole."

He wet his lips and let his eyes run the length of her body. "Why do you think you haven't already?"

Red colored her cheeks as the storm clouds in her grey eyes grew darker. "I prefer not to sleep with the man who murdered my sister."

Caius watched her anger rise, and for a split second, the temptation to tell her everything overwhelmed him, but she wouldn't believe him. He couldn't risk her safety, anyway. Her reaction to him tonight was proof he was right. She would go straight to Gedeon and get herself killed.

"Why do you think I killed your sister?" he asked instead.

"I saw you with my own eyes, and I know you have her

soul," she sneered. "This might be a dream, but I will find you, and when I do, I will enjoy watching the life drain from your eyes."

Yes. He definitely made the right decision in not telling her.

The truth in her words reminded him of how she killed Tallent and condemned Nina. She was her own brutal version of the Scales of Justice, who waited for no one to pass judgment on the wicked, not when she could do it herself.

She was a stunning little savage, inside and out.

"Have you ever heard of twins, Miss Raven?" he asked. "Shapeshifting potions perhaps?" Rubbing his jaw, he winked. "I am quite handsome. It would not be unheard of for someone to desire my looks."

A flicker of doubt crossed her features so quickly that he would have missed it if he didn't know her like the back of his hand.

It didn't last long. "I know what I saw." The anguish in her eyes killed him.

"I didn't kill your sister, Rory." He hadn't meant to say it, but her pain would always be his weakness.

"Don't call me that," she fumed and walked away.

Much to her obvious dismay, he followed her, and when she whirled on him, he couldn't help but smile at the annoyance on her pretty face. "Go away."

He'd never smiled so much in his life, and his cheeks hurt from it, but seeing her again was a new kind of high. "No."

She studiously ignored him and sat on the plush ground. His long legs folded as he sat across from her. When he leaned back on his hands, her eyes landed on his naked torso, and pain pricked his tongue as he bit down to keep from laughing at her flustered state.

"Do you like what you see, Miss Raven? You can touch if you'd like."

Her lip curled. "You are vile."

"That's not what you said last time." He fought off a laugh as the apples of her cheeks turned red again. He ached to trail a hand across them.

The room shimmered. **"Not yet,"** *he pleaded silently, not ready to let her go.*

"What's happening?" she asked, waving her hand through the glittering air.

Caius sighed and stood. He didn't want her to know who actually killed her sister, but he didn't want her to hate him every time they met, either. She didn't need to know it was Gedeon. She only needed to know it wasn't him.

"I didn't kill Cora." He took one last look at her before she was taken away by the morning light. "I'll make you see that one day, but for now, it's time to wake up."

Caius stood in the shower with his head bent as the hot water pelted his skin. All he wanted was Rory in his arms, but even in the soulscape, she hated him. He'd hoped since their bond solidified before she left that her soul would remember him.

Theoretically, that should be the case, but his mate had always been a wild card. *Everything about her was wild.*

Remembering their last day together, he groaned as blood rushed downward.

They'd had sex too many times to count, and her moans were burned into his mind. He could hear them as if she were here with him now, and he could almost feel her beneath him, battling for control. She would relinquish it to him in the end. She always did.

Wrapping his hand around his cock, he stroked slowly, thinking of her perfect body and the way her arousal covered him as he slid in and out of her. He missed the soft pants she made when he pulled her nipples into his mouth and sucked them between his teeth, only to bite down to hear her cry out.

His head fell back as his hand squeezed around the tip of his dick before sliding back down to the base. The palm of his hand was nothing compared to her pussy, and there was no slapping of skin in the air, but he could pretend.

His imagination ran away from him as his strokes came faster with the image of his cock slamming into her while shadows held her arms above her head.

He'd slow down to a painful pace, relishing in the way her inner muscles throbbed around him. It was a sensation like no other.

"Faster," she'd demand, and he'd refuse to give her what she wanted.

Torturing her was an addiction. He'd wrap one of her legs around his waist and throw the other over his shoulder as he lifted her hips for a new angle that allowed him to dive deeper.

Then he'd give in, unable to help himself, and slam into her hard enough to make her scream.

"Yell for me," he'd command as he slammed into her again, and she'd obey because she always did. His name would echo around their room, and when his thumb found her clit, she would tumble over the edge.

Her cries were music to his ears, and he slapped the shower wall with a moan as his cum mixed with the water dripping down the marble. As he emptied himself, his strokes slowed with his heavy breaths.

The wall was cool against his skin as he rested his forehead against it.

She'd always been his fantasy, but now she was one he couldn't have.

CHAPTER 5

ERDIKOA

Rory sat up, covered in sweat, with a racing heart. She placed her hand over her chest and willed herself to calm down. *It was only a dream.*

Seeing Bane had shaken her, but what unsettled her more was her soul whispering to believe him. At least in her dream, it did. *Had her time in Vincula made her an idiot?*

Her soul whispered things her entire life, whether it was colors or simple gut feelings. It'd never steered her wrong.

Throwing back the blanket, she stood and padded to the bathroom to splash water on her face. She'd never seen Bane up close, and it was nauseating to learn he was the most beautiful man she'd ever seen, but he looked different somehow. Why did she remember him differently? Had too much time passed?

She splashed more water on her face and relieved herself before sitting back on the bed, unable to shake the dream. Bane didn't seem surprised when she attacked him; he expected it, but he'd never seen Rory before. That she knew of, anyway.

He bested her. Was her mind telling her to train harder? Her breath hitched, and she clenched her fists in her lap, reminded of Cora's soul trapped somewhere.

No. She'd been given a second chance at a life, and she couldn't throw it away to seek revenge. A day ago, she would have made plans to continue her search for him, but now, she realized some things were more important than vengeance.

Bile rose in her throat. She had to choose between putting her family through hell again to save Cora's soul and leaving Cora's soul trapped forever in order to keep her family from suffering more heartbreak at her hand. The word *unfair* didn't do her situation justice.

She sighed, telling herself not to seek Bane out, but if the opportunity to kill him arose, she would take it.

Standing, she grabbed the clothes she wore yesterday and pulled them on. She'd ask Lauren to take her by her old apartment to pick up her things.

Besides, she wanted to see Keith and Kordie, assuming Dume told the truth about them wanting to see her. Buying a cell phone was a top priority. And a job.

Rory stepped into the hallway and ran into her father. A smile tugged at her lips as she hugged him.

"Good morning," he greeted and kissed the top of her head.

"Good morning." She untangled herself from his arms and stepped back. He looked tired. "How was work at the clinic? I didn't realize there was a night shift."

He patted her shoulder and started toward the stairs. "Come eat breakfast with me, and I'll tell you all about it."

As she approached the stairs, she groaned as something inside her recoiled. Her feet faltered. *Since when did stairs bother her?*

Her father looked concerned when he turned around. "Is everything okay?"

She mentally slapped herself and ran down the stairs, eager to be done with them. "Just tired." A sweet smell assaulted her as she entered the dining room. "What's for breakfast?"

"Waffles," Lauren said as she set down a bottle of syrup and took a seat.

Rory sat opposite of her and stared at the tall stack. "I didn't realize they were a golden color." Her father and Lauren looked up, and she felt her neck heat. "They used to look grey to me."

"I can make them different colors," Lauren said to break the awkwardness. "I just have to add food coloring to the batter."

Rory shot her a grateful smile. "I love waffles no matter the color."

"Cora hated them but loved pancakes," Patrick recounted with a chuckle. "Do you remember that?"

"How could I forget?" Rory snorted. "It didn't matter how many times Mom told her it was the same batter. She refused to eat them." Laughing, she soaked her waffles in syrup, filling her entire plate.

"They're not the same," Lauren replied before popping a forkful of waffle into her mouth.

Rory and Patrick looked at her and burst out laughing.

"It's the texture," Lauren insisted, waving her fork over her plate.

"Don't tell me you don't like pancakes," Rory teased with a wide grin.

"They feel like a sponge." The guard's nose wrinkled. "What's to like?"

Rory's father was still laughing when he pointed his fork at Rory and said, "This one right here will eat anything."

Rory shrugged and shoveled a piece of waffle into her mouth. "Life's too short to pass up food."

"Your mother used to say the same thing," her father remarked, cutting his waffle into tiny triangles.

She tried not to let the reminder of her mother pull her into the all-too-familiar dark place that plagued her thoughts and swallowed her bite without chewing.

"Lenora doesn't have her abilities there," Lauren said softly, meeting Rory's gaze. "Her mind is clear, and you might not believe me, but the inmates are treated very well. Some prefer it to Erdikoa."

Rory stared at her plate. "I believe you."

"Tell me about your job, Dad," she said, changing the subject. "When did they start needing a night vet?"

Patrick picked up his napkin, wiped his mouth, and took a drink, stalling. "I quit the vet's office and took a job at the library downtown to stay with your mother during the day." Rory's mouth fell open. He loved treating animals.

Her mother was not trapped in her mind anymore. She was treated well. She was not trapped in her mind anymore. She was treated well, Rory chanted silently. Maybe if she said it enough, it would make her feel better.

She set down her fork. Her father was one of the best veterinarians in the realm. People traveled across the city with their pets instead of using the offices closest to them. "Can you get your old job back?"

His mouth lifted a fraction. "I like the quiet calm of cleaning the library."

"You clean the library?" Cleaning was a respectable job, but he *hated* cleaning. Patrick nodded with a genuine smile, and Rory returned it. "You really love it."

"I do. I love animals, and there is nothing more rewarding than saving someone's beloved pet, but telling someone that not even potions can help took a toll on me." He dropped his napkin on his empty plate. "Don't tell my boss, but sometimes I sit and read while I'm there."

Lauren's silence didn't go unnoticed by Rory. "And what about you? How did a non-*Aatxe* become a guard?" Jealousy struck her hard in the gut. Had they allowed her to be an enforcer, would she have still become The Butcher?

Lauren smirked. "Because I'm an *Angel*."

Rory and Patrick looked at each other, and while her father looked star-struck, Rory laughed. "Are you a *Seraph*? Should I bow down?"

Tears were forming in her eyes as she continued to laugh. It wasn't that funny, and she knew that, but it was the first truly funny thing to happen since her arrest.

Lauren stood, and wings shot out of her back, making Rory yelp as she pushed back from the table. Her chair toppled over, and her father moved to help her up. They stood, and Rory's eyes popped out of her head as Lauren crossed her arms and gave them an '*I told you so*' look while sporting two beautiful white wings that wouldn't fit through a doorway.

"What the fuck?" Rory breathed. "Shit, are you really a *Seraph*?"

Lauren scoffed. "No. In their true form, they have wings

on their legs, back, and face." She shivered. "Could you imagine feathers tickling your nose all the time?"

"I read a book on *Angels* recently," Patrick said with awe still in his voice. "There are different types and a hierarchy." He looked thoughtful before snapping his fingers. "You protect—you're one of the *Principalities*, aren't you?" She nodded, amused. "You can shapeshift into any animal."

Rory rubbed her eyes. *Was she still dreaming?* When she looked back at Lauren, the wings remained. "Holy aether."

Lauren's wings disappeared, and she gathered their empty plates. "Something like that. Put away the syrup, please."

Rory grabbed the bottle and trailed the *Angel* into the kitchen. "I'm sorry for laughing. I didn't know *Angels* existed outside of storybooks."

Lauren rinsed the dishes before loading them into the washer. "There are a lot of things you don't know."

"No shit," Rory mumbled under her breath. "And Sam?"

Lauren nodded. "His wings are bigger than mine. It makes him look like a giant bird."

"How often will you two switch out?" Rory asked, moving around the kitchen island.

"Every few days, maybe every week." She dried her hands on a towel and took the bottle from Rory's hands to put away. "We have different duties in Vincula and need to check in often to ensure everyone is doing their jobs."

Rory's interest was piqued. "What do you do in Vincula?"

"I run patrols around the town and take reports from other enforcers in the legion. Sam handles patrols in the palace and processes incoming inmates."

"He's a paper pusher?" Rory bit back a laugh.

"Please ask him that," Lauren said with a wicked glint in her eye. "No. When an inmate is stationed in the palace, he assigns them a room, takes them to Caius for their assignment, and tells the head of the palace staff what room they're in so they can issue an inmate mystic card."

"Caius?" Rory barely heard anything Lauren said after hearing that name.

The guard's eyes raised to hers. "That's all you got from that? Interesting. He's the Umbra King."

"Oh," she said lamely. She knew who the Umbra King was; she just didn't know why his name felt *important*. "Did I meet the Umbra King?"

Lauren stopped moving for a beat. "Every inmate does."

Rory wished she could remember. *What was he like?* If Vincula was not as they'd been told, did the same go for the king? She frowned. That can't be right. He killed his own sister.

She pushed the thought from her mind. "I need to go to my old apartment and get my things."

"No, you don't," Lauren said. "Your friends are bringing them later today."

"Friends?" Rory squeaked. "Will Keith and Kordie come too?"

"They wanted to be here last night, but we didn't want to overwhelm you."

Rory's chest constricted. Dume said they wanted to see her, but when you're a convicted serial killer, it was hard to believe.

～

That evening, after her father left for work, Rory flipped mindlessly through the ES channels, stopping on an arrowball game.

The prickling feeling returned, like there was something she should remember about the sport. Did all returned inmates experience this sensation? She stared at the screen, watching the players run down the field.

Arrowball never interested her. Sure, she enjoyed going to games with friends and drinking amongst the energetic crowd, but other than that, she couldn't care less.

Frustration made her want to punch the pillows on the couch. Would she always have this sense of vague recognition, feeling her memories just out of reach?

Not for the first time today, her mind replayed her dream from last night in vivid detail. There was a familiarity between her and Bane, making her want to throw something. *Nice to know Vincula didn't dampen her violent tendencies.*

Killing him had always been her goal, but now the thought gave her pause. It was completely fucked. If Bane killed others and not just Cora, perhaps he was caught and sent to Vincula as well.

"Fuck," she muttered as she turned off the ES.

Someone pounded on the door, and she jumped up to answer.

"Don't touch that," Lauren warned as she descended the stairs.

Huffing, Rory folded her arms across her chest. "No one knows I'm here, remember?"

Before she could open the door, Lauren stopped her. "Get back, or I'll make you get back."

Narrowing her eyes, Rory moved out of the way.

When Lauren opened the door and stepped aside, a whirl of purple rushed past her and looked around. Kordie spotted Rory and burst into tears, throwing her short arms around her, almost knocking her over.

Once she was over the shock, Rory returned the hug nervously. Part of her hadn't wanted to face them, not yet, but the other half was elated.

Kordie eased to the side, and Keith picked Rory up in a big hug. Before he let go, he whispered into her ear, "I knew you were a supermystic."

Tears threatened to spill down her cheeks, but she forced them back as she looked between her friends. Words evaded her, but thankfully, Kordie spoke first. "We missed you so much."

"I'd say I missed you too, but it feels like I just saw you," Rory tried to joke.

Keith's eyes lit with understanding. "Because you don't remember the past three months."

She nodded and turned back to Kordie. "You kept your hair purple."

Her friends stilled. "How did you know that?" Keith asked, giving her a once over.

Rory motioned for them to have a seat in the living room. "When I woke up in Erdikoa, my grey-scale sight was gone."

Kordie gaped at her. "How?"

"I have no idea." Rory fell into one of the oversized chairs and sighed heavily.

Keith pointed to his chest with a goofy grin. "What color is my shirt?"

She pinched her brows together, feeling like she'd done this before. "Blue, like your eyes."

He clapped as he laughed, and Kordie perked up. "Does this mean I can dye your hair pink?"

"Absolutely not," Rory responded immediately. The two were sitting awfully close to one another, and Keith's hand rested on Kordie's leg.

Kordie noticed her staring and smiled sheepishly. "We're together."

"I'm glad you two finally worked that out," Rory said, unsurprised.

"What is that supposed to mean?" Keith asked and rested his arm behind Kordie's shoulders.

"I've been watching you two circle each other for years." She tucked her legs under her. "If you didn't get together soon, I was going to have an intervention. How did it happen anyway?"

Kordie's cheeks pinked as Keith threw her a devilish grin. "She finally took me up on my offer."

Rory recalled what *offer* he spoke of and snickered. "I'm glad she did."

Lauren opened the front door, carrying two suitcases, and Keith rose from his seat. "Let me help you with those. I was going to grab them later."

The guard gave him a look that stopped him in his tracks. "I am not a fair maiden who needs a man to do something I can do myself."

He returned to the couch without arguing. "She is terrifying," he whispered, making the girls laugh.

"You haven't seen the half of it, puppy," Lauren called from the stairs, making Keith pale and the girls laugh harder.

"She's an *An-*" Rory began, but Lauren's voice carried down the stairs, cutting her off.

"Don't finish that sentence."

Rory smirked. "I was going to say you were an angry beast," she called back.

Lauren's snort could be heard from the second floor. "Liar."

"Does she have super hearing or something?" Kordie asked, glancing at the stairs.

Lauren reappeared and sat in the chair next to Rory's. "Don't worry about me."

Battling another smile, Rory turned back to her friends. "I need to get out of this house."

Kordie glanced at her skeptically. "Is that a good idea?"

"I'm going," Rory replied. "Besides, this one won't leave my side." She tipped her head toward Lauren.

"Fuck, yeah," Keith agreed. "We'll go to Night Potions."

Night Potions was a bar near the edge of the warehouse district, a seedy part of town where Rory had a storage unit. The others avoided it at all costs. "Why there?"

Keith gave her a wry smile. "Because no one there will care who you are, and those that do will want to hire you."

"I wonder how much they'd pay?" she joked without thinking.

Her breath caught in her throat, unsure how her friends would respond, but her lungs loosened when Kordie's eyes twinkled. "Make sure it's enough to buy us a round of drinks."

The three laughed, Lauren smirked, and after an hour of catching up, they stood as the couple readied to leave. Lauren sauntered outside and brought in more boxes of Rory's things from Keith's truck.

Kordie's arms banded around her middle and squeezed with impressive strength. "Never leave us again," she commanded with a hitch to her voice. All Rory could do was pat her back reassuringly.

Keith gave her a quick hug, and after the two left, Rory stood motionless, staring at the door.

"Your friends love you," Lauren said as she locked the deadbolt.

"Did I have friends in Vincula?" she asked the *Angel* quietly.

Lauren had Rory follow her upstairs, and when they stepped into Rory's room, she opened both suitcases and began unloading one.

"You did." She pushed the other suitcase toward Rory. "They aren't much different from your friends here." She paused. "Well, they're criminals, but they didn't bat an eye at your crimes. Your friends here don't hold them against you either."

A hollowness settled in Rory's chest at the mention of friends she didn't remember. The thought of forgetting Dume, Kordie, or Keith devastated her, and she wondered if she'd feel the same about the others if she remembered them.

As casually as she could, Rory asked, "Was there an inmate named Bane?"

Lauren's movements ceased, a shirt dangling from her fingers, and Rory already knew the answer.

"Tell me. Please." She couldn't be bothered to be embarrassed about the desperation in her voice.

"There was no one named Bane," Lauren said carefully. "But there was someone you thought was Bane."

Rory sat on the bed. Half of her hoped Lauren would say no, but she never expected this. She *thought* they were Bane? "What does that mean?"

Lauren continued putting away Rory's things. "That's all I can say. Don't ask me anything else."

"Please, Lau—"

"No," Lauren clipped. "I've told you too much as it is. You have been given a fresh start. Live your life and stop worrying about the past."

Rory's resolve thickened. Something important was being hidden from her, and she needed to find out what. Returning was an emotional shock, but it was time to pull herself together.

Lauren was right about one thing. Rory needed to enjoy the time she'd been gifted with her friends and family. The guilt about her mother's incarceration was still there, but the knowledge that her visions no longer plagued her and that she was treated well, helped ease it a bit.

She pulled shoes from the other suitcase, thinking. Her intuition was telling her something, and if her dream last night and the prickling sensation she felt were any indication, there might be a way for her to lift the magic blocking her memories.

She just had to figure out how.

Later that night, Rory stared at the ceiling, willing herself to fall asleep. Her visit with Keith and Kordie lightened her mood, and tomorrow the group was going to Night Potions after everyone got off work.

Tossing and turning, she decided to swing by a pharmacy tomorrow to pick up a sleeping potion. *Would she dream about Not-Bane again?*

She didn't know why it mattered. It wasn't like she wanted to go back to prison, but the elusive recognition was driving her crazy.

Sleep never came.

CHAPTER 6

VINCULA

Caius sat up and scrubbed his face with both hands. There was no soulscape last night, and he was obsessing over why. She was safe, otherwise he would have had a vision, but any number of non-life-threatening things could be wrong.

After getting ready for the day, he slipped through the corridor from his and his mate's bedroom to his office. He allowed himself to grieve in private but not in front of others. Being a king meant he could not let his problems affect his subjects, even if his life was falling apart.

He also needed to get out of this *Seraphim*-damned realm to kill his brother before he discovered Rory.

The only way to kill a *Royal* was by decapitation or stabbing them in the heart. Caius was the only person strong enough to get close enough to his brother to do it. Gedeon would fry anyone else before they reached him, but Caius' shadows could smother Gedeon's light.

Asking Adila to lift his sentence was out of the question, but there had to be information about the magic trapping the inmates in Vincula somewhere. He needed to find it.

When he entered his office, Sam was waiting. "What is your plan, *Your Grace*?"

The *Angel* stood in front of Caius' desk, looking pissed. It was a look he'd permanently adopted since Caius sent Rory to Erdikoa.

Sighing, he sat down at his desk. His chair squeaked lightly as he leaned back and drummed his fingers against the arm. "Research. I'm certain there are no useful books in my office, and I need to speak with Rory's friend who works in the library. I believe her name is Kit."

Paper crinkled as Sam pulled a small bag from his pocket. Reaching inside, he produced a donut and bit into it.

Caius eyed the pastry as a memory of Rory biting into the sugary food with a taunting smile invaded his thoughts. The corner of his mouth lifted at the image. "Why do you always have food in your pocket? You're like a walking vending machine."

Sam smiled for the first time in days. "I am a growing boy." He sat on the bench, his large wings tucked tight against his back. "What are you researching?"

"I need information on Adila's power or the magic sealing Vincula from Erdikoa." He rocked his head from side to side, pondering his own statement. "Or that seals Erdikoa from Vincula."

He wasn't sure which it was. The realms were, topographically speaking, mirror images of one another. One of the history books his parents forced him to read as a child described them as being stacked on top of each other, sky to sky. It's why you practically fell into whichever realm you were entering.

He needed his full power to break through the barrier, but without access to Erdikoa, it felt impossible. *There had to be a way.*

Sam stared at him like he was an idiot. "If you think there is a book accessible to inmates detailing how to break out of Vincula, you need to be reassigned."

"Just bring me the librarian," Caius replied crossly and rubbed the slight stubble on his jaw. He needed to shave, but more important tasks consumed his time. *Like finding a way to save his mate.* "Did you see Rory's mother this morning?"

Sam shook his head. "She either has not woken yet or is already in town meeting new people. My bet is on the latter."

Caius smiled inwardly. Lenora was a force to be reckoned with.

Later that afternoon, Sam knocked on the door a millisecond before charging into Caius' office with Kit in tow. The woman was tall with brown hair and an annoyed look on her face.

"Hello, Miss Cooper." He'd studied her file after Sam left. She burned a school administration building to ash for banning books and was exactly who he needed.

"Hello," she returned as she took a seat across from him. "Is there a problem, Your Grace?"

"Yes," he replied, clasping his hands in front of him.

Her eyes flared. *Maybe not.* "Is she okay?"

"She's fine." He hesitated. "For now. I need your expertise to help make sure she stays that way." Kit leaned forward, listening intently. "What do you know about mystic abilities?"

She fixed her gaze on him with a dubious frown. "Can you be more specific? That's a vague subject."

Caius glanced at Sam. He shouldn't reveal much to an inmate, but he was on the edge of not giving a fuck. "The *Royals'* magical abilities, specifically the Scales of Justice."

Kit's brows nearly hit her hairline. "You know more about your sister than I do, Your Grace."

"I don't care about my sister." He sat forward, leaning his elbows on his desk. "I want to know how her power works."

Kit's face screwed up. "She has essence like everyone else." Caius held his breath while the woman sorted out her thoughts. "Actually, the *Royals* are given powers."

His face remained a mask of indifference as he tried not to bang his head on the desk. "I meant anything that is not common knowledge."

She looked up excitedly. "No, Your Grace, I mean *Royals* are *given* power. Other mystics are born with a mark behind their ear, and it takes a few years for the essence of their soul to fully develop."

He sat up straight. "*Royals* don't possess marks."

Kit shook her head excitedly. "And the story of you and your siblings is legendary. The shadow power skipped Gedeon and passed to you, and when you killed your sister..." She had the decency to wince before she continued. "Her power transferred to your brother. That doesn't happen with mystics."

Sam shifted into his wingless form and sat beside Kit. "What does this knowledge mean?"

"I'm not sure, but the power isn't attached to them." She thought for a moment. "It must be attached to the realm."

"The shadows," Caius murmured and glanced at Sam. "The shadows I control make up the realm, and the light Gedeon controls is from the suns." He furrowed his brow. "Where does Adila's power originate?"

Kit raised her hand slightly, and Caius signaled for her to speak. "It's common knowledge that the original Lux *Royal* was born a *Fey*. That's why *Royals* have the *Fey* ears," she said, glimpsing at Caius' slightly pointed ears.

He considered her, not understanding her point.

She blew out an exasperated breath. "The Scales of Justice ability is basically enhanced *Fey* ability. Rory once said that when she still had grey-scale sight her soul would whisper the colors of other people's souls to her. That is likely how your sister knows people's perfect sentences," Kit clarified. "Her soul tells her."

"What is enhancing her *Fey* abilities?" Caius mused.

The librarian lifted a shoulder. "Beats me, but her other ability to lock people in Vincula or send them to hell must come from the magic separating the realms."

Caius leaned on the arm of his chair, unable to sit still. It was the closest thing they had to an explanation, but only the *Seraphim* knew if it was correct.

"The librarian makes sense," Sam said finally. "Each *Royal's* power is drawn from the essence of the realms, not their own essence."

"Do *Royals* have essence at all?" Kit wondered, glancing at Sam suspiciously.

"Yes and no," he replied. "They receive a fraction of it when they turn six, but they do not inherit the full power until they inherit their positions. They also possess a small amount of their *Aeternum's* essence."

"Do you hear yourself?" Kit asked him. "You aren't making a lick of sense."

"I am not licking anyone to get my point across." He motioned to Caius. "Each *Royal* possesses a twisted version of their mate's abilities. It is why Caius can sense black souls without touching them."

Kit contemplated the king. "That's not in any book."

Caius knew she was right, but he refused to give up hope. "You've been a great help, Miss Cooper," he replied, ignoring her question. "If you remember anything else, please let us know."

She nodded and followed Sam to the door, hesitating before turning back. "If you have someone who can cross into Erdikoa with their memories." Her eyes slipped to Sam. "Then ask my parents. They're two of the best historians in the realm."

Caius smiled tightly. "Thank you, Miss Cooper."

She gave a curt nod and stepped around Sam to see herself out, and Caius held back a laugh when Sam glared after her.

Shortly after, Caius left through the side door to his office, breathing in deep. With his eyes closed, he called on the shadows in the dark room, imploring them to give him the answers he desperately needed.

They snaked around him, their cool caress encasing him fully as he focused on the power filling his body. He would break the magic holding him here, and then he would kill Gedeon.

Failure wasn't an option.

CHAPTER 7

Kit grabbed a table at the bar, waiting for Bellina and Cat to arrive. She couldn't get the conversation with the king out of her head. She also couldn't help but notice that he didn't leave Vincula with Rory, despite not letting her out of his sight ever since Nina tried to have her killed.

The information he sought must be important, and tomorrow, she would comb through the library's catalog for anything promising.

A woman's voice startled her, and she glanced over her shoulder. "Hello, dear."

Rory's mother, Lenora, appeared next to the table. They'd been introduced briefly by the legion commander, but she'd not seen her since. "Hi, Ms. Raven."

Lenora waved her hand. "Please, call me Lenora. May I join you?"

"Of course." Kit waved toward another chair, telling her, "Bellina and Cat should be here soon."

Lenora perked up. "That little curly-headed one is something else, isn't she?"

A snort escaped Kit before she could stop it. "You could say that." When they were introduced to Lenora, Cat asked her how it felt to go crazy and come back.

"Would you like another drink, dear?" Lenora indicated Kit's almost empty glass.

"I can get both of ours," Kit offered as she stood.

Lenora pushed her chair back and motioned for Kit to sit. "The king gave me unlimited credits."

She accepted the gift better than Rory had, Kit thought with a chuckle. "Thank you. I'll have a brandy and lemon-lime soda, please."

Lenora grabbed Kit's glass and walked off, returning shortly with a server holding a tray of shots.

"What's this?" Kit asked, eyeing the tiny glasses of liquor.

Lenora set their drinks down and began unloading the tray. When she was done, the server smiled and left. "They're shots." She held up her beer, motioning for Kit to clink her glass with the bottle. "Cheers!"

There were four shots, and when Lenora saw Bellina and Cat weaving through the crowd, she lifted her hand to flag them down.

"Hey, Lenora," Cat said, going in for a hug.

Lenora smiled and handed Cat a shot. "It's nice to see you girls again."

She passed a shot to Bellina, and the seamstress stared at it before smiling. "I knew I liked you."

The women sat, and Kit reached for her shooter as Lenora held hers up and said, "To the king being a dumbass." She threw it back as the other three stared with wide eyes.

Cat shrugged. "Hear! Hear!" She threw hers back and scrunched up her face.

Bellina and Kit exchanged a glance and took theirs too. "What did the king do?" Bellina asked casually, but Kit could tell she was worried.

Lenora took a swig of her beer, looked around, and leaned forward. The other three mimicked her, and when they were huddled close, Lenora said, "What has Rory told you about her sister's murder?"

The three looked at each other. "We didn't know her sister was killed," Bellina whispered. "I'm sorry to hear that."

"Rory had a twin sister named Cora and, when they were fifteen, Rory watched as Caius' identical twin brother, Gedeon, killed her," Lenora explained.

Bellina gasped, and Cat swore under her breath.

"That's why Rory hated the king when she first arrived," Kit remarked. "She thought he was Gedeon."

Everyone knew of the anomaly that was the current generation of *Royals*. Four *Royal* children were unheard of, but there was nothing in the books about the boys being *identical* twins.

Lenora nodded. "I don't know what happened between him and my daughter, but I imagine she hated him until she learned the truth." She shook her head and chuckled. "With as stubborn as she is, it's a wonder he convinced her at all."

"What does this have to do with the king being a dumbass?" Cat asked impatiently.

The four were still leaning in close. "As you are aware, I am a *Sibyl*." The group stayed quiet. They knew of the lives *Sibyls* endured. "I saw Rory and the twin *Royals* in two different futures. One where Gedeon kills her, and one where Caius saves her."

"Oh, fuck," Cat hissed.

Bellina's hand flew to her mouth, but Kit watched with rapt attention. She needed to catalog everything Lenora said in order to help the king because whatever information he needed was literally life and death.

"I tried to break out of my mind to get here to make her stay with him," she said grimly. "I knew there was a way she left the prison realm, but I didn't know what it was, and by the time I arrived, it was too late."

"How did she get out?" Kit inquired, needing to know every detail.

Lenora met their gazes with unwavering intensity. "Caius took over her contract."

"What does that mean?" Bellina demanded, and Kit knew their friend was hanging on by a thread. Tallent beating her half to death changed her. She was no longer the fun-loving woman she once was.

"It means Rory was released on *his* release date, and he must finish out the rest of her five-hundred-year sentence," Lenora explained with a pained expression. "And Rory doesn't remember her time here. Or him."

"Or us," Bellina murmured, and a somber silence descended on the table.

Kit sat back in a daze. "You're right. He is a dumbass." She signaled for the server and ordered another round of shots as they digested the information. When the server returned, Kit downed hers quickly. "He can't save her if he's locked in here."

Lenora took her shot. "He has to. Rory's life depends on it." For a mother whose daughter was sent to her death, she was eerily calm.

"He gets out, doesn't he?" Kit guessed.

Lenora nodded. "Yes. In one future, he's too late." Unchecked emotion laced the older woman's words. "In another, he makes it without a minute to spare."

Kit understood why the king wanted information on the magic possessed by the Scales of Justice. He needed to either break through it or use it to get through the barrier.

"What can we do to help?" Cat asked, and Kit was taken aback by how serious she was. "We are criminals. Doing things the illegal way is our specialty, and we will do whatever it takes to break him out."

Lenora turned slowly to look at Kit, pinning her in place. "Yes. You will."

It was then that Kit understood. Saving Rory's life depended on her finding the correct information. Her pits began to sweat.

She'd never been great under pressure.

That night, after leaving the bar and parting ways with the others, Kit found herself standing in front of the library. Despite being tipsy, she wanted to start looking right away.

The jangle of her keys cut through the quiet night as she let herself in and hurried toward the back. She was thankful the torches were still lit, albeit low, and when she retrieved the large catalog and plunked it on the desk, she flinched at the sound.

She would kill for an electronic catalog, but she'd work with what she had. While history was her passion, as a child, she collected old storybooks with tales of the first days. They were fantasy, but she always suspected they were rooted in truth, which proved to be correct when she met Samyaza.

Her plan was to pull every historical text and storybook this realm possessed. As she found them, she would take them to the king, but they couldn't comb through them alone.

They needed help.

CHAPTER 8

ERDIKOA

The following day, after eating breakfast with her father and Lauren, Rory went to her room to find shoes and a cap to wear in the city. As she tied her hair into a low ponytail, she stared at her long hair in the mirror. The urge to cut it was strong enough that she considered searching the house for a pair of scissors.

The thought took her off guard. She loved her long hair, always had. Shaking off the uneasiness, she found Lauren in the kitchen. "I need to go shopping."

Lauren turned. "What for?"

"I need a new phone, a sleeping potion, and a few other basic things." Rory paused. "Shit. Never mind, I need to apply for jobs first."

"You don't need a job," Lauren informed her as she grabbed a knife out of the drawer and began picking at her nails.

Rory shuddered at the sight and walked out. "I can't buy

anything until I have moedas," she said, searching for the keys. "And to get moedas, I need a job."

"Looking for these?" Lauren asked, dangling a set of keys from her finger. "You can't leave without me."

Rory walked forward, assessing the *Angel* for a way to swipe the keys without getting killed. "I wasn't going to, but I figured if I drove off, you'd have to give in."

A wide smile spread across Lauren's face. "There you are." She walked to the door and stepped outside. "Come on, little butcher. Let's get your shit and grab lunch on the way back."

Rory followed her to the same vehicle they'd arrived in. Sam must have flown back to Vincula. Or disappeared back, however they did it. "I don't have any moedas, and I'm not borrowing from you."

Lauren jumped in and started the engine as Rory climbed into the passenger seat. "You will never need a job again," Lauren replied. "Don't ask me any more questions." When they pulled onto the highway, she added, "We need to stop and get your new mystic card before running by the bank to pick up your bank card."

"New mystic card?" Rory parroted. "What's wrong with my old one?"

Lauren kept her eyes on the road. "You're getting a new identity."

"The fuck I am," Rory replied crisply.

Lauren smirked, and it struck Rory as odd that the *Angel* seemed to like her better when she was a bitch. "It's non-negotiable. Everything is set. We just have to pick everything up."

"I haven't chosen a name yet. How is it ready?"

"Your new name was chosen for you." She glanced at Rory, trying not to laugh. "You are now Lo Senka."

Rory blinked. "What kind of name is Lo? Where's the rest of it?"

Lauren shot her a death glare. "It doesn't matter if you like it or not; that's your new name when you're in public."

A new name was the least of Rory's worries, and she gave up the battle. When they pulled into the warehouse district, she slid her eyes to Lauren. "You can get in and out of The Capital without being searched, but you need the underground market to get a new mystic card?"

Lauren opened her door when they stopped and threw over her shoulder as she walked away, "Stop asking questions."

Rory stared out the window at the place she'd been one too many times. Fiona, the *Alchemist* she bought illegal potions from, hurried down one of the side alleys, and though they weren't friends, they were friendly.

The car door swung open as she hopped out and called Fiona's name without thinking. The *Alchemist* looked up and stopped in her tracks. *Shit.* Getting used to her new life would be challenging, but it was too late to turn back now.

Her lips parted as she scanned Rory's face. "Rory?"

"Yeah," she replied and closed the distance between them.

Fiona clasped both of her hands around Rory's. "The news said you were sentenced to five-hundred years. Did the protests really work?"

A nervous laugh scratched Rory's throat as she averted her eyes. "Something like that, but no one knows I'm out. I would be dead within the week."

"You're right," Fiona agreed, nodding. "The public is split down the middle on your case. Some think you're a monster." She eyed Rory up and down and shrugged. "I suppose you are, but not all monsters go bump in the night."

She did.

"Thanks, Fiona." She glanced back at Lauren's SUV. "I have to go. I just wanted to say hi."

Fiona nodded with a small smile. She was a tough businesswoman, and her soul was a darker shade of grey, but there was good in her, too. She was far enough away from black that her soul didn't suffocate Rory when they touched. "You stay safe, girl, and come see me at the market sometime."

"I will." She waved as she crossed the street and jumped back into the car. Approaching Fiona was stupid, and she didn't shirk the rules intentionally, but she thought it'd be fine. *Hopefully.*

When Lauren came back and climbed into the car, she handed Rory her new identity. It was the picture from her old card, but all the information was different.

"Memorize that," the *Angel* ordered as she pulled into the street.

Rory grunted and looked around for her purse, realizing she didn't grab it. "Can you hold on to it until we get home?"

"You'll need it at the bank," Lauren reminded her. "When we get there, hand them your mystic card and tell them you need to pick up the new bank card you ordered."

Rory blew out a long breath. "And if they recognize me?"

Lauren lifted a shoulder. "Say it's a coincidence. Say

you're a cousin. Say whatever you want. It doesn't matter because everyone thinks The Butcher is in prison."

As Rory neared the entrance of the bank, a man thrust a flyer into her hands. "He's coming any day," he cautioned. "Guard your loved ones." The man sounded delusional, and when she scanned the paper in her hands, she sucked in a sharp breath.

The end is almost near.

The Umbra King has returned.

"What does this mean?" she asked the rambling man.

His wide eyes met hers. "He has been released. His sentence is over. Everyone forgets, but not me."

She sidestepped him with a tight smile. "Okay, thanks." Her mind drifted to Caius. If he was the Umbra King, and he was free, would he find her? Shaking off the notion, she hurried toward the door.

Once inside, Rory adjusted her cap to conceal her face. She wasn't nervous, but her senses were on high alert in case she needed to defend herself.

"Hello, what can I do for you?" the woman at the counter asked. Her smile faltered when she saw Rory's face.

Rory slid her mystic card across the counter, forgoing pleasantries. "I ordered a new bank card, and I was told it's ready."

The woman forced a toothy smile. "I'll check on that for you."

She set Rory's card down next to her computer keyboard, and when she looked at it, her entire body sagged with relief as her eyes scanned the information.

The woman glanced up. "Senka? That's a beautiful name."

"Thank you," Rory replied with a close-lipped smile. "I got it from my father."

The joke didn't land. "One moment, Miss Senka," the teller said with a tight smile. "I'll grab your bank card from the back." She handed Rory's mystic card back and disappeared through a side door.

About five minutes passed before the woman returned, holding Rory's new bank card and a packet of paperwork.

"This is your new card," she explained, handing the card over. "If you lose it, call us, and we'll replace it the same day." Rory nodded along as the woman rattled off general information, showing Rory where to sign. "Thank you for banking with us, Miss Senka. You're a gold client, and we are at your disposal anytime, day or night, at this phone number." She pointed to a number on the front of the packet.

Gold member? Rory glanced at the paper and almost passed out when she saw the balance. She couldn't spend that many moedas in her lifetime if she tried. "Thank you," she uttered and left quickly. Lauren said not to ask questions, but this was too big to ignore.

"What the hell?" Rory snapped when she opened the car door. "What is this?" She waved the packet at Lauren and shut her door.

"It looks like a stack of papers," the *Angel* deadpanned. "Where do you need to go next?"

"You need to explain why there is an unfathomable amount of moedas in my new bank account," Rory replied, refusing to drop it.

Lauren glanced at the papers. "I told you I can't, but the person who put it in there doesn't take no for an answer. You're keeping it. Now, where do you need to go?"

Rory sat back in a daze. "To get a phone, or did my mysterious benefactor already get me one of those, too?"

An amused smile spread across Lauren's face. "He wouldn't be able to use a cell phone if you held a knife to his throat."

Rory stared straight ahead, knowing nothing she said would convince the guard to break her vow of secrecy. Fucking *Angels*.

Rory twisted side to side as she admired herself in her bedroom mirror. On the way home, they stopped by a clothing store to pick up a few new things for her wardrobe. She needed to break away from The Butcher's persona, and to do that, she needed more than black hoodies and leggings.

The red top she wore reminded her of her mother's soul, and she couldn't stop staring at it.

"It's time to go," Lauren shouted from downstairs.

Rory took a deep breath, grabbed her purse, and joined Lauren on the main floor of her new home. "I'm ready."

They parked next to Night Potions, and Rory hopped out, excited to see everyone. Would they fall back into their old routine, or would it be awkward for a while?

Lauren wore all black, and she imagined the guard jamming her stiletto into someone's eye. Rory could never fight in heels, but she bet Lauren could fight with her hands tied behind her back and blindfolded.

When they stepped inside the bar and combed through the unsavory crowd, Keith stood and flagged them down. Rory grinned as she hurried across the room toward him.

They hugged when she approached the table, and the

affection felt weird because they usually never hugged when meeting up at a bar, but she reminded herself they'd not seen her in months. "What's everyone drinking?" she asked. "Tonight is on me."

"You're not paying for anything," Dume objected. "Have you even found a job yet?"

Rory glanced at Lauren, who gave a subtle nod. "Actually," Rory taunted with a smug smile. "For whatever reason, I've been given more moedas than I can spend in a lifetime. I'm filthy rich."

Dume's eyes shifted to Lauren as the others gaped. "No shit?" Keith blurted.

"No shit." Rory chuckled. "Is everyone having their usual?"

"I'll have another one of these," Dume said, holding his beer bottle in the air. "And Sera usually drinks a petal pusher."

Rory stared at the bottle in his hand. "Since when do you drink?"

After chugging the rest of his beer, he averted his gaze. "Since you've been gone."

Unfamiliar small arms wrapped around her, and she yelped, breaking from their hold to spin around. A tiny woman with red hair and freckles beamed at her.

The woman grimaced and offered Rory her hand. "Sorry. I'm Sera."

A pretty cyan soul pulsed between them when Rory returned the gesture. "Rory." She didn't say much else as she remembered the night she'd first seen Sera.

It was maybe a year ago, and a man Rory had been tracking followed the tiny redhead out of a sandwich shop one night. Sera had been looking at her phone, not paying attention to her surroundings, when he grabbed her and dragged her into an alley.

Rory had followed the man at a distance, and when he snatched Sera, she had to sprint after them. By the time she turned the corner, the man had Sera on the ground, tearing at her clothes.

Rory ripped him off and told her to run. She hadn't seen the girl since.

"You remember," Sera murmured, noticing the recognition in her eyes.

Rory noticed a man who looked a few years younger than her father standing behind Sera. When she noticed him, he smiled and bowed his head in greeting. "I'm Bruce. I hope we've met before."

An awkwardness settled over her. "I don't think we have."

He cleared his throat and looked morose. "I was in Vincula for a month after your sentencing. I needed to thank you for saving my baby girl, but had I known you'd be released, I would have waited."

Rory reared back. If she found out another person went to prison for her, she would lose it. "Why would you do that?"

"You deserved to know that people on the outside admire you," he said with enough conviction to make a knot form in her throat.

Rory looked back at her friends, who stayed quiet. "Did anyone else go?" she demanded.

Kordie shook her head. "Not that we know of."

"Thank the *Seraphim*," she muttered. "If I go back, don't come for me." She made eye contact with everyone, daring them to object. "Bruce, what can I get you to drink?"

He opened his mouth to protest, but Keith cut him off. "Don't bother. She's rich now and won't take no for an answer. Killing pays."

Kordie slapped her boyfriend in the stomach, Bruce smirked, and Rory blanched. "A whiskey and dark cherry soda please," he replied.

"Petal pusher?" she asked Sera, and the woman grinned with a nod.

As Rory stood waiting for a bartender, she glanced around. She'd seen some customers at the underground market before, but to her knowledge, none of them were black souls. If they had been, they wouldn't be here, and her kill list would be longer.

"What can I get you?" The bartender placed a napkin on the bar, but his smile wavered when he saw Rory's face.

She looked away and rattled off her order, and the man's voice shook a little when he asked for her mystic card. When she handed it over, his eyes scanned her information quickly. It was amusing to see the relief flit across his face.

Handing back her card, he smiled kindly. "Coming right up."

She looked over her shoulder and jumped. "You scared the shit out of me," she hissed at Lauren, who stood right behind her. "I thought you stayed with the others."

Leaning leisurely on the bar, Lauren eyed the crowd. "Get used to it."

Once back at the table with everyone's drinks, they pushed two tables together to fit their large group, and Rory slid onto a chair next to Dume.

She sat quietly as the group slipped into easy conversation as though nothing had changed, and gratitude filled her heart, along with something else. An unexplainable longing.

Her mind drifted to her faceless friends in Vincula, and the pang of sadness she felt surprised her. Lauren looked at her knowingly and leaned over. "Enjoy your life here, Rory. Everyone wants that for you."

She nodded and turned back to her friends, listening as they talked about recent events she had missed. She felt like an outsider looking in, and they couldn't ask her about what she'd been up to because she didn't remember.

After a few weeks of being back, it would feel normal again.

At least, she hoped it would.

CHAPTER 9

Rory stared at her ceiling, begging sleep to pull her under.
When it was clear that would not happen, she sat up to grab
her new sleeping potion. Potions were her least favorite
things to put in her mouth, and that's saying a lot. But if she
wanted to see Not-Bane again, she needed to choke it down.

The instructions on the bottle said to fill the cap once
and chase it with water. Tiptoeing downstairs to avoid
waking Lauren, she slipped into the kitchen, took a shot of
the potion, gagged, and then chased it with water.

When she settled into bed, her eyes closed, and she
quickly drifted into the shadowy abyss.

~

*"You came," a man's voice said behind her. Rory whipped
around and came face to face with Bane, or Bane's look-alike.
She still didn't know.*

*Looking around, she noticed they were in the woods near
the old treehouse she'd found with Dume and her sister as a*

kid. It was a place filled with memories, and she walked toward it, touching the old wooden ladder.

"What is your real name?" she asked without turning around.

Goosebumps spread across her skin as he approached, his dominant aura wrapping around her.

"You called me Bane before. What's changed?" Curiosity laced his words, as did something else she couldn't decipher.

"Nothing," she lied. "But it's likely a murderer would give a false name."

She felt him shift behind her. "Then it doesn't matter, does it? If you think I killed Cora, call me whatever you wish."

She spun on him, shoving him. "Don't you dare say her name."

The sadness in his eyes took her aback, and she cursed the pang of empathy in her chest. Why did her brain conjure this man and make her doubt what she knew?

"Tell me," she whispered.

The side of his mouth lifted as he took a step forward. "And what will you give me in return, Miss Raven?"

She stepped back, hitting the ladder attached to the tree. Without a word, she turned and climbed until she was sitting inside the spacious fort. It pleased her to see that their childhood treasures still remained in decent condition. Before her arrest, she cleaned the place often, unable to let their memories decay with time. Had Dume taken over the responsibility while she was in prison?

Bane, or Not-Bane, hoisted himself inside and looked around silently with a furrowed brow. He bent forward and picked up Cora's favorite book, opening it. "This isn't my copy," he said absentmindedly.

Rory stood and snatched the book from his hand. "It's my sister's."

Looking around the room with interest, he moved slowly as he drank everything in. "None of this is mine."

Rory gazed around the room, seeing nothing but **her** childhood memories. "Why would any of this be yours?"

The curtains Cora stole from their mother's linen closet glided between his fingers as he walked past. "Because my sister and I built this when we were children." He knocked on the wooden wall. "How is it still here?"

"That's not possible," she insisted, tracking his every move. "When we found it as kids, it looked ancient."

He ignored her, murmuring to himself. "It must be the potion-based lacquer the contractors used to seal the wood."

"What are you talking about?" She was losing her patience with him. "You can't be more than thirty years old. I'm twenty-five, and when we found this place, the wood looked old."

"It doesn't look old now," he said pointedly.

"We showed my dad, and he bought magic repairing lacquers to coat the wood and fixed it up for us." Rory motioned around her. "Before I was arrested, I maintained it."

An eternity passed as he stared at her before finally shaking his head with a small smile. "Of course you would find it." He walked to a built-in bookshelf where Rory, Cora, and Dume kept trinkets and some of Cora's favorite books.

Not-Bane kneeled on the floor, running his hand along the underside of the bottom shelf before stopping. A wide grin smiled across his face. "It's still here."

"What are you doing?" she demanded, wanting to slap his hand away from her sister's books.

"Looking around," he replied with a smirk and sauntered toward her. "Tell me the truth." His voice was seductive, and she forced herself not to react. "Why do you think Bane isn't my real name?"

"Last time you said you didn't kill my sister."

He nodded slightly. "Knowing my name will not help you find what you're looking for."

"How would you know what I'm looking for?" she challenged. **She** didn't even know what she was looking for.

"Because I know you." He brushed a piece of hair out of her face, and she swatted his hand away, making him smile. "I know you sleep with your mouth slightly open. Your favorite color is red, and you hate reading. I know how your eyes swell when you cry, breaking my heart into a million pieces."

Stepping into her space, he leaned down, and his voice was husky. "I know what sounds you make when you ride my face and how your back bows off the bed when you want me to replace my fingers with my coc—"

"Stop," she practically yelled as her entire body flushed. Clearly, she needed to get laid, but she would worry about that later. "You only know me because my mind has conjured you into existence. I need to know why."

He walked across the room and peered out of the small window at the wildflowers blanketing the ground. "What makes you think this dream isn't mine?"

There it was again, that sense of familiarity. It was a phrase she'd heard somewhere before. What did it mean, and why was it important enough for her mind to remind her?

"Who are you?" she breathed. Was he important to her in Vincula, or was he Bane, and she was subconsciously trying to let go of her need for vengeance?

He looked over his shoulder. "I am no one to you, not anymore."

The treehouse shimmered, and Not-Bane hung his head. "Time to wake up, Miss Raven."

Rory sat up, covered in a sheer layer of sweat. Despite the magic blocking her memories, her brain remembered. Why else would she have such lucid dreams that caused feelings so strong she thought they were real?

Something in her chest stuttered with heartache, like watching the third-act breakup of a romance movie. The only difference was she had missed the beginning of the movie and didn't know what was happening. That's what her life felt like.

Frustration wasn't a good enough word to explain how she felt. Who was this man in her dreams, and why did he feel familiar? She longed for someone she didn't know anymore because her memories were packed away, just out of reach.

She wished the vague recognition didn't plague her so she could move on with her life, but it did, and she couldn't.

Not without knowing who she left behind.

CHAPTER 10

VINCULA

"She's remembering," Caius said the second Sam walked into his office. "I could see it on her face."

Sam's wings tucked tightly against his body as he ambled across the room. "That is impossible. The magic cannot be broken."

"She's my *Aeternum*. Maybe the magic doesn't work as well on her," Caius replied. "We can't let that happen, or at least, if she remembers, we need to convince her it's all in her head."

He wanted her to remember him so he could touch her, kiss her, tell her how much he loved her, and hear her say she loved him, too. But it wasn't safe. His chest ached every time he looked into her questioning eyes.

"She is not remembering," Sam asserted as he reached into his pocket and took out an apple. "It is your heart fabricating what you want to see."

Maybe he was right. Caius ran a frustrated hand through

his hair. It'd only been four days since she left, but it felt like a lifetime. All he wanted was for her to live a full life before they were reunited in the aether, but if Gedeon ruled Erdikoa forever, that would never happen. If Cora was Gedeon's *Aeternum*, and he trapped her soul, then he would never have children, and Caius and Adila had to stay in their positions as well.

The *Royals* ruled in their positions until the Lux ruler had three children to inherit their powers and positions. If Gedeon had no children, there would be no one to inherit their thrones, and he'd rule forever. They all would.

Unless he allowed Gedeon to kill him. He shook off the intrusive thought. His brother could not be allowed to rule forever. There was no telling what type of ruler he would become. Nothing was amiss in Erdikoa as of now, but that could change at any moment. Power could corrupt even the purest of souls.

Gedeon's soul was already black, and Caius shuddered to think of what too much power would do to his twin.

"I need you and Lauren to spy on Gedeon when you switch shifts," he said abruptly. "Do it at night. Rory will be asleep and unaware of what you're doing."

Sam dropped onto the bench, and Caius thought it might break with the force. "How are we to do that undetected?"

He ignored the *Angel's* sarcasm and flicked his hand in Sam's direction. "You can shift into whatever animal you wish. I have faith you will find a way in without drawing attention to yourself." Sitting back, he studied his friend. Any other time, Sam would tell Caius to fuck off, but it was for Rory, and the commander would do anything for her.

"What are we looking for, exactly?" Sam asked after a brief pause.

Caius tried to suppress his triumphant smile. "We need to monitor my brother to ensure he doesn't know about Rory."

The smile slipped off his face. If Gedeon found out about her, Caius didn't know what they'd do. His only choice was to break through the barrier before then.

"Just do it," he said with finality. "And find Kit before you go. See if she's made any progress."

Kit stood on a ladder, reaching for a book on the top shelf, praying to the *Seraphim* she didn't fall to an early death.

"What have you found?" a booming voice said from behind her.

She jerked, making the ladder wobble, and she knew her time had come. Two large hands grabbed the ladder, holding it still.

"You are not very coordinated," Sam said and stepped aside for her to climb down.

When she stepped off the last rung, she sniffed indignantly. "And you are an asshole."

He ignored her. "You did not answer my question."

She held up the book she almost died for. "I found a few so far that might be promising." His pounding footsteps echoed through the quiet library as he followed her to the back room. "We need people to help go through them."

The torchlight reflected off of his armor when he crossed his arms. "No one can know."

She snorted and tossed the book onto the table with the

others. "It's too late for that. Lenora told Cat and Bellina about her vision and the king needing to find a way to Erdikoa." The commander's permanent frown deepened. "They're both smart. Cat loves history too, and we need to utilize them."

"I will have them removed from their jobs," he replied. "How many more books do you have to look through?"

Kit pointed to the massive catalog. "I'm not even a fourth of the way through, and I read most of the night and all of today."

"Read faster." Sam turned, and she briefly considered pelting him with a book.

"Send the others here as soon as possible," she called after him.

He left without responding, and Kit decided she didn't like the giant cockatoo.

Lenora, Bellina, and Cat burst into the library and called out for Kit.

She poked her head out of the back room. "In here." Seeing Lenora enter with her friends didn't surprise her.

The women meandered through the shelves, and when they piled into the room, Kit handed them each a book. "Look for anything pertaining to the barrier, breaking out of realms, the powers of the *Royals* or stronger beings, and anything else that sounds even vaguely related to breaking the king out of here."

Lenora grabbed Kit's hand. "Thank you for what you are doing for my daughter."

"She isn't just your daughter," she replied. "She's our friend."

"Yeah," Cat added. "She beat the shit out of Tallent for hurting Bellina. The least we can do is keep her from getting killed."

Bellina stiffened, and Kit wanted to slap Cat for being insensitive. "She's right," Bellina clipped. "Let's get started. The sooner we find something, the better."

CHAPTER 11

Sam knocked on Caius' bedroom door just before nightfall. He would leave for Erdikoa shortly, and irritation crawled up his arms at what he must do to enter the palace.

The door slid open, and Caius stepped aside. "I thought you'd be gone by now."

Sam walked past him and looked around the room. Caius refused to let anyone move Rory's things, and other than the bed and Caius' clothes, nothing had been touched. "You need to let Gracie clean in here."

The king ignored him and picked up a glass of amber liquor from the table beside his reading chair. "Why are you here?"

Gone was Sam's playful friend, and in his place was a broken man whose heart was dying at his own hand.

"Other than seeing Gedeon and protecting Rory, is there anything else you need?" Sam asked dutifully.

Caius stared at his drink, tossed it back, and turned his glassy eyes to Sam. "Would you kill me if I asked you to?"

Sam's indifferent facade cracked at the seriousness in

Caius' tone. "No," he barked back and then lowered his voice to a slight yell. "You can undo this. Let me tell her the truth."

Caius' fist tightened on the glass as the room darkened with his anger, the shadows forming a living coffin around them. "No matter what I do, she is in danger." He looked up. "But not if I'm dead. Gedeon wouldn't need to find a way to torture me or covet what is mine if I'm gone."

There were few things in existence that could shake the fearless Samyaza. The truth and conviction in his best friend's words were two of them.

He stepped forward, towering over the king. "Do not ask that of me. You would hurt not only yourself but Rory, too. If she is regaining her memories, as you say, what do you think will happen to her mind when she finds out you forfeited your life?" The shadows closed in around Sam, and he kicked at them. "Calm down so we can discuss this rationally."

Caius squeezed his eyes shut and massaged his temples. "I really fucked up." The darkness receded slightly. "I would have fucked up no matter what I chose."

Sam's wings disappeared as he sat in one of the other chairs. "What I do not understand is that you were going to marry her. *You* pursued *her* with marriage in mind. What changed?"

Caius looked weary. "What changed was my access to Erdikoa." Defeated eyes rose to meet Sam's, and instantly the commander understood. "I would have been able to kill Gedeon, and she would have been immortal, but then..." His voice cracked. "Her guilt would have sucked the life out of her, and I couldn't keep her here. Had we married, she still would've had to serve her sentence."

Sam wished he knew how to comfort people because the sight before him was crushing to see. Caius picked up his glass and threw it across the room. It shattered against a bookshelf, spraying the floor with razor-sharp shards.

"Had I married her and then taken over her contract, Gedeon would have felt the awareness of a new *Royal* and went looking for her. I wouldn't have been strong enough to protect her. She would *still* be in danger, immortal or not." He hung his head. "Had I known Lenora would show up, I wouldn't have traded contracts. I would have married her because being with her mother would've absolved her guilt. But I didn't know, and I did what I thought was best."

"And what of Adila?" Sam asked. "Have you tried speaking to her about Gedeon?"

Caius' features darkened again at the mention of his sister. "She won't speak to me."

Sam's brows pulled together. "Why not?"

"The last time I spoke to her was about bringing Lenora to Vincula for Rory's sake," Caius spat.

Sam remembered the day well. Adila wouldn't even let Caius tell her Lenora's name. She'd cut him off, told him not to ask her for anything, and hung up on him. "Have you tried calling her since then?"

Caius laughed humorlessly. "What's the use? She knows my sentence is up, but I've heard nothing from her."

The *Royals* each had a phone that only the other *Royals* had access to, and when they called, it indicated who the caller was. The phones lacked technology, but the magic in them was old. It was impossible for Adila not to know he called.

"Do you think she is working with Gedeon?" Sam asked carefully. He had only seen the Scales of Justice sporadically over the last five-hundred years. He stayed in Vincula mostly unless Caius sent him to Erdikoa. He preferred the relaxed atmosphere as opposed to the bustle of the light realm.

Because of his ability to detect lies, Sam knew Caius didn't kill Atarah. He wasn't sure how Adila's ability worked, but he'd always assumed it allowed her to see if the mystics on trial were guilty or not. Caius' sentencing never made sense.

He once asked Caius why he didn't fight Gedeon then, why he let himself be taken before the Scales of Justice in the first place. The king's response was, *"I thought my sister and I would stop him together."*

It struck Sam as odd that Gedeon never tried to kill Caius in the name of avenging their sister. *Unless the Lux King feared his brother.* Caius' power was strong, even when cut off from Erdikoa. It shouldn't be stronger than Gedeon's power, but Sam often questioned the fact.

Something resided within Caius, an ancient strength Sam sensed when they first met. Perhaps Gedeon recognized Caius' strength and feared he wouldn't win against him in a fight.

But what had he planned to do when Caius was released?

"How could she not be working with him?" Caius asked. "A part of me always hoped she sentenced me without hearing my side because she thought I was guilty and that if I confessed, she would have to sentence me to hell." He shook his head, lost in his own mind. "But that makes little sense. Her ability would have known my deserved fate, no matter what I said." Unfocused eyes stared at nothing as he voiced Sam's exact thoughts. "It was a lie I told myself because she was all I had left."

Sam sat quietly, letting his friend vent. He did not speak

about Adila often. Her betrayal cut deeper than Gedeon's ever did.

Sam stood, his wings fluttering as they reappeared. "Do not abandon Rory now," he said, looking down at his friend. "In Lenora's visions, only you can save her."

He turned to leave, but Caius' voice stopped him. "'*Only the golden child can save her*,'" he recited, giving Sam a tight smile. "It's more likely to be you than me."

Sam pushed the button to open the bookcase door and turned back before stepping into the corridor. "If I thought I could save her, I would have already done it."

***

Erdikoa

Sam appeared in the arrival bunker and ripped at his uniform more aggressively than was necessary. He ground his teeth together in frustration at all the things he had to watch happen, knowing his help would kill them all.

The power he possessed could make his clothes disappear, but there was something satisfying about ripping things when angry.

He yelled as he pulled the leather shirt from his body, threw it on the ground next to his breastplate, and tilted his head back to yell at the aether. "I will never forgive you if something happens to them."

He shifted into his wingless form, dressed in street clothes, and tied his hair back. Like shifter magic, he could shift in and out of animal form with his clothes still intact.

Once outside in the night air, he surveyed the area before shifting into a creature of the night. His sleek black fur would keep him well hidden, and his enhanced night vision would help him navigate his way.

He hurried across the courtyard that separated the bunker from the palace. The palace, the bunker, and the judgment chambers were separate buildings that sat close together.

It allowed each *Royal* complete control over their own domain.

Sam stayed close to the side of the building and waited near the back staff entrance. He was shrouded in darkness, keeping him hidden as he waited for someone to open the door.

Being in his mystic form put him at risk of discovery, but if no one came, he would be forced to shift back to let himself in.

The Lux Palace was a replica of the Umbra Palace, but where the Umbra Palace was all black and greys with silver accents, the Lux Palace was light, neutral colors tipped with gold. The staff wore the same uniforms, but instead of black, the Lux staff wore khaki and white.

The biggest difference was that the entire Lux Palace ran on essence and technology as opposed to the Umbra Palace, which lacked energy, save for Caius' quarters.

They were the same, but not.

Once inside, he would shift the color of his fur to blend in with the walls to remain unseen. A maid who looked to be in her thirties hurried toward the entrance, mumbling to herself about being late, and Sam inwardly grinned at her flustered state.

She wore her mousy brown hair in a low bun, and her beige uniform made her seem unremarkable. The woman was perfectly average in all aspects.

And very pretty, Sam noted when the essence light above the back entrance illuminated her face. She wouldn't draw attention when she entered and would hopefully be too distracted to notice him slipping in beside her. He stepped away from the building, readying himself, but she halted with a gasp.

She bent over with a face-splitting grin, showcasing two dimples, and he caught a glimpse of her *Eidolon* mystic mark. It must be frustrating for her at the palace because the walls and doors were infused with iron, rendering her ability useless.

"Aren't you the cutest little thing?" she cooed. "What's a sweet little cat like you doing out here all alone?" She picked him up as his tailed flicked furiously.

He considered scratching his way free but refrained. The last thing he needed was for the staff to be on the lookout for a rabid cat. She continued to pet him and murmur into his fur.

"Are you hungry? What's your name? Do you have a home?"

Sam's feline face was set in a disgruntled scowl as he bounced around in the maid's arms with each step she took. *He was inside the palace, at least.*

The maid rounded the corner into the staff breakroom and held Sam up like a trophy. "Look what I found!" He thrashed around, vowing to bite people if she didn't put him down. "Ope!" The maid giggled and brought him close to her chest again. "I'm sorry, little guy. I didn't mean to scare you."

Against his better judgment, Sam stayed still. As irritated as he was, he wouldn't risk hurting her. Chuffing, he tried to figure out how to extract himself safely from her arms and disappear into the palace without causing an uproar.

He should have shifted into a mouse.

"Where did you find that mangy thing, Stassi?" an older man's voice asked, and Sam hissed, glaring around Stassi's arm.

She hugged Sam closer. "He's not mangy, Herb. You can't even see that far."

Herb mumbled under his breath as he walked away, and another hand joined Stassi's on Sam's fur. "He looks mean, Stass."

Stassi nuzzled the top of his head. "You're not mean, are you?"

He tried to growl, but it came out as a purr, further damaging his cause.

"See?" Stassi mumbled against his head. "I'm taking him home with me."

"Sweetie," the other woman said. "You know you can't take anything outside of The Capital walls."

Sam felt Stassi slump, and he would have felt sympathy for the girl if she wasn't treating him like a common house cat.

"Even if it's just a house cat?" she asked, making Sam's scowl deepen. "Where is it going to live? It must have snuck in the gates somehow."

The woman sighed. "You can ask, but be prepared for them to say no."

Stassi gave Sam another squeeze. "I need somewhere to keep him until my shift is over." If she stuck him in a cage, he would have to shift and blow his cover.

"I think I saw a box in the supply closet near the kitchens' entrance," another man offered.

"Thanks!" Stassi called over her shoulder as she left the breakroom with an extra bounce in her step.

He wondered what she would do if he peed on her because if she didn't set him down, he would be forced to do it.

As they neared the kitchens, a man dressed like a palace guard stepped into the hallway, and Stassi's steps faltered as her heart rate sped up. Sam braced himself. This man scared her, and he didn't like it.

The man wasn't an *Aatxe*, but he wore a guard's uniform. Like enforcers, only *Aatxe* could be guards because they wouldn't abuse their authority. It was why the legion in Vincula, save for Sam and Lauren, were all *Aatxe*, as well.

"Hey, Stassi," the man said in an oily voice. "Cyrene said you took last night off."

Stassi's head jerked up and down, a movement that made her seem childlike and showcased her fear. Sam tensed, and despite being afraid, Stassi stroked his fur to calm him.

The man advanced toward them, and she took a step back. "Have you thought any more about my offer?" he asked, his beady eyes filled with lust.

She stopped retreating, took a deep breath, and steeled her spine. Her face hardened, and if Sam didn't know she'd been terrified only moments before, he'd think she wasn't bothered at all.

"I already told you my answer," she snapped.

The man laughed, and the sound made Sam want to rip his voice box out. "You don't have much of a choice." Sam lunged with a hiss when the man stepped closer, but Stassi held his feline body tighter against her chest. The man's lip curled when he looked at the cat. "You can either say yes to the arrangement I have *graciously* offered you, or you can consider yourself terminated, effective immediately." He rocked back on his heels, looking smug. "The other women chose wisely."

Stassi made a sound of disbelief. "You can't do that! I'll file a complaint with The Crown!"

The man was repugnant, and Sam made a mental note to return and make him bleed. "Mmm, and why haven't you reported me already?"

Her grip on Sam tightened, and he struggled to breathe. "Because you are not the first pervert to proposition me in my life, but blackmailing me is a new low. I'm reporting you."

The man feigned concern. "You will? Did you discover a way to reverse the effects of the memory magic?" Stassi's heart pounded harder, and Sam battled to keep his temper in check.

The man sucked air through his teeth with satisfaction. "I'll escort you to the gates myself, letting them know of your unwanted advances on palace staff." His smile was sinister. "You won't be able to get a word in before you're kicked out of The Capital permanently." He leaned forward, and his putrid breath made Sam gag. "And if you try to report me once we've completed our arrangement tonight, I'll tell them you're a lover scorned, and you'll lose your job, anyway."

"I am thirty-one years old, and you will not blackmail me into fucking you," she spat. "I would rather be clueless and jobless on the other side of the gates than let you lay a finger on me."

Sam would never know what was said after that because all he saw was red before he shifted and slammed the man against the wall. "In what realm do you think it is acceptable to fire a woman who does not wish to have sex with you?" His voice was low and barely restrained as he fought to keep his power suppressed.

The man in his arms thrashed, but whatever he tried to say was garbled by Sam's hand squeezing his neck. Stassi was sprawled out on the floor, and her eyes widened with fright. Blood dripped down one of her elbows, and she cradled it against her body.

Sam dropped the man and ran to her, crouching down, but she scooted back.

"St-stay back," she stammered and held up a bloody hand to ward him off.

"I need to make sure you are not hurt." He tried to make his voice as unimposing as possible, but when her skin leached of color, he knew he had failed.

A shuffle sounded from behind them, and Sam turned with a growl, forgetting he was no longer in animal form. The guard wet himself and begged for his life, but Sam heard none of it as he told the man to stay put.

When he turned back to Stassi, his eyes flicked to her injured elbow. "See someone about that and tell no one what happened." She nodded rapidly, watching him turn away. He hesitated, wanting to take her to the infirmary himself, but word would get back to Gedeon if he was seen with a bloody maid.

Before he did something stupid, he grabbed the guard and dragged him down the hallway. "If you make a sound, I will snap your neck to keep you quiet," he told him.

The man said nothing. *Good.*

∼

Sam quietly led the man through the hallways, and when he passed an *Aatxe* guard he recognized from his training course a couple of years back, he tipped his head by way of greeting. The woman's eyes slanted to the guard in his grip, but she said nothing.

Sam had free rein of the palace, but if news traveled back to Gedeon that the Vincula commander was there in the middle of the night right after Caius' release, it would raise red flags. It was why he must go undetected, but this poor excuse for a guard could not go unpunished.

Sam pushed open the staff entrance and stalked around the building toward the judgment chambers. Another *Aatxe* guard stood outside. Sam didn't recognize him, and when the guard asked him to state his business, Sam exposed his wings, fanning them out wide.

The guard was mesmerized, and the man in Sam's hold whimpered. "Samyaza?" the *Aatxe* asked.

"Yes," he rumbled to make his voice sound even more imposing. "This man committed a heinous crime and must be seen by the Scales of Justice."

"We can put him in a cell, but he will need to be scheduled for a trial," the *Aatxe* replied.

Sam nodded once. "I understand the way things work, but this cannot wait. I will speak with Adila myself."

The *Aatxe* dutifully stepped aside. Sam was the commander of the notorious Vincula legion, second only to the *Royals*. Before walking inside, he turned to the *Aatxe*. "I would like you to come inside to witness the trial, but I am commanding you to speak of this to no one."

The guard bowed his head. "Yes, commander."

Sam followed the *Aatxe* to the holding cells and shoved the man inside.

"I haven't been accused of anything by the law!" the man protested. He must feel brave with iron separating them. Sam's arm shot forward, bending the bars slightly, and his hand clamped around the man's throat.

"I am the law," he snarled, pushing a violent promise into every word.

The man shook, and Sam released him, turning to the *Aatxe* guard. "No matter what anyone says, you do not let him out until I return with the Scales of Justice."

"Yes, commander."

Sam nodded, left the holding cells, and wound his way through the building. As he walked, he examined his arm with a frown. The iron bars of the holding cell hadn't cut his impenetrable skin, but they tore his favorite shirt.

When Sam approached the guard outside of Adila's quarters, his wings were still out, revealing his identity. To her credit, the woman's expression remained stoic, but her pale cheeks filled with color as she said, "Commander." Sam glanced at her tiny bull-like horns to see if they were red too.

"I need you to help guard a defendant in the holding cells," he said. "I will bring the Scales of Justice down." The guard hesitated. "That is an order."

"Yes, commander." The guard left her post and hurried to the holding cells.

Sam stomped up the stairs to Adila's floor, tension radiating off of him in waves as he readied himself to see the woman who betrayed his best friend. His purpose was to have the imposter guard punished before Gedeon discovered his arrest, but Sam had a few questions of his own for the Scales of Justice.

Pressing his fingers to the keypad on the door at the top of the stairs, he unlocked it with ease and stepped inside.

The small amount of power he could use in the realms afforded him small conveniences, including tripping electronic locks.

Sam had a badge to grant him entry, but he wanted no record of him being here tonight.

The air was thick, and he knew someone was there, but the hallway was empty.

Adila materialized in front of him, and he stepped back. Sam was not one to gawk, but his lips parted with the urge to. She deflated with relief. "What is this?" Sam demanded. She had been invisible, but that wasn't possible. *That he knew of.*

Adila shook her head and held her finger to her lips. She paused before speaking, and her words threw him off guard. "I've been waiting for you," she purred.

He stiffened and opened his mouth to ask what was wrong with her, but then she mouthed, *"Play along,"* and tiptoed to the door he'd just come through to lock it.

"Good," was all he said back as he waited for her to lead the way.

Once inside her main chambers, she locked her bedroom door before waving her hand toward the bathroom. "Do you mind a little mood music?" she asked in a husky voice.

"No," he replied as his senses heightened, wondering why they had to continue with this charade inside of her private chambers.

She turned on music and stepped into the bathroom. "Take your clothes off," she said with a giggle before shaking her head furiously and mouthing, *"Don't you dare."*

He smirked as she hurried around the room, turning on every faucet.

Adila's small hands fisted his shirt and yanked him close.

"Keep your voice as quiet as possible." Sam pulled his head back and stared at her. He didn't know her well, but he knew she was telling the truth. "Gedeon has eyes everywhere. I don't know why Caius switched places with Aurora Raven."

Sam moved back to ask how she knew, but her hand clamped over his mouth. He nodded and bent forward to whisper. "How do you know he switched places? No one knows."

She muttered something about men and idiots. "I waited for Caius in the bunker," she admitted. "I saw you and Lauren enter a room, and I stood outside waiting, but instead of my brother's voice, I heard you speaking with Aurora." She twisted her mouth to the side. "The shapeshifting potion you used to change her face was impressive."

"You couldn't have been there without us seeing you," Sam replied. She couldn't have been there. The shape of the hallways in the bunker made it impossible to remain unseen.

She quickly disappeared into thin air and reappeared, making Sam jump. "Stop doing that."

"I think my *Aeternum* is a *Sylph*," she explained. "I can't manipulate air, but I can turn into it."

Sylphs were mystics who controlled air like Caius controlled shadows. Invisibility was an impressive skill not even he possessed. She shrugged and grabbed his shirt to pull his head down to hers.

"As I was saying, I don't know why Caius allowed Aurora to leave, but she must mean a great deal to him." She stared at Sam intently. "Gedeon can never find out."

Sam nodded. "It is a long story. Why did yo—"

Her hand clamped over his mouth again. "We don't have

time for questions. Gedeon has spies everywhere in the palace. My chambers are the only place without them because I control who guards and who doesn't." She ground her teeth together. "But it's still not safe to speak freely. I can't prove it, but somehow, he listens in on my conversations. I'm not sure if he bugged my phone or room, but anytime Caius calls, he visits the next day, asking if I've spoken to our brother."

She clenched her jaw so tight that Sam was concerned for her teeth. "It started right after I sentenced Caius to Vincula. After a few times, I realized something was wrong and limited my conversations with him as much as possible. Caius called recently, and Gedeon insisted I assign some of his other guards to patrol my chambers in preparation for Caius' return." She pulled her shoulders back. "I refused."

Other guards? He thought back to the man in the cell downstairs but rerouted his attention to what she said about the phones.

If only Caius knew. This entire time, he thought his sister hated him, but she had no choice in the matter. Her ability offered her no defense against Gedeon's light, and the fact must have scared Adila into submission.

Sam walked into Adila's room and closed his eyes, letting the surrounding essence call to his. He followed every little tug—the essence screen, remote control, music player—he stopped at her nightstand and opened the top drawer, freezing.

A dainty hand reached around him and slammed the drawer shut. Her eyes promised a slow murder if he opened it again.

He winked and closed his eyes, allowing himself to be pulled to a large painting.

She elbowed him out of the way and opened the frame like a door. A safe stared back at them, and after entering the code, Adila opened it to reveal her *Royal* phone.

The slide-out shelf under the phone drew him in, and moving the phone aside, he pulled out the shelf and examined it, realizing it was hollow. The shelf came apart with ease, and he cursed when he looked inside, removing a tiny microphone no bigger than his fingernail.

Adila snatched it from his hand to throw on the ground, but before she could stomp it to bits, Sam took the wire from her, set it on the table, and led her to the bathroom.

When he closed the door, she whirled on him, but he put a finger to his lips. "You need to keep it, or Gedeon will know you found it," he whispered. Sam needed to leave soon, and they would have to discuss everything at length at a later date. "I also need you to come to the cells with me."

Adila regarded him carefully before nodding and making her way to the door. He was surprised she agreed without question. When they were on the stairs, she whispered, "I don't think he has anywhere else bugged, or if he does, he gives no indication of the fact. I think it's only my phone he monitors remotely."

Sam nodded. Once downstairs, he led her to the man's cell, and they both studied him silently.

"You two are dismissed," she said to the two *Aatxe* standing guard. "Thank you."

They bid them goodbye and disappeared.

The imposter guard sat in the corner of the cell, crying. "Why are you in a guard's uniform?" Sam demanded.

The man's face was red and puffy. "Because I'm a guard."

Sam turned to Adila with a questioning look, and she

looked angry. "Gedeon started hiring non-*Aatxe* mystics as guards." Her eyes turned to slits as she stared down the guard in the cell. "I think he is finding people he believes will serve his agenda."

Sam opened the cell and dragged the man out. "Why did the Lux King hire you?"

"He'll kill me," the man whimpered.

Adila leaned forward and with an eerily calm voice said, "You will be judged today, and if you cooperate, I will consider sending you to Vincula instead of hell."

The man's eyes widened. "W-We report everything we hear to him," he stammered.

"What type of things are you listening for?" Sam asked and traded a knowing look with Adila.

The man glanced at Adila. "Anything about the *Royals*, even if only gossip. Especially the Umbra King."

"You've been spying on me," Adila stated flatly.

The man nodded. "When you are out of your chambers, yes."

Tilting her head, she watched him closely. "Why?"

"I don't know." *Truth.* Sam was grateful for his ability to detect lies. It made interrogations easier. "He pays us more than we'd make anywhere else for our loyalty and discretion," the guard blurted. "He also said he would torture us for a lifetime if we betrayed him."

"And you have the luxury of doing whatever you want," Sam seethed, thinking about Stassi's pounding heart. "It is why you thought you could fire a maid if she did not fuck you."

Adila's eyes burned with a quiet rage, and the man swallowed hard. "Yes."

An eerie calm fell over Adila, and Sam recognized the

power of the Scales of Justice as it took over. She inclined her head and softly said, "Give me your hand. It is time for your trial."

The man held out a trembling hand, and when Adila took it, she squeezed. "Your sentence is death."

Before the man could protest, he disappeared. The serenity of the Scales of Justice dissipated. "I knew my brother was spying on me, but I don't know why," Adila said.

Sam scratched his jaw as he thought. "He must suspect you will conspire with Caius to kill him. You two were close as children, yes?"

She cleared her throat and looked away. "I've never given Gedeon a reason to suspect me since Atarah's death," she said meekly. "I laid low and bided my time because I thought when Caius was released, he would come to me about Gedeon, and we could hash out a plan together."

"Why do you think Caius would come to you?" Sam scoffed. "You have barely spoken to him in five-hundred years."

"Because I know my brother," she snapped, and tears filled her eyes. "He knows me enough to know I had a reason for what I did. I hope."

Sam felt for the woman. She was put in an impossible position, and while he wanted to know why she hadn't joined forces with Caius initially, there was no time to discuss it. "We need to find a way to communicate. Can you go to Vincula?"

"No, but I can go into the city," she offered instead. "It wouldn't appear strange to venture into Erdikoa for a day or two, but if I disappear without a trace to go to Vincula, he might get suspicious. There's a place Caius and I would go camping as kids," she whispered. "Gedeon doesn't know about it. We can meet there."

"I know of it," Sam lied. They had no time to draw maps. He would ask Caius. "Meet us there in six days' time at dusk."

"I will," she promised him. Sam made to leave, but her voice stopped him. "Tell him I love him."

He looked back. "One day, you can tell him yourself."

CHAPTER 12

Gedeon stood in his office, staring at the head of his *elite* guard unit. Titus was a *Visitant* with the ability to sway people's emotions. It was useful amongst lesser mystics, putting them at ease around him and having them spill any secrets they may know.

"He's gone, Your Grace," Titus informed him.

One of his *elite* guards didn't turn in his report last night, and according to the gate log, he never left The Capital.

"And we are sure he is not with some maid somewhere, drunk and fucking?" Gedeon asked, clasping his hands behind his back.

"Not to our knowledge," Titus answered.

If something was amiss, he knew Caius was responsible. His brother's release should have been a few days ago, yet Gedeon heard nothing of him. He had prepared for his brother's possible retaliation. Planned on it, even.

His brother's wrath was unmatched. It was ironic, really,

how Caius was deemed the gentle child despite having the worst temper of the four *Royal* heirs.

But Gedeon was prepared. He had loyal guards placed within The Capital, as well as spies throughout the city.

One thing that both surprised and pleased Gedeon was that Adila seemed to want nothing to do with their brother. Caius was close with their sisters growing up, and as always, Gedeon was forgotten.

Forgotten by the *Seraphim* when his rightful position went to Caius, forgotten by his siblings, and forgotten by the world. He was merely the *Royal* everyone passed over.

The room brightened as Gedeon's irritation grew. "Scour The Capital. If he is not found by the end of the day, report back. Tell the others to be diligent. Something is amiss."

When Titus left, Gedeon filled his office with white-hot light. It would blind another mystic, but not him. Not the Lux King.

His power had grown stronger, and he'd spent years honing his skill to lethal perfection. He'd only just gained his light power after killing Atarah, and there was no way he could have killed Caius, but for five-hundred years, he worked to build his strength and control.

Gedeon felt ready to take on his brother when the time came, but with Caius hiding in Vincula, he wasn't sure when that time would be. *What was his brother planning?*

Walking to a cabinet against the far wall of his office, he pulled a key from his pocket to unlock it and reached inside the cabinet to pull out a jar that glowed bright pink.

Caressing the glass, he murmured, "Hello, darling."

The day he met his *Aeternum* was burned into his mind,

and the feel of her blood coating his hand squeezed his chest. He hadn't wanted to do it; she'd been so young.

A teenage girl with dark hair and bright grey eyes stared at him across the busy cafe. Her eyes were wide and curious, and Gedeon felt compelled to ask her why but refrained.

He ignored her and pulled out his cell phone to text one of his regular fucks. It was the reason he ventured into Erdikoa today. There wasn't enough selection in The Capital.

"Excuse me," a melodic voice said beside him, making him turn to see the pretty teenager he'd caught staring at him.

Something pulled him toward her, and he moved away. She was a child, and while he obviously didn't feel sexual desire for her, he felt something odd.

"I—you...," she started, fumbling over her words.

He quirked a brow. "Yes?"

Gedeon bit back a smile when she stood tall and lifted her chin. "You are in color, and I want to know why."

Their surroundings ceased to exist when her words sunk in, and he was unsure if he was breathing as he stared at her. Asking her was pointless because he knew what it meant.

She huffed when he said nothing. "I have grey-scale sight. I see everything in—"

"I know what grey-scale sight is, darling. Most unfortunate for you, but I'm afraid I must be going."

"No," she rushed, grabbing his arm. He was glad he wore long sleeves that day because if she touched his skin, he was fucked. "I see you in color." She waved her hands, motioning to his face. "Your eyes are gold. I don't know how I even know what gold looks like, but I do."

*Fuck. This wouldn't do. He didn't kill his sister and frame his brother just to lose his position. After hundreds of years, he thought the **Seraphim** deemed him unfit for an **Aeternum**.*

*Most **Royals** met their mates within the first one hundred years or so of their reign. It'd been almost five-hundred years for Gedeon, and much to his dismay, here his mate stood with wide eyes and a curious expression.*

No. He wouldn't give up everything he'd worked for. "I don't have time to sit and chat. Let's meet for lunch later this week and try to figure it out. Say, Friday?"

She swallowed. "You're old. I'm not going anywhere alone with you."

The smile he fought to conceal broke free. "And you're young. Too young for me, but I'd like to find out why you claim to have grey-scale sight yet see me in color."

She bristled. "I'm not lying."

"So you say," *he replied wryly.* "While I have no interest in you outside of finding out your little game, I'd rather you not speak of this to anyone until we find out what's going on, assuming you are telling the truth. I'd hate for us to become an experiment." *Noticing her backpack, he asked,* "Do you have a pen and paper?" *Without answering, she pulled a notebook and pencil from her bag.* "Write down your address, and I will pick you up."

She chewed on her lip, considering his offer. If she was as smart as he expected, she'd say no.

"No," *she said finally, making his smile widen.* "I'll meet you here after school."

"Very well, darling. What was your name?"

She stuck out her hand, but he ignored it, causing her to drop her arm with a frown. "Cora Raven. And you are?"

"Cora Raven," *he murmured, testing out her name.* "You can call me Bane."

After she left the cafe, he went back to the palace and inves-

tigated her. She was fifteen. Her parents were divorced, and she lived with her mother and twin sister, Aurora.

He cursed when he saw her mother was a **Sibyl.** **Sibyls** *were written off as insane, but what they spouted was true. Thankfully, no one listened.*

He pulled himself from the memory. The day he killed her was one of the hardest days of his life. Killing the other half of oneself wasn't easy, but it had to be done. Something within him burned at the memory.

When he'd held the dagger to her chest, he'd had a vision of himself through Cora's eyes and *felt* her fear. It had been a miracle he'd pierced her heart on the first try because the vision had rendered him blind, and when she died, it'd been excruciating. Even though he'd wanted to fall to his knees from the pain, he couldn't. The *Merrow* he'd paid off had to drag him away.

The recent news about Cora's sister took him by surprise. He hadn't thought about her family since killing her. When Adila sentenced Aurora to Vincula, he wondered if her power wasn't as all-knowing as everyone thought because Aurora was a fucking serial killer for aether's sake.

It's not the first time he questioned the validity of Adila's abilities. When he killed Atarah, he was young and impulsive. She'd told him the day before that he could no longer live in The Capital. She thought he needed to live amongst the regular mystics to lead a normal life. Gedeon wasn't immortal, or at least he didn't possess the healing power of his siblings.

He was young at the time, only twenty-nine years old, and Atarah's decree was just one more way his family alienated him. He decided they wouldn't push him out, and that night, he planned her assassination.

He hadn't planned on framing Caius outright; he only dressed as his brother in the rare event someone saw him but planned it to where the chances of anyone seeing him were almost non-existent.

Adila finding their brother guilty shouldn't have happened, but when it did, he was giddy; his brother deserved death for what he'd taken from Gedeon. The Umbra throne belonged to *him*, not Caius.

But the biggest question, the one he was sure Caius wondered as well, was *why* did she find him guilty? Gedeon had a theory, but he couldn't prove it. Adila could see the souls of all mystics except *Royals*. It made him think none of her abilities worked on *Royals*.

When one of the staff caught Caius standing over Atarah's body, covered in blood and holding a dagger, Gedeon didn't think there would be a trial. He's a king, after all.

But there was, and by some miracle, their sister found Caius guilty.

Did she instead use the evidence presented when deciding Caius' fate but didn't have the heart to damn him to hell? And if her power didn't work on him, *how* did she lock him away? The questions ate at Gedeon, but there was nothing he could do about it.

He shook himself from his spiraling thoughts and stared at Cora's soul. If only there had been a way to have her without eventually relinquishing his throne. The only way would've been to convince her not to have children, but he couldn't risk it. He'd known once their bond solidified, he would have denied her nothing.

Old storybooks mentioned reincarnation, but no one knew if the tales were true or not. He couldn't risk it, and so here she rested in a jar, tempting him every day to set her free.

The door to his office opened, and he turned around, shoving Cora's jar back into the cabinet when a maid entered with her cleaning cart.

She shrieked and placed a hand over her heaving chest. "I apologize for not knocking, Your Grace. I'm used to coming at night when no one is here."

Anastasia worked nights, and judging by the bags under her eyes, she'd not gone home from her shift yet. "You did not get to my office last night," he remarked, and she ducked her head, staring at her feet.

"No, Your Grace. My other duties took me longer than expected."

He approached her and reached his hand out, wrapping it around her neck to yank the meek woman forward. Her eyes widened with fear as he squeezed.

She was a mousy little thing and not someone who would typically catch his eye, but he always loved women who frightened easily.

His warm breath fanned her face when he leaned in and said, "From now on, even if you come to my office in the dead of night, you will knock first, or I will cut off your hand."

Why did his guards let her in without announcing her first?

A whimper escaped her quivering lips, inciting him to lick his own with a malicious smirk. He pushed her back and stuck his hands in his pockets, watching her with satisfaction as she trembled.

"Y-yes, Your Grace."

"Go home." He flicked his wrist in her direction and

crossed the room. "Get some sleep and return early for your shift to finish your duties. I will have a staff member call your phone number on file to remind you to return early."

"Thank you, Your Grace," she said and grabbed her cart to hurry from the room.

The fear on her face was delicious, and he considered taking her upstairs. How loud would she scream when cold steel punctured her delicate skin? How many slices would it take before she passed out from the pain?

He finished locking Cora's cabinet and cursed himself for allowing the thought of his mate to turn him soft, if only for a few minutes. The urge to release her soul was strong, but the need to keep her close was stronger.

He learned long ago that fear was more potent than love, and so fear is what he bestowed upon those around him.

There was a knock on the office door, and Titus entered, announcing Fiona, an *Alchemist* from the underground market in his employ.

"Bring her in," he said as he sat behind his desk.

"Has something happened?" he asked when she walked in. Whatever information his spies brought to him was more imperative than ever now that Caius was free to move between realms.

Fiona hesitated. "I'm unsure, Your Grace. You told me to report anything unusual I heard regarding your siblings, and this seemed unusual."

Gedeon motioned for her to sit. *Was Caius in Erdikoa?*

"I am not sure if this directly includes your siblings, but one of them must be responsible for it, and I thought you ought to know." She was a wise woman fueled by moedas, and if she thought it would earn her more, it must be important. "Aurora Raven has been released from Vincula early."

Gedeon stopped moving. *How was this possible?* "You're sure it was her?"

Fiona eyed him warily. "Yes. I sold her intoxicant for a few years, though I didn't know she was The Butcher at the time. She was waiting outside of the underground market, and when she spotted me, she said hello."

Gedeon sat, stunned. *Why would his sister release an inmate early, especially one as notorious as Aurora Raven?* It didn't make sense, nor had there been any news of it.

"Thank you, Fiona. You will be rewarded." He unlocked the bottom drawer of his desk and counted out a handsome amount of gold moedas. Handing them to the *Alchemist*, he said, "Keep your ears open, and let me know if you see her again."

Her eyes widened at the amount he handed her. "Yes, Your Grace. Thank you."

After she left, Gedeon picked up his office phone and called Titus. "I need a detail on everyone Aurora Raven was affiliated with before her arrest. She was released from Vincula, and I need to know everything about her and her associates. Be discreet. If any of your men breathe a word about this, I will kill you all."

Titus agreed and hung up. The light from the windows became blinding with his growing anticipation.

Aurora Raven was important to one of his siblings.

But which one?

CHAPTER 13

Rory jumped when the front door burst open, and Sam stomped in with an annoyed look on his face. She was beginning to think it was his default setting.

Standing abruptly, Lauren planted her hands on her hips and glared daggers. "Where have you been?"

It was around midnight, and Lauren had been on edge since dinner. Instead of answering, Sam said, "We need to speak in private." He opened the front door and gestured for Lauren to step outside.

"You should go to bed," she suggested to Rory with a look that brokered no argument.

Rory bristled at being ordered around like a child but didn't argue. "Fine."

She strolled toward the stairs, and when the front door shut, she ran the rest of the way to her room and cracked open her window. The large eave below her window blocked her vision, but Sam couldn't speak softly if he tried.

"Explain why you were hours late," Lauren demanded.

"I was at the Lux Palace," he replied, loud enough for the dead to hear.

"Why would you be there?" Lauren asked, reining back her attitude. "You hate that place."

"Caius wants us to spy on Gedeon during our shift changes," Sam explained.

Caius and Gedeon? As in the Lux and Umbra Kings? No one in Erdikoa knew what the *Royals* looked like, but they studied them in school. Everyone knew their names.

"I tried tonight, but I was intercepted." Something about his demeanor suggested there was more to that story.

She heard one of them shift before Lauren asked, "Intercepted by whom?"

"A maid," Sam replied. *Why did he sound uncomfortable?* "I shifted into a cat, hoping to move around undetected, and she caught me and tried to take me home."

Lauren laughed loudly. Rory slapped her hand over her mouth to keep from doing the same.

"We will cover more ground together," he replied in a gruff voice that made Rory want to laugh again.

"Next time, shift into a rat," Lauren suggested, trying to hold in another laugh. "No one will touch you then."

It was impressive how calm he sounded after telling someone he almost became a domesticated pet. "You must shift, as well," he said, all business. "We cannot chance being seen because the king is hiring other mystics as guards, not just *Aatxe*, and paying for their loyalty."

Rory swallowed the urge to yell, *'What?'* at the same time Lauren asked, "Why?"

"He hired them to spy and report back with anything pertaining to his siblings," Sam answered, sounding tired.

Nothing they said made sense. Why would the king spy on his own siblings?

"We can't leave her unprotected," Lauren said, grabbing Rory's attention.

"Patrick can take off those nights," Sam reasoned. "You will wait to leave until after she is asleep."

Rory heard rustling. She hated not being able to see them. "Someone can attack just as easily at night," Lauren pointed out.

Sam grunted. "No one knows about this house, and I am more worried about her sneaking out. It is better if she does not know."

How stupid did they think she was, and why did they think she had a set bedtime like a toddler? The coddling was driving her insane. Sam's words offended her. She understood the gravity of her situation, and unless an emergency arose, she wouldn't sneak out.

"Fine," Lauren conceded. "I'll see you at the bunker next shift change."

The two fell quiet, and Rory heard the front door open and close. She stared in a daze, trying to make sense of what she had heard. A shadow crossed over her face as Lauren appeared on the eave with her phone pointed at the open window, and Rory muffled a scream.

The *Angel* laughed at her phone and tucked it away in her pocket. "I knew you were listening."

Rory pursed her lips and tried to look like she didn't almost shit her pants. "I don't appreciate being treated like a child."

"Sometimes you act like one," Lauren replied immediately, making Rory scowl. "You don't understand the danger you're in, and I know you'll figure out our schedule soon enough. I am asking you to stay here."

"How selfish do you think I am?" Rory asked incredulously. "I know what is at stake, and I know my family will hurt the most if something happens to me. Don't pretend to know anything about me."

"I do know you, and I know you still want to avenge your sister." Lauren's wings appeared and spread wide. "I am asking you not to."

Without another word, Rory watched as her guard disappeared into the night sky.

Despite being restless, Rory refrained from gulping down her sleeping potion after crawling into bed. It was late, and she didn't want to sleep the next morning away.

Instead, she mulled over the *Angels'* conversation. Why would they spy on the Lux King, and why would the Lux King spy on the Scales of Justice? As with everything else in her life since she returned, she felt like she already knew the answer but couldn't reach it.

Sighing, she tugged on her comforter and berated herself for worrying about things out of her control. Her mother would return in a year, and everything would go back to normal.

Unless Rory's soul was trying to warn her about something.

"Fuck it," she muttered and grabbed the potion from her nightstand, hoping she found answers in her dream.

Wildflowers tickled the bottoms of her feet as she meandered through a garden. There was no sign of Not-Bane yet, and she walked faster along the winding path.

The walkway opened to a small pond, and the sight made heat pool low in her stomach. The closer she got, the more aroused she became. She **really** *needed to get laid.*

Did she have a pond fetish now?

"Hello, Miss Raven."

The silky voice sent a sensual shiver down her spine, and she cursed her body for betraying her. Without turning, she said, "Hello, whoever you are."

The heat from his body caressed her back as his breath fanned over her hair. "Are you still on that?"

Lifting a shoulder, she feigned nonchalance. "You say you're not Bane, yet you tell me nothing about yourself. How would you feel?"

She felt his hesitation and held her breath, hoping her mind was conjuring up another memory. "You can call me Caius."

"You're named after the Umbra King?" Another thought occurred, and her eyes widened. "Are you the Umbra King?"

His lip tugged to the side. "I imagine many people name their children after the **Royals.***"*

He was right. She'd gone to school with a Gedeon and an Atarah. "Where do you live?"

His breath against her ear made her shiver again. "Not close enough to you."

She tried to put much needed space between them. "Did we know each other in Vincula?" If he still lived in the prison realm, what were the odds he wasn't the king, and why would the king look like Bane?

He stuck a hand in the pocket of his sweatpants, drawing

her eyes down to a prominent bulge. At that moment, the desert had more moisture than her mouth, and she licked her lips before returning her eyes back to his devious grin.

"Do you see something you like, Miss Raven?"

Crossing her arms to cover her hardened nipples, she huffed. "Don't avoid the question."

He raked a hand through his messy blonde hair, and Rory tried not to watch his muscles flex with the movement. If someone had asked her that morning if the oblique muscles turned her on, she would have said no. Her answer had since changed.

The amusement in his voice suggested he knew what she was thinking. "Why do you think we met in Vincula?"

She stepped closer to him, hoping her proximity would muddle his mind like it did hers. "One of my guards said there was a man in Vincula I thought was Bane." He stiffened, making her smile. "So, it's true."

"You need to stop digging," he commanded tersely. "Forget your past and enjoy your future. It's all that matters now."

Her face twisted indignantly. "Our past matters because it put us where we are, no matter if it was good or bad. We learn from it, grow from it. If it didn't matter, we would forget it without magic, but it does, and it always will."

He reached out and touched a piece of her hair, letting it slide through his fingers. "If you focus on the past, you will never move forward. You will obsess over what you did wrong." His imploring eyes met hers. "You don't learn from your past because you learned your lesson as it happened." The muscle in his jaw fluttered as he looked away. "And then you learn to let go."

"What if I don't want to let go?" she whispered. "What if

I left someone in the past I was supposed to bring with me to the present?"

His golden gaze met hers again. "What if they purposefully pushed you into a future without them?"

Pain struck her in the chest at his harsh words. The same pain reflected in his eyes, and in that moment, she knew he was important to her, and she to him.

"Who are you?" she asked, barely above a whisper.

Reaching out a hand, he tenderly ran his thumb across her bottom lip. "I am a man who dreams of you, even if you don't dream of me, and when you forget me and move on with your life, I will dream of you still." He dropped his arm and backed away with a resigned expression.

The room shimmered, and she lurched forward, reaching for him. "Wait!"

Rory sat up with tears rolling down her face, knowing, without a doubt, that Caius was the missing piece. Nothing about it made sense, and despite him looking like Bane, she *knew* he wasn't.

Just as she knew colors without being told, she knew this too.

That only meant one thing: the real Bane was still out there, and despite everything in her telling her to find him, Caius' words echoed in her mind. *"You learn to let go."*

CHAPTER 14

VINCULA

Caius threw back his comforter as pain consumed him. Seeing her was bittersweet, but she was questioning things, meaning her memories were trying to return.

Every night he fought the urge to tell her, and he was second-guessing his decision not to. If he told her, could he convince her to stay hidden from Gedeon until he found a way out?

He didn't know. It should be impossible for Gedeon to know about her, and for all intents and purposes, Gedeon should think Caius was released.

Lenora's warning could not be ignored, but how would Gedeon find out? Could her friends really be trusted?

Padding across the room to the bathroom, he splashed water on his face. When he looked in the mirror, flashes of Rory assaulted him. Her cleaning his toilet while glaring daggers over her shoulder; the way she stubbornly refused his help bathing, despite needing it; seeing her curled on the floor, drowning in her grief.

His pain morphed into anger toward his brother and himself. A guttural cry tore from his throat, and shadows erupted around him, destroying the room. Bits of porcelain from the tub rained down, along with glass from the shower and mirror. He stared at his hands.

The veins turned black, creeping up his arms like roots. He lifted his hand and flexed his fingers, enthralled with his skin. This wasn't like the day the two men attacked Rory. The shadows had crawled *over* his skin then, creating the same illusion, but this time, they flowed through him like venom.

As he calmed down, the black receded, and he questioned if it had been there at all.

Bits of glass crunched under his bare feet as he walked into the bedroom without flinching.

He welcomed the pain.

Caius stalked through the halls of his palace, looking for Lauren. She didn't report to his office that morning, and he hoped she was still in her room.

Once outside her door, he lifted his hand to knock, but it swung open. Lauren's mouth quirked to the side. "Eager to hear about Rory, are we?"

Caius stepped aside, allowing her to exit her room and follow him to his office. "How is she?"

"You don't know?" the *Angel* asked. "I know you've seen her in the soulscape."

He came to a full stop. "She talks about me?" Could Lauren hear the galloping in his chest?

"She's asking questions." Lauren said, lowering her voice. "Did you tell her something, or is she remembering?"

"You tell me," he replied, walking with her toward his office. "She said you told her there was someone in Vincula she mistook for Bane."

The *Angel's* short legs kept pace with his long ones, and she side-eyed him as they walked. "I don't enjoy lying to her, and she asked me directly if Bane was in Vincula."

Shadows started snaking across the walls as Caius' agitation grew. *What if telling her things puts her in danger?* "You should have said nothing at all. I didn't say you needed to lie."

Lauren flicked her black and white hair behind her shoulder. "I told her nothing of importance. Do you want her hating you in the soulscape?"

He remained quiet.

"That's what I thought." Once inside his office, she turned to him with a tight, sympathetic smile. "It's okay to let yourself be happy, if only in the soulscape. You're spending time with her almost every night, and as far as she knows, they're only dreams."

"I think she's remembering," he admitted.

"Then let us tell her everything," Lauren pressed. "It will be easier to keep her safe if she knows the truth."

Caius laughed bitterly. "She doesn't have her memories, and if she doesn't think we're lying, she won't understand the gravity of the situation because she doesn't remember. It won't make her love me, and it won't make her jump back into the life she had with us." His words were thick. "Telling her will only put her in danger because she will go to Gedeon."

Lauren closed her eyes, and Caius wondered if she was counting to ten. Controlling her temper was not her forte. "You don't know that," the *Angel* said, emphasizing each word. "It's not fair to assume how she'll react. She is smarter than you are giving her credit for."

Caius clenched his teeth, fighting not to spew words he couldn't take back. His grievance wasn't with Lauren, and she didn't deserve to be on the receiving end of his anger. He was pissed at himself because he didn't know if his decisions were keeping her safe or putting her in more danger.

"Nothing you've done has made sense, Caius," Lauren said, and his restraint snapped.

"*Nothing about love makes sense,*" he thundered, making the shadows go in every direction. "*Nothing.* I did what I thought was best, and I know now I fucked up. Do you think I didn't know the moment I saw Lenora's name on that contract?" He fisted his hair, and Lauren's eyes widened as she watched him fall apart. "I don't know what to do. What if my decision is the one that sends her straight to Gedeon?"

"I think you should sit," Lauren said carefully, focusing on his hands. "Calm down."

His body ignited with fury; or maybe it was grief, pain, sadness, or all four. He couldn't tell the difference anymore and was losing his sense of self. "I will not calm down when my other half is in danger. Every second I'm awake, I'm consumed with her, and I can't see her, go to her, protect her, and it's no one's fault but *mine.* Don't tell me to fucking calm down."

"*Caius,*" Lauren shouted above the sound of the

shadows crashing around them. *"Something is happening, and you need to calm down."*

Her eyes focused on his hands, and when he saw the black veins covering his skin, he cursed and forced himself to control his emotions.

Fresh air dragged into his lungs and cleared the red haze around his mind. The sound of things crashing to the ground filled the room, and he opened his eyes to a familiar disaster. Anything not bolted down lay on the floor, most of it broken.

Lauren still stared at his hands, and they watched as the black veins slowly receded.

She stepped forward and grabbed his hand to examine it. "The last time that happened, you ripped a man's jaw off."

"I was angry," he replied, extracting his hand from hers. It was different this time, but she didn't need to know that. Hopefully, whatever Kit found would explain how the *Royals'* powers worked.

"Don't tell Rory anything," he said, getting their conversation back on track. "I'll test the waters in our soulscapes. It can be written off as a dream if needed." He sat down in one of the unbroken chairs, feeling defeated. Sending her to Erdikoa had been a mistake, and no matter how he tried to justify his actions, he'd been wrong. *What if he was wrong now?*

"If she regains her memories, do you think she would do the smart thing and lie low?" he asked Lauren, looking up.

She perched on the edge of his empty desk with a wry expression. "You know it's impossible for her to gain her memories back."

"It might not be," he argued. "As my *Aeternum*, she is *Seraphim* blessed."

His head rested in his hands as he mulled over every plausible scenario. Eventually, he came to a decision and prayed it was the right one. "I'll try to jog her memory in the soulscapes, and in the meantime, I will ask Kit to add memory recovery to her research list."

If looks could call you an idiot, Caius would be thoroughly offended by Lauren's. "First, you demand I tell her nothing," she recounted acrimoniously. "Now, you want to tell her in the soulscape to bring her memories back? You're giving me whiplash."

He was mentally exhausted. "Have you never battled internally? Thought you did the right thing, stuck to your decision, then realized you might be wrong?"

"I'm always right," she quipped and jumped off the desk. "I need to show Lenora and Rory's friends something, and when I return, you can tell me your thought process. We'll work it out."

"Can you bring Lenora here when you're done?" he asked before adding, "Why do you need to see her?"

Lauren pulled her phone from her pocket, laughing. "I scared Rory and recorded it."

"There's no service here," he reminded her. He'd never owned a cell phone because there was no service in Vincula. What would be the point?

"It doesn't need service to play a recorded video." She pointed at the small device and pushed a button. "It only needs to power on."

There was enough of his essence in his office to power up the small phone, and once the display was illuminated, he held his hand out. "You weren't going to show me?" he asked, masking his hurt.

Lauren placed the phone in his hand but shook her head. "You see her every night."

He pushed a button, and the screen went off. Pressing it again did nothing, and he frowned, flipping it over in search of another button. There were different ones on the sides and one on the front.

No matter what button he pushed, nothing happened. "I think it's broken."

Lauren was quiet, and when he looked up, her face was split with the biggest shit-eating grin he'd ever seen. "You shut it down. Hold down the button on the bottom for three seconds to power it back on."

He followed her instructions, and once the screen lit up, he looked at her expectantly.

"Tap the icon that looks like a painting."

While searching the screen, he kept tapping on different things by accident. "Why do you have so many files on here?"

She snickered, and he ignored her as he continued to look for the painting. He pushed another button, and his face filled the screen, startling him. Lauren roared with laughter.

"Forget it," he muttered and dropped the phone on his desk.

The *Angel* grabbed it, tapped on the screen a few times, and handed it back. It was a movie showing the front of a log cabin, a blur, and then Rory jumping back with a silent scream. The video stopped, and his heart pounded against his ribs as he played it again, smiling at the glare she shot the camera.

She transfixed him with every replay, and he wanted to watch her forever.

"Can Lenora record Rory a message to let her know she's okay?" Lauren asked, taking her phone back. "Rory will want to send her one, too. I know it's against the rules, but she needs this."

Any form of exchange between an inmate and the outside world was expressly forbidden by the *Seraphim*.

Caius couldn't care less about the *Seraphim* and their rules if he tried. If they wanted his loyalty, they should have sent Gedeon to hell when he killed his own sister. "Can you get me one?"

Lauren quirked a brow. "You two talk regularly. Why would you need one?"

It took him a minute to register her meaning. "Not a personalized video. A phone."

She rubbed her hand across her mouth to hide a smile. "Why do you want a phone when you can't use it here?"

"I want to look at her whenever I please," he answered honestly. "Take as many pictures of her as those things will hold and as many videos as you can record." One day, it might be all he had of her.

Lauren's face softened. "I'll get you one and fill it with her when she's not paying attention. Otherwise, she'll break the camera if I stick it in her face every day," she joked, and Caius laughed lightly at the thought of Rory threatening Lauren. The *Angel* stood and crossed the room to leave.

"Lauren," he called out as she closed the door behind her.

The door swung back open, and she poked her head in. "Yeah?"

"Record her laughing for me."

Emotion passed over her face, followed by a smile. "I'll tickle her if I have to."

A couple of hours later, Lenora bustled into the room with Lauren and Kit on her heels, and Caius smiled, genuinely happy to see her.

His eyes landed on Kit before sliding to Lauren. The *Angel* stepped in front of Lenora and kicked her a path through the rubble. "She needs to weigh in. If anyone will know anything, it's our resident bookworm."

Kit and Lenora looked around at the wreckage. "Did you do this?" Lenora tsked at him. "Start cleaning this up."

He straightened defensively. "I have staff to do that, and those who do will receive extra credits this month." Lenora didn't seem impressed, and three men stepped into the room with extra chairs, stopping her from scolding him further.

"What happened?" Kit asked, jumping to the point.

Caius glanced at Lenora. "Will restoring Rory's memories help?"

She regarded him thoughtfully, and Kit muttered something under her breath.

"I know my daughter, and if you tell her, she will try to avenge her sister. Even if she resists at first, she won't be able to help herself. It's who she is."

Caius shook his head. "I don't mean telling her." He paused. "I mean, yes, that is an option, but I'm talking about *restoring* the memories she lost."

Kit mumbled again, and Caius turned to her. "Is there something you'd like to say?"

The librarian looked at the other three, baffled. "Restoring her memories is no less of a feat than breaking the magic holding you here. It was put in place by the *Seraphim*, not a *Munin*."

A *Munin*. They were mystics with the ability to manipulate memories. Caius hadn't considered having Rory see one.

"It won't work," Kit said, interpreting his thoughts. "You think mystics haven't tried?" She snorted. "They have, and not only did it not work, but it's also illegal."

Lenora sat quietly, listening to the exchange, and Caius cleared his throat. "That's *if* we decide restoring them is the best course of action."

"Right," Kit agreed, nodding her head sardonically. Shadows wound around Kit's ankles, and she shrieked, kicking at them.

He smirked. "As I was saying, our choices are to tell her nothing and allow her to live as she is now, *tell* her what's happened the last three months, or find a way to restore her actual memories."

Kit glared at the retreating shadows, and Lauren gave her a look that said, *'You should have known better.'*

Ignoring them both, he turned to Lenora. "I can try to jog her memory in our soulscapes, and if I believe it's working, we can try to restore them completely."

"What is the difference between telling her about her missing memories and you jogging her memory?" Lenora asked, leaning forward.

Caius adjusted in his chair. "If the *Angels* and I tell her, she might not understand the seriousness of the situation and go after Gedeon herself."

"She will," Lenora agreed.

Caius' mouth pressed into a grim smile. "That's what I'm afraid of. If I try to remind her in our soulscape, it can be explained away as a dream if it doesn't work. But if it does and she remembers bits and pieces, then maybe a *Munin* can bring the rest of her memories back."

"Why do you think she will remember anything?" Kit questioned him. "It has never happened in the history of Vincula, as far as I know."

"I believe it's already happening," he said, glancing at Lauren.

Kit sat straight up, and Lenora sucked in a sharp breath.

"Holy aether," Kit breathed. "Are you sure?"

He nodded. "She's asking questions she shouldn't be asking. As my *Aeternum*, she is blessed, and it's possible the magic doesn't work as well on her," Caius said, repeating what he'd told Sam days earlier.

"By that logic, the magic holding you here might not work as well on you, either," Kit pointed out.

Caius considered her theory. It made sense, but *where* did he start? There were memory restoring methods they could try to break the magic binding Rory's memories, but there weren't any 'break out of prison' methods to try.

"Before I decide, I need to consider the consequences of every possibility." The weight of the silence between them was heavy, and he sighed. "I've already made a mistake that put her in danger, and I can't risk doing it again."

"She's in danger as she is," Lenora interjected, surprising them all. "If she stays in the dark, she is as good as dead." Her eyes glazed over slightly with her last statement, and Caius and Lauren shot to their feet.

"Did you see something?" he asked the *Sibyl*. "Lauren, did she keep any of her abilities?"

The *Angel* shook her head. "I didn't think so."

"I can hear you two," Lenora huffed. "No, I do not have my abilities, but I remembered a part of a prophecy I saw."

"What did you remember?" Caius asked, losing what little patience he had left.

"Watch your tone, young man," she scolded him. "I've told you I only remember pieces. Well, more like tiny shards. In one potential future, Rory knows, and she's in the Lux Palace, screaming your name as Gedeon chokes her."

Caius' body turned cold. "What? You're sure?"

Lenora nodded. "I don't get the sense that she's dying, only suffering, but in a future where she doesn't know, she's on the floor, dying, with blood pouring from her mouth as Gedeon stands over her. I-I don't know if she actually dies or not. I know that in both futures, she dies if you don't arrive soon enough, but I'm not sure which one gives you more time."

"You see different futures of different futures?" Kit asked.

Lenora nodded. "Every future can go different ways, and when I have my abilities, I see them all."

The librarian gaped at her. "I didn't realize it was that bad."

Caius cursed under his breath, and shadows snaked up the walls.

"Whoa," Kit breathed, looking around.

Lenora reached forward and grabbed his hand. "Stop."

Her touch made the shadows recede almost instantly. "We have to restore her memories," he said with finality. "We know she is on the path to Gedeon as she is. I cannot allow that."

"She is on the path to Gedeon no matter what," Lenora reminded him. "But I don't think keeping her in the dark is the best option."

"If we can't restore her memories, we have to tell her," Lauren added, and Kit bobbed her head in agreement.

He looked around the room, remembering when he once made Rory clean up his mess. Would telling her of memories where her emotions ran high be the key?

The others were waiting for him to respond, and he rolled his shirtsleeves up, bending over to pick up a piece of wood. "I know we have to tell her if she doesn't remember, but first, we try it my way."

He continued to collect as much debris as he could hold. "Lauren, you and Sam find everything available in Erdikoa that involves restoring memories." The armload he carried clattered loudly when he dropped it near the door. "Kit, add anything to do with memories to your research list." His throat tightened as he turned to Rory's mother. "Lenora, tell me if you remember anything else."

The *Sibyl* remembering minor details about her visions was helpful, but he feared what they revealed could break him.

CHAPTER 15

ERDIKOA

Rory had a stare-off with Sam across the dining table as they ate an early lunch with her father.

"Why are you looking at me?" he grunted, sticking half a sandwich in his mouth.

"Who is Gedeon?" she asked, satisfied when he choked on his food.

Her father stood with his plate in hand and reached across the table for Rory's. "I'll give you two privacy."

"Thanks, Dad," she called after him.

When Patrick disappeared into the kitchen, Sam said, "No one you need to concern yourself with."

A mischievous grin that would make Lauren proud spread across her face. "I shouldn't concern myself with my king?" She grabbed her glass and took a long drink. "That's odd."

Sam pushed his plate away and folded his arms on the table. "If you knew who he was, then why did you ask?"

She leaned forward, mirroring his position. "Because I knew you'd lie. Why?" Before he could answer, she added, "Why would the king assign non-*Aatxe* mystics as guards?"

Sam's face was blank, making her think he wouldn't answer, but he surprised her. "We do not know. It goes against the decree of the *Seraphim*."

"Then why don't they swoop down and stop him?" She twirled her glass around, smearing the condensation on the table.

She smirked at Sam's annoyance. "They cannot '*swoop down*.'" His massive arms bulged with his tension. "If the *Seraphim* use their full power in the realms, it will destroy the realms, killing everyone. It is a last resort. Even then, it is not a decision made lightly."

Rory paled. "Have they had to destroy the realms before?"

"Other *Seraphim* have wiped their realms clean to start over, but not ours," he assured her. "There has been no evil bad enough to warrant that level of action."

"Have you been in the realms since creation?" She motioned to his body. "Since you're an *Angel* most people don't think exists."

"No. I arrived not long after the current Umbra King took the throne," he replied. His eyes seemed distant, as though reliving a memory before saying, "Do not ask me about Gedeon again."

Rory's father walked into the dining room, holding a book. "I picked this up at work last night." He placed it on the table.

Leaning over the cover, she read the title aloud. "*Re-entry: Life After Vincula.*"

He placed a hand on her shoulder and gave it a squeeze.

"Inmates are put through an extensive re-entry program when they are released from prison to help ease them back into their normal lives," he said, sliding his eyes toward Sam.

"You cannot go through the program," the *Angel* informed her. "No one—"

"Can know I'm back. Yeah, we've been over that," she grumbled.

"I see you struggling, sport," her father said with a sad smile. "I thought this might help."

The knot in her chest burned. She wasn't just struggling; she was drowning. Life moved on without her, and she hadn't even realized it, and now she spent every waking moment playing catch up. "Thanks, Dad."

"I'll see you tonight before I leave for work," he promised.

"I love you," she said before he disappeared upstairs, leaving her alone with Sam once more.

The silence stretched between them, and she eyed the *Angel's* broad shoulders. "Can I see your wings?"

He scowled at her, and she bit back a smile. "No. What do you need to do today?"

Standing, she collected her glass and Sam's empty plate from the table, but he reached over and took them from her, grabbed his own glass, and followed her into the kitchen.

"Today is Wednesday," she told him over her shoulder as she took the dishes and loaded them into the washer.

"And tomorrow is the Plenilune," he deadpanned. The Plenilune happened once a month when the moon was full. It was nothing special to ordinary people.

But once a year, it was important to her.

She mentally ran through the months she missed. The Plenilune was the twentieth of every month, and if her calculations were correct, tomorrow was the anniversary of Cora's death.

"What month is it?" she asked stiffly.

Sam's hand touched the top of her back. "It's Avril. Is something wrong?"

Numb, she straightened, closed the washer, and wiped her hands on a dish towel. "Tomorrow is the anniversary of Cora's murder."

Sam did not look at her with pity, only understanding. "Would you like to hit something?"

His voice was so formal that she couldn't help but laugh a little. "Dume and I meet at a special place and drink in her honor. We trade stories and those kinds of things."

An awkward silence stretched between them, but she was too distracted to care as darkness blanketed her.

Holding her sister's lifeless body as she screamed was something she would never forget. Not that anyone would forget seeing their sibling murdered, but it often replayed in her mind in vivid detail.

"Do not get lost within yourself," Sam said with such tenderness that it took her aback. "I know what it is like to lose a loved one, and if you allow your grief to pull you under, you might not reach the surface again."

Her watery eyes met his. "I coped by killing," she whispered. "I thought I would feel better if I could prevent others from going through what Cora did. Without it, I'm not sure if I want to reach the surface anymore."

He leaned down and placed both hands on her shoulders, commanding her attention. "I know it is hard, but I learned that the ones we have lost are not the only people in our lives. A part of you will always be buried under the grief, but the rest of you belongs with those still here. Do not rob yourself of that joy."

A tear slipped down her cheek. What he said was true, and she owed it to herself and the people she loved to be present. "Thank you."

With a curt nod, he straightened. "Stop crying."

A laugh bubbled out of her as she looked at her robotic guard. "You are strange, but I like you."

Was that a flush she saw creeping up his neck?

"Earlier, you said today was Wednesday. What is the significance?" Sam asked, changing the subject.

She was still smiling at his obvious unease. "Yes. Dume, Kordie, Keith, and I used to meet every Wednesday afternoon. We decided last night in our group message to play catch-shot against another group from the rec. Sera knows them. She's filling in for Kordie."

Catch-shot was a sport Rory didn't care to watch, but it was fun to play. It's basically a big game of keep away with a batter, bases, and a lot of running.

Their group only played a few times before Kordie swore she would never play again.

Sam looked Rory up and down skeptically. "You play a sport?"

She pushed him, but his massive body didn't move. "I'm a *Fey*. I'm athletic."

"If little Sera cannot play, I will take her place," he offered, and Rory thought she saw a hint of excitement flit across his face.

"Come on, big boy, we need to stretch."

That afternoon, Rory stared at her long hair with scissors in her hand. Despite loving it long, she couldn't shake the urge to cut it off. There was no explanation for it.

"Drop those scissors, or I swear to the *Seraphim* I will dump an itching potion on your head!" Kordie's voice yelled from her bedroom door, and Rory jumped at least a foot in the air with a screech. *Why did people always sneak up on her?*

Kordie made Keith drop her off earlier so she and Rory could ride to the rec center together. They'd hung out that afternoon, talking about her and Keith, much to Sam's dismay.

Rory stared at her friend in the mirror like a deer shifter caught in the headlights.

"What are you doing?" Kordie hissed as she snatched the kitchen scissors from Rory's hand.

"I don't know," she confessed. "I need to cut my hair."

Kordie picked up a lock of her long hair, examining it. "Why?"

Rory rested her hands on either side of the sink. "It doesn't matter." She pushed off the counter and walked into her room to grab a hat from her closet.

"It does matter," Kordie said lightly, trailing behind her. "I'll cut it for you, but over my dead body will you do it yourself with kitchen scissors." She was an *Alchemist* with an esteemed salon, and if her best friend walked around with whacked-off hair, Rory knew she'd be mortified.

"Thank you. We can do it later," she said gratefully.

Kordie breathed a dramatic sigh of relief. "Come to my salon tomorrow. How short do you want it?"

"I don't want it easy to grab," Rory replied automatically and winced at her answer. She didn't know why she said that, but it was true. The sense that she was missing a piece of the puzzle ran down her spine, and she wanted to break something.

Kordie slid in front of her. "We'll start out small and cut it to here." She touched just below her shoulder. "Not too short, in case you change your mind."

"If I change my mind, can't you use a potion to grow it back?"

The *Alchemist's* mouth twisted to the side. "I can, but I'd still like to err on the side of caution in case you have to keep it for a few days."

Rory put her hair in a ponytail and donned her cap. "Alright. Are you ready to watch us kick ass?"

Kordie rolled her eyes. "You and Keith are too competitive for your own good." Rory grinned, and her friend added, "But wait until you see Sera in action. Don't be fooled by her small stature. She's tough."

A hint of jealousy wormed its way into Rory's chest. *Did they replace her with Sera when she was gone?*

Shaking off the notion, she scooted around Kordie into the hall and bounded down the stairs. "We'll be late if we don't leave now."

They loaded into the car with Sam, who had changed into athletic clothes and tied his hair back. Rory spotted the edge of a book peeking out from under the backseat and picked it up, remembering she had it in her lap the day they brought her home.

Flipping it over, she scanned the title, wondering why she had one of Cora's favorite books from when they were kids. Rory set it under her purse on the seat so she wouldn't forget to take it inside when they returned.

When they arrived at the rec center, Rory pulled her hat

lower to cover as much of her face as possible as they approached the field.

Dume met them halfway and handed Rory a glove. He was the most responsible of the group and always kept their equipment until they needed it.

"The team we're playing seems tense," he warned the two girls and Sam. "They aren't speaking much and keep glaring at us."

"Why?" Kordie wondered and peeked around Dume at the other team. "Have we played them before?"

"That's the thing," he replied, leading them to the dugout. "We have, and they were friendly."

Sera waved with a broad smile when they approached the field and held up a travel cooler. "I brought you three drinks."

"Thanks," Rory said with a grateful smile.

Keith stepped forward and hooked his arm around Kordie's waist, planting a loud kiss on her cheek. "I was beginning to think you wouldn't show," he teased.

"We're batting first," Sera said and clapped her hands together, rubbing them back and forth.

Rory chuckled at her enthusiasm. She liked her, but the thought of her with Rory's friends while she was gone stung.

Sam sat on the bench, and Rory felt the tension radiating from him. "What's wrong?" she asked.

He was staring at the other team. "Be careful when you're out on the field."

The other team glared at them, and he glared right back. "What is their problem?" she muttered.

Keith stood next to Sam and crossed his arms as he stared down the other team. "They know we're going to beat them again."

That wasn't it, and they all knew it.

"Kordie, we need you to play today," Keith said apologetically and handed her a glove.

She stared at it like it would bite her. "Why?"

He jerked his thumb toward the other team. "They said we're playing five on five today. I think they thought we would forfeit since we told them we only had four when we set up the match. Assholes."

"I'll play," Sam's deep voice rumbled as he stood.

Everyone stared at him, and Keith whooped loudly. "Fuck yeah. They're going to piss their pants when they see you."

The bench shook as Kordie plopped down with relief.

"What position am I playing?" Sam asked, taking the glove from Keith.

As Keith, Dume, and Sam talked gameplay, Rory stared at the other team. She felt the animosity from across the field.

The men broke apart, and everyone ran to their positions near the players they were covering as Sera grabbed a bat and stood over the fifth plate.

When Rory reached her position, the girl near her looked at her and stumbled back. "What the fuck?" she shouted as she continued to back up. Her teammates moved closer as she pointed at Rory. "It's The B-Butcher."

Rory cursed under her breath and shook her head. "Aurora is my cousin, not to mention she's in prison." She walked forward and offered her hand. "I'm Lo."

The other team looked uneasy, but they believed her. Why wouldn't they? "The resemblance is scary," the girl replied, tentatively taking her hand.

Rory put on her best act and laughed. "You should have

seen her twin sister. It was impossible to tell them apart."
Lie. "Please don't hold my cousin's crimes against me. We
were as shocked and hurt as everyone else."

"They were her friends," the other team's pitcher
accused, motioning to the rest of Rory's friends. "We
remember playing against her, and that one," he said,
turning to glare at Sera. "Holds rallies and praises her like a
hero. You're all sympathizers." He spat on the ground.
"Disgusting."

Rory's eyes caught movement behind him, and she
watched Sera stalk across the field like a predator as she
twirled her bat in her hand like a professional catch-shot
player.

Dume realized what she was about to do and bolted
toward her, and when she cocked the bat back with impressive form, he picked her up from behind.

The bat swung inches from the pitcher's head, and he
jumped back. "You crazy bitch!"

"Fuck you," she shouted as she struggled to free herself
from Dume's hold.

Rory couldn't help but double over with laughter at the
fury on Sera's face, the fear on the pitcher's, and the annoyance on Dume's.

"I will bash your fucking head in if you utter another
word," Sera vowed when Dume lowered her to the ground.

Rory, Keith, and Kordie joined Dume and Sera, and the
pitcher folded his arms across his chest, ready to spew more
insults, but he didn't realize Sam was behind him. The *Angel*
closed his massive hand around the pitcher's neck and
slammed him face-first onto the ground.

"I do not need a bat to kill you," he snarled. "I suggest
you and your friends go back to whatever filth you crawled

out of." The man on the ground screamed, and his team ran. "Your teammates are cowards. Leave." He released the guy's neck and backed away, watching him scurry after his friends.

Rory had yet to move when Keith approached her and slung an arm around her shoulders. "Don't listen to them, and never insult yourself to avoid upsetting people. I'd die before I let anything happen to you."

It was the same thing Dume said to her before she was arrested, back before they knew she was The Butcher. The knowledge that they still felt that way lightened a bit of the heaviness in her heart.

"I don't deserve any of you," she confessed, meaning every word.

"I will bash your head in, too, if I hear you put yourself down again," Sera yelled across the field. Rory snickered, understanding why everyone liked the girl so much. She took no bullshit.

Still laughing, they made their way to the parking lot, recounting the fear on the other team's faces when Sam went supermystic on the pitcher.

Rory peeked at him and swore she saw the faintest smile.

CHAPTER 16

VINCULA

Lenora, Cat, and Bellina sat around a large table in the library with books stacked around them as Kit flipped through the catalog. The king excused them from their jobs, and they'd been in the library from the time they woke until well into the night.

So far, they'd found nothing, but Kit refused to quit.

"I think I found something," Cat announced with impeccable timing.

Everyone crowded around her to look at the storybook. The design of the pages suggested it was old, as were most of the books in Vincula. They rarely received new ones.

Kit knew it was more likely they'd find information in the storybooks than anywhere else. There were no history books dating back to the beginning, but many of the old storybooks were retellings of earlier events. The books were doused in a preservation potion periodically to keep them intact.

Cat pointed at a picture of a large figure shrouded in black shadows that sparkled. "Listen to this. This guy Aemas," she pointed to the glittery shadow man, "created the realms for his wife, Lora." There was a picture of a woman who appeared to be dipped in gold. "It says she wanted stars, but I think it's a metaphor for something, because the next part doesn't match that."

"I don't understand," Bellina interjected.

Cat glared. "Will you wait? It's right here." Her excitement returned. "Aemas wanted to prove his love by giving her golden stars, and with his darkness, he created two realms.

"Lora marveled at the power of his love as she stood in the realms, watching the stars, but the shadows left no light." Cat thumped the book. "See? No sense. Stars *are* light. Anyway, it goes on to say that she called on the suns, spreading their energy to each of the realms, but to remind her of her husband's love, one realm was dark, and the other was light. Like them."

Cat stopped reading, and they stared at her. She huffed. "Don't you see? It's the creation. Our realms were *created* by the shadows and powered by the light. The dark realm is Vincula, and the light realm is Erdikoa."

Kit turned the information over in her mind, and Bellina clapped excitedly. "The king's shadow power! He controls what created the realms!"

"And it says his darkness is more powerful than Lora's light." Cat scanned the page again and pointed. "Here."

"Then he should be able to change the realm," Kit remarked. "Or rearrange the barrier to let him through."

Cat nodded, and her dark curls bounced with the movement. "Yes!"

Standing, Bellina rounded the table. "We need to tell him. The sooner he knows, the sooner he can try to bust out of here."

Lenora leaned forward and hugged Cat with a tender smile. "I am proud of you." She looked at the other two girls. "I am proud of all of you and what you're doing."

"Come on," Bellina said. "Bring the book."

Cat reached for the page to fold it over, and Kit slapped her hand. "Don't you dare dog ear that page. Hold on." She hurried to the desk, grabbed a bookmark, and made her way back. "You two stay here and keep looking. Focus on memory magic. Lenora and I will take this to the king."

Bellina and Cat murmured their agreement and returned to the books scattered around them.

～

Lauren entered Caius' office and stepped aside as Lenora and Kit walked inside.

When Caius registered who arrived, he stood, almost knocking his chair over. "You found something."

Kit grinned from ear to ear. "We think so." She opened an old storybook and placed it on his desk. "This is a tale about creation. According to the story, the shadows created the realms, and the light powers them."

He stared at the picture of a man with skin like a starry sky. It literally looked like his skin was jet-black with twinkling stars. A solid gold woman stood next to him. "Why is this significant?" Looking up, he was met with stares that insinuated he was an idiot.

"The shadows *created* the realms," Kit repeated. "If you control the shadows, you control creation."

"The realms are separated by magic, and magic is holding me here," he reminded them, shaking his head. "If the light powers the realms, then it controls the magic." He pointed to an essence light. "The magic possessed by mystics gives us power, and it stands to reason that light gives magic its power."

Kit jabbed the page so hard that he was surprised it didn't drill a hole. "It says darkness is stronger than light. You should be able to create something to break the magic holding you here or create a way through."

Caius flipped the page, skimming the story. He was disappointed in himself because he already knew this information about the shadows, but he never thought he could *create* something new. "I only know how to move the shadows, not *create* things. I wouldn't know where to begin unless there's a book telling me how, which I doubt."

"You need Sam," Lauren said from behind the women, and they all turned their attention to her.

To Caius, Sam's magic appeared to be no different from Lauren's. "If Sam knows, then you should know, too."

She huffed out a quiet laugh. "Sam is much older than I am. If anyone knows how it's him." That made sense. The way Sam spoke and held himself suggested he was older than Lauren and Caius combined.

"How old are you?" Kit blurted out, studying the *Angel*.

"Older than you," Lauren quipped, and the librarian glowered back.

"Where is Sam?" Lenora asked, breaking her silence. "You boys need to try breaking through."

"Sam will be back in a couple of days," Lauren answered her.

Nodding, Lenora spoke to Caius. "You will break through."

Hope and shock took root as he met her confident stare. "You've remembered something?"

She sat in a chair and smiled, but it wasn't one of joy, and Caius' hope evaporated. "I have. You—" Her brows knit together. "Explode. Or something like it."

The blood drained from his face at her foreboding words. "That doesn't sound promising."

Her lips moved as if having a conversation with herself. He didn't know how or why she was remembering parts of her visions. Maybe the *Seraphim* were helping them, or maybe without the assault of new visions, her mind could sort out the old ones stored within her memory.

"I can't explain it," she said finally. "But you get out."

"Do I get out in time to save her?" He wasn't sure he wanted to know her answer.

"You can," she replied, but her grim expression deepened his dread. "That doesn't mean you will."

The ominous response hung over their heads like a dark cloud. "Please, keep looking for anything that might help," he told the women. "And thank you."

They filed out of his office, and he retreated to his bedroom, praying sleep came easy tonight.

～

Caius stood in the palace gym on a field of wildflowers. His heart beat fast at the prospect of seeing his mate. As if he conjured her with hope alone, Rory walked out of the shower room and looked around.

When her eyes landed on him, they were frozen in time. "You're here," she whispered.

He raked a hand through his already messy hair and tried to keep himself from smiling like a lunatic. "I'm always here, Miss Raven."

"Why are we in a gym?" She pushed a punching bag as she walked by. "Have I been here before?"

"We have, many times." He met her in the middle and traced his eyes down her body. She wore a sleep set, not much different from the ones she wore in Vincula. "We've used this room for many things." Heat filled his eyes as they met hers. "Some were quite loud."

Her breath hitched before she spun around to survey the room. "Were we loud often?"

She peeked over her shoulder at him, and he sauntered across the room, pressing his chest to her back. With a featherlight touch, he brushed her hair aside and kissed her neck tenderly, half expecting her to elbow him in the face.

She stopped moving, and he smiled against her skin. "We were." On instinct alone, his hand snaked around her middle and pulled her body tighter against his. He closed his eyes, thankful to be close to her.

"We were together, then?" she mused, leaning her head back to rest on his shoulder.

Pressing his cheek against the side of her head, he nodded. "We were."

"I wish I could remember," she murmured. He did too.

The prospect of her memory returning lit him like a match. "Do you remember anything at all?"

*She swung around until they were face to face, his hand now resting on her lower back. All he could think was, **she's letting me touch her.***

"Sometimes I get this feeling." She waved her hand around her head. "Like whatever I'm doing is familiar. The memory is on the edge of my mind, but I can't reach it." She tilted her head up to meet his gaze. "Does that make sense?"

"What things?" He assumed the magic affected her differently, but no one believed him.

A pensive mask fell over her face, and her mouth bunched. "I hate stairs now."

Chuckling, he pushed her long hair over her shoulder, exposing her neck. "You didn't have your **Fey** strength in Vincula, and the stairs killed your legs when you first arrived." Another memory made his face darken. "And someone pushed you down a stairwell. You almost died."

Her lips parted. "Who pushed me?"

This was his opening to help her remember. "A woman named Nina was infatuated with me. She thought you stole me from her and convinced men to kill you." The image of Rory lying broken at the bottom of the stairs turned his stomach. "Once we proved it was her, you slit her throat."

Rory blanched. "I killed someone in prison? Why am I not in hell?"

"You were going to be my queen, and it was your right to pass judgment and dole out the punishment you saw fit."

"Queen?" she exclaimed with wide eyes, and he nodded. "You **are** the Umbra King!" She stepped away from him, and he regretted saying anything at all. "Why didn't you tell me?"

"I thought if I told you anything about your time in Vincula, there would be consequences, but I changed my mind." Silently, he pleaded for her to come back to him.

"Why me?" she whispered.

This woman was always too hard on herself. He closed the

distance between them, unable to stay away. "It was always going to be you, bond or not."

She frowned. "Bond?"

A wry smile formed on his lips. "You are my **Aeternum**."

No longer able to hold back, he kissed her. She hesitated but soon opened for him, and the feeling was like no other. Kissing her again was rapturous, and when she pulled away, he felt the loss deep inside.

She pressed her fingers to her lips. "What is an **Aeternum**?"

The room shimmered, and he hung his head. "Wear a dress tomorrow night," he said, kissing her cheek.

She looked around and groaned. "It's time to wake up."

CHAPTER 17

ERDIKOA

Rory jumped out of bed and rushed to the bathroom to get ready. Hurrying to her closet, she yanked on whatever clothes her hands landed on and hopped as she pulled her socks on before running downstairs.

She'd never lived in a house with stairs, and as her sock slid, she learned a valuable lesson: never run down a set of stairs unless you want to tumble. She screamed, but two meaty hands caught her before she hit the ground.

"I thought you were athletic," Sam said after setting her on the ground.

Her track record with stairs was getting increasingly worse, she thought as her heart pounded.

Ignoring his jab, she grabbed the shoes she left by the door and pulled them on. "I need to go to the library."

He pointed to a window. "It is still dark outside. The library is not open."

She reached into the pocket of her hoodie and called her

father, who picked up on the second ring. "Hey, is everything okay?"

"Can you let me into the library? I need to find a book." She grimaced at her rudeness. "Sorry. Nothing is wrong, but I need to look for anything on *Aeternums*."

Sam stared at her. "Why are you looking into *Aeternums*?"

She twisted around, and his expression made her turn to him fully. "Tell me what you know."

"If I find anything on them, I'll bring it home," her father promised, reminding her he was on the phone.

"Thanks, Dad. Love you," she said quickly and hung up.

"That was rude," Sam remarked.

She poked his chest. "Don't change the subject. What do you know about *Aeternums*?"

He turned from her and walked toward the kitchen. "I know nothing."

"You're lying," she accused and grabbed his arm to stop him.

He shook her off like a pesky fly and kept walking. "You ask too many questions."

"You will tell me what you know, or you will regret it," she threatened.

He laughed a little too hard, and she flipped off his back. He spun around and grabbed her hand. She stared at his hand holding hers, and when he tried to pull back, she stopped him. "We've done this before."

He ignored her. "Your threats do not scare me. What will you do to me? String me up from one of your hooks?"

"I won't kill you," she shot back. "But I will make you wish you were dead. Do you know what glitter is?" She gave him a saccharine smile. "Or what happens when it gets on your clothes or in your pretty hair?"

He grabbed eggs from the refrigerator and set them on the counter before grabbing a glass. "You are a child."

She watched him crack the eggs, drop them into the glass, and gulp them down in one drink. It was impossible to hide her disgust.

It surprised her that egg yolks were yellow. She never thought to ask what color they were when she had grey-scale sight.

"You were not this immature in Vincula," he remarked. "Is this how you act here?"

She tried a different approach. "Please, Sam. Caius mentioned it last night, and I need to know what he meant."

Sam's eyes flared, and she narrowed hers. Judging by the *Angel's* face, Caius told her the truth. "I know he's the Umbra King," she added. "And I know we were together and that a woman named Nina tried to have me killed."

Sam said something under his breath, shaking his head.

"I dream of him," Rory continued. "And the look on your face confirms it's true." She swallowed hard. "My mind is remembering and showing me through my dreams, isn't it?"

His eyes flicked to hers. "I cannot tell you what transpired in Vincula. It goes against the rules of the *Seraphim*."

"Who was Nina?" she tried again. His face remained stoic, giving away nothing. *Dammit.*

"Do not ask me questions." Sam rinsed his glass, placed it in the washer, and left the room, leaving her to stew.

It was evident he wouldn't budge, and staying in the dark wasn't an option. Rory made her way to the living room, eager to leave the house, but as Sam pointed out, it was too early for anything to be open. She didn't know where she'd go, anyway.

When she fell onto the comfortable couch, her mind wandered to last night.

Caius told her to wear a dress tonight. It felt silly, but she would do it. She needed to go shopping for the sexiest dress she could find. Her eyes closed at the memory of his lips on hers. It should have bothered her how easily she believed he didn't kill Cora, but something inside her trusted him.

A devious smile spread across her face as she sought Sam out, delighted to tell him they were going shopping. He would hate it.

Her smile fell when he held out a book. "You left this in the car."

The leather cover was smooth against her fingers when she took it from his outstretched hand. "Thank you." She'd been too distracted by the events at their game. Another thought occurred to her. "Why did I have this in the car the night I returned from Vincula if I never took it with me?"

Sam's stoic expression never changed. "I do not know."

Did she take it to Vincula, and if so, how? Dume arrested her at the bar, and she only had her small purse. "Are inmates allowed to bring things back?"

"No." He offered no explanation, and she was tempted to throw the book at him, but instead she ran upstairs to her room and tossed it on her bed.

When she returned, Sam wasn't in the living room, and she yelled, "I need to go shopping today!"

He stalked into the room with a disgruntled look, and she pressed her lips together. "I need a new dress."

"We will leave at a reasonable hour," he grunted and

looked pointedly at the window. "The stores are not yet open."

She nodded and headed toward the kitchen. "I know. Do you want breakfast?"

The look he gave her was one of utter confusion. "You saw me eat breakfast already."

She stared at him, remembering the raw eggs. "You are disgusting."

His eyes danced with amusement. "I am many things, but disgusting is not one of them." Brushing past her, he opened the fridge to grab ingredients. "Do you like omelets?"

"Everyone likes omelets," she replied, and after making a cup of coffee, slid onto a stool at the kitchen island. He cooked quietly as she observed him. The *Angel* was a big softie, even if he would die before admitting it.

The plate clanked against the counter when he set it down. "Eat." Staring at the plate, the feeling of déjà vu returned.

Her eyes were fixated on the food. "Is it not to your liking?" he asked, interrupting her spiraling.

Lifting her eyes to his, she tried to work out what she was feeling. "You've given me food before."

His face neither confirmed nor denied her guess. "Eat," he repeated and walked out of the kitchen.

First, the hand grab, now the food. Were they friends?

Eating quickly, she took out her phone and texted Sera to help her brainstorm ways to restore her memories. Her other friends would try to stop her—maybe not Keith, but he would tell Kordie, and she wouldn't agree and would tell Dume.

Something told her Sera would agree without hesitation.

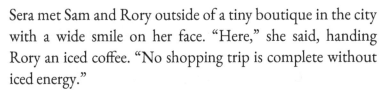

Sera met Sam and Rory outside of a tiny boutique in the city with a wide smile on her face. "Here," she said, handing Rory an iced coffee. "No shopping trip is complete without iced energy."

Rory took a sip and moaned. "You are a blessing from the *Seraphim*."

Sera turned to Sam. "You don't seem like the iced latte type. I got you a hot one instead." She removed another drink from the cup holder and held it out.

Rory worried he would hurt Sera's feelings with his blunt nature because he didn't drink coffee. If he tried to refuse it, she was making good on her previous threat.

Accepting the drink, he lifted it to his nose and sniffed. "Thank you. You are a thoughtful person." Rory relaxed but chuckled at his formality. "Let's get this over with."

Sera grabbed the door and shooed him away. "You stay out here. It's girl time, not massive-bodyguard-scares-away-the-associates time."

"Fine," he resigned and sat on a nearby bench.

The girls hurried inside and started looking through the racks. "Do you really need a dress, or are we scheming?"

Rory laughed despite herself. "We could have schemed on the phone. I really need a dress, and I thought it'd be fun to have someone help," she said honestly. The jealousy she once felt toward Sera was gone, and in its place was a desire to get to know her better.

She realized her friends wouldn't replace her, and it didn't surprise her they welcomed Sera into the group.

Sera held up a dress to Rory's front. "Is it for a special occasion?"

Rory shouldn't be embarrassed, but she was. It sounded ridiculous to admit she was buying a dress because a man in her dreams told her to.

"You can tell me." Sera lowered the dress. "I won't laugh or judge."

Rory sipped her coffee and considered her options. Worst-case scenario, her new friend thought she was delusional and told the others. *Screw it*. She grabbed a random dress and indicated for Sera to follow her into a dressing room.

"This is going to sound insane, and I know that," she began.

Sera grinned deviously. "I love insane. Tell me everything."

Rory lowered her voice to a whisper. "Since returning from Vincula, I keep getting these weird feelings when certain things happen like I've done it before. It happened when I met your dad."

Sera stared, wide-eyed. "Do you think you're remembering things from your time in prison?"

"That's the thing." Rory took another drink, giving her time to articulate her thoughts. "I'm not remembering, but it's like the memory is just out of reach."

"That would bug the shit out of me," Sera mumbled, sliding her eyes to the dress hanging on the door. "But what is the dress for?"

"This is the insane part. Almost every night, I have these dreams, and I'm either in somewhere I know from Erdikoa, or in an unfamiliar place that feels familiar." She hesitated, genuinely worried about how Sera would react. "The same man is always there. At first, I thought he was the man who killed my sister, but Lauren slipped up and said when I was in Vincula, there was a man I thought was Cora's murderer, but he wasn't." Sera watched her with rapt attention, encouraging her to continue. "His name is Caius."

"As in Caius the *Umbra King*?" Sera whispered with big eyes.

Rory nodded. "Yes. He said we were dating, and the worst part is that I believe him. I can feel it. Every time we're in a dream, we're wearing what we wore to bed." She swallowed, praying Sera would take this in stride. "Last night, he asked me to wear a dress tonight."

Sera flapped her hands excitedly. "Like for a date?"

Relief flooded Rory's body at the lack of judgment on her friend's face. "I don't know, but that's why I need a dress."

"Do you think you're *actually* meeting the king in your dreams?"

Rory straightened and looked down at Sera. She never considered the possibility that the dreams were real. "I assumed my memories were trying to come back, which is why I need to pick your brain." Sera shifted to all business as she waited. "There is something important I'm missing. I need to get my memories back, but I don't know how or if it's even possible."

"We'll think of something," Sera promised. "I'll think on it, and we can ask—"

"No," Rory said, cutting her off. "No one else can know. You seemed to be the most likely to believe me, but the others won't. Even if they did, they would tell me to leave well enough alone and enjoy my time back." *Like Lauren, Sam, and Caius.*

Sera beamed with pride. "Okay. You know, Keith's

parents are *Munin*. If you're almost remembering things, maybe their abilities will work on you."

"I can't ask them to do that, and that would involve telling Keith." She paused. "That will be our last resort." Even then, she didn't know if she would risk getting someone else in trouble for selfish gain.

Sera slumped and said something under her breath before perking up. "Wait! Do you remember the Glassman movie where the villain had a mind eraser weapon?" Rory nodded, unsure where she was going with this. "Glassman went to some super lab and asked them to create a potion to reverse the effects."

Glassman was a supermystic who turned into unbreakable glass. He was one of Dume's favorites when they were kids. "Potions like that are illegal." A light went off in Rory's head, and she shook Sera's shoulder. *Fiona*. "You beautiful genius! I know someone."

"Who?" Sera whispered, peeking out of the curtain.

"An *Alchemist* who sells illegal potions in the underground market. Whatever you need, she can make." Rory and Sera stared at each other, smiling like idiots.

"How are we going to ditch the giant on the sidewalk?" Sera asked, chewing her thumbnail.

Rory shook her head. "The underground market is dangerous. I won't risk you getting hurt."

Sera's face transformed into one that would scare Sam. "I am going, and if you say no, I'll go by myself."

"You're scary as fuck sometimes," Rory muttered with a hint of admiration.

Sera tightened her bright red ponytail. "I know. Now, when are we going?"

"Is everything all right in there?" an associate asked from the other side of the curtain, startling both girls.

"We're fine," Sera called back. "Just discussing boys. We'll be out in a moment."

"Let me know if I can help with anything," the woman responded before walking away.

"At some point this week, Sam and Lauren will switch shifts, leaving me alone with my dad." Their scheming brought on a wave of guilt. Rory berated Lauren for saying she would sneak out, and now she was planning to do exactly that. "We can leave then. The only problem is I won't know they're switching shifts until the night of."

Sera shrugged. "I'll be on standby. Call me, and I'll come get you."

"You have a car?" Most people didn't.

"Yes. My dad lives on the outskirts, and taking a cab that far is too expensive," she said.

Rory clasped Sera's hands in hers. "Thank you."

Sliding open the curtain, Sera stepped out and waved Rory off. "No problem." She looked around and found an associate. "We need help to find the perfect dress."

Rory's heart jumped in her chest at the prospect of seeing Caius tonight and the prospect of retrieving her memories.

CHAPTER 18

Rory sat on her bed, clutching a picture of Cora to her chest. The excitement of buying a dress for tonight and getting her memories back had occupied her every thought and temporarily distracted her from what today was.

But when she brought her shopping bags to her room, Dume messaged her, and her happiness shattered on the floor. Today was the eleventh anniversary of Cora's death, a stark reminder of why Rory went to prison to begin with.

She paused. That meant her twenty-sixth birthday was during her incarceration. Did she celebrate? Probably not. She'd hated birthdays since Cora died and tried to forget the day when at all possible. It wasn't the same without her twin. Her friends and family knew not to bring it up, and after years of avoidance, it sometimes slipped her mind until days or weeks later. Add in a life-changing event like going to prison, and she could almost guarantee it was the last thing she thought about while in Vincula.

Good.

She knew seeking vengeance for her twin sister's murder

would only bring more heartbreak to her friends and family, but knowing Bane had Cora's soul trapped somewhere made her decision excruciating. *Assuming he still had it.*

The sound of the car starting was Sam's way of letting her know it was time to go, and she crept down the stairs quietly to keep from waking her father. This day was hard on their entire family. Before getting ready, she'd left him a note and slid it under his door, telling him where she went and how much she loved him.

When they arrived at Dume's apartment building, he stood outside and waved them down.

Rolling down her window, she leaned her elbow on the door. "Ready to go?"

He nodded with a somber smile. "I've never been more ready for a drink in my life."

Every year they bought a shit ton of liquor and sat in the treehouse, reminiscing about old times when Cora was still alive. It was the one time a year Dume drank. At least, it used to be until Rory drove him to drink more.

Once at the park, they hopped out of the car and wove through the woods until they reached the massive tree that housed their childhood.

Sam surveyed the old structure. "This is impressive."

Dume and Rory exchanged smiles. It was one of their favorite places in Erdikoa, and when they came here, even on this day, it lifted their spirits.

They hurried up the ladder, and seconds later, Sam's head popped through the floor. "May I join you?"

"This place is big enough for even you," Dume joked.

Sam wedged his colossal body through, and Rory held in a laugh as his broad shoulders got stuck. "Do you need help?"

He glared at her and Dume as they lost control and burst out laughing. With a final grunt, he freed his shoulders and shimmied inside.

"How will you get out?" Rory asked, imagining his feet dangling in the air.

"I will shift. Had I known the door was made for infants, I would have shifted to come up," he replied, rendering Dume speechless.

Dume eyed him warily. "Shift?"

Sam brushed splinters of wood from his shoulders. "I can shift into any animal."

Dume shrugged and unloaded whiskey and cola soda from his backpack cooler like it was everyday news.

Rory began mixing their drinks as Dume dropped ice into plastic cups. "Are you drinking, Sam?"

"Someone must drive you two home." He scanned the treehouse. "Did you build this?"

After taking a drink, she smacked her lips with a loud pop. "No. We found it when we were kids. It was in terrible shape, but we used a restoration potion lacquer and elbow grease to restore it."

"We always wondered who built it," Dume chimed in. "Cora used to say it was the *Seraphim* themselves."

"She read too many adventure books," Rory said with a chuckle. "She saw the world through fresh eyes."

"Remember when she asked your mom to put her in sword fighting lessons 'just in case' the realm was attacked by creatures from other realms?" Dume asked, throwing his head back with a booming laugh.

"And when Mom said no, she tried to build her own sword out of our shower curtain rod," Rory recalled, and they both roared with laughter.

"I would have taught her," Sam said with a small smile. "I wish I could have met her."

The tender words touched Rory. They were unlike him, and her heart lurched for the man sitting across from her. "If she met the infamous Samyaza, she would have fainted."

Dume spewed his drink all over the floor. "Samyaza?" he choked out.

Rory bit her lip, and Sam gave her an '*I'm going to kill you*' look.

"*Sorry*," she mouthed.

Dume gulped, looking starstruck. "You're *the* Samyaza?"

"No," Sam said as Rory said, "Yes." He shot her another look, and she winced.

"No fucking way," Dume breathed.

"Yes," Sam grumbled. "You cannot tell anyone." The look he gave Dume made the *Aatxe* scoot closer to Rory.

She laughed for the thousandth time that night. "Don't be afraid of him. He's secretly nice."

"How would you know?" Dume challenged. "You've only known him for a week."

Sam didn't react to her teasing and instead asked, "How *do* you know I am Samyaza?"

She opened her mouth to answer but came up short.

Did Lauren tell her? No, she would remember that conversation. Shocked, she looked at the two men. "I don't know. I just do."

Sam cleared his throat and turned away from her while Dume assessed her carefully, but before he could ask questions, another memory surfaced.

The dream she had of the treehouse. Caius said he and his sisters had this place built. She shot to her feet and faced Sam.

"Caius and his sisters built this place."

Sam scratched his jaw as he regarded her without so much as a peep.

"Who is Caius?" Dume asked, rising to his feet.

Rory began searching for anything that might suggest the information was true. "Did we keep anything that was already here when we found the place?"

The men watched her frantically overturn the entire place. "No. It was unsalvageable. We brought in the pillow seats, knick-knacks, and Cora's books."

Rory heard nothing else he said as she made a beeline for the bookshelf. Caius felt for something under the shelves, but he never said what he was looking for. Dropping to her knees, she ran her hand under the top shelf as he had done. *Which shelf was it?*

When she ran her hand on the underside of the bottom shelf, her fingers grazed over something carved into the wood. She pulled out the books, threw them on the ground, and tugged at the wood.

"Help me," she pleaded through gritted teeth as she yanked hard enough to hurt her fingers.

Dume pulled her back and pinned her arms to her sides. "How drunk are you?"

She wiggled free and shoved him lightly to make him move. "I only had one drink. I need to see the bottom of this shelf."

Sam quietly watched the exchange. She could use his strength, but it was apparent he wouldn't help. "I need something to break the shelf."

Dume stepped between her and the small piece of furniture. "Calm down, Rory. Why are you destroying Cora's bookshelf?"

Realizing she wanted to destroy Cora's favorite thing in their hideout gave her pause. "I'll buy potions to fix it," she promised. "But I need to see the bottom of the last shelf."

Dume's eyes met Sam's before he sighed and kneeled beside her. "Watch out. I don't want any wood hitting you."

She scooted back and watched as he grabbed the entire shelf and pulled with every bit of his strength. It released with a loud crack, and Dume fell back on his butt, holding the shelf in his hands.

Rory stood and took the shelf from him. "Sorry. Thank you."

She laid the shelf on its back, inspected the bottom of the wood, and gasped when she saw two names carved there. *Caius and Adila*

She stumbled back as tears filled her eyes. "How would I know that was there? It's not possible. There's no way I could remember that because I've never seen it before."

If it wasn't knowledge she already possessed, her brain couldn't tell her in a dream.

Did Caius tell her in Vincula? How would they even broach the topic of the treehouse, let alone know they shared memories of the same one? When he found out she'd been there, he seemed surprised.

Her conversation with Sera resurfaced as she examined the wood. *What if her dreams were real?*

Sam cursed behind them, and Rory turned on him. "Are my dreams real? Is he really there?"

"What dreams?" Dume demanded. He reached down and grabbed the wood to examine it. "Will someone tell me what's going on?" Reading the names, his eyes widened. "Oh, shit. Are these who I think they are?"

"It is not my place to say," Sam replied. Rory didn't know if he was answering her question or Dume's.

Dume dropped the wood. "What aren't you telling me?"

"I'll tell you in the car," she said, starting toward the entrance. In her haste, she stepped on a book, making her foot slip and her arms windmill. Dume steadied her, and when she looked down, her heart stopped.

"That's impossible," she breathed, snatching the book off the ground.

Rory flipped it open as the others watched her quietly. Her hands shook when she saw Cora's name written in childlike handwriting on the inside cover. "I have this book in my bedroom at the safe house. It's the one I had in the car after returning from prison." She looked at Sam. "How is it here? I didn't bring it with me tonight."

His eyes flashed knowingly, but he said nothing.

"I need to get home," she insisted, shouldering past Dume. Neither man tried to stop her, and when they were loaded up and driving back to her new home, she told Dume everything.

She didn't care if anyone believed her or if they thought she was crazy.

～

After dropping Dume off, Rory peppered Sam with questions, but he refused to answer any of them. As soon as he parked in their driveway, she jumped out of the SUV with Cora's book and ran to her room.

Sam's loud footsteps sounded on the stairs, and she turned to glare at him. "Don't bother coming up here if you won't help."

"Knowing and remembering are two different things," he said quietly. "Knowing will only further your frustration, and remembering might break you."

His words were a blow to her resolve. "If you were me, would you stop trying?"

The muscles in his shoulders tensed before he eventually said, "No."

A sort of understanding passed between them. Sam wouldn't help her, but he wouldn't stop her, either. She took a shaky breath and opened her nightstand drawer to retrieve the book that matched the one in her hands.

Holding them up, she realized the one from her nightstand was in better condition than Cora's well-loved copy. The bedsprings creaked when she lowered herself to the mattress, and she placed Cora's book beside her to open the mystery one.

Nothing was written on the inside, but when she flipped through the pages, a scrap of paper fell out.

Rory,

The oversized buzzard won't let me in. I guess your royal boyfriend hasn't changed his mind about letting you attend the ball. Tell him to fuck off for me. The bird, too. I'll be back tomorrow, and if the brute doesn't let me in, I will light his wings on fire.

-Bellina

Rory read the note repeatedly. "Sam, who is Bellina?" she yelled, not expecting him to answer.

He appeared at her door, sympathy painting his features. "May I see the note?"

She placed the paper in his outstretched hand, and when he read it, he scowled. "My wings look nothing like a buzzard."

Despite herself, Rory laughed. "Can you tell me if the note is real?" It felt like a stupid question since it was tangible evidence, but she wanted to hear him say it.

After handing the paper back to her, he walked to the door and said, "It is."

Rory's breath caught as she watched him go.

Looking back down at the paper, she carefully placed it back into the book that wasn't Cora's. Her dreams were real because if her brain had tried telling her things from her time in prison, someone as important as Bellina would have surfaced.

Remembering her new dress, she grabbed it and took a shower to get ready. When she was primped and polished, she slipped under the covers.

Not taking any chances, she grabbed the potion from her nightstand and drank more than necessary.

Her last thought before sleep pulled her under was, *"He's real."*

CHAPTER 19

VINCULA

Wildflowers covered Caius and Rory's bedroom floor, and he looked around, hoping everything he set up transferred to the soulscape. A long breath pushed past his lips when he saw the twinkling lights, refreshment table, and music box sitting exactly where he left them.

"Caius," came Rory's frantic voice from behind him, and when he turned around, he was stunned.

Her hair hung straight around her face, and her skin was radiant against the golden silk of her floor-length dress. He wanted to stare at her for an eternity. "You look good enough to eat, Miss Raven."

Alarm bells blared in his mind when he saw the expression on her face as she hurried across the room. "What's happened?" he demanded.

"You're real," she claimed as she closed the distance between them. "Don't deny it because I know I'm right." Her

teeth dug into her bottom lip, and he could tell she was staving off tears.

Wrapping his hand around the back of her neck, he pulled her closer. Their lips were only a breath apart, and he couldn't help but smile. "Am I?"

Her hands pushed against his chest. "I found your names."

Keeping his composure, he smirked at her. "Are you stalking me, Miss Raven?" He couldn't keep his distance and moved into her space again. "Tell me. Were you looking for my pictures to hang above your bed?" Her eyes flared, and he brushed his lips over hers. "Do you want to touch yourself as you stare at my face?"

She drew back. "Do you always think with your dick?"

"Yes," he answered immediately, and she pursed her lips as he fought a smile. What she told him was monumental, but he couldn't let her panic. Teasing her always calmed her down.

Caius longed to tell her that, no, he didn't always think with his dick because his thoughts **were** consumed with all of her, not just her body. He missed everything about her. Their late-night talks in bed, her temper, her teasing, the way she'd bring him sweets or a book if he had trouble sleeping. He loved this woman more than he'd ever loved anything, and without her, he felt broken.

"In the treehouse," she snapped, and he grinned widely. There she was. "The names you carved into the bookshelf. I found them."

Her golden dress swished as she paced back and forth. "I thought this was a dream." She twirled her finger in the air and redirected her steps toward him. "I thought **you** were a dream."

When she looked up, he winked. "I am."

*Her scowl was as beautiful as her smile. "Will you be serious? **Seraphim**, are you always this arrogant?"*

*He opened his mouth to answer, but she pressed a finger to his lips. "It was a rhetorical question." When he nipped at her finger, she pulled it back. "How is this possible?" she whispered. "You're real. I **know** you are."*

*He shrugged out of his suit jacket and laid it on the bed. "It's possible because you are my **Aeternum**, and this is our soulscape." Her eyes were glued to his chest. "My eyes are up here, Miss Raven."*

Jerking her head up, she glared at him. "It's not my fault your shirt doesn't fit properly."

He looked down at the material stretched across his broad chest. "It's buttoned fine, and while we're on the subject, you look beautiful in that dress."

"You should see what's underneath it." Her eyes widened as though she hadn't meant to let those words slip from her mouth.

He ate up the distance between them and grabbed the side of her neck, ghosting his thumb across her jaw. "I will."

A smile almost appeared on her pretty face before she remembered herself and pressed him back. "This is serious. What is a soulscape?"

"A soulscape is where our souls meet when we're apart," he explained. "We meet here when we are both asleep." He watched her absorb the information and added, "We've been meeting in the soulscape since you turned twenty-one, but neither of us remembered them. Mates don't remember their soulscapes until they solidify the bond."

Rory scanned the room, distracted by the decorations. "Did you do all of this?" When he nodded, she reached up and ran

her finger over a strand of low-hanging lights. "Why are we
dressed up, Caius?"

"You're not in Vincula to attend our Plenilune ball." He
strode to the music box and cranked the volume a little higher.
"I made us our own."

"Plenilune ball? What is that?"

"You don't know what the Plenilune is?" he teased. "I
thought the education system in Erdikoa was top-notch."

"I know what the Plenilune is," she said through clenched
teeth. "But we don't have Plenilune **balls** in Erdikoa."

Caius knew this because there was nothing special about
the Plenilune there. In Vincula, it was the one night a month
when they could see the stars and full moon that revolved
around the Vincula sun. He never understood the anomaly,
but it was beautiful and something to be celebrated. "We do in
Vincula."

He saw the moment of recognition in her eyes and the look
of concentration as she chased the memory. "You've done this
for me before?"

"I have," he confirmed with a soft chuckle. "But instead of
surprising you, you barged into the room in a murderous
rage."

She eyed him curiously. "Why was I mad?"

He shrugged. "You were always mad at me for one thing
or another." Two flutes of champagne sat on the table, and he
handed her one. "You were planning my murder when we
met."

After taking a long drink, she licked her lips. "Because I
thought you killed Cora."

He nodded. "I won you over then, Miss Raven, and I will
do it again."

"Oh? And how do you plan on doing that?" Her voice held a challenge he was happy to accept.

Tracing his eyes down the length of her, he slowly unbuttoned his shirt, savoring how her eyes darkened with desire. "Sleep with me."

Champagne spewed from her mouth. "No. You can't go around asking people to fuck you. What is wrong with you?"

The smooth fabric of his shirt slid off his shoulders and onto the floor. "I didn't ask you to fuck me, Miss Raven. I asked you to sleep with me, but if you'd like me to, I'd be happy to make you come before I hold you."

Her mouth moved wordlessly as he unbuckled his pants. There would be no dancing tonight, and some of his favorite memories with Rory were the nights they lay awake, talking.

He folded the comforter back, grabbed one of her old shifts from her dresser drawer, and moved across the room toward her. Never breaking eye contact, he kneeled and grabbed the hem of her dress, dragging it up, but she stopped him.

"There's a zipper," she said softly, setting her glass down.

His fingers trailed down her legs as he lowered the hem of her dress. Goosebumps cascaded across her skin, and when he stood to unzip her, he couldn't help but place a kiss on the nape of her neck.

He reached for the shift and held it out to her without looking. He knew her body as well as his own, but she didn't know that yet.

While he held out the garment, he heard the bed dip and glanced over to see her tucking herself in. The shift slipped from his fingers without a second thought as he slid into bed beside her.

Was she naked under the blanket, or was she wearing a

bra and panties? Had there been a bra when he unzipped her? He couldn't remember, and it was all he could think about.

Flipping onto her side, she stuck her hands under her head and watched him do the same. "It's strange," she murmured. "To have no memory of someone you love."

His breath caught in his throat. "How do you know you love me?"

She brought her hand to her chest, pressing lightly. "Here. I know it as well as I know my name. I may not remember falling, but my heart remembers loving you."

A tear trailed down her cheek, and he leaned forward to kiss it away. "Don't cry. I will find my way back to you," he vowed as the room shimmered. Smoothing her hair back, he kissed her forehead. "Time to wake up."

～

Lying in bed, Caius stared at nothing and rehashed every word Rory said in their soulscape. He knew she was on the verge of remembering, and he needed to give her the extra push. *But how?*

When he looked back on all the poor decisions leading to their current situation, he hated himself. Everyone ostracized him for his choices, but had they been in his shoes, would they have followed their own advice?

Love blinds your brain and binds your will, and once it takes hold, you become a slave to it. He'd read that in a book somewhere but never understood it until now.

Getting up, he prepared for the day and took the corridor to his office, determined to learn to *create*. Without access to Erdikoa, he didn't know if he possessed enough power, but he had to try.

He needed Sam, but the commander wasn't due back for another couple of days. Caius would send Lauren to Erdikoa early to switch places, and he needed to assign an enforcer to finish her work.

It took a lot to run and maintain an efficient town, let alone a prison town. And despite it being relatively peaceful, there were those who teetered on the edge and required close monitoring. Lauren took daily reports from every legion member to know which prisoners to watch. She barely had time to do her work as it was.

Sam, too.

Caius didn't trust anyone else to do their jobs, nor did anyone else possess their power. All the legion enforcers were *Aatxe* with honest souls, but even *Aatxe* could unknowingly be manipulated by others.

A few weeks ago, a legion guard stopped Lauren to report a disturbance. She detected no lies from the guard because the guard herself believed her story to be true, but they later learned she had been poisoned by Nina's back-alley potion, allowing Nina to manipulate her mind with falsities.

Thinking back to the day when Nina's henchmen attacked Rory in the banquet room made Caius' rage seep into the air.

Seeing her bloody on the ground was an image he'd never forget, and the men deserved to suffer far longer than they did. Shadows crawled over his skin, mimicking the black veins from days prior.

As he flexed his hands, the shadows retreated. Since learning he'd sent Rory into danger, his anger had been harder to control, and the darkness crept into his heart like a poisonous spider ready to inject its deadly venom.

A quick knock sounded, and Lauren waltzed in. "It's like you read my mind," Caius said in way of a greeting. "I need to speak with you about something."

She handed him a paper. "Here is yesterday's report." Caius set it on his desk as she sat down. "What do you need?"

"I need you to go to Erdikoa tonight and switch places with Sam."

Her long nails drummed on the arms of the chair. "Why?"

"I need to train using the shadows to *create* a way through the magic."

She flicked her long hair over her shoulder. "I think that's smart."

Caius expected pushback about her leaving early. "Thank you. Is there a trusted enforcer that can do your job in your absence?"

"I'll hand in today's report before I leave, along with the name of someone who can handle the rest while I'm gone," she replied and stood to leave.

"Lauren," Caius called out, stopping her retreat. "Thank you."

"I will do anything if it means saving Rory," she said and slipped out of the room without a backward glance.

There was another knock, much softer than Lauren's, and Caius called upon the shadows to open the door. Lenora stood on the other side with a bag and drink carrier. "May I come in?"

"Always," he said with a demure smile. "Is something wrong?"

She loomed over his desk and opened the bag. He watched as she pulled out napkins, placing one in front of him and keeping one for herself, followed by two travel mugs. "I don't need a reason to see my son-in-law," she chided and pulled cookies out of the bag, laying them on the napkins. "Rumor is you love sweets, and the bakery downtown has the best macadamia nut cookies in both realms."

She called Caius *son-in-law* as though she knew Rory would give him a second chance. If only he were as confident. He knew Rory, and if she regained her memories, she would try to kill him for sending her to Erdikoa.

"You didn't have to do that," he said. "I know you're still adjusting to life here."

She harrumphed and set down one of the cups. "I have adjusted fine. Eat and relax."

He puffed out a quiet laugh and bit into a cookie. They were his favorite, and he wondered if someone told her or if it was a lucky guess. "Thank you."

She tapped the top of her mug and pointed to his. "Hot chocolate. I'm not sure how, but things here taste better than in the other realm."

Picking up his drink, he took a tentative sip and hissed. It was scalding hot. "I agree. Everything is made from scratch."

"Being clear of mind is something I never thought possible." She sighed and sipped her drink. Either her coffee was cooler than his, or she had a high pain tolerance. He scowled down at his boiling hot drink.

"It seems unfair that the magic exists to take away essence, yet *Sibyls* are forced to succumb to their abilities for most of their lives," she said, and Caius didn't miss the bitterness simmering beneath her surface. "Why would the *Seraphim* do that?"

"They wanted *Sibyls* around to predict any great disasters that may arise," Caius replied robotically. It was something he'd wondered himself, and as a teenager, he'd often researched different mystics. He'd always loved reading and devoured anything he could.

"But no one predicted Atarah's murder." Bitterness overwhelmed him. "Or if they did, they didn't come forward. It seems unfair to force *Sibyls* to live that way for nothing."

Lenora dabbed her mouth with a napkin. "Vincula is the only place that takes a mystic's essence, and it wouldn't be fair to allow *Sibyls* to live forever while others suffer mortality."

She was right. In Vincula, mystics did not age, but they could die by force. Caius wouldn't be able to stomach ending a *Sibyl's* life after a certain number of years to avoid their immortality; therefore, keeping them in Vincula was not an option.

The silence stretched between them, but it wasn't uncomfortable. Quite the contrary, it was comforting to have someone who cared for him other than Sam. And maybe Lauren. She was a wild card.

Speaking of, he grabbed her report and opened his drawer to file it away, but Cora's emergency report stopped him.

Lenora noticed the tension and set her drink down. "What is it, dear? Is there a ghost in that drawer?"

Bringing up Cora's death seemed like a bad idea, but before he could lie and say it was nothing, Lenora said, "Don't even think about lying to me."

Closing his eyes, he pulled out the file and set it on his desk. "It's a copy of Cora's emergency report." He took a glimpse to gauge her reaction, but instead of looking distraught, she looked curious. "When Rory accused me of killing her sister, I wanted to know why, and I had a copy of her report brought to me."

Lenora reached her hand across the desk. "May I?"

It was amusing to him that she felt the need to ask. He would deny her nothing. "I'm sure you know everything in there."

After placing the file in her hand, she flipped it open, and he watched pain contort her face when she saw the pictures of Cora's body. The urge to snatch the file back was strong, and he had to grip the arms of his chair.

"How did the king have a *Merrow* erased from the database without raising any flags?" she asked without looking up. "The *Merrow* database is controlled by enforcers in The Capital, is it not?"

"It is," he confirmed. *Merrows* were soul stealers whose abilities were bound by a mandatory monthly elixir. He never understood why *Merrows* were created in the first place.

The books said they were created to capture souls, keeping the black ones trapped in jars and releasing the others to ascend into the aether. But why not let black souls descend to hell like they do now? He stopped trying to understand the *Seraphim's* motives a long time ago.

She snapped the file shut and passed it back to him. "What if *Sibyls* could take the elixirs the *Merrows* are forced to take?"

Caius rubbed his chin, surprised no one had suggested it before. "The elixir has only been around for a few hundred years or so, and if I'm not mistaken, it was curated specifically for *Merrows*. But if the formula was altered to cater to *Sibyls*, hypothetically, it could work."

If anyone suggested using it on *Sibyls*, he doubted Gedeon would approve it, especially if he feared a *Sibyl* would predict his transgressions. No one would listen to them if they weren't coherent. "When we kill Gedeon, I will see that it is tested."

"It's a wonder that wretched brother of yours approved the *Merrow* elixir in the first place," Lenora spat, and the tops of her rounded ears turned a bright shade of red.

Caius grabbed his hot chocolate and sipped, forcing himself not to make a face at the now cold drink. Did the drink burn him and then cool extra fast to spite him? It felt like it. "*Merrows* cannot help themselves when their abilities are unbound," Caius explained. "The temptation to take and use souls for their own gain slowly blackens their own. The crime rate among *Merrows* was astronomically high. Finding a solution has been a priority since before my time. My brother couldn't deny using a solution if one was found, lest he risk the wrath of the *Seraphim*."

Not that the *Seraphim* cared anymore. He bit off a piece of cookie and chewed slowly.

"He killed your sister," Lenora countered. "Was that not a risk?"

"It was, but I cannot begin to understand the way my brother's brain works." He grabbed a napkin and wiped his hands, thinking hard about Lenora's observation.

Blackened souls saw no issue with the most heinous crimes known to man. It wouldn't surprise Caius if a mystic's black soul slowly ate away at their sanity.

Lenora gasped, leaned forward, and grabbed Caius' hand, turning it over. He watched her curiously. "You must tread carefully," she cautioned.

"You do not have your abilities here, but you speak in riddles," he remarked. "Have you seen something?"

"No, but pieces come back." Lifting a plump finger, she tapped the side of her head. "My memory is a large filing cabinet filled with visions I've had. Now that I don't have millions of new visions coming in, I can focus on sorting through the pieces of old visions in my memory."

He nodded, not understanding. "And what pieces have you put together that involve my hands?"

She let go of him and stood. "You are feeding the darkness inside you, and you must stop."

"I know I've been a bit of a downer since you arrived in Vincula," he said, moving to walk her out. "But surely my company has not been so abhorrent that you think me a monster."

His bad joke put a faint smile on her lips. "You are a good man, Caius. Do not lose yourself." She patted his arm. "Rory is lucky to have you."

"It is I who am lucky to have her, Ms. Raven. It was never the other way around."

CHAPTER 20

ERDIKOA

Rory and Sam walked into the restaurant she and her friends agreed upon for lunch, and when Kordie saw them, she stood and met them by the door, giving Rory a hug.

Sera sat on the end next to Dume and scooted out of the booth for Rory to slide in.

Sam looked at the space between the table and bench and back at the group. "Is this a joke? I cannot fit here."

Keith tried not to laugh, and Sera patted his arm. "I'll grab you a chair."

Rory noticed Dume zero in on Sera's hand touching Sam's arm, and she elbowed his side. "Is there something you want to tell me?"

He lifted his glass of water and mumbled something before taking a drink. Sam trailed behind Sera, and when she found a spare chair, he grabbed it and held it in the air with one hand. Sera wove her way back to the table while Sam barreled through, bumping into other people's chairs. It didn't escape Rory's notice that women turned to watch him pass.

He was a handsome man in that big, burly way with his shoulder-length blonde hair tied back, light stubble, thick body, and arms that made you think he could snap a log in half with his bare hands. *He probably could.*

Once everyone settled in and ordered their food, Keith pulled out a bag and set it in front of Rory. She peered around the gift at him. "What's this?"

"Open it." His face split into a mischievous grin, and her hackles rose.

Kordie was shaking her head, Dume and Sera were watching her expectantly, and Sam couldn't have cared less. Giving in, she pulled out the tissue and peeked inside, spying a black sweatshirt.

Keith's smile practically touched his ears, and Rory was hesitant to see what had him so giddy.

When she unfolded the hoodie and read the front, she gasped and slammed it back into the bag. "Are you out of your mind?" she hissed as he burst out laughing.

Kordie pushed his shoulder. "Shut up. I told him not to do it, but he refused to listen."

"What does it say?" Sera asked, grabbing for the bag.

Rory's reaction caught Sam's attention, and she had no choice but to show the table. "I am going to kill you," she promised Keith. "And I'll wear this when I do it."

He couldn't stop laughing, and she flipped him off. While threatening Keith had her occupied, Dume plucked the shirt from her hands and held it up before she could show everyone herself. His deep laugh made her elbow him in the side. "It's not funny!"

"Let me see!" Sera nagged until he flipped it around.

Her eyes scanned the shirt quickly before her hand clapped over her mouth, and her eyes reflected the laugh she was holding in for Rory's sake. Even Sam's lips pulled into a half-smile when Dume passed it to him.

"It is funny," Sam admitted.

"You're all traitors," Rory grumbled and snatched the shirt back, holding it up again. It had the logo for a local butcher shop called Erdikoa Meat Co across the front with a picture of a pig, and at the bottom, it said, *'Employee of the Month.'* "Why would a butcher shop sell merchandise, anyway?"

"They don't sell them to the public, but the employees wear them. I paid some kid behind the counter for it and had *'Employee of the Month'* added." Keith looked proud, with the stupid smile still plastered on his face.

Rory pressed her lips together and tried not to laugh. "You're an ass."

She put the shirt back in the bag and locked eyes with Keith. His wide smile conveyed his actual gift, and gratitude overtook her. He knew she was worried her crimes would make them see her differently.

They might have, but not enough to shy away from her, and his ability to make light of it proved that.

"Do you remember when the old lady at Whiplash mauled Keith?" Dume asked her and Kordie. "The *Sylph* who kept ruffling his hair?"

The girls burst out laughing at the memory. Once when Rory was working, the other three came in after work, as usual, and a woman in her early one-hundreds took the seat next to Keith. She wouldn't leave him alone the entire night.

Keith narrowed his eyes at Dume. "No thanks to you three."

Tears ran down Kordie's cheeks, and she fanned her face. "And you kept scooting closer to me, but every time you did, she pushed your chair back next to hers with her air ability."

Rory slapped the table as she laughed, Dume drew the attention of the entire restaurant with his own booming laugh, and Keith threw back the rest of his drink. "You are terrible friends."

Sera and Sam were quiet, and when Rory turned to them, Sera was watching Dume dreamily while Sam watched Rory with an emotion she couldn't describe. It wasn't pride, but it was akin to how a parent or older sibling would look at someone they loved when they were happy for them.

Rory already assumed she and the *Angel* were close in Vincula. If only she could remember it.

That night after dinner when they got home, Rory's father told her to stay put while he grabbed something he had picked up for her. If it was another butcher shirt, she was hanging them all from hooks.

He returned, holding a large book with a worn leather cover. "I couldn't find a book on *Aeternums*," he said apologetically. "But this one is about the history of Erdikoa. I thought it could be useful."

She set the book on the coffee table and pecked him on the cheek. "Thank you." It was doubtful there would be anything about *Aeternums* in the book, but her father's thoughtfulness made her chest warm.

"Anything for you, sport." He patted her on the head and reached for the remote to the ES before settling in on the couch.

"Are you not going to work tonight?" she asked, sitting next to him.

He glanced at Sam when the *Angel* descended the stairs. "No, I have the night off."

Her father never had Fridays off. Remembering Sam's words to Lauren, she forced herself to look unaffected. He'd said her father would take off work on the nights they changed shifts.

This might be her only chance to grab potions from Fiona for another week. "I'm going to take a shower," she told them and hurried to her room without waiting for a reply. After turning on the water to ensure they couldn't hear her, she called Sera. Hopefully she was free.

Her friend answered and asked, "It's go time, isn't it?"

Rory snorted. "Yes, but we have to wait until Sam leaves and my father is asleep," she whispered.

"Excellent. Remember to wear a hat and a hood to cover your face." She stopped talking, and Rory heard rustling. "I'll bring you a pair of glasses, too."

"Sunglasses?" Rory wouldn't be able to see with a hat, hood, and sunglasses at night.

"No." Sera giggled. "They're a pair of reading glasses with fake lenses. It'll make you less recognizable."

Rory didn't think it would, but she went along with it. "Okay, thanks. And Sera?"

"Yeah?"

"You don't have to go. This might be dangerous." Silence stretched between them, and she worried she had hurt Sera's feelings. The thought of anything happening to one of her friends made her ill.

"I'm coming." Sera sounded pissed. "If you try to stop me, I'll go to the underground market alone."

Rory grinned into the phone. "Okay. I'll call you."

"You better," Sera snapped before hanging up.

Rory stared at the phone. "Damn."

Rory sat patiently on her bed with her window open, waiting to hear Sam's car leave and her father go to bed. As far as they knew, she was already asleep.

It felt like hours before she heard the front door shut and Sam's SUV roar to life. Her father had turned in earlier, and she texted Sera, sharing her location through her navigation app.

Rory slipped on her signature black hoodie, leggings, and boots before grabbing a hat and pulling it low over her eyes. Her hair hanging long over her shoulders still bothered her, and she pulled it through her cap, wrapping it in a tight bun.

She made a mental note to tell Sera they needed to stop by an ATM and take out moedas before heading to the underground market. After ensuring she had her things, she tiptoed downstairs and noticed a red light flashing on a panel next to the door.

"Fuck." How would she get out, and how did she not know there was a security system?

Wait. When they set the house alarm, her window was open, meaning the sensor wouldn't trip unless she closed it and opened it again. Slipping back upstairs, she pushed her window all the way open and waited to make sure it didn't trip the alarm.

"Rory, you beautiful genius," she praised herself as she

carefully stepped onto the roof and hesitated. *Maybe she didn't think this through.*

Scooting to the edge on her butt, she cautiously peered over the side. The awning over the porch was lower than the roof of the house, and if she could lower herself onto it, she could try to shimmy down one of the pillars.

Moving as quietly as possible, she crab-walked sideways until she was over the porch, then slid off the edge, scraping her back. She cursed as her skin burned. *So much for getting down unscathed.* She stared warily at the edge of the porch awning and sighed.

She'd come too far now. This time, she turned around on her stomach, lowered herself until she hung by her finger-tips, and dropped into the flowerbed. Scaling buildings looked easier in the movies.

A dark blue car pulled into the driveway with its lights off, and Rory tensed. What if it wasn't Sera?

All of her anxiety melted away when Sera rolled down the window. "Get in bitch. We're going to get your memo-ries back."

Rory laughed as she careened around the hood and slid into the front seat.

Sera held out a pair of black square-frame glasses. "Put these on."

Rory obliged her friend, and when she looked in the mirror, it surprised her to see that Sera was right. Yes, anyone who knew her or who really looked at her would know who she was, but between the hat, glasses, hood, and the dark, it would be tough for a passerby to recog-nize her.

"Good call." Rory held out her phone. "Here are the directions to the market."

Sera grabbed the phone and attached it to her phone holder on the dash. "Thanks."

After twenty minutes of random conversation and a stop by an ATM, they pulled into the warehouse district. Despite the name, the underground market wasn't underground; it was in an unmarked group of warehouses in the heart of the warehouse district.

To gain entry, you had to know somebody who knew somebody. Rory was thankful Fiona told her she could drop her name. She really liked that old bat.

They approached a large man sitting near the dumpster that hid the entrance. He looked drunk and homeless, an act they'd used for years. "I'm here for Fiona," Rory told him.

The man sized her up. Standing, he pushed the dumpster slightly, revealing an open doorway. It quickly sealed behind them, and Sera ate up the bustling scene filling the extensive building.

"Holy shit," she marveled.

Rory grabbed her wrist to guide her through the throng of people. "We need to get in and out as quickly as possible. Keep your head down, and don't speak to anyone."

She searched the building, looking for Fiona's familiar face. The *Alchemist* kept certain potions on hand, but sometimes she took orders to be picked up later. Rory prayed they wouldn't need to come back.

Fiona's familiar booth caught her eye, and she released a sigh of relief.

As they approached, Fiona glanced up and smirked at Rory across the way.

Sera tugged on Rory's arm, stopping her. "Are you sure you want to take a potion from someone in this place?" Her voice was barely a whisper so as not to be overheard.

"I've known Fiona for years," Rory assured her, glancing at the *Alchemist*.

Sera followed her gaze, and for the first time since Rory met her, she looked nervous. "And you're positive you want your memories back? I will help you however I can, but I want you to be one hundred percent sure you want this. It could be traumatizing."

"No more traumatizing than having a gaping hole in my memory," Rory countered. "I need to know what happened in Vincula. There are too many unanswered questions that I can't let go. My guards are spying on the fucking Lux King for aether's sake, and apparently, some woman named Nina tried to kill me, but I killed her first. Do you know how unsettling it is to know you killed someone but can't remember?"

Sera blanched. "How were you not sent to hell for killing someone again?"

"I don't know," she admitted. "That's why I have to get my memories back."

Sera pulled her wrist from Rory's hold and adjusted her ponytail. "We'll get them back. Even if this potion doesn't help, we'll think of something."

Rory led the way to Fiona's booth and gave the woman a wide smile. "Hey, Fiona. We're interested in buying a memory-restoring potion."

Fiona's eyes were hard, and she looked *pissed*. *What happened in the last five minutes?* "What kind of memory potion are you wanting?"

Rory glanced at Sera and back to the *Alchemist*. "We weren't aware there were different types."

Fiona looked unimpressed. "Is it for you? No one has restored their memories from Vincula." She crouched down as she searched through a shelf of bottles. "I have a potion that reverses the effects of a *Munin's* magic and another that helps with old age memory loss." She stood and placed two bottles on the counter.

Rory felt uneasy with Fiona's hostile tone, but she dismissed it. It was likely a shitty customer trying to swindle her. "We'll take them both. How much?"

Fiona bagged them quickly and held out her hand. "Ten gold moedas each."

Rory narrowed her eyes. "That's steep, even for you."

"Then find someone else," the woman quipped.

"Fine." Rory pulled twenty gold moedas from her bag. "We'll take them."

Plunking the potions on the counter, Fiona swiped the moedas and waved Rory and Sera off with her hand. "Leave."

Sera was quiet during the exchange, and once they were out of earshot, she whispered, "I thought you two were friends."

Rory glimpsed over her shoulder and saw Fiona still watching her with slitted eyes. "I thought we were too. I saw her recently, and she told me to come see her."

Sera glanced back and pulled her along faster, but Rory stopped and veered her to the right. "The exit is over here."

Sera flipped off the headlights as they pulled into the driveway of the safe house. "Are you going to take them now, or do you want to wait?"

Rory pulled the bottles from the bag and nodded. "I need you to stay here in case they're poisoned."

"It's strange that she had two memory potions in stock, don't you think?" Sera asked with a hint of suspicion.

Rory stared at the bottles in her hands. "Yes, but what other choice do I have?"

Sera unbuckled her seatbelt, signaled for Rory to do the same, and pulled out her cell phone. "In case you start to die, and I need to call for help and give you mouth-to-mouth or something," she explained when Rory stared at her.

"Okay." Rory took a calming breath before throwing back the first potion. She covered her mouth as she gagged. "I hate potions." Her eyes watered as she gagged again.

"Don't throw it up," Sera commanded. "I don't want to go back."

Rory breathed in through her nose and out through her mouth until the nausea passed. Gulping down the second one, she willed herself not to puke. "These are worse than any potion I've ever taken in my life."

They waited for what felt like forever, but nothing happened, and Rory cursed. "I don't know if she gave me fake potions or if they don't work."

Sera inspected the bottles, turning them over in her hands. "You said you two were friends. Why would she lie?"

Banging her head against the headrest, she closed her eyes. "I don't know."

"We will try every memory recovery tactic in the realms before we give up," Sera assured her. "But for now, go back inside before we're caught by one of your guards."

"Thanks, Sera." She hopped out and leaned down to peer into the car. "I'm glad you harassed my friends while I was gone; otherwise, we wouldn't have met."

When Rory shut the door, Sera rolled down her window and poked her head out. "Get some sleep!"

After waving goodbye, Rory turned back to the house with a groan. She jumped onto the porch railing and clung to a pillar, climbing until her fingers grabbed the awning's edge.

There were no gutters on this house, and while dangling in the air, Rory wondered if that was bad for the roof. She used a pillar to push off with her feet, and her arms had never ached so much in her life.

Picking up anything tomorrow would be impossible. When she tumbled through her bedroom window, she stayed sprawled on the floor, huffing. Even with her *Fey* strength, that was hard.

She wouldn't be surprised if her heavy breathing alone woke her father. Would it be ridiculous to crawl to the shower? *Yes.*

Rory managed to get up and dragged herself to the bathroom. Once in the shower, she stood under the stream until the water ran cold. She practically fell into bed, but instead of sleeping, she lay awake and hoped the potions would kick in, eventually.

They didn't.

CHAPTER 21

Fiona always took a hearing-enhancing potion before setting up her booth in the market. It helped target potential customers or sort out those who thought to swindle her, but tonight, it instilled such hatred in her heart that she may never recover.

Her daughter, Nina, had been sentenced to a few years in Vincula for scamming men out of hundreds of thousands of moedas, but a week ago, she received word they executed Nina for treason.

Devastation didn't describe what Fiona felt when she learned of her daughter's death.

Rory's early release had piqued her curiosity. She'd been happy to see the girl, but now, here the little bitch was, whispering about needing to remember killing a woman named Nina. She would have no such luck retrieving her memories with the potions she bought. They were useless bases that Fiona had not yet mixed.

Fiona didn't believe in coincidences, but what she *did* believe in was revenge. The girls also mentioned Rory's guards were spying on the Lux King. It was precisely the type of information he wanted, and Fiona knew, without a doubt, he would bring Rory in for questioning.

She hoped for a long, tortuous execution, but if the king left the girl unharmed, Fiona would take care of it herself.

CHAPTER 22

Sam stood in the back courtyard with Lauren as she explained why Caius needed him back early. They agreed to search the Lux Palace before Sam returned to Vincula. He would look for more information on the planted guards while Lauren searched for Gedeon to see if he said anything of worth.

They glanced around to ensure no one saw them open the staff entrance, and Lauren transformed into a small bird, flew inside, and signaled that it was safe for him to enter.

He couldn't risk being scooped up like last time and transformed into a cat the same pale color as the walls. Once at the end of the hallway, he gave Lauren a slight nod, and they split up.

As he approached Gedeon's office, he saw a non-*Aatxe* guard keeping watch. Sam assumed the king would have his trusted spies guarding places he deemed important, and if they were here, then something inside was noteworthy.

What he did not expect was to see Stassi appear around the corner of an intersecting hallway. Something made her pause and whip her head around. Her eyes widened when she saw *him*.

He saw her gulp, and before she could say anything, he trotted over and hopped onto the bottom shelf of her cart, knocking over a few bottles. He peered up at her, but when he heard the guard approaching, his fur stood on end.

"Clumsy today, I see," the man teased. He didn't sound menacing, but as one of Gedeon's spies, he couldn't be trusted. The guard's legs bent to pick up the bottles on the ground, but Stassi dropped beside the cart, shielding Sam from view.

"It's okay, Tag, I've got it," she said, stumbling over her words.

She grabbed the bottles quickly in her arms and stood. Concern filled the guard's voice. "Are you okay, Stass? You're jumpy."

Sam tensed at the familiarity in his tone and released a low hiss. Stassi laughed nervously to cover up the sound. "Yes, just tired."

The man shuffled his feet, and Sam's irritation grew. "I was wondering," Tag started to say, but Stassi grabbed the cart handle and pushed.

"I'm sorry, Tag. I have to finish my duties before my shift is over. We'll talk soon, okay?"

The disappointment in the guard's tone gave Sam a sick satisfaction. "Yeah, okay. Do you need into the king's office?"

"No," she replied a little too quickly. "I... I have to clean his quarters tonight. I'll see you around."

She grabbed her cart and whipped it around so fast that Sam almost fell out. When she was far enough away, she pushed her cart into a random room and flipped on the light.

Her head popped into his line of sight as she peered under the cart. "Is it you?" Pressing her lips together, she righted herself. "I'm going crazy. Of course, it isn't him. His fur was black."

She continued muttering as she paced back and forth, and Sam jumped from the cart to shift.

"Stassi," he said, his deep voice filling the room.

She screamed bloody murder and jumped as she spun around. "You—" Her shaking hand pointed from the cart to Sam. "You shouldn't be able to change colors. Weren't you black last time? Y-you were because you shed on my uniform."

He wanted to argue that he didn't shed, but he couldn't get a word in as she continued to ramble. "And now you're an awful beige color, but you were black. Shifters can't change anything about their animals. What are you?" Her breaths were rapid as she shook out her hands. She was hyperventilating, and Sam only had a few seconds to catch her before she hit the ground.

Hoisting her into his arms, he surveyed his surroundings. It was a banquet room with long tables filling the space. *The tables would be too cold*, he thought and laid her gently on one of the plush, ornate rugs instead.

His eyes traced her sweet face, and a foreign feeling filled his chest. He scanned the rest of her, confirming she wasn't hurt, and the thought of her fainting because of him didn't sit right. She didn't faint the first time she saw him, but she was probably more focused on the guard trying to take advantage of her.

Her eyes fluttered, and he tensed, waiting for her to scream again.

"What happened?" Her voice was weak as she rolled her head sideways, her eyes landing on him. "Shit," she cursed and rolled away.

Giving her space, he assured her, "I will not hurt you."

Stassi rubbed her eyes and opened them again. "It's not possible. You were a black cat before. Shifters can't change their animal forms." Shaking her head, she sat back on her haunches. "I'm losing my mind."

"You already said that," he reminded her. "Why did you faint? It did not bother you last time."

Her face transformed from shock to annoyance. "You would faint too if cats kept shifting into giant, beautiful men."

When she called him beautiful, something inside him warmed. Frowning, he rubbed a fist over his chest. "I am not a shifter," he replied after a beat. "I am going to show you something, but do not faint again."

Before she could reply, his wings flared to life behind him, and he watched her, worried she would run.

There was no logical reason for him to divulge his identity to her, but he *had* to. He couldn't explain it.

"*Seraphim,*" she breathed and stood on shaky legs. "I thought *Angels* lived in the aether?"

"Most people do not think *Angels* exist," he countered. "At least you are smarter than most."

She fought a smile, and he wanted her to set it free.

Her hand reached up as if to touch his feathers but paused midair. "Why are you here?"

"What do you know of the new guards?" he asked instead of answering, which irritated her more.

She pushed a wisp of hair out of her face. "You mean the non-*Aatxe* guards?"

"Yes. When did this start?"

He noticed a slight blush creeping up her neck. "I almost took you home." Sam choked on air, forgetting his reason for being here as an image of her in his bed flashed through his mind, but before he could reply, she narrowed her eyes at him. "As a *cat*."

"You can take me home any way you would like," he drawled before he could stop himself, relishing how her skin reddened.

"Uh, the new guards started arriving about a year ago," she mumbled, changing the subject. "They oversee the staff and guard certain areas of the palace."

Sam scolded himself for getting distracted by this woman when there were more important issues at hand. "How do they treat the staff?" The man he took to Adila was vile, but the guard from today was respectful. His lip curled at the memory of how familiar Tag was with Stassi.

"It's hit or miss. Most are nice, though everyone knows they're snoops." She wrinkled her nose. "Some are assholes, but you already know that. Thank you, by the way."

"You are welcome."

"Did you kill him?" Her voice was so soft he almost didn't hear her.

Sam studied her expression. After everything the man did to her, did she still worry about him? "I took him to the Scales of Justice, and she sentenced him to hell."

She averted her gaze, but Sam saw the tension melt from her shoulders. "Thank you."

He didn't like that she wouldn't look at him. "You already said that."

She huffed, making him smile. Her demeanor was sweet, but she had a little fire in her as well. He liked this woman who saved a cat but stood up for herself against a seedy guard, and who feared an *Angel* but still made her annoyance clear.

"Why are you looking at me like that?" she mumbled, smoothing a hand over her hair. Tonight, it was half up and hanging halfway down her chest.

"My name is Sam." He held out his hand.

She chewed on the inside of her cheek before tentatively shaking it. "Anastasia."

His lips twitched. It suited her better than her nickname. "You have access to the king's office?"

Yanking her hand back, she backed up. "Whatever you're about to ask, the answer is no."

"You are afraid of the king," he observed. "Why?" The Lux rulers were often known for their kind nature, even Gedeon. He was a talented actor.

Anastasia fidgeted, and Sam involuntarily took a step toward her. "I'll lose my job. Staff members are fired for even *mentioning* the new guards or questioning anything the king does," she replied. "Especially the *Aatxe* guards."

"Why would they fire *Aatxe* guards?" Sam asked, switching to commander mode. It was rare for an *Aatxe* to be fired. They're honest and good at their jobs.

Anastasia pursed her lips. "I just told you. Gossiping, asking questions, looking at a new guard wrong; take your pick. Imagine what would happen if someone was caught snooping around the king's office. Not even to help an *Angel*."

"I would let nothing happen to you," he promised her, meaning every word.

She puffed out a disbelieving laugh. "Is that so? Tell me, have you seen me since you were here last?" Before he could answer, she continued. "Because I haven't seen you, and unless you are trailing me every second of every day, your word means nothing."

His wings ruffled with his anger. She was right, and if Gedeon hurt her, he would kill everyone in the realms without question. "If there comes a day that I need your help to get into Gedeon's office, I will take you with me when I leave and never let you out of my sight again."

She stood still enough to be mistaken for a statue before she burst out laughing. "What the fuck?" Her laughter made him want to bend her over his knee and spank her.

"This is not a laughing matter, Anastasia." The laughter stopped abruptly. "We do not know what will happen in the long run if the Lux King goes unchecked, but as of now, a friend's life is in danger, and by proxy, the Umbra King's life, as well."

He knew if Rory died, Caius would soon follow. The king's grief would pull him into an early grave.

"The king who killed his sister?" she squeaked. "There are Umbra King worshipers who think he's coming back any day to take over Erdikoa. They say a battle will destroy half of the realm."

He rubbed a hand down his face. "Now is not the time to discuss conspiracy theorists. Lives are in *real* danger."

"You're serious," she breathed. "What the *fuck*?"

His eyes narrowed. "You already said that."

"Stop telling me what I've already said," she snapped. He rubbed his mouth to hide his smile but wasn't fast enough. "This is not a laughing matter, *Sam*."

"I know it is a lot to ask, and I will not ask it of you

today, but there might come a time when I need you. I will not let you do anything dangerous alone."

He saw the moment he won her over, but it didn't make him happy. The defeated look on her face made him hate himself. "Okay." Her brown eyes found his. "You promise you won't get me killed?"

"With everything I am." He moved closer and kneeled before her. Her lips parted slightly. "I, Samyaza, commander of the Vincula legion and heir to the Aravoth throne, promise to protect you in this life and the next. If I fail, I will find you in the aether."

"Samyaza?" The color drained from her face.

He stood and placed a large hand on her shoulder. "Do not faint again."

She shook his hand off her shoulder and rubbed her forehead. "I can't believe I'm trusting someone who is heir to a made-up kingdom, but okay." Without looking at him, she grabbed her cart and wheeled it toward the door. "If I die, I'll kill you."

He'd never smiled so big in his entire life.

Sam met Lauren at the bunker behind the palace. She leaned against the doorframe as he approached and lifted a perfectly manicured brow. "Why does your face look like that?"

His smile dropped instantly. "My face always looks like this."

It was the wrong thing to say. "No, it doesn't. Why do you look happy? Did you fuck someone when you were supposed to be working?"

He and Lauren had warmed each other's beds, but that

was as far as it went. They'd been friends forever, and Lauren often found comfort in other companions. Sam did occasionally, but it was rare, and now she smelled blood in the water.

Something about referring to Anastasia as a 'fuck' set him off, and he turned on her. "Do not speak that way about my personal matters again."

Most would have run screaming at the promise of violence in his voice, but Lauren's face lit up like a Plenilune festival. "You *like* this person. Spill."

"I do not *like* people," Sam countered. "We have a job to do. Did you learn anything or not?"

Lauren planted both hands on her hips. "It's okay to want something for yourself, Samyaza." Her voice softened. "It's okay to be happy." When he ignored her, she dropped her hands to her sides. "No. Gedeon was fucking someone, unimpressively, might I add, but there was nothing amiss."

Sam rolled their tiff from his shoulders. "Gedeon hired non-*Aatxe* guards to be spies around the palace, which I already knew from Adila, but Anastasia confirmed it. According to her, staff members are fired for mentioning anything negative where the king and new guards are concerned."

"Damn," Lauren said finally. "What is he hiding?"

"I do not know," he replied.

"That doesn't tell us much, but at least it's something," Lauren said and patted Sam on the shoulder. "I need to get to Rory."

He stalked back to the bunker to change.

It's okay to be happy.

CHAPTER 23

VINCULA

Caius sat in the sandwich shop, staring at the chair across from him where Rory once sat. She wasn't in the soulscape last night, and he was miserable.

"Your Grace?"

He turned toward the delicate voice to see a pretty young woman standing beside him, holding a sack. Her hair was a soft blonde, and she had a gentle air about her.

Caius struggled to place her. "What's your name?"

A slender hand brushed a wisp of hair away from her face as she smiled politely. "Brynne."

Brynne Taylyr. A light went off in his head. "Convicted of theft and assault."

She averted her gaze and shifted uncomfortably. "Yes, Your Grace."

He gave her a once over, remembering her arrival. It was shortly before Rory's, and unlike his mate, Brynne had been polite and cooperative when she arrived.

The girl was caught with groceries shoved into her large bag. Most people did not need to steal food because The Crown provided a certain number of food credits for every person in Erdikoa each month. She was sentenced to Vincula because when the shop owner grabbed her arm to stop her, she decked him in the face, earning an assault charge.

Caius meant to seek her out and figure out why she'd stolen food, but Rory arrived, and everything else was pushed aside.

"Sit down." He stood and pulled out the chair across from him.

"Your Grace, I only wanted to borrow the chair." She pointed to a small, chair-less table across the crowded deli. "There were no extras."

Caius tapped the back of the chair. "Sit."

She snapped her mouth shut and sat tentatively, clutching her sack lunch like a lifeline.

The girl looked ready to bolt, but he knew she wouldn't leave. He was the king, after all. "Why did you steal food?"

Her fist tightened around the top of the sack, and she swiveled toward the counter. "I paid with my credits, Your Grace."

He chuckled at her stricken expression. Rory would have thrown her food at him, but Brynne sat obediently, maintaining her innocence. "I know that, Miss Taylyr." She shivered slightly and slowly set her sack of food on the table. "I am asking why you stole food in Erdikoa. The Crown provides its citizens with enough food, does it not?"

She looked ashamed. Not guilty, but ashamed. "Tell me," he urged quietly.

"I had to trade some of our food credits for moedas."

Refusing to look at him, she prattled on before he could ask questions. "My older brother is a *Sibyl*. He's almost forty years older than I am. My mother shouldn't have been able to get pregnant with me at her age, but she did, and the pregnancy took a toll on her body." A dismal quiet settled over their table until Brynne spoke again, "She was almost seventy-five, you know?"

"She was a *Fey*," he guessed. They live longer than other mystics, and he'd heard of *Fey* women having children in their sixties, but in their seventies was unheard of.

Brynne nodded. "My father did his best, but it was hard since my older brother is a *Sibyl*. His abilities manifested when I was five, and by the time I was sixteen, I had to drop out of school to care for him."

Caius didn't know a simple question would have such a complex answer, and a part of him wished he'd never asked, but the other part of him needed to know why she wasn't taken care of by The Crown.

"My father was a *Visitant*," she continued. Caius wondered if he ever used his abilities on Brynne to provide her with a happier childhood. He hoped so. "He died when I turned twenty-one. I never graduated, and I had trouble finding a job that paid enough to cover our bills and a day nurse for my brother while I worked."

"And you had to sell your food credits to pay for his care," Caius concluded, and she swiped at a rogue tear. "Did you go to the mystic services office and petition The Crown? There are programs available to help."

Her eyes hardened. "I did. They said their funding had been cut drastically, but that they'd put me on their waitlist. Their very *long* waitlist."

Sitting back in shock, he scratched his jaw as he thought. Why would Gedeon cut the funding to the assistance programs? He didn't need the money. On top of being the Lux King, each of the *Royals* had an inheritance from their parents. It was what Caius transferred to Rory in Erdikoa.

"Is there anything else you need, Your Grace?" Brynne asked politely.

He looked at the woman, who was so unlike Rory, and smiled to himself. His mate would have liked Brynne and demanded he apologize for making the poor girl cry.

Fuck, he missed her.

"I apologize, Miss Taylyr. The Crown failed you." He stood and pushed his chair under the table. "Tomorrow morning, find the legion commander and give him your brother's name. We will look in on him and see that he is taken care of."

Her hand flew to her chest. "You would do that?"

"The happiness of my subjects is important to me." With a small wave, he turned to leave. "Have a good afternoon, Miss Taylyr."

Caius strolled down the streets of Vincula, watching the inmates go about their day-to-day. He couldn't stop thinking about his conversation with Brynne. Gedeon's greed now affected the people of Erdikoa. This was no longer about revenge for his and Rory's sisters or saving Rory's life. It was about protecting the people, too.

Everyone thought Gedeon was a decent ruler for the last five-hundred years, but was it possible things were worse than they appeared? If not for Brynne, Caius wouldn't know about the funding cuts to Erdikoa's assistance programs. What else didn't he know about?

"Caius," Sam's deep voice called across the street.

Caius smiled and crossed the road they had no use for. There were no carriages or horses in Vincula, but the *Seraphim* wanted it to be as familiar to the inmates as possible. As time passed, renovations were done to keep up with the changing times.

"Good to see you," he said to Sam, slapping him on the shoulder. "Lauren told you why I needed you back, I presume?"

"Briefly." Sam eyed him with scrutiny. "You want to learn to *create* using the shadows?"

Caius waved at a passing inmate before answering. "Yes. I need something to get through the barrier or break it altogether."

"I am unsure if your plan is sound," the *Angel* remarked as they walked side by side.

An anger Caius rarely experienced toward the commander reared its ugly head. "What other solution have you come up with? From where I'm standing, this is our only lead." He ran a frustrated hand along the side of his styled hair. "If you aren't capable of helping, I need to know now."

"I will try to help. Where did this idea come from?"

Caius gave him the rundown of the information Cat found in the old storybook, and when he finished, Sam looked impressed.

"That was an excellent observation," Sam replied. "While that story is false, it is rooted in truth. A *Seraph* did create the realms for his wife. She'd always wanted children but thought she couldn't have any, and it was his way of giving them to her." Sam's voice grew sad. "The darkness of the universe is a powerful thing."

Caius saw the *Angel* in a new light. He wasn't speculating; he *knew*. Sam and Lauren were the only two *Angels* in the realms, and when they arrived, they claimed it was to help with the inmates but never stated why.

"It's possible, then?" Caius felt the shadows move around him as his hope flared to life.

His friend chuckled. "It is for a *Seraph*. If a *Seraph* used their full power within the realms, it would destroy everything."

"Even if they used them to create?" Caius was befuddled. They created the realms with their power; how would it destroy it?

"They created the realms while still in the aether," Sam replied. "The capacity of power the aether can house is limitless, but these realms were not made for that."

Caius' hackles rose with suspicion. "Have you ever created anything?" *Was Sam a fucking* **Seraph**?

The *Angel's* brows furrowed. "Of course not, but I have seen it done."

It made sense. *Angels* were from the aether. While it was a resting place for the souls of mystics, it was also a realm. Caius wasn't sure what happened to souls when they reached the aether, but different races of *Angels* resided there under the *Seraphim's* rule.

According to their history books, anyway.

"If I can manipulate the darkness," Caius said, pressing forward. "Then, by logic, I can manipulate the realm itself."

"If logic were the basis for magic and creation, then yes." Sam reached into his pocket and pulled out a chocolate bar. "But nothing about magic is logical."

Caius visualized shoving the candy down Sam's throat. "I have to try, with or without your help."

Swallowing, Sam licked the chocolate from the corner of his mouth. "I will help, but do not put all of your eggs into a picnic basket."

Caius barked out a laugh. The rapport around the palace had been dark since Rory left, and seeing his friend had not changed was nice. "It's '*in one basket*,'" Caius told him. "Not a picnic basket."

Sam threw the chocolate wrapper into a trashcan as they approached the palace gates. "Does the size of the basket matter?"

Caius continued to laugh on their way to his office. "When can we start?" he asked, circling back to what was important.

"Tomorrow. It will be taxing, and you need to be well-rested. We will meet at the arrowball field at sunrise." Sam opened the office door. "I must check in with the enforcer in charge. Send for me if you need anything."

"Wait," Caius called out. "How is she?"

"She's asking a lot of questions," Sam replied, crossing his arms. "Because you are telling her things in the soulscape."

Shit, Caius thought. Sam didn't know of their plan to help Rory remember.

"I'll explain everything before you return," he promised the *Angel* as they parted ways.

After pouring himself a drink, he fell into his reading chair, opening the drawer of the side table out of habit. His favorite book was missing. He hadn't read it in years, but Rory said it was Cora's favorite, and he'd started to reread it before Rory went back to Erdikoa.

It was comforting to have something she held dear, but now it was gone.

Sighing, he pulled out another book and turned to the bookmarked page. His thoughts were loud, and today he hoped the characters could occupy his mind for a little while until the real world came crashing back in.

CHAPTER 24

ERDIKOA

The next morning, Lauren stood at the bottom of the stairs with her arms crossed, stopping Rory in her tracks. "You said you wouldn't leave."

Rory didn't bother lying. "It was an emergency, and how did you know, anyway?"

"You don't look hurt," Lauren accused, blocking her path to the kitchen. "And I know everything. Please do not make our jobs harder than they need to be. If there is somewhere you need to go, ask me."

Rory threw her hands up. "Sam wouldn't even tell me what an *Aeternum* was! He wouldn't have taken me to buy an illegal memory recovery potion."

She expected Lauren to be pissed. What she didn't expect was for the guard to say, "It's a *Royal's* eternal mate."

Rory's mind took a second to catch up to her words. "What?"

Lauren turned and beckoned Rory to follow her into the

living room. "An *Aeternum* is a *Royal's* eternal mate. Two souls made for each other at the same time."

Rory let the information sink in. Caius said she was his *Aeternum*, but it was impossible. "Caius is hundreds of years older than I am." She wrinkled her nose. "It's weird that I am—*was* in a relationship with someone hundreds of years old." *Especially when they look like sex on a stick.*

"Who else would he have a relationship with?" Lauren asked. "His siblings are the only other immortals, and seeing as you are the only person he can marry for life, that leaves him no choice but to date a woman with a *significant* age difference."

"It's still odd," Rory muttered. "But if our souls were made at the same time, how am I only twenty-five?" A thought occurred to her. "Have I been alive before?" Cora read about this once in a book. *What was it she called it?* "Reincarnated?"

Lauren smirked. "Reincarnation doesn't exist in these realms."

Her wording irked Rory. *Did it exist in other realms?* "Then how is it possible?"

Lauren shrugged. "Your soul rests with Moira until your mate needs you the most."

Who the hell is Moira? "How can we share dreams?" There was more to being an *Aeternum* than Lauren was saying, and Rory needed to know everything.

Lauren leaned back and crossed her legs with her arms spread wide along the back of the couch. "When you are both asleep, your souls meet in a soulscape. To simplify it, you share a dream that's real."

Rory thought back to Caius' hands on her and shivered. *It felt real, all right.* "And what else?"

"When one of you is in danger, the other will get a vision. You see through the other's eyes." *Would Caius be in danger in Vincula?* "*Aeternums* are born with grey-scale sight, and when they meet their mate, they see them in color. Skin-to-skin contact lifts the grey-scale sight permanently, confirming the bond."

Touching her cheek, she frowned as a memory tried to push through. *Red.* "The bowl was red," she whispered.

Lauren dropped her arms and straightened. "What are you talking about?"

She chewed on her lip, unsure where the words came from. "I don't know, but there was a red bowl. I think."

"Caius thinks because you are *Seraphim*-blessed as an *Aeternum* that it's possible the memory magic doesn't work the same on you," Lauren commented, more to herself than Rory. "I think he's right."

Rubbing her eyes, she groaned. What a mess. "Why was I released early?"

Lauren hesitated. "That is not my story to tell."

"Cora had grey-scale sight, too," Rory said, standing. If she'd fallen for his lies, she would never forgive herself. "Was she his real *Aeternum,* and I took her place after she died? Did he really kill her?"

"No," the *Angel* said quickly as she rose from the couch. "She was not his *Aeternum*, and he didn't kill her, but that is something I can't explain to you. You need your memories back; otherwise, you'll do something stupid."

Rory bristled. "You don't know that."

"Yes, I do," Lauren countered with a snort, making Rory purse her lips.

Irritation bubbled in her chest. "Either you can help me get them back, or you can stay here while I do." She brushed past Lauren toward the kitchen for a much-needed coffee.

"Open the front door," Lauren said to Rory's retreating back.

She regarded the *Angel* as she rerouted to the foyer and opened the door.

Lauren followed behind her and pointed outside. "Throw your attitude out, and then we'll talk."

She stood stunned before laughing. When she regained her composure, her shoulders slumped as she massaged her temples. "I'm sorry, Lo. This whole thing has me on edge." She looked at Lauren's shocked expression and realized what she said. "Why did I call you Lo?"

The *Angel* debated internally before gesturing for Rory to follow her outside. Lauren stood in the front yard, and within seconds, shifted into a murderous-looking panther.

Shrieking, Rory pressed herself against the front door, but recognition quickly replaced her panic when she met the panther's gaze. Lauren shifted back and waited.

"You're a cat," Rory said lamely.

"I'm a panther, and you used to pet me." She smirked when Rory's jaw fell open.

"You don't seem the type to let someone pet you," she mumbled as they walked back inside. "Besides, what does that have to do with me calling you Lo?"

"Lo is what everyone calls my panther form."

"You named my new identity after your *cat*?" Rory asked incredulously.

"Panther, and yes." She guided Rory toward the kitchen. "I know everything is overwhelming, but I will not hesitate to lay you out if you continue to speak to me the way you did."

"Or eat me," she said under her breath.

"I heard that."

After pouring them both a cup of coffee, Rory slid onto a stool at the island. "Sera and I went to the underground market for memory potions," she admitted. "They didn't work. I'm not sure what else to try other than asking a *Munin*, but I refuse to involve an innocent person."

Lauren tapped her red nails on the side of her mug. "You're nicer than you look. Dumber, too. Never go to the underground market without me again."

"I'm going to call Kordie," Rory announced and put her cup down to grab her phone. "I need to get my hair cut."

Lauren eyed Rory's long locks. "Why?"

She ran her fingers through the ends of her hair. "I don't know, but I have to."

The *Angel* blinked, and then a look of understanding crossed her face. "I think I might have an idea," Lauren said, glancing at Rory's hair again. "You always wore it down or in a long ponytail."

Uneasiness raced through Rory's body. "How many times was I attacked?"

"A few." Lauren hiked a shoulder nonchalantly.

Rory shuddered and lifted the phone to her ear. She all but yelled, "I need a haircut today," when Kordie answered.

"Hello to you too," the *Alchemist* returned. "Come in whenever. I'll fit you in between clients."

"See you soon." Ending the call, she stood. "Can we leave now?" Her anxiety over her hair was higher than ever after hearing Lauren's admission.

She rushed across the kitchen, cleaned the coffee maker, reloaded it, and programmed the auto setting to start around the time her father woke up for work. Their schedules were so different that they rarely saw each other during the day.

He'd kept her grounded since returning from Vincula, and the least she could do was make sure he had coffee.

Rory and Lauren walked into the salon, and when Kordie spotted them, she squealed and flitted across the room. Her hair was a deep blue today, and it looked great.

"I just finished my last client, and I have half an hour before the next arrives." She directed Rory to sit in a nearby chair and ran her fingers through Rory's hair, placing it in front of her shoulders. "How short did you decide to go?"

Lauren sat in the waiting area flipping through a magazine and, without looking up, said, "Short enough that it's harder to grab when she's running or fighting."

The blood drained from Kordie's face, and she leaned forward to whisper in Rory's ear. "Is she serious?"

"I can hear you," the *Angel* informed her. Kordie jumped slightly and widened her eyes when they met Rory's in the mirror.

Rory shifted in her seat and stared at her reflection. "Yes. Cut it to here." She motioned slightly below her shoulders. "Can you change it back to my normal color?" Rory liked the black, but she wanted to see what her natural brown hair looked like now that her grey-scale sight was gone.

"If someone grabbing it is what you're worried about, why don't you just wear it in a bun?" Kordie mused.

"It's doubtful I'll be prepared for a fight at all times," Rory pointed out. "I'd rather not wear a bun every day."

Her friend nodded and clapped with a giddy smile. "Perfect. I'm going to give you waves too. It will look great with your new length."

Lauren ran to grab a new cell phone, claiming her old one broke while Rory sat in Kordie's chair for an hour. She returned shortly before Rory stood from the chair with a satisfied smile to examine her hair. It was a shiny dark brown and hit just below her shoulders in soft waves.

Her face fell slightly. *What would Caius think?*

She ignored herself. He could fuck off if he didn't like it.

"Smile," Lauren said, snapping a picture when Rory beamed into the camera.

A disgruntled client sat in the waiting room with several chairs between him and Lauren, but when Kordie apologized for running late and offered him three free haircuts, he seemed fine. Not wanting her friend to lose out for helping her, Rory hid enough moedas to cover ten free haircuts in Kordie's purse.

"We should go to a Phantom House tonight," Kordie said deviously as she walked the other two to the door. "It's been a while since we've been."

Rory smirked. Phantom Houses were fun houses where *Eidolons* tried to scare people, and their group usually went once or twice a year. "I'll call Dume and Sera, and you tell Keith."

Kordie nodded. "We'll meet at the Phantom House on 13th at sundown."

Rory grinned. *This should be fun.*

Sera bounced on the balls of her feet. "I haven't been to a Phantom House in ages!"

Dume, who had looked disgruntled until then, glanced at Sera fondly when he thought no one was paying attention.

"These places are for kids," Keith grumbled. "Let's go for a drink instead."

Lauren looked bored, and Rory thought the *Angel* would scare the *Eidolons*, not the other way around.

After paying for their tickets and waiting in line for half an hour, they finally entered the dark hallway filled with artificial fog. A dim red light lit their way, and the air filled with screams, banging, and evil laughter.

As they made their way through the dark maze lined with creepy props, Rory's heart raced at the prospect of *Eidolons* popping out at any moment.

The girls forced Dume and Keith to the front of the line, and when they turned a corner, an *Eidolon* fell through the ceiling with a loud screech. Dume jumped a foot in the air, and Keith screamed like a child.

The girls all doubled over with laughter until Rory's side hurt. Seeing the boys scared shitless never got old.

Rory caught Lauren videoing them on her phone and waved. "Text that to me. I want to remember that scream for the rest of my life!"

"It's not fucking funny," Dume hissed from the front, causing them to laugh harder.

"I hate you all," Keith shot over his shoulder at the girls.

Clapping as she laughed, Lauren said, "This is the best idea you all have had yet."

Another *Eidolon* crawled through the wall and stood with a wicked grin. Dume slammed into the opposite wall with a terrified look, Keith froze, and the rest of the group bumped into him from behind.

"How much longer is this stupid thing?" Keith griped. "This is ridiculous."

When they made it to the end of the house and stepped outside, a masked man with a chainsaw ran around the side of the building.

Keith and Dume hollered and took off running, leaving the girls behind. It didn't matter how many times they came; it was funny every single time. Once the girls rounded the corner to the front of the building, they found both men with crossed arms and sour expressions.

"We're not doing this again," Dume informed them gruffly.

Reaching up to pat his cheek, Sera wore a sugary sweet smile. "Yes, we will."

Dume tried to look annoyed but failed.

"Can we get a drink now?" Keith griped. "I deserve one after that torture."

Kordie snaked her arm around his waist and leaned her head against him. "It was worth it."

He pecked his girlfriend on the lips, and Rory's heart warmed. It made her feel such a deep longing that it almost took her breath away.

Lauren fell into step beside her and nudged her shoulder. "You'll see him again."

Hot tears prickled the corners of Rory's eyes. "I don't remember him, and all I can think is, what if I never do?" She stopped and turned to the woman, who was becoming a close friend. "Even if I get them back, how will I get back to Vincula to see him?"

Lauren placed both hands on Rory's shoulders and pulled her down to eye level. "There isn't enough magic in either of the realms to keep him from getting to you."

"But there is," she whispered back. "Otherwise, he'd be here."

"Do not underestimate the power of Caius' love. He will break out of Vincula, and when he does, the entire realm will feel his wrath." Lauren released her and joined the others as they chattered away, leaving Rory standing in the dark, wishing her words were true.

CHAPTER 25

VINCULA

Caius stood in a small apartment and stared at the walls covered in erratic handwriting.

Two were one, and one is yours. Do not let him fool you. His darkness is poison. Only the golden child can save you.

The prophecy. Lenora said he had to be the one to save Rory, but nothing about him was golden other than his eyes. She misinterpreted her vision.

***Sibyls'** visions weren't black and white, and he searched his memories for any clue of who it could be. It could be someone from Erdikoa he hadn't met, and the thought drove him mad, but then again, all thoughts involving Rory did.*

This was Rory's old apartment, he realized, and curiosity got the better of him. Turning in a circle, he looked at the worn couches, small Essence Screen sitting on a small entertainment center, and framed pictures of Rory's family covering the walls.

*He ran a finger down a picture of Rory and her sister as teenagers. He recognized Cora from the pictures in her emergency report and seeing her before her short life was snuffed out made his stomach turn. An **Aatxe** boy around their age stood between them with his arms slung over their shoulders, and their smiles were huge. This must be Dume. Seeing the pictures, he finally understood their familial relationship. It was as clear as day.*

He moved on to other pictures, seeing Rory grow up through moments captured in time. A picture of a young Lenora and a man, Rory's father, he guessed, holding twin baby girls sat on a side table.

The gentleness in her father was evident in his eyes, and Caius chuckled at Lenora's words. Rory was like her mother, indeed, but there was a piece of her father in her as well.

Meandering down the hall, he stopped in front of an open bedroom door. In the middle of the wildflower-covered floor was the most beautiful woman he'd ever seen, but something was different about her.

"Your hair." He stepped forward, and her grey eyes found his.

Rising from the floor, she stared at him in challenge, raising her chin defiantly. "I like it."

Reaching out a hand to run through her short brown waves, he grinned. "I love it. Who knew I had a fetish?"

"A fetish for what?" Amusement tinged her words.

His hand threaded through her hair and pulled her close. "You. For every physical change you could ever have." He brushed a kiss across her lips, and she smiled.

Suddenly, she jerked back. "The bowl was red."

It took a second for her words to register, and when they did, his knees almost buckled before gaining his bearings and pulling her into his chest. "You remember," he murmured against her hair, but his relief was short-lived.

*"No, but when Lauren explained **Aeternums**, she mentioned my grey-scale sight, and that popped into my head."*

He nodded. "It was the first thing you saw when your sight lifted." His hope returned in full force. This wasn't a feeling something was missing; it was an actual memory. "Did you try something to get your memories back?"

A sheepish smile pulled at her lips. "I bought illegal memory recovery potions, but they didn't work."

*"They did," he insisted. "Even if it's only one memory, it's still a memory." He wore a path through the wildflowers as he paced. The magic could be broken. Hell, it **had** been broken, but only a little. What else could she try? He stopped and turned to her. "A **Munin**. Their ability is powerful, and with the memory magic already cracked, a **Munin** might be able to break it fully."*

"No," Rory said so quickly that it was obvious she'd already considered it. "I will not put someone at risk of being arrested."

She had to. "I will take over their contract," he promised. "They will go back home immediately."

Her head tilted slightly. "You can do that?"

The air grew heavy, and he nodded, unwilling to admit what he'd done.

"It could make them a social pariah," she admonished. "I can't do that to someone."

*"I will do anything to make them happy once they return." He was desperate. A **Munin** could do this. And then it hit him. "Max."*

"Who is Max?" she asked him.

Caius rubbed a hand down his face. Max wouldn't remember Rory, but their souls would know one another. It was the soul that changed in Vincula; their souls remembered, even if their minds didn't. "He was an inmate, and you two were close. He's a **Munin** who lives in the compound with his wife. His contract ended a little before you left. He won't remember you, but I would bet anything he will help you."

"If we were friends, then I really won't do that to him," she replied. "I've hurt my friends enough."

He had to convince her. "You have to. This isn't just about saving your life anymore." **Yes, it was.** "Gedeon is neglecting the people."

Not a lie. He knew his next words were a low blow because she'd think of her mother, but he needed her to regain her memories for her own safety. "Brynne was arrested for stealing food. She cares for her **Sibyl** brother, and they faced hardships. The funding for the assistance programs was cut by order of The Crown, and no one knows why. She couldn't even afford food."

Rory's eyes became slits. "Who is Brynne?"

He recognized the hint of jealousy in her tone and fought a smile. "An inmate. You'd like her."

Rory sniffed and looked away. "Are you two close?"

Grabbing her chin, he turned her face to his, descending on her for another kiss.

"No. We spoke once." He cupped her cheek and implored her to believe him. "I am yours, Aurora Raven. Every part of me belongs to you. Another woman couldn't hold my attention if they tried."

"Have they tried?" was her only response, and he fought another smile.

"After what you did to the last woman who wanted me as her own, they wouldn't dare."

"You did that on purpose," she accused, removing his hand from her face. "Using the greater good of the realms was a shitty thing to do, and now I can't say no."

He tried and failed to hide his triumphant grin, earning him a glare. "Find Max Story. His wife's name is Tammy, and they live in the **Munin** *compound."*

"I'll make Lauren take me tomorrow," she reluctantly promised. "If he is caught and arrested, you send him back immediately, or I **will** *cut your heart from your body."*

His smile faded. "You already hold my heart in your hands, Aurora Raven. One day you'll believe me, whether you remember me or not."

Her misty eyes made him want to reach for her, but the blaring alarm sounded through the room, and Caius cursed Sam for demanding they meet early. Rory looked around in confusion, and Caius sighed. "Time to wake up."

CHAPTER 26

ERDIKOA

Rory sat up. "Max Story," she said repeatedly as she jumped up and ran to the bathroom, afraid she would forget.

Once dressed, she ran downstairs, calling Lauren's name, only to find her sitting with Patrick in the living room, drinking coffee.

"You've been waking up early," Lauren commented as Rory leaned over to kiss her father on the cheek.

"Caius' alarm went off in the soulscape last night," she told her.

Patrick looked between the two women. "Do I even want to know?"

"It's a story for another time," Lauren replied with a shake of her head.

"How was work last night?" Rory yelled as she padded to the kitchen for coffee.

Her father waited to answer until she returned and sat down, presumably not wanting to scream across the large house. "I found something else you might be interested in." He grabbed a book from the side table and held it out to her. "It's a history book about the *Royals*." Her excitement piqued. She'd only scanned the last book he brought her, finding nothing useful, but this one sounded promising.

Opening the cover, she read the table of contents and grinned widely. There was a section on Caius and his siblings. "Thank you," she said mindlessly as she flipped through the pages. "This is perfect."

There were no pictures of the *Royals*, but what she read about the brothers made her gasp. They were identical twins. "Bane," she hissed as she looked at Lauren. "Gedeon killed Cora, didn't he?"

Patrick sat forward and turned to Lauren as well. "The Lux King? He killed my baby girl?" Cora was born second and thus the baby of the family. Something Rory never let her forget. Their father had always called her his baby girl, which drove her sister crazy. Hearing the endearment almost did her in.

Lauren looked unsure as she looked between the two before giving her full attention to Rory. "Don't do anything stupid that will get you killed."

It wasn't a straight answer, but it was close enough. Rory's first instinct was to find the king, kill him, and make him suffer. She thought of ways to get into The Capital. Seduction? No. He would know she was Cora's sister. They looked too much alike. Besides, the thought of seducing any man other than Caius made bile rise in her throat.

"I said don't do anything stupid," Lauren fumed, and Rory reared back. The *Angel* had been nothing but calm until that point. She was *really* mad. "It's why we didn't tell you anything about Vincula when you first returned. Caius knew you would try to go after Gedeon and get yourself killed."

Rory repressed a snide remark, irritated that they knew her so well. "Fine," she spat back. "I need to go to the *Munin* compound today. Caius told me to find a man named Max and ask him to break through the memory magic." She would at least try to regain her memories before making any rash decisions.

"He thinks Max is strong enough to retrieve your memories?" Lauren asked, her previous anger gone.

"He thinks the magic binding them is already cracked since I remembered a red bowl." She chewed on the side of her lip. "Apparently, it was the first thing I saw when he lifted my grey-scale sight."

"What red bowl?" her father asked.

Rory winced. "I'll explain later, but he thinks a *Munin* can break the magic the rest of the way."

Her father scratched the top of his head, looking tired. "How will you get into the compound?"

The *Munin* compound was locked down as tight as The Capital. *Munin* kept to themselves, mainly because people tried to convince them to wipe their painful memories or use them against their enemies. Rory didn't blame them, and guilt chipped away at her resolve. She was about to do the same thing.

The only way in was if you knew someone and were on their approved guest list. "I haven't figured that out yet." She blew out an exasperated breath. "Could you get us in with your clearance?" she asked Lauren.

The *Angel* huffed out a laugh. "I can do whatever I want in The Capital, but there's no way they'd let me into the compound without a written demand from The Crown."

"And we can't ask Gedeon," Rory concluded with a groan.

Patrick snapped his fingers. "Keith! His parents are *Munin*, no?"

Rory straightened with an excited gasp. "They are!" She dug her phone out of her pocket and dialed Keith's number. When he answered, she explained the situation, and he agreed to call his parents without asking questions. He must have heard the seriousness in her tone. She'd tell Keith and Kordie everything today.

She beamed as she hung up. "He said he knows his parents will say yes, and he'll take us this afternoon."

Lauren sighed. "This is going to be interesting."

CHAPTER 27

VINCULA

Sam stood with his arms folded across his chest, waiting for Caius to follow his instructions.

Caius stared at the shadows swirling around him and wondered how in the fuck he was going to make them do anything other than move. "I don't understand what you mean."

"The shadows *are* the realm," Sam explained. "You are not actually *creating*; you are manipulating them to form into something else."

Caius thought about a rock, willing it to form. The shadows made the shape of a small boulder like a fucking shadow puppet. "This isn't working."

"You have been trying for five minutes," Sam reminded him. "When the King of Aravoth created the realms, it was out of love for his wife. Dig up the strongest emotion you have and use that."

"Will annoyance work?" Caius asked with feigned seriousness.

Sam's wings tightened, and Caius smirked. While the *Angel's* face showed no emotion, his wings were a front-row seat to how he felt. "You are impatient."

Closing his eyes, he thought about Rory, how she laughed with her friends and cried over her mother. The reminder of sending her away flooded his memories, and his anger and anguish overrode his other emotions.

"Stop," Sam commanded, and when Caius opened his eyes, they widened.

A small boulder sat before them, and black veins coated his hands. Pushing up his sleeves confirmed his suspicions; the veins stretched to his elbow.

Sam grabbed Caius' wrist and turned it over, examining his skin. "You do not look surprised by these."

"You do." An ancient *Angel* being surprised by anything couldn't be good, but he wasn't focused on that. He was focused on the boulder. *He'd done it.*

"This has not happened to others who have *created*," Sam observed, still studying the veins. "But they were *Seraphim*, and you are only a mystic."

"Can my body handle this much power?" Caius would cover himself in scars if it meant saving his mate, but if he died breaking free, it defeated the purpose.

"I don't think so. Do you have more of these?" Sam asked, flicking his eyes over Caius' tall frame. "This has happened before, yes?"

He flipped his arm over, looking at the veins. "Yes, on my hands, but they faded quickly."

They didn't hurt or itch as they appeared on his arms;

they burned, but not in the physical, painful sense. It was an icy fire that heightened his anger, fanning the flames.

The veins were the living embodiment of his fury, strengthening him. It was euphoric.

"They are not fading now," Sam remarked. "You need to find a different way. I do not know what this means."

Caius yanked his sleeve down. "This is the only way."

The commander stepped back, shaking his head. "I will not help you kill yourself. If Lauren and I must try to kill Gedeon ourselves, we will."

They would die trying.

"I've succeeded," Caius said, motioning to the boulder. "I can practice on my own. Gedeon is powerful, and I will not risk you or Lauren."

"And what good will you be if you are dead?" Sam demanded, his wings spreading wide.

Caius used shadows to push the boulder off the arrow-ball field. "We don't know if it's going to kill me. It makes my veins darker, nothing else," he lied.

"It looks like poison." They left the field, walking around the pond and through the garden. "This could be what the prophecy meant, Caius. You cannot risk it."

"I can, and I will."

CHAPTER 28

ERDIKOA

Sera, Dume, Rory, and Lauren rode in Lauren's vehicle, while Keith and Kordie met them at the compound in Keith's truck. Rory called Keith and Kordie earlier and explained everything. They were shocked but agreed to do whatever they could to help.

Keith pulled up to the security gate first, giving them their names and his parents' names, and after presenting them with their mystic cards, the gate opened, allowing them through.

Keith used Rory's new name, which made Rory stare at Lo. She couldn't believe she named her after her cat form.

This was really happening. Rory might leave the compound with her memories today, and the idea both terrified and excited her.

As they piled out of their cars at Keith's parents' house, Rory trembled.

Dume's hand squeezed her shoulder reassuringly. "Are you sure you want to do this?"

"She drank a mystery potion. I think having a *Munin* try is safer than that," Sera piped up.

Dume frowned. "I'm still not happy about that."

"Me either," Kordie added. "Why wasn't I invited?"

"Yeah," Keith threw in for good measure, and Rory's nerves eased a fraction.

"I knew you'd try to talk me out of it." She nudged Sera with her elbow. "She's crazier than I am."

"That place was awful," Sera complained with a shudder. "But I'll go back if we need to."

Rory smirked at the others as if to say, *See?*

"Are your parents okay with me being here?" Rory asked, looking at their front door. "Not everyone is fond of serial killers. Or did you tell them I'm the cousin named Lo?" She glared when Lauren smirked.

Keith waved her off. "They know you saved people. Besides, they wouldn't have agreed to put you on the list otherwise."

"Did you tell them why we're here?" Lauren asked, narrowing her eyes at Keith, making him step back.

"No. That's where they draw the line. They're very protective of other members of their community."

They all nodded and ambled up the porch steps and into the house.

Keith's mother hugged Kordie tightly, looking at her like she was the best thing to exist, and Rory smiled. It was hard not to like her, and anyone would be lucky to have her as a potential daughter-in-law.

She and Keith hadn't been dating long, but they were such good friends that Rory knew they wouldn't risk ruining their friendship unless they were serious about one another.

Dume shook Keith's father's hand and exchanged a few words while Sera introduced herself to Rina, Keith's mother. Rina bustled around the group to stand in front of Rory and placed her hands on her shoulders.

"Don't be nervous, honey." She glanced at Clark, her husband. "We know your heart was in the right place, no matter how unsavory your methods were."

Rory's stomach tumbled. "Thank you. I don't plan on hanging people from hooks anymore." More people were accepting of her than she expected, but the more people that found out she was back, the more uneasy she felt.

Telling Keith's parents was necessary, but after the way Fiona treated her at the market, she couldn't let anyone else know unless she had to.

Clark released a loud belly laugh. "You're all right, young lady. Now," he said, looking at Keith. "Your mother and I worked all afternoon in the kitchen. Come eat willingly, or I'll force-feed you."

Keith clapped his dad on the back and looked over his shoulder. "I went through a stage where I refused to eat at the table. He'll never let me live it down."

After dinner, they sat around chatting about random things. Even Lauren joined in, telling stories about Sam that kept everyone laughing.

Finally, Rory cleared her throat. "Do either of you know Max and Tammy Story?" She struggled to keep her voice steady.

Rina grinned widely. "Everyone knows Max and Tammy. If they didn't before, Max breaking that Cleary boy's legs did the trick."

Rory choked on her water and glanced at the others. Lauren neglected to tell her what landed Max in Vincula.

"He had it coming," Clark grumbled. "That boy was making fun of Tammy's limp. Now he has one to match."

Sera stood and began gathering plates, and Dume got up to help.

"They are friends of my mother's," Rory lied through her teeth. "I wanted to deliver the news of her worsening condition personally, but I've never been to their home before. They always came to ours, but they haven't been in quite some time. My mother is not well, and I would hate for them to hear secondhand."

She prayed they bought it. Everyone knew *Munins* rarely left the compound, and it was doubtful they'd heard of her mother's incarceration.

Rina placed her hand on her chest. "Oh, honey. Is she sick?"

"No. She's a *Sibyl*." Not a lie. Her condition *was* worsening.

Rina leaned forward and patted her arm. "I'm sorry to hear that. Let me jot down their address for you."

Rina grabbed the paper with Max's address on the counter and handed it to Rory. "Tell Max and Tammy we said hello."

Rory looked at the address. *Would Max help her?* Releasing a nervous breath, she nodded. "Thank you. We'll be back shortly."

It was agreed upon that only Rory and Lauren would go.

They weren't sure if a big group would make the couple nervous or not.

"We'll be right back," Rory told them as she and Lauren slipped out the front door.

They loaded into the SUV, and Rory shook out her hands to expel her nerves. "This is your last chance to back out," Lauren said, starting the engine.

"I'm not backing out. This is my last option." Rory handed Lauren the paper with the address, and within minutes, they arrived at a cute white house with beautiful landscaping. There were flowers and plants of all colors to accompany the lush grass.

"Let's get this over with," she mumbled and opened the car door.

As they walked along the sidewalk, an old man appeared around the edge of the house holding a weed eater. His skin was weathered, but his eyes were kind, and Rory felt a sense of familiarity.

"Are you Max?" she asked when he approached them.

"I am," he said, leaning the weed eater against the porch. After wiping his hands on his overalls, he stuck them in his pockets. "And who might you be?"

He hadn't taken his eyes off Rory, and she hoped he wouldn't send her away once he realized who she was. "I'm Rory, and this is Lauren," she answered, adding another person to the roster of those who knew she was back.

He stepped forward and held out his hand. "You're The Butcher." She winced, and her heart sank. "We must have met before."

Her eyes snapped to his. "You remember me?"

"No, but we were in Vincula together. It's why you're here."

Rory and Lauren exchanged a bewildered look. "Can *Munin* read minds?"

"I can't reveal all my secrets." His eyes ticked between Lauren and Rory. "Well, say what you came to say."

Lauren pushed Rory forward, and she shot the *Angel* a sharp look over her shoulder. "Before you say no, hear us out. Please."

Max stood watching and waiting, and when she said nothing, he motioned for them to follow him. Once in his backyard, he ushered them inside his garden shed. "You want me to restore your memories or at least attempt to?"

She needed to read up more on *Munin. Could* they read minds? "Yes."

Lauren's wings burst from her back, and Rory startled with a yelp, but Max didn't flinch. She smirked at Rory. "This is the fastest way to convince him we are telling the truth." She turned back to the old man. "I work under the Umbra King, and long story short, we need Rory's memories back. Her life depends on it, and she's a very important person."

Max stayed quiet for an eternity before nodding. "All right, come here."

She hadn't expected him to say yes. Lauren moved behind Max and laid a hand on his shoulder. He glanced at her hand. "Trust me," she said.

He turned back to Rory. "I need to touch your temples."

She stepped closer, and he grabbed the sides of her head. "Keep your eyes open," he instructed.

His eyes bore into hers and turned a bright blue, making her gasp. She felt a buzzing under his hands right before they sparked, throwing them both backward.

Rory shrieked as she fell to the ground, but she couldn't

focus on anything but her memories as they came flooding back.

The Scales of Justice.

Falling into Caius' throne room.

Her friends, her foes, her life hanging on by a thread.

"Hello, Miss Raven."

She sobbed on her hands and knees as memory after memory pounded into her.

Lo ripping a man's throat out.

Running through the garden.

Max.

Asher.

Bellina.

Cat.

Kit.

Tallent. Her stomach roiled.

Running through the garden.

The red bowl.

Destroying his office for her to clean.

Their bedroom filled with twinkling lights.

His hands against her skin, murmuring in her ear.

Finding him in his office with Lauren and Sam.

He sent her away. A scream tore from her throat as hurt and betrayal ripped her in two.

"I love you more than anything, and I always will."

"LIAR!"

Voices were in the background, but she couldn't understand what they were saying. Hands tried to pull her up, but she slapped them off as she cried. "How could he?"

Her sobs were loud, and she could hear Lauren soothing her. "How could he do this to me? To us? That fucking bastard."

With her head in her hands, she let her anguish salt the pieces of her heart scattered on the ground. She stood on shaky legs and wiped her face with her shirt.

"I need to go to sleep." She had to see Caius.

"I remember," Max murmured, and both women swiveled to face him. Lauren cursed under her breath.

"You remember me?" Rory asked weakly, choking down another sob.

"You're a terrible gardener." He smiled, and she saw a single tear trail down his face.

Her shoulders shook, and she crushed him in an emotional embrace. She didn't know how long they stayed like that, her crying and him rubbing her back. How did she forget her friends?

Max kneeling in the garden, meeting Asher in the clothing store, Kit and Cat bickering.

She laughed through her tears.

Bellina laying on the floor, bloody and bruised. Tallent's head smashed in as her fists flew.

She *forgot* them all.

"I'm sorry I asked this of you," she rasped as she pulled back. "Caius said the realm is suffering because of his brother."

"I would have helped you no matter what," Max replied. She remembered now he couldn't read minds; she'd asked him once, but he always knew things others didn't. "Have your memories ever been altered while manipulating someone else's?"

He shook his head. "It's unheard of."

Lauren cleared her throat, and the other two turned their attention to her. "I might have given you a tiny push with my power." Rory sputtered, wide-eyed. "It seems to have worked a little too well."

"You could have given me my memories back this whole time?" The betrayal stung.

"No," Lauren replied, looking hurt at Rory's accusation. "I merely boosted his abilities." Turning to the *Munin*, she said, "Thank you, Max. We have to get back to the group."

His eyes, still bright blue, moved to Rory. "I'm putting your name on our list. Come and see me. I want you to meet Tammy sometime."

She hugged him again, swearing she'd be back.

When the group stood in Rina and Clark's driveway, they asked her about getting her memories back, and she could only nod. Lauren had a hushed conversation with them while Rory stood in a daze, and they backed off.

Dume and Sera rode back with Keith and Kordie, and Rory switched between wallowing in grief and stewing in rage.

Caius had a lot to answer for.

CHAPTER 29

Gedeon sat behind his desk, still furious over Fiona's visit the day before.

She'd spewed nonsense about Aurora Raven killing her daughter as if he gave a damn. When he told her to calm down or lose a finger, she stopped yelling and explained everything she heard.

Caius had people spying on Gedeon.

He'd heard nothing of his brother, despite his sentence ending, but Aurora Raven was released early and sought a way to retrieve her memories at the behest of Caius.

And what's more unsettling is the knowledge that Aurora was his brother's *Aeternum*. He chuckled darkly at the cliche of it all. Twins fated to twins.

When he glanced at Cora's cabinet, his fingers flexed, wanting to hold her. Every time he held her, he felt his anger and intrusive thoughts fade a little, and he couldn't have that. Remaining diligent was important, especially now.

Pushing thoughts of his mate aside, he focused on the

matter at hand. He needed someone to infiltrate Aurora's inner circle.

Would they be welcoming of a newcomer?

He pulled out the files his men collected on those she associated with. Finding their identities proved to be easier than he thought, thanks to the loose lips of her old coworkers.

Whether Aurora had her memories didn't matter. Any harm done to her would torture Caius, and when she died, Gedeon knew his brother would follow.

Because once the *Aeternum* bond was in place, it was impossible to live without them.

CHAPTER 30

Rory stood in the middle of Caius' office with a field of wildflowers under her feet. It was peculiar that the flowers remained, no matter where the soulscape took them.

"Hello, Miss Raven," Caius purred.

She spun around, and the sight of him stole her breath. Seeing him in their soulscapes before had been one thing, but seeing him with her memories intact impaled her heart.

Closing the distance between them, he studied her pained expression. "What's wrong?"

Instead of answering, she cocked her arm back and slapped him as hard as she could, and before he could register what happened, she shoved him as a sob tore from her chest.

"How could you do this?" she cried, pushing him again.

He staggered back with a bewildered look that soon turned to relief. "You remember," he whispered, catching her wrists as she tried to pound on his chest.

Her head fell forward as she sobbed. "How could you?" The words were weak, and she battled to reclaim her composure.

"*I know I was wrong,*" *he said, tipping her chin to look at him.* "*I'd give anything to go back and make a different choice.*"

She slapped his hand away. "*That's just it,*" *she seethed.* "*It wasn't your choice to make. It was* **mine***, and you stole it from me.*"

The helplessness on his face gutted her. "*I know.*"

"*Did I mean so little to you that you could give me up so easily?*" *She hated the way her voice wavered.* "*There isn't anything in this realm I would have let come between us.*"

Caius grabbed her face and looked at her with such intensity that she had to close her eyes. "*Open your eyes and look at me,*" *he commanded, and her lids involuntarily fluttered open.* "*I sent you back because* **I love you***. When you hurt, I'm helpless, something I never want to feel toward the one person I'm supposed to protect. I would have done anything to take away your pain, and because of that, I made one of the biggest mistakes of my life. I'm sorry. I shouldn't have made a decision that affected you without asking, and I will spend the rest of our lives making it up to you.*"

"*What if I don't want you to make it up to me?*" *she croaked.*

That wasn't the case. He was ingrained in her very being, and she refused to let anything else tear them apart, but he had to understand how unacceptable his actions were.

He looked broken. "*I won't let you go without a fight, but if that is your final decision, I will watch you from the sidelines, taking the punishment I deserve.*" *His golden eyes were brighter than she'd ever seen them before.* "*And if you ever decide to take me back, I will drop to one knee wherever we are and make you mine in every way.*"

She drew back, hurt invading every cell in her body.

"You've said that before." He reached for her, but she snatched her arm away. "You lied."

They stared at each other in a stalemate, and while she was furious, all she wanted was him. The reminder that she may never see him again outside of the soulscape won out over needing to stand her ground. "Never do that again," she whispered. "I won't tolerate it, no matter how destroyed I am without you. I'd rather live a life of misery than a life controlled by someone else. You don't get to make my decisions."

Caius pulled her into his chest and buried his face in the crook of her neck. "Never again," he swore like an oath and planted a trail of kisses along her jawline until his lips found hers. "Say you still love me."

The agony and desperation in his voice were her undoing. "I love you, Caius, even when it hurts to."

She pressed her lips to his, and his tongue caressed hers with a hunger that would never be satiated. Their hands wandered in a frenzy to compensate for the week they lost. A week. That's all it'd been, but it felt like years.

They were racing against the sun, needing to take everything they could. She wanted to taste him, fuck him, feel him against her. This wasn't the tender need one expected of two lovers torn apart. It was a primal need.

He picked her up and carried her to his desk, the only flat surface large enough to hold them other than the floor. Once she was perched on the edge, he maneuvered around the desk and swiped everything to the ground.

She twisted her body to watch him, and lust overtook her at the predatory gleam in his eyes. A wicked smile spread across her face when she remembered something she learned in her early twenties. She'd fulfill her first need: tasting him.

Her body slid to the middle of the desk, and she lay back, silently beckoning him to stand near her head.

His gaze traced every inch of her body, and his hand caressed her ankle. A single brow lifted as his hand trailed slowly up the inside of her leg. "I haven't explored your body yet." The low timbre of his voice sent a shiver down her spine.

She wanted him now. They'd been crazed only moments ago, and all she wanted was him in her mouth, coating her tongue, but he had other plans.

A trail of goosebumps followed his fingers, and his attention returned to exploring her skin. His touch was featherlight, and she couldn't help but squirm as he neared the top of her thighs.

"I wonder," he murmured. "If your pussy still weeps at my touch."

"It's only been a week," she taunted.

"A single day without you is too long," he returned, lifting his gaze to hers. "Seven might as well be a lifetime."

The throbbing between her legs grew in intensity. She tried to squeeze her thighs together, but he grabbed her opposite leg with his other hand, stopping her. "None of that," he tutted, running both hands slowly up her thighs.

She moaned and lifted her hips slightly. "If you don't touch me now, I'll do it myself."

The whisper of a smile graced his handsome face. "Is that so?"

His words distracted her, and she didn't realize his hands were on her panties until his finger hooked around the middle and dragged them down her legs.

"Caius," she breathed, unable to stay still.

"Patience, Miss Raven." His voice was her own personal aphrodisiac. Soon, his hands trailed up her legs again, and

when he got to the apex of her thighs, his fingers dipped to her entrance and ran up and over her swollen skin at a torturous pace. "You're fucking soaked," he groaned.

His fingers stopped at her waist, and in one swift move, he ripped her nightie down the middle, making her gasp. His fingers continued their perusal, caressing her skin.

She wouldn't survive this if he didn't fuck her soon. Skimming over her breasts, he lightly brushed her hardened nipples.

"I am going to devour you in every way," he promised. "You will wake up screaming my name, and all you will think about tomorrow is my tongue on your body, my cock filling you, and this." He grabbed her chin and yanked it so that she was facing him as he descended on her. As his tongue demanded entrance, his hand slid to her throat.

She felt him squeeze the sides of her neck as he continued to fuck her mouth with his own. His hand squeezed harder. Not enough to hurt, but enough to make her lightheaded.

Her back bowed slightly as a soft moan escaped her lips. He pulled back, loosening his hand, and ran it down her breastbone, staring with such heat that she thought she would burn alive from it. "What did you want to show me before I take you?"

As the fog cleared from her brain, she licked her lips. "Take off your pants and stand by my head," she instructed. He obeyed, and when his erection was even with her head, she slid on her back to the edge and hung her head over the side.

His eyes darkened, and he ran his thumb across his bottom lip. The gesture was so familiar that it made her miss him more. Clearing away the emotion, she reached her hands over her head, grabbing his hips as she opened her mouth and pulled him forward.

"Not yet," he murmured and grabbed his sleep pants,

rolled them up, and slid them under her neck as a cushion. She grabbed him again and opened.

Understanding, he wrapped his massive hand around his cock and guided the tip into her mouth. She learned to deepthroat this way, and the need to take him in her mouth was overwhelming. She sucked him in, and his head fell back with a deep groan that had her rubbing her thighs together.

Catching the movement of her lower body, he leaned forward, gently pushing in and out of her mouth, and spread her legs wide. With his height, it was nothing for him to lower his head to her core and give her a long lick.

Bucking her hips, she gagged on his cock as it pushed into her mouth. Her hands squeezed his tight ass as she sucked harder, trying not to lose her mind as he lazily ran his tongue all over her pussy.

She pulled him forward as she sucked hard, gagging again, and he cursed against the skin of her inner thigh. It became a competition as he dove in, pushing his tongue into her and rubbing his chin against her clit. One of his hands held her left thigh while the other braced on the desk.

His tongue left her opening and ran along her sensitive skin before his mouth covered her clit and sucked. She whimpered and lifted her hips for more friction. His heavy balls tightened against her face as his cock throbbed. He was close, and so was she.

Something like a growl rumbled from his chest, followed by a deep moan. She sucked harder, and her pussy clenched. Straightening slightly, he hooked both hands under her thighs and pulled her hips off the desk, allowing him better access.

She jerked as her orgasm crashed through her, crying out against his cock. As her body convulsed, he gently laid her hips down and stood to grab her head on each side. "You're doing good, baby," he praised as he pulled out slowly before pushing back in.

"Did you daydream about this?" His hand caressed her throat. "Have you been waiting to fuck me in every way possible, waiting to taste me?"

Throwing his head back, he groaned. Moving one of his hands to protect the back of her head, he pumped faster. "Fuck, your mouth is beautiful." He thrust deep, and her eyes watered as her grip tightened around him. His wild eyes found hers. "Open wide, Miss Raven. I want to hit the back of your throat as you drink everything I give you."

She did as she was told, and he thrust deep as his cock swelled. Before long, his hot cum coated her tongue, and she struggled to swallow with his dick still filling her mouth. His thrusts slowed, and his hand moved to cup her jaw. "Seal your lips around me." Closing her lips tight, he slid out bit by bit. "Clean me," he murmured with his eyes glued to her mouth.

She intended to run this show, but there was a certain thrill to his domineering persona in the bedroom.

Or on the desk.

He traced his eyes over her body. "I am going to fuck you hard enough that you'll be sore when you wake up," he promised, but as he moved around the desk, the room shimmered.

A string of curses left his lips. "We will pick up where we left off tomorrow," he promised and kissed her. "Time to wake up."

~

Rory rolled over and groaned, aching for another release. Their soulscape felt real, and had Caius left marks on her, she'd check to see if they remained.

If luck was on her side, tonight, he would.

But even lust couldn't stop the pain in her heart. She forgave him, but the fact remained that she was here while he was there.

Focusing on the issue at hand was impossible because her chest tightened at the loss she suffered and the opportunity she gained. Seeing her friends and family again was a sweet torture. Mere weeks ago, she would've given anything to be here, but now that Caius forced them apart, she wanted to go home.

She vowed to find her way back to him that night, and killing Gedeon was the last thing on her mind, despite what everyone thought. They promised to kill him together, and she intended to keep that promise.

How would she get back? Caius didn't mention his sister often, but when he did, they weren't on the best of terms. Could Rory plead her case and convince the Scales of Justice to send her to Vincula?

If the *Royal* refused, did that mean Adila was helping Gedeon? How could she call herself the Scales of Justice when she offered none the day she locked Caius away?

Justice bloomed from empathy, but injustice fueled the need for blood.

Rory wanted Gedeon's blood. She hoped she wouldn't thirst for Adila's too.

Killing Adila would be easy. She felt the itch of The Butcher, and watching the *Royals* who wronged her mate swing from a hook was tempting. If the intrusive thoughts made her a monster, so be it. She was already one, anyway.

Sitting up, she threw her legs over the side of the bed and spotted Caius' book sitting on her nightstand.

Chuckling humorlessly, she revisited the night he sent her back. She'd thought he couldn't sleep, nervous about his return to Erdikoa, and had wanted to give him his book to read, hoping it would calm his nerves. That's why she held it when she disappeared.

How stupid she'd been. Thinking of Vincula, her eyes burned at the loss of her friends. *Would she ever see them again?* By the time Bellina returned, Rory might be dead, and Kit and Cat wouldn't remember her.

Her mother. Rory pressed a hand to her chest to stop the ache.

If she hadn't been overcome by anger, hurt, and lust last night, she would've sent Caius with a message for her mother. She perked up.

Sam and Lauren. One of them could carry a letter back to her mother and friends in the prison realm. She knew they wouldn't deny her that. It was a viable solution until she could return.

Staying in Erdikoa wasn't an option, and hiding her departure from her friends and family wasn't an option, either. Honesty was what they deserved, and they would understand once she explained her situation. *She hoped they would.*

Once dressed and downstairs, she sought out her father and Lauren, finding them in the kitchen, deep in conversation. "Good morning."

They turned to her, and her father's lips lifted into a small smile. "I heard you have your memories back." She nodded, and he crossed the room, wrapping her in a hug. "I'm sorry."

She needn't ask what for. Being taken away from her friends and family, only to later be taken away from her soulmate and other friends, was hard, and her father always knew how she felt. Cora had been the same way.

He kissed her forehead. "I have an errand to run this morning, but I'll see you before I leave for work."

She said goodbye, made herself coffee, and leaned on the counter next to Lauren. "Can you deliver a letter to my mother and friends in Vincula for me?"

Lauren smirked. "Want me to take a few nudes to Caius, too?"

Coffee spewed all over the floor as Rory choked. "What is wrong with you?"

Laughing, Lauren pushed off the counter and handed Rory a hand towel to clean up the mess.

"Why would he need a picture when he can see the real thing every night?" Rory asked as she wiped at the mess.

Lauren pulled out her phone and snapped a picture of Rory glaring over her coffee cup. "He misses you during the day, too, you know."

Rory missed him, too. "I'm still not sending nudes."

The *Angel* lifted a shoulder. "Suit yourself, but instead of a letter, you can send them a video."

"How?" Rory asked, excited. Could they send her one too?

Lauren waved her phone. "There's no service in Vincula, but Caius can power a phone with his essence. I'll record a few videos and show them. I don't need service to play anything from my camera roll." The *Angel* paused. "And I had your mother record you something, too."

Rory's heart stuttered in her chest. "And you're just now telling me? Can I see?"

After tapping a few buttons on her phone, Lauren handed it to her. "I wanted to wait until the time was right. I'll let you watch them in private."

Tears threatened to make themselves known, but Rory pushed them down. "You act tough, but you're secretly nice."

Lauren snorted. "I'm kind, not nice, and I don't *act* tough. I am. I'll be in the living room. Come find me when you're done."

Rory's hands shook as she stared at the phone in her hand, and when she tapped play, the tears sprang free. "Hello, love," her mother said into the camera with a familiar smile. Rory clamped her hand over her mouth to stifle a sob. "I know you're already crying, so I'll make this short. I'm proud of you, and I've always known what you did for the people you saved." The sob escaped past her hand, and Rory hung her head in shame. "Stop feeling ashamed," her mother scolded, making her laugh. "I am well and enjoying myself. The only thing missing is you and your father." Her mother's eyes sparkled at the mention of her ex-husband. "Don't worry about me here, and I'll see you soon, love. I love you."

She grabbed a towel and dried her face, willing herself to stop crying. Lauren gave her this, and no matter what the *Angel* said, she was one of the best people Rory had ever met. Telling her would only end in Rory getting her ass kicked, but she would find a way to repay her.

When she walked into the living room and handed Lauren back her phone, the *Angel* pocketed it. "Any plans today?" she asked before Rory could thank her. She cleared her throat, and her friend narrowed her eyes. "What pain in the ass thing are you planning today?"

The corner of Rory's mouth lifted slightly. "I need to speak to Adila, but before that, I need a meeting with everyone here."

She lifted her eyes to meet Lauren's. "Why do you need to speak with the Scales of Justice? Better yet, *how* are you planning to?"

"I'm going to ask her to send me back to Vincula," she replied, tilting her head. "And I need to tell everyone my plans to leave. After what I put them through, I owe them that."

Lauren threw her head back, laughing. "You're just going to waltz into The Capital and demand to speak to Adila? By yourself?"

Taking another drink of coffee, she glared at the *Angel*. "I thought you or Sam could take me, or at least, get me into The Capital."

Lauren shook her head. "If what Caius says is true, he and his sister rarely speak. Pair that with the fact that she sentenced him to five-hundred years for a crime he didn't commit, and I'm guessing she won't send you back out of the kindness of her heart."

"Then get me clearance into The Capital," Rory tried again. "Please."

"I will not send you to your death." Lauren stared at her with a dull expression. "Because that's what going to Adila could mean for you."

She tried to be patient, but it was hard. She took a few calming breaths and gritted her teeth. "I am sick of everyone making decisions for me. I might not be older than the fucking dirt beneath our feet, but I am still an adult capable of making my own decisions, and everyone keeps stealing that from me."

Lauren looked amused before shaking her head. "It's good to have you back, Rory." Rory blinked. *What?* "I'll try to find out more about Adila first. Next time Sam and I search the Lux Palace, I'll see if I can sneak into her quarters. We need to know who we're up against."

Rory knew Lauren might knee her if she tried to hug her, so she refrained. "Thank you." Under her breath, she added, "You *are* nice."

Lauren wiped down the already pristine counter, and Rory suspected she was a bit of a clean freak. "I'm not nice."

Rory grinned. "Whatever you say."

CHAPTER 31

VINCULA

Sam tucked his wings tight and stepped into Caius' office, looking as formal as ever in his outdated uniform. It couldn't be comfortable to wear leather and metal all day like a warrior from an old storybook.

Caius filed away the contract of their newest arrival and set his hands in his lap to hide the black marks that refused to fade. It wasn't Sam's business, but the *Angel* seemed to think it was, and he didn't feel like arguing today.

After their soulscape last night, anger stronger than anything he'd ever felt burned him from the inside out. Time with Rory was limited; he couldn't worship her the way she deserved, hear her laugh whenever he wanted, or simply stare at her for no reason at all.

With his waking anger came the blackened veins; only this time, they didn't fade. It was localized to his hands, but it would only spread until he had her in his arms.

"What are you thinking, brother?" Caius' thoughts dissipated at the sound of Sam's voice, having briefly forgotten he was there.

"Rory," he admitted. "As always."

Sam crossed the room with a look of sympathy, and Caius ground his teeth together. He didn't want pity; he wanted his mate.

"I am meeting with Adila tonight," the *Angel* informed him.

Caius didn't know what he expected Sam to say, but that wasn't it. "She speaks to you?" Hurt and betrayal coursed through him, giving way to fury. The veins on his hands spread to his wrists, and he focused on his breathing to calm himself.

The *Angel* sat on the bench, resting his elbows on his knees. "She has not abandoned you as you think." Caius rotated slowly to look at his friend. "She could not tell me much because Gedeon not only has her *Royal* phone bugged, but he also has spies watching and listening to her every move outside of her chambers."

"What do you mean?" Caius demanded, stunned.

"I am meeting with her to find out more, but Anastasia said Gedeon started hiring non-*Aatxe* guards a year ago. According to the guard we questioned, Gedeon hired them to spy and listen for anything of interest, specifically pertaining to the *Royals*."

Caius didn't know what to say. He had a million questions running through his mind. *Was Gedeon's extra precaution because of Caius' scheduled release? Why did Adila sentence him all those years ago? Did she know it was Gedeon all along?*

"We are meeting at the place where you two camped as

children," Sam said, interrupting Caius' downward spiral. "Where is this location?"

Caius' brows rose. When he and his siblings went to school in Erdikoa under aliases, they were split up. He and Adila lived with one foster family, while Atarah and Gedeon lived with another. Four ethereal-looking children at the same school drew more attention than only two.

Caius and Adila would venture into the park near their foster family's home, and when she said she wished they had a hideout, he begged his real parents for moedas to have one built. He was thirteen, and Adila was eleven, and they viewed the treehouse as their own little palace.

They never told Atarah or Gedeon. It was an unspoken rule that it was for them and no one else.

Looking thoughtful, Sam scratched at the stubble on his jaw. "Rory and Dume have a treehouse they visit. She found your names carved on a bookshelf. Is it the same place?"

Caius' heart warmed at the thought of Rory in the place that held his happiest childhood memories. He'd been surprised in their soulscape when she claimed it as her own.

"Yes, it's the same," he confirmed. "Take Lauren with you. You will return to Rory after, and I will get a full report from Lauren on the meeting." *What he really wanted was a full report on Rory. What does she do during the day?*

After Sam left, Caius slipped through the passageway that led to the pond.

He stood by the water, surrounded by memories of her. The first night he watched her come undone was on this bank. *Seraphim*, he missed her.

He needed to train, or he'd lose her forever. Concentrating, he imagined a large boulder, bigger than the last, hovering over the pond, but after several minutes, nothing happened.

"Fuck." How could the *Seraphim* let this happen? They went through the trouble of creating a failsafe no one understood, yet a murderer with a black soul presided over an entire realm for half a millennium, and they'd done nothing.

Ever since Caius sent Rory away, anger trailed him like a shadow, coiled and ready to strike. He hadn't been in this dark of a place since Atarah was murdered, but even then, it wasn't like this.

That familiar feeling seeped into his skin, fueling his resentment toward the creators for turning their backs on him and everyone else in the realms.

A delicious burn crawled across his arms with a rush of power not far behind. Staring out over the water, he silently commanded a boulder to appear. Shadows rushed around him, shooting forward and colliding with the shadows around the pond.

Merging, the darkness turned solid, forming a boulder the size of Caius' desk, and he stared at it hovering in the air, fascinated by what he'd done.

The large rock balanced on a shelf of shadows, and Caius released them, watching the boulder plummet into the water.

By the time he registered the splash, he was drenched from head to toe with his hair matted to his forehead, but he didn't care because he was getting stronger.

The burning faded, and he glanced down, rolling up his sleeves. The veins had climbed higher without fading.

Whatever they were made him stronger, and strength was what he needed.

CHAPTER 32

ERDIKOA

Rory and Lauren walked into Night Potions after eating lunch and found the rest of the group waiting on them with drinks in hand. Rory smirked despite her nerves when she saw Kordie's bright blue hair and blunt bangs.

"I like your hair," she told her as they sat. Dume slid Lauren a water and Rory her usual.

"Just tell us," Kordie blurted out. "Never text *I need to tell you something* unless you plan on shouting it as soon as you walk through the door."

Smiling sadly, Rory took in her friends' worried expressions. If Adila sent her to Vincula, would she be able to come back soon, or would the Scales of Justice force her to complete her original sentence?

Keith set his drink on the table, and his mouth turned down. "Judging by your face, it's nothing good."

Dume stayed quiet, staring at Rory with a deep sadness.

He knew her better than anyone here, and he probably already knew her plan.

"You're going back," he guessed, but there was no venom in his voice. Only disappointment, and somehow that was worse.

"You can't," Kordie protested, standing.

Keith placed a gentle hand on his girlfriend's shoulder, stopping her. "We need to hear her out."

Sera stayed quiet, which struck Rory as odd. She talked more than Kordie. "Caius is my mate," Rory began, earning her an incredulous scoff from Dume. "The Lux King is his identical twin brother and the one who killed Cora." That shut Dume up. "He also killed Atarah and took over the Lux throne. Caius was falsely accused, and now, instead of being free to exact his revenge, he's locked in Vincula for another five-hundred years because of me."

"How is it your fault he was sentenced longer?" Kordie demanded. She wasn't taking this well.

"Because he took over my contract to free me." Her voice was barely a whisper and riddled with guilt. He'd done it for her, sacrificing his own freedom to give her a chance at a full life with her loved ones.

She swiped at a tear running down her face. "Not only that, but my mother's prophecy was true."

Everyone sat forward, listening intently. "In what way?" Dume asked.

"Caius and Gedeon are identical twins. '*Two were one, and one is yours,*'" she recited. "Caius is my mate, and he and Gedeon were once one egg in their mother's womb."

Kordie's mouth hung open, Dume looked down at the table, and Keith stared at her. "The end of that prophecy says you're in danger."

Sera still sat silently, looking perplexed.

"Who is the golden child?" Dume asked. "They're the only one who can save you, according to the prophecy."

"Caius," Lauren said. "Lenora's head is clear in Vincula, and parts of visions are coming back to her with more clarity."

Rory's stomach clenched at the mention of her mother.

"Lenora claims if Caius can't break out of Vincula in time, Rory will die. If the golden child saves her, and Caius also saves her, either he's the golden child, or she'll be in danger twice." Rory hadn't thought about that. *Great.*

Sera chugged the rest of her drink and set the glass down with a loud clunk. "Is Gedeon trying to kill you?"

"Yes," Lauren answered for Rory. "If Caius cannot get to her in time, Gedeon will kill her."

"Then why is she going to Vincula?" Kordie asked. Her already pale face had leeched of what little color it already had.

"Maybe I'm the key," Rory guessed. "Or maybe my mother misinterpreted her vision, and we need to be together, not necessarily in Erdikoa." From the corner of her eye, Rory saw Lauren press her lips together.

Dume glanced between the *Angel* and Rory. "How do you plan on getting back to Vincula?"

She took a drink to stall. Her plan was shotty, but what other choice did she have? "I'm going to ask the Scales of Justice to send me back."

Dume's face twisted in disbelief. "Are you out of your mind? You can't go before the Scales of Justice and ask for a ticket to Vincula. You can't go before the Scales of Justice *at all* unless you're an enforcer or on trial!" He was on a roll now. "You can't even walk into The Capital without reason, Rory. You're smarter than this."

"Lauren can get me in," she said defensively. "I know it's a shitty plan, but it's the only one I can think of. I'm going to die if I can't get to Caius. What have I got to lose?"

"Us," Sera said, making the table fall silent. "You have us to lose." The small woman released a loud breath. "But you're in danger either way." Her pale eyes met Rory's. "What can we do to help?"

Gratitude overwhelmed her because Sera understood her on some level the others couldn't. "I don't want you all involved. I wanted to let you know so we can say proper goodbyes this time."

"Rory, please don't do this," Kordie begged as she grabbed her hand. "We just got you back, and it's too dangerous for you to be in The Capital with the Lux King. What if you're delivering yourself to him on a silver platter?"

"If it was Keith, what would you do?" Rory challenged.

Kordie's lip trembled. "Caius is not the one in danger. You are."

She couldn't deny what Kordie said, and she knew they would never agree. How could they? Her love for Caius was unlike anything she'd ever known. He was like a phantom limb; there, but not, and all she wanted was to have him back.

But it was more than that; she couldn't shake the notion that he was in danger too.

"It's not up for debate," she said with finality. "I promise to send letters and videos back and forth through Sam and Lauren."

Lauren turned to her with a look she couldn't decipher but said nothing.

"There's no talking you out of it," Keith guessed ruefully.

"No." She looked around at her friends. "I'm going, and I'd like to leave on a happy note, unlike last time."

"It's not just her life on the line," Lauren added, surprising Rory. "The Lux King is up to something. He is hiring non-*Aatxe* guards in the palace and removing anyone who asks questions or speaks about the changes."

"I knew something was going on," Dume said, furrowing his brow. "There has been a large influx of *Aatxe* enforcers being transferred from The Capital to city departments. They can't remember why, and the transfer papers they're given at the gates don't give a reason."

Lauren nodded. "They must have become suspicious."

They sat quietly, absorbing the information, and Rory's throat dried. She couldn't promise them anything, so she didn't. They were important to her, and she would do her damndest to see them again once she and Caius reunited and figured out their next steps regarding Gedeon.

Sitting back, Dume exhaled loudly. "I'll go with you."

Rory couldn't hide her surprise, and once his words sank in, she shook her head. "I already told you I didn't want any help. It's too dangerous. I'll have Lauren or Sam." When Lauren snorted, Rory realized Sam might not help her. It would have to be Lauren.

Kordie wiped her face with a napkin and threw her hair over her shoulder. "Then we have things to plan."

Everyone turned to the *Alchemist*, and she forced a smile. "We're spending as much time together as possible until she leaves." Turning to Rory with watery eyes, she whispered, "I don't understand, but I know you wouldn't leave us again without reason."

"Thank you," Rory replied. "And you're right, I wouldn't. It will be one of the hardest things I'll ever have to do."

Keith raised his hand to grab the server's attention, and after ordering everyone new drinks and a round of shots, he gave them his signature devilish grin. "We'll start tonight. First one to throw up has to pick up the tab."

Rory's head swam as she laughed along with her friends. They traded stories from their past, reminiscing as Sera listened with an amused smile on her face, interjecting playful jabs here and there. *She's funny*, Rory thought.

Lauren's phone rang, and she stepped away to answer it. When she returned, she plucked the drink from Rory's hand and set it down. "We need to leave."

Squinting, Rory tried to focus on Lauren's face. "You're really pretty. Have I told you that before?"

The *Angel* looked annoyed instead of flattered. "I shouldn't have let you get this drunk, but thank you. I have to meet Sam, and I can't leave you alone in public."

She scanned the group before landing on Dume. "Are you sober?"

He was already rising from his seat. "Yes."

"Mr. Stick-in-the-mud," Keith taunted, raising his glass.

Dume ignored him and returned his attention to Lauren. "I'll stay with her," he told the *Angel* and turned to Sera. "How are you getting home?"

Sera waved her phone in the air. "I'll call a car."

"I don't want you riding in a stranger's car alone while you're drunk," he protested. "We'll drop you on the way."

Sera smiled at him. "My hero."

"You can stay with us!" Rory exclaimed.

After getting up, Sera clapped excitedly. "Let's go."

"I want to come, too," Kordie whined, crossing her arms like a petulant child.

"Me too," Keith added as he stood. "Lead the way, Dumey."

Dume shot eye daggers at the *Shifter*. "I will leave you here."

Keith's toothy smile was lopsided when he said, "No, you won't."

"Good luck," Lauren told Dume under her breath. "Do not let anyone near her, and do not answer the door for anyone once at the house."

"You have my word," he promised, watching the drunkards. "Wait here, and I'll close out our tab."

She rummaged around in her purse for her bank card and thrust it into his hand, making him scowl. "I'm rich now," she reminded him. "I'm paying."

Reluctantly, he took the card, and when he returned, he and Lauren herded the group to Keith's truck.

"How would you have taken us home if Keith hadn't come?" Sera asked him.

He smirked. "Keith's truck. He was never going to drive home. He'd either take a car, or I'd take him."

Sera used Dume's shoulder to hoist herself into the backseat, and he grabbed her safety belt, buckling it for her.

Lauren bid them goodbye and stalked off, and Rory frowned. *Where was she going?* She forgot to ask.

The group pulled into the safe house and piled out of the truck. "Isn't everything beautiful?" Rory asked her friends.

Dume chuckled. "I haven't seen you this drunk in a while." It was true.

"I missed the greenery of Erdikoa," she admitted softly. "I mean, there are some plants in Vincula. We had a beautiful garden, but it was nothing like this."

Keith slung his arm around her shoulders. "I want to hear all about it."

"We're not supposed to tell," she whispered behind her hand. "Everyone is supposed to think it's a horrible place, but it's better than here in some ways."

"Will you marry the king?" Kordie asked with a hint of intrigue. The sadness from earlier disappeared, thanks to the copious amounts of alcohol they consumed.

"Yes, and when I do, I'll bring you to Vincula for a visit," she proclaimed.

Sera's eyes widened. "You can do that?"

"No." Rory shrugged. "But I can try."

All but Dume burst out laughing again. "All right, everyone in the house," he grumbled, opening the door.

They all stumbled inside and threw themselves on the living room furniture. Rory heard the door lock automatically and the alarm set. *Fancy.*

The group sat around, talking and laughing until they all passed out. As Rory's eyes drooped, she looked around from her spot on the couch. Keith was on the floor, curled around Kordie, Sera lay sideways in one of the oversized chairs, and Dume draped blankets over everyone before disappearing upstairs.

Seraphim, she hoped she would see them again.

CHAPTER 33

After Sam ended the call with Lauren, informing her where to meet him and Adila, he stepped into the courtyard of the Lux Palace, breathing in the night air. He halted at the sight of Anastasia rushing across the grass toward the door. Before entering, she glanced over her shoulder, and her eyes flared when they landed on Sam.

He could see her internal struggle with what to do, and without thinking, he closed the gap between them.

"Commander," she said, bowing her head slightly, and her formal tone grated on him.

"Call me Sam, Anastasia," he corrected her with what he hoped was a friendly smile.

Her nose wrinkled. "I will call you Sam if you call me Stassi. Only my parents call me Anastasia."

He would do no such thing; her name was beautiful. "Why were you running? Are you late?" It was before dusk, and if the schedules were the same as the Umbra Palace, she was early.

Pursing her lips, she planted a hand on her hip. "Are you my keeper or something?"

"Yes," he replied automatically and grimaced. *Why did he say that?*

She looked around and crept forward, lowering her voice. "Are you here to do more recon?"

"Not tonight," he replied, attempting to keep the amusement off his face. "Have you heard anything of importance?"

She lightly shook her head. "No, but I work the night shift. Everyone is asleep, other than the staff."

"I thank you for your willingness to help," he told her, still in awe of her selflessness.

She regarded him, and he wanted to know her every thought. "Why do you speak like that?"

Any thought but that. "I do not speak like anything." Did she consider his speech unpleasant? He never cared what others thought of him until her. *The stress of everything must be getting to him.*

"If you say so," she muttered.

Her brown eyes turned to his, making her hair rustle with the movement, and he longed to touch it. It was thin but well cared for, and he thought it would be soft against his skin.

The slight lines next to her eyes told him she smiled a lot, and he wanted to see them crinkle with laughter. Did she have a husband who made her laugh often?

He scowled.

"Why are you staring at me?" she demanded, suddenly irritated.

"I find you to be pretty." His answer caught her off guard, and he smirked.

"Thank you," she replied, awarding him with a shy smile. "Are you always this blunt?"

The smile spreading across his face couldn't be stopped. "I am honest."

Looking away, she fought another smile.

The sun was almost gone, and he realized he was late for his meeting with Adila and Lauren. "I apologize, Anastasia, but I must leave."

Turning, she started toward the palace and called over her shoulder, "Have a good night, Commander."

He smiled the entire way to his destination.

When Sam approached the treehouse, Lauren stood at a window like a gargoyle statue. "It took you long enough."

He ignored her and shifted into a bird to fly through the open hatch. If Lauren saw him get stuck, she would never let him live it down.

Adila looked around the treehouse, touching knick-knacks left by the Raven sisters and Dume. "Someone comes here." Her voice was quiet as she continued her perusal.

"Aurora Raven," he replied, with no explanation.

Adila set down the figurine in her hand. "What are the odds?"

"I am not a mathematician," he replied, making her frown. *Did she expect him to calculate things when they had more important issues to discuss?*

"Let's get to the point," Lauren said as she glared daggers at Adila. It occurred to Sam that he had never told her about his previous conversation with Adila. To her, the woman betrayed Caius. Lauren was loyal, and she would claw Adila's eyes out if given a chance.

"It is not what you think," Sam said, touching her shoulder. "Hear her out."

Lauren pushed him off. "Then speak."

Adila sighed. "I understand your anger, but I assure you, I have not intentionally harmed my brother."

"Gedeon or Caius?" Lauren shot back.

Adila flinched. "Caius." She took a calming breath and continued. "I knew Caius didn't kill Atarah. He wouldn't do that."

"Why sentence him?" Sam asked. It was something he'd always wondered.

Holding her hands out, she shrugged helplessly. "He was accused of a crime, and therefore I had to give him a trial. Once a trial starts, I cannot override what the Scales of Justice decides, even if I don't understand it."

Lauren looked ready to pounce. "You *are* the Scales of Justice."

Closing her eyes, Adila whispered to herself, likely asking for strength not to strangle Lauren. "Yes, and no. I am called the Scales of Justice, but when someone is on trial, I am no longer myself. The power takes over, and the Scales of Justice judges the accused. I could not change the sentencing if I tried, and trust me, I tried."

"But *why*?" Sam asked again. "He is innocent. Does your power give you a reason?"

"In a way." She paused for a moment. "It's hard to explain. I just *know*, and at my brother's trial, I saw Caius' beautiful golden soul darken before my very eyes."

"You can't see the souls of *Royals*," Lauren interjected.

"You're correct," the *Royal* agreed. "But Caius was on trial. I have to see their souls when they're on trial." She smiled sadly. "Caius would have tried to kill Gedeon. He was angry and hurt, whereas Gedeon was ruthless and cunning. Our brother would have anticipated Caius' retaliation, and he would have killed him." She looked off, almost in a daze. "Why it was five-hundred years, I'm not sure. All I knew was he needed something."

Leaning against the wall, Lauren crossed her arms. "Needed something?" Her voice lost its edge.

"I didn't know." Adila gave them a meaningful look. "Until three months ago."

Sam and Lauren both stood at attention. "Rory," Lauren concluded.

"Aurora? Yes. I don't know why or how he needs her, just that he does."

"Even pissed off, Caius would have won against Gedeon," Sam argued, unable to push the thought from his mind. "Gedeon could not have known Atarah's power would pass to him. Caius had years to learn to control his power."

"He killed Atarah." Adila and Sam looked at Lauren, who stared back at them like they were idiots. "He killed her with only a dagger, and she could have turned him to ash. Do not underestimate him. Ever."

The three stared at each other. Sam didn't understand why the *Seraphim* waited five-hundred years to send Rory to Caius, or why Adila's power didn't think he could kill Gedeon. Why not send his *Aeternum* immediately, and why did they give Gedeon the Lux power, anyway?

Nothing the creators did made sense to him.

"Rory wants to speak with you," Lauren told Adila.

"Her memories are back, and she wants you to send her back to Vincula."

"Her memories are back? When?" Sam barked before Adila could reply. Lauren glared at him.

Did Caius know? If so, why did he not inform him? Sam wondered. The king was distracted earlier, but something as crucial as Rory regaining her memories shouldn't have slipped his mind. He'd not been the same since Rory left, and Sam was afraid he was headed to a place where he could not be saved.

"Yesterday," Lauren answered. "We went to Max, and I gave him a little boost. It worked."

Sam stared at her incredulously. "A boost? You could have killed them both." An *Angel's* power was beyond anything in the realms, and if too much was used, it would destroy everything. Using it on a mystic was a risk. Sam had considered helping Caius, but the amount needed to complete his task would kill him.

Lauren faced him and matched his imposing stance. "I am not an idiot, Sam. It was a small push. Small enough that I didn't think it would work."

"I cannot send her back," Adila cut in.

Lauren whirled on her. "Why? You said yourself Caius needs her."

Adila looked stricken. "I can only send someone to Vincula if they are on trial. I have already explained the Scales of Justice to you. If she commits a crime, there is no guarantee she will be sent to Vincula."

She could be sent to hell.

Lauren swore under her breath. "Can you break her contract Caius took over?"

Adila's sadness turned quickly to annoyance. The quick

change almost made Sam laugh. *Almost.* "If I could, don't you think I would have already?"

"We need to discuss Gedeon," Sam reminded them. "A maid told me anyone who questions the reason for the non-*Aatxe* guards is fired."

Adila looked surprised. "What maid? She's a brave woman, speaking with a stranger about something that could get her fired or worse."

Sam shifted slightly. "You are dwelling on the wrong thing. You said his guards are spying on you, but why would they need to if your room is compromised?"

"I don't sit in my room all day like an old maid," she replied hotly. "But anywhere I go within the palace, a spy is always nearby. When I noticed what was happening, I hired an undercover guard, a woman named Heather. As far as everyone else knows, we're best friends."

Lauren wrinkled her nose. "What kind of name is Heather?"

Sam shot Lauren a *'Not now'* look.

Ignoring her jab, Adila kept talking. "She is a *Fey* and very strong."

It was a relief she was smart enough to hire protection, but it made him weary. "And if she turns on you?"

Adila stood taller. "Gedeon is not the only one who pays handsomely, nor is he the only one with the loyalty of the staff."

"What did you mean when you said her room was compromised?" Lauren asked Sam.

"Gedeon bugged her room."

Adila tucked a strand of hair behind her slightly pointed ear. "He's paranoid—always has been since we were kids. I don't know when he had time to plant a listening device in my room after Atarah's death or how he got into my room in the first place."

"Your doors are not magic," Sam returned. "It is easy to pick a lock."

Lauren walked to the window and stared outside, thinking. "If he planned Atarah's death far enough in advance, he could have done it before." She stopped and looked at Adila. "You and Caius were close, weren't you?"

Adila nodded. "He had to have thought Caius wouldn't be sentenced because he was innocent. Why spy on me?"

A realization struck him. "What if he spied on all three of you?"

Adila looked at him like he was stupid. "Gedeon never went to Vincula."

Sam pressed his lips together and prayed for patience. Explaining things was not his forte. "Caius stayed in Erdikoa often."

Still staring outside, Lauren addressed Adila. "Let me make sure I'm understanding. Gedeon has somehow been spying on you for five-hundred years."

"Yes."

"You realized it not long after Caius was sentenced."

"Yes."

Lauren pivoted on her heel, incredulous. "Why the fuck wouldn't you take the device out of your room?"

"I couldn't find it," Adila snapped and pointed at Sam. "He used his *Angel* power and discovered it in my safe."

Lauren's eyes turned to slits. "I don't believe you."

Sam stepped between the two women when Adila took a menacing step forward. "I don't care if you believe me or not. It's the truth. I am no match for either of my brothers, and you will have to forgive me if I didn't play hero against my psychotic brother while the other was locked safely away in another realm." Her eyes blazed as she glared around Sam at Lauren.

"I wasn't even thirty years old when everything happened. I was scared shitless, and I had no one to talk to. Our parents had their memories wiped and were sent to Erdikoa. Atarah was gone, and Gedeon was a murderer, spying on me, preventing me from speaking to Caius. What would you have had me do?"

Sam stayed quiet because Adila was right. There was nothing she could do because rocking the boat with Gedeon would have gotten her killed. They couldn't presume there was a method to Gedeon's madness other than hatred and a thirst for power.

When one longed for power, logic was pushed aside for instinct, and a greedy mind instinctually did whatever it took to get what it wanted.

Lauren smirked at Adila. "I didn't know you had it in you, little golden girl."

Adila scoffed. The fastest way to earn Lauren's respect was to stand up for yourself, and Lauren's response meant she believed Adila. Sam released a sigh of relief. They'd get nothing done if those two were at each other's throats.

Sighing, Lauren waved an exasperated hand in the air. "Let's look at the facts. Gedeon has spies everywhere. Rory can't go to Adila because Adila's power is rogue." Adila scowled at her. "Adila can't do anything within The Capital without Gedeon monitoring her. Rory will die, and Gedeon will continue to rule forever unless Caius can break through the *Seraphim's* magic locking him in prison."

When she said it like that, their situation sounded even worse.

"Where does that leave us?" she asked the other two.

The three fell silent. Their only hope was Caius breaking free, as impossible as it seemed, because there was no way to send Rory to Vincula without risking sending her to hell.

Reuniting the Umbra King and his mate was their priority because Gedeon could not be defeated until that happened. Caius would destroy himself without Rory, and Gedeon was too smart to let anyone close enough to decapitate him or stab him in the heart. Only someone with a power strong enough to rival his own could kill him.

That someone was Caius.

CHAPTER 34

Rory heard the door open shortly before midnight, and moments later, the living room light flicked on. Some of the alcohol had left her system, and the room no longer spun.

She yanked the blanket over her head with a groan. "Turn it *off*."

Sam chuckled softly as the sound of his footsteps grew closer. She lowered the blanket and tried to kill him with her eyes. "Why are you always loud?"

Sera stirred in the chair, but Keith and Kordie were unphased in their drunken slumber.

"You are loud," Sera agreed, shielding her eyes. "Turn off the light."

"We will talk in the morning," he told Rory before switching the light off.

Rory grumbled and turned over, slipping back into a deep sleep.

CHAPTER 35

VINCULA

Caius stood in the middle of the arrowball field with nothing but his pajama pants on. The wildflowers covering the turf made him smile. Their soulscape.

He searched for his mate, and panic set in when he didn't see her. "Rory?"

A giggle sounded from somewhere down the field, and he smiled as he followed it.

An arm shot up from the tall flowers. "Here I am!"

When he approached, he smiled at the sight of her sprawled out like a child making snow Angels. "What are you doing?" She giggled again, and he crouched down. Rory didn't giggle. "Are you all right?"

Blindly reaching for his hand, she pulled him down beside her. "My friends and I had a few drinks tonight."

He chuckled lightly. "Are you drunk, Miss Raven?"

She held her hand up and flipped it side to side. "Tipsy."

Leaning forward, he placed a chaste kiss on her lips. "I've missed you."

"Mmm, I missed you, too." She threw her leg over his lap and straddled him. "A lot."

When she twined her arms around his neck, her breasts pushed against his chest, and she pressed her mouth to his, running her tongue across his bottom lip. He deepened their kiss as a hunger that would never be satisfied took over.

Fisting her short, brown locks, he tilted her head back and moved his lips down her neck. She moaned and rocked forward. His want was all-consuming, but she was drunk, and he reluctantly stopped his descent.

"You're drunk," he murmured.

Her wide eyes blinked at him. "And I would still fuck you if I were sober. You promised you would finish what you started last night." Grinding against him, she whispered, "You're my mate." The shine in her eyes almost did him in. "Please, Caius. I need to feel you."

He returned his mouth to her neck, licking and sucking, unable to get enough of her taste.

"Fuck me," she pleaded.

They flipped over, and he stared down at her. When their eyes met, she nodded slightly. "I'm only tipsy, I swear. We passed out hours ago."

Looking down at the tight jeans and low-cut shirt she wore, he bit his lower lip. She was a fucking wet dream. He needed her naked. In the blink of an eye, both of their clothes disappeared. He'd forgotten this was only a dream.

Hovering his mouth above one of her nipples, he blew until it pebbled. She arched her back with a moan when he flicked his tongue over the tip. "No time," she panted. "Fuck me before we wake up."

The reminder stirred the anger he'd become familiar with, and a quick glance at his arm confirmed his suspicion. The veins, which still had not faded, moved past his elbows.

Her eyes followed his, and she gasped. "What is that?"

Straightening, he grabbed her hips and pulled them closer. "It's nothing." Before she could ask again, he lined up his cock and slid into her, almost yelling from the sensation.

"Caius," she breathed and immediately squeezed around him.

It felt like she was actually here. His dick dragging against her smooth muscles was too much, and he didn't know how long he could last. "Are you okay?" he breathed, praying she said yes.

Her hips lifted. "If you don't move faster, I might die," she groaned.

He grinned, pushed deeper, and watched as she threw her head back. "Fuck, you're beautiful."

With one hand under her thigh, he leaned forward and kissed her as he thrust into her warm body. "I will fuck you every night if you'll let me." Moving faster, he dropped his forehead to her shoulder, and she clawed at his back, writhing beneath him.

"I love you, Caius," she breathed.

Lifting his head, he kissed her again. "I love you, too." His movements came harder and faster, the slapping of their bodies filling the air.

Without thinking, he bit her neck with an animalistic need to mark her as his. The sounds she made were driving him over the edge, and he wished he had his shadows to move against her clit so his hands could touch her everywhere else. He couldn't control them here, so he propped himself up and moved his fingers between them.

She got louder, and satisfaction made his body buzz. He sat on his knees and removed his thumb, making her groan. "I need to come."

"You will," he drawled as he slowed his strokes. As she palmed her breasts, he pushed deep and slow, wanting to savor the feel of her. His thumb ran around the soft skin of her pussy, teasing everything but her clit.

It took everything in him not to pull out and replace his fingers with his tongue. The refusal to touch her clit made her squirm, and he coasted his thumb across the sensitive spot, giving her what she craved.

"Fuck, Caius, touch it again," she begged.

"Mmm." He grinned. "I love every part of your cunt, Miss Raven, and it is not to be ignored." Adding more pressure, he continued to slide his fingers along the slick area as he fucked her slowly, brushing over her clit again.

When she tried to lift her hips, he flipped his hand palm side up to slide his middle finger inside of her with his next stroke. His digit moved in and out with his body, and he curled it forward.

Pushing as deep as he could, he moaned when her panting came faster as he flicked the tip of his finger. Her cries were a symphony he would recall in his darkest hours, and he watched where their bodies connected.

"I wish you could see your pussy swallow every inch of me," he told her as he slowed to enjoy the sight. Again and again, his cock and finger disappeared inside of her, and on the next outstroke, he paused to add another finger, groaning at how she tightened around him.

She squirmed and made incoherent noises, and when he curled both fingers, she came undone.

He moved faster, grunting as she convulsed, and once her

muscles relaxed, he removed his hand and felt his balls grow tight. "Fuck, baby," he breathed when her glazed-over eyes looked into his.

She grinned and flipped them over. "It's my turn to take a ride," she said in a sultry tone as she lifted her body. He hissed, and when she sheathed him with her cunt, his hips slammed skyward.

With her hands braced on his chest, she rolled her hips, and it was too much. He wanted to see her come again, and holding off his own release would be a challenge.

He ran his hands up her sides and over her breasts to massage them as she rode his cock. "Caius," she breathed and rocked faster, grinding her clit against his pelvis.

"Come," he commanded, and her hooded eyes flashed wide. His hips swiveled beneath her, and she bounced up and down, throwing her head back with a long moan.

Her pussy clenched around him, and she cried out, making his dick throb right before he came, filling her completely. Their movements slowed, and their chests heaved as their surroundings shimmered.

"Shit," he breathed, and she leaned forward to kiss him. "Time to wake up."

∼

Caius stood in the kitchens with a bowl of ice cream just before dawn. Their soulscape ended earlier than usual, and he didn't know why. Did someone intentionally wake Rory?

He shoveled another spoonful into his mouth and licked his lips after he swallowed. Sugar de-stressed him, always had since he was a child. His mother would catch him hiding in the kitchen cupboards with a piece of cake clutched in his hands and crumbs covering his shirt.

"Did you leave any for the rest of us?" a teasing voice asked from the doorway.

He glanced behind him, surprised to see Lenora up this early. "I don't mind sharing," he said, holding up his bowl.

Rory's mother scurried around the island and into the other kitchen. She popped back into the room with her own bowl and sidled up next to him. Peeking at his snack, she tsked. "I didn't take you as someone who ate plain vanilla." Her gaze lingered on his hands. "What is this?" She reached out and poked the black veins.

He twisted toward her and glanced at her bowl, grinning at the chocolate syrup and nuts sprinkled on top. "They're tattoos," he lied. "And I didn't picture you as someone who ate ice cream for breakfast."

Her eyes ticked to his hands one last time before she popped a bite of ice cream into her mouth. "It's no different from syrup on waffles or jelly on toast. Sugar is sugar."

"I like the way you think." He licked the back of his spoon and set his bowl on the counter. "Why are you wandering the palace this early?"

Mixing the contents of her morning dessert, she avoided his gaze. "Pieces of visions are coming back with clarity but no context. I am painfully aware I hold the key to saving my daughter with no way to access it at will."

"What did you see?" Caius couldn't comprehend receiving visions and not understanding what they meant. Wasn't it like watching a movie?

Her eyes glazed over, staring at nothing. "Maybe I shouldn't call them visions because it's not always visuals. It can be anything from whispers to feelings to pictures, and if

I only have one or the other regarding a specific event, the meaning is unclear. At least that's how it's been since arriving here." She set her bowl down. "I have seen you grab Gedeon away from Rory and snap his neck, just as I have seen him drive his power into her chest while she lay lifeless on the ground. I can *feel* what those visuals mean. I know if you don't break free in time, she will die, but..."

Her hesitation made him nervous, and he struggled to steady his voice. "But what?"

"But I suspect the prophecy of the golden child differs from the visions of you saving her." She shook her head, frustrated. "I can't see that part of the prophecy. I only hear it over and over. It's connected, but not the same. *'Only the golden child can save you.'* I know those words are true." Her tired eyes lifted. "This *'golden child'* is her only hope."

An unfamiliar sensation filled Caius' veins: fear. "Is it possible I am also the golden child, and I must protect her from more than my brother?"

Would he have to protect her from himself if darkness took him over? He almost glanced at the veins marring his hands but didn't want to draw her attention to them.

The sigh she released was heavy with defeat. "Yes. Anything is possible."

"Lenora, you have helped Rory and me more than anyone else. We know I must find my way to her, and when I do, I'll protect her from everything. I swear it."

Lenora grabbed both of their bowls and carried them to the sink. Her silence hung heavy between them, and her next words rocked Caius to the core. "Do not make an oath you cannot keep."

His feet were lead as he stood rooted to the floor. "I

know you have your doubts that I will escape in time, but I am not making an empty promise. I *will* get to her in time."

Lenora nodded weakly. "I'm counting on it, dear." She went rigid, staring at him with unseeing eyes, and when she blinked back to reality, she covered her mouth, looking at his hands. "*His darkness is poison,*" she whispered as she continued to stare. "Whatever you are doing, you must stop."

He was thankful he'd gotten dressed before coming to the kitchens. Otherwise, she would see how far the veins went. "They're just markings." Wiggling his fingers, he smiled. "I am the shadow king, after all. It only makes sense that I have shadows in my blood."

She grabbed his arm and shook it. "You cannot save her if you are dead, Caius." Her voice broke. "I saw the darkness consume you."

"That doesn't mean it killed me," he replied carefully. "Consume and die are vastly different. What did you see?"

Her brow furrowed as she stepped back. "I saw the darkness cover you completely, and then you..." She trailed off and looked to be searching for the correct word. "Were nothing."

The experience had shaken her, and Caius couldn't deny that her words were haunting, but earlier, she admitted it was hard to interpret her visions.

With tears in her eyes, Lenora backed away and left him standing alone with nothing but the shadows for company.

～

Caius stood in line at the deli and twisted his hand as he stared at the veins. He liked how they looked, and briefly, he pictured his marked hand around Rory's throat as she came.

Yes, he definitely liked the way they looked. "I knew I'd find you here," Lauren said from behind him.

He glanced at her with a wry grin. "I like sandwiches." The deli reminded him of Rory, of the way she squirmed when he declared his intentions to marry her. The memory made him happy, and he needed more happiness in his life right now.

Lauren ordered and moved to his side as they waited for their food. "I put my reports on your desk."

"No issues, I take it?" he asked, sticking his right hand into his pocket.

She side-eyed him. "With the legion or with Rory?" He mindlessly twirled the ring on his left hand, drawing Lauren's attention. "What is this?" she demanded, reaching for his wrist.

Caius pulled his hand from her grasp and stuck it in his other pocket. "A side effect of my training." The man working behind the counter called his name, and after grabbing his food, he asked, "How is she?"

Lauren stared at the hand clutching his to-go sack. "She was planning on petitioning the Scales of Justice to send her back here, but Sam and I met with Adila last night." Her face was grim, and Caius crumpled the top of the bag in his hand. "She can't send anyone here unless they're on trial, and even then, she has no say in where they go."

Caius' jaw ached from how hard he clenched. "Bullshit," he ground out. "If she had no say over my sentencing, then why am I here?" The worker called Lauren's name, and after grabbing her food, they stepped outside onto the cobble-

stone sidewalk. "Her power would have known I was innocent. I didn't deserve a punishment."

"She knows that," Lauren returned defensively, taking
Caius aback. "The Scales of Justice ability is like a separate
entity from her, for lack of a better explanation. It—" She
lifted two fingers and made air quotes. "'Tells her' why,
though."

Caius stopped and turned to her. "I'd love to hear why
the Scales of Justice decided I needed to be locked away for
five-hundred fucking years." His anger was mounting. How
dare she defend his sister's actions? The cool burning sensation spread to his shoulders, and he knew what he'd find
beneath his shirt.

"Because you were grieving and angry," she snapped
back. "You would have gone after Gedeon with nothing but
pure rage while he laid in wait. He would have killed you,
Caius."

"You have got to be kidding me," he fumed. "I am
stronger than Gedeon when I have access to both realms. He
didn't even have power until he murdered my sister. He was
completely untrained!"

Lauren held up her empty hand. "Calm down, Caius,
and let me finish." He took a deep breath, nodding. "The
Scales of Justice said you needed something before you could
defeat your brother."

He wanted to ram his fist into a wall. "What exactly
would I need? If she sentenced me because I was angry, why
not only a year or two?"

Lauren looked at him pointedly, and it clicked. "Five-
hundred years after I was sentenced, Rory arrived in
Vincula."

The *Angel* nodded. "Adila doesn't know why or what it means, but that's everything."

"Did her power tell her to avoid me for five-hundred years, as well?" he asked, unable to hide the bitterness in his tone.

"I gave her hell, if it makes you feel better," Lauren offered. "Until I realized she had no choice. Gedeon has been spying on her since your arrest, possibly longer." Caius opened his mouth, but Lauren held up a finger. "This is a conversation you need to have with her, but until then, know she had a reason for her actions. Some were out of her control, and some were self-preservation, but what's important is if you can get out of here, she's on your side."

Caius wanted that to be true, but he wasn't dense enough to believe anything his siblings said without proof.

They passed through the palace gates and crossed the courtyard to the main entrance.

He and Lauren greeted the guards as they walked inside. "Keep Rory as far away from Gedeon as possible." He smiled at a passing butler. "That includes keeping her out of The Capital."

"She'll have no need to go to The Capital once Sam tells her Adila can't send her back," Lauren assured him.

That didn't make him feel better.

They settled into his office, and Lauren propped her feet up on his desk as she unwrapped her sandwich. He frowned and used a pen to push her boot off the edge.

"I need to see Lenora and Rory's friends," she mumbled as crumbs fell into her lap.

His hands froze midair with his sandwich halfway to his mouth. "Why?"

Lauren set down her food and pulled her phone from

her pocket. "Rory recorded video messages for them." She pulled out another phone and handed it to him. "This one is yours to keep."

He couldn't grab the device fast enough. The screen was black, and he looked at her expectantly. "Hold the bottom button down for three seconds to power it on," she explained.

Following her instructions, he watched the screen light up, and Rory's eyes glared back at him from behind a coffee mug. He stared in wonder as he ran a finger down the screen, but it changed, and a few file icons appeared.

Frowning, he tapped the bottom button again, making the screen black.

Lauren's cheeks were puffed out, and her body shook from holding in a laugh. "I set that picture as your main background."

His face screwed up as he flipped the device over in his hand. "What does that mean?"

Leaning forward, she tapped the button, illuminating the screen. "The first screen is her picture, and when you swipe sideways, your apps come up."

He swiped back to her picture, knowing he would stare at it an infinite number of times every day. "Thank you for bringing me this." Looking up, he held up the phone. "When you go back, can you bring one of her entire face?"

Lauren stood quietly and rounded the desk. "I already did. Tap here and swipe side to side whenever you want to see them."

His heart rate picked up, and he tapped the icon. There were tiny square pictures and videos, and when he clicked one, it enlarged to fill the screen. The first was a video in a dark hallway, and two men scrambled and screamed as an

Eidolon fell from the ceiling. Rory and two other women laughed so hard they were bent over.

"Text that to me. I want to remember that scream for the rest of my life!" Rory said with a wide smile as she laughed.

He covered his mouth with his hand and pushed down his swelling emotions. *She was happy.* When he swiped the video, a picture of her smiling with her friends stared back at him. *Swipe.* Her in a hair salon with a small woman behind her, beaming at the camera. *Swipe.* Rory sitting on the couch with her father. *Swipe. Swipe. Swipe.*

He set the phone down, and the first tear fell. The number of times Caius cried in his life could be counted on one hand, but seeing her, living her life and happy, *broke* him. It was everything he wanted for her, and if she weren't in danger, he would live his life in misery if it meant she stayed that way.

But she *was* in danger, and they had to force her memories upon her, causing her pain.

With his head in his hands, he let his anguish free. Dark spots appeared on the papers beneath his elbows, but he didn't care.

"I took that blind happiness from her," he choked out.

Lauren's hand touched the top of his back. "She misses you. Yes, she's happy to see her friends, but all she wants is *you.*"

He looked up with red-rimmed eyes. "And what if something happens and to save her, she has to stay in Vincula?" he asked. "She will resent me, and we both know it."

Lauren shook her head. "This is Rory, Caius. If she didn't want to leave Erdikoa, she wouldn't. She plans on coming back, and last night, she gathered her friends to tell them she was leaving because that's what she wants to do.

You are what she wants." She walked back around the desk and sat down. "If you had to choose between Rory and never seeing me, Sam, or Adila again, which would you—"

"Rory," he said without hesitation.

Lauren scowled. "You didn't have to say it that fast, but that's my point. You love us, but you love her more, and we understand. Her friends do too. You are two parts of a whole."

He grabbed a napkin from his lunch sack and wiped his eyes and nose. "Thank you for bringing me a piece of her," he said, powering up the phone again.

As he watched videos of his mate, Lauren slipped out quietly, leaving him to break alone.

CHAPTER 36

ERDIKOA

A blanket hung over Rory's head as she gripped a cup of coffee for dear life.

Keith, Kordie, Dume, and Sera left around eleven thirty that morning, and Rory had been too tired to move from the living room. Despite going to sleep at a decent time, she was exhausted.

It didn't help that she woke up before dawn to puke before drifting back to sleep. Thanks to her hangover, their soulscape ended early last night.

She was pissed at herself for barely registering Sam's arrival last night, and her eyes hadn't moved from the stairs since she woke up.

The front door opened, and she jumped, spilling her coffee all over her legs. "Shit! Shit! Shit!"

Sam snatched the blanket from her head and quickly wiped the scalding liquid from her skin.

His biceps bulged as he motioned to the coffee-stained chair. "You should be more care—"

He grunted when her entire body crashed into his with the force of her hug. He was so large that her hands barely met behind his back, but she squeezed anyway. "I can't believe I forgot you," she mumbled into his shirt before drawing back.

His mouth tugged to the side. "Do not be hard on yourself. I have a forgettable face."

Rory shoved him as she laughed. "Who taught you how to tell jokes?"

White teeth flashed with his quick smile. "I am glad you are back," he told her sincerely. "We need to talk."

"Way to ruin the moment." She sighed and fell back on the couch. "When did you go outside?"

"Before you and your friends rose," he replied as he took a seat. "The weeds in the flowerbed needed to be pulled."

A quick glance at his clothes confirmed he recently handled dirt, and she looked away to hide her smile. Weeding seemed mundane for a mystical being like the infamous Samyaza. Leaning back against the soft back of the chair, she shot him a tight-lipped smile. "Give me the bad news first."

His forehead wrinkled. "What else would I give you?"

The blood drained from her face. "I can't tell if you don't know the phrase or if there isn't any good news to give."

"Both."

"I'm going to need more coffee for this. Do you want any?" she asked as she padded across the room.

Sam leaned back and rested his ankle on the opposite knee. "No, thank you." He didn't drink coffee, other than the one Sera bought him when they went shopping. She'd spotted him through the window.

When she returned, she sat across from him and put her mug down. "Just rip the bandage off."

His body went rigid, and he shot to his feet, rounding the coffee table between them. "Where are you hurt?" he asked as he lifted her arms to examine them.

She pawed at his hands and pushed him away. "Will you sit down? It's a saying."

"Then what is that?" he demanded as he zeroed in on her neck.

She tried looking down like an idiot. "What is what?"

Crouching down, he moved her hair and leaned in. "Who bit you?"

"What?" She covered the area and stood. "That's not possible."

Sam ducked as she hurtled over him and ran to the bathroom on the main floor. She pulled her hair back and stared at herself in the mirror. "Holy aether."

Sam filled the doorway and shot her an accusatory glare. "You do not know who bit you? How drunk were you last night?"

She was too shocked to be offended. "Caius bit me." Her eyes never left the bruise on the crook of her neck.

Sam's hand covered her forehead, then moved to each of her cheeks before pinching the bottom of her earlobe.

She dodged his hand. "What are you doing?"

"Checking for fever." She tried to protest, but he started searching her hair like a grooming monkey.

Slapping his hands away, she ducked under his arm to exit the bathroom. "Keep your banana hands to yourself. I'm not delusional."

His face conveyed that he wasn't kidding. He thought she had a head injury.

"He bit me in the soulscape last night," she explained.

Sam studied the teeth marks, and she instinctively covered them with her hand.

The *Angel's* silence was worse than his Mother Hen Mode. "Say something."

"It seems if something happens to you physically in the soulscape, it stays with you," he observed.

"You don't say?" she deadpanned and pointed at her neck. "Did you not know this?"

"No."

She waited for him to elaborate, but it was Sam. Elaboration was not in his vocabulary.

"What does this mean?" she tried again.

"It means you two should be careful where you mark each other."

Her jaw fell open. "This isn't funny! What's gotten into you?"

"What would you like me to say?" he asked her honestly. "It does not matter as long as you do not kill each other."

*Thank the **Seraphim** Caius was stronger than her because she **did** try to kill him in one of their soulscapes.*

"You already tried," Sam guessed with a booming laugh before turning serious. "You need to train more."

She sputtered out a laugh. Leave it to the commander to take offense at her failure to kill his best friend.

"We still need to talk," he said, interrupting her thoughts.

What did they need to talk about? From the look he gave her, nothing good. Trailing behind him toward the living room, her mind ran through every bad thing that could have happened. With her luck, it was all of them.

"Just tell me," she groaned.

"Adila cannot send you back to Vincula," he informed her, sucking the wind from her sails. "It is not that she chooses not to; it is because that is not how her power works."

Rory stared at him, unblinking. "What do you mean *that's not how her power works*?"

Strands of blonde hair slipped free from his hair tie, framing his face. "She does not choose where people go. The Scales of Justice power does not allow her to. It decides, and she must obey."

Rory's mind was reeling. "Why are you speaking as though her power is a separate entity?"

"Because it is," he replied flatly. "In a way. She cannot send you back unless you are on trial, and if you are on trial, you risk being sent to hell."

"Even for something small, like punching Dume in the face?" she asked. He was an enforcer, and assaulting an enforcer would get her in front of the Scales of Justice.

Sam snorted. "You would punch your friend?"

"Yes." Her reply was automatic, and his laugh shook the walls. "But only for something important," she amended.

Still smiling, Sam shook his head. "As entertaining as that would be, it is unlikely you would be sent to Vincula a second time. Inmates do not get a second chance once they are back."

Rory knew this, but she was Caius' mate. That had to count for something.

"Not even an *Aeternum*," Sam added.

Leaning forward, she studied him closely. "Can you read

minds?" He ignored her, and the disappointing news about Adila sat on her shoulders like a weight. She wasn't stupid enough to get herself arrested and risk hell. "There has to be another way."

Sam stood and walked toward the stairs. "There is no other way, and going to The Capital will put you at greater risk of being discovered by Gedeon."

"Where are you going?" she demanded. "We're in the middle of an important conversation."

He pointed to his dirty jeans. "I need a shower, and this conversation is over. You cannot reenter Vincula. What more is there to say?"

She threw her hands up. "I don't know, but people don't just get up and leave in the middle of a conversation."

"But the conversation was finished." He looked genuinely confused, and she gave up.

"Go shower." Before walking away, she called after him, "Don't forget to use your strawberry mango conditioner!"

He gave her his back and raised his middle finger in the air as he ascended the stairs.

Later that evening, Rory and Sam went to a local pasta spot for dinner. It sounded like a good idea until they stood in front of the restaurant, and she remembered Caius taking Nina on a date in Vincula.

"Why do you look like that?" Sam asked her.

"You need to learn to rephrase your questions," she muttered. "Can we eat somewhere else?"

The *Angel* glanced between her and the restaurant. "You

wanted to eat here. I see no threat inside. What is the problem?"

"Bad memories," was all she replied. It was enough for him, and he held out his arm as if to say, *'lead the way.'*

As they walked down the street, people stared at Sam. The last thing they needed was unwanted attention.

"Can't you shift into something?" she hissed. "Everyone is staring at you."

Sam looked around and flashed a charming smile at the two women ogling at him from across the street. "I am considered handsome."

Rory couldn't help it; she burst out laughing. "We need to work on your social skills. You don't go around telling people how good-looking you are."

He glanced sideways at her. "You would rather I lie?"

The *Angel* was hopeless. Rory spotted a pet store up ahead and pointed. "I'll buy you a collar and leash if you'll shift into one of those little dogs that hates everyone. No one would look at you then."

"I am not the one who wears a collar in my relationships."

She choked on air. "I don't want to know how you fuck."

"I said nothing about fucking." The smirk on his face said otherwise.

"Umbra Queen," a frantic man whisper-yelled as he ran up to the two, making Rory jump back. Sam snatched him up by the throat.

The man looked about ten years younger than her parents, with dark, thinning hair and sallow skin. His eyes were wide as they bore into hers. He didn't seem to notice Sam dangling him in the air.

People stared and whispered to one another. They didn't need the attention, and she placed a hand on Sam's arm. "Everyone is staring. We need to leave."

His hand squeezed, and the man finally realized he was being choked. "Please," he pleaded. "I have seen her, just as I have seen him. He will ink the sky." His ramblings were familiar, and she didn't need to see his mark to know he was a *Sibyl*.

A crowd gathered, and Rory tugged on Sam's arm that held the man. "We need to go. *Now*. Bring him with us."

Sam's eyes blazed bright blue as he set the man down and gripped his nape. "Walk." The *Angel's* voice was deadly, and Rory's mouth went dry. She'd never seen him like this.

"My apartment is a block away," the man stammered. "I want to help her, not harm her."

Sam's grip loosened. "Take us."

"You were ready to snap his neck three seconds ago," Rory said, incredulous.

"He is telling the truth," Sam replied. ***Angels** can detect lies.*

"What's your name?" she asked the man.

"My name? Oh, right. You can call me Turney." He jogged to keep up with Sam's long gait, and before long, they arrived at a Crown-sanctioned housing complex.

Rory was disgusted at the condition it was in. Old wallpaper peeled off the walls in the hallways. The stairway railings were loose, and the carpet lining the floors was disgusting.

"I thought The Crown did the upkeep of sanctioned housing," she said to no one in particular. No one deserved to live like this, no matter their financial status.

The anger on Sam's face startled her. "They are supposed to."

Her voice lowered so no one else could hear. "Caius said Gedeon cut funding to different assistance programs. How can he allow people to live in a place that should be condemned?"

Sam's eyes moved over every inch of the building. "Gedeon must be stopped."

She couldn't agree more. Once they'd climbed three flights of stairs, Turney looked both ways as though someone would pop out and attack. He scurried down the hall and unlocked an old blue door, ushering them inside.

"Do you live with someone?" She looked at him expectantly. He seemed to be in his late forties, meaning his powers had not completely manifested yet, but would soon. If he was a *Sibyl*, he needed care on his bad days.

Shaking his head, he disappeared through a door in the tiny hallway. She looked at Sam. "He can't be alone on his bad days." Something in her panicked for the man. They had no relation, but no one deserved to be alone while locked within their own mind. He could hurt himself or become an easy target.

"I will make a call this evening to arrange care," he promised her, and her shoulders drooped with relief.

When they followed the *Sibyl* into the room, Rory swallowed a gasp. There were words and drawings covering the walls. Papers with things scratched in illegible handwriting and torn out book pages were pinned everywhere.

Her mouth opened as she inched closer. Some of the drawings were of her. She snatched one from the wall and shook it at him. "What is this?"

Turney turned to her. "I have seen you for years," he

said, waving his hand haphazardly in the air as he shuffled around the room.

"What is the meaning of this?" Sam asked as his keen eyes examined the room.

Turney whirled on them and pointed at Rory. "The Umbra Queen will die unless the day is destroyed."

Sam and Rory traded a quick glance. "My mother is a *Sibyl*. She predicted my death unless the Umbra King breaks out of Vincula in time." *Did Turney see something different?*

He shook his head wildly. "The day will disappear, or you will die."

"Do you mean to say she will live if she is attacked at night?" Sam asked as he studied the walls.

Turney's agitation was obvious in the way he moved around the room. "You are not listening. The day will *disappear*."

"Does the sun explode?" Rory joked under her breath. She was beginning to think coming here was pointless. His visions were as clear as a brick wall.

He crossed the room and reached for her shoulders, but Sam grabbed him. "Do not touch her."

The man's eyes were wild. "The light will no longer shine *on* our realm," he stressed. "It will shine *from* it."

Sam eyed him. It was the first sign he'd given that the weirdness of it all affected him, too.

Turney's eyes glazed over, and he looked at Rory in a daze. "He fills himself with poison, eating the light," he murmured. "And the sun explodes."

Rory narrowed her eyes. *Was he fucking with them?* He said the sun didn't explode.

He turned in a daze and grabbed a marker from the floor before approaching a wall.

"He fills himself with poison, eating the light, until the son explodes."

"Son?" Rory read. *Not sun.* **Son**.

Sam's eyes slid to her midsection before meeting her own. Her hand flew to her stomach. *It couldn't be.* She was pretty sure she couldn't get pregnant until Caius passed his throne to the new Umbra *Royal*. Kids weren't something she'd thought about. Hell, she didn't even think she *wanted* kids, and now her stomach might explode? No fucking way.

Turney continued to write. *"The son will save her."*

"Only the golden child can save you," she whispered to Sam, gripping his arm.

Sam showed no reaction other than the corners of his eyes tightening. She rushed to the messy desk and searched for a blank piece of paper and something to write with to jot down the prophecy.

Turney dropped the marker and stumbled back as he read what he wrote. He looked over his shoulder at Sam with clarity. "She will die by the Lux King's hand if the son is not found in time."

"Thank the *Seraphim*," Rory breathed. Her stomach wasn't going to blow up if they had to *find* whatever son he spoke of.

Turney left the room and went about his business as if they were no longer there. Rory and Sam made to leave, but she stopped and turned to the *Sibyl*. "Thank you."

The man ignored her, and she shrugged. Once she and Sam were in the hall, the lock clicked.

"How did he move that fast?" she asked, staring at the door. He'd been across the room.

Sam grabbed one of her shoulders and guided her

toward the staircase. "It is not important. We need to go home."

"I'm still hungry," she protested.

His mouth jerked to the side. "I will make you an egg smoothie."

Gagging, she followed him out of the building, wondering what had just happened.

～

Rory stood in the middle of Turney's apartment on a field of wildflowers. Their soulscape was at Turney's place? **Interesting***.*

"There's my favorite girl," Caius' silky voice said from behind her.

A smile spread across her face, and when she turned, her breath caught. He was shirtless in pajama pants, and black veins covered his arms and torso like tattoos. It was hot as fuck.

"What is this?" She ran her hands over his chest, and his pec jumped under her touch.

He caught her hand and brought it to his mouth, kissing the inside of her wrist. "They are nothing to be concerned with." Bringing her to his chest, he descended on her lips. "Fuck, you taste sweet," he groaned into her mouth and swept his tongue against hers.

Her mind went foggy as she lost herself in him. Slowly, he ran a hand down her side toward the waistband of her sleep shorts. She leaned back to look at him, and her eyes caught on their surroundings.

"Stop." She placed her hand on his chest. "We need to talk."

The arrogant mask he wore conveyed nothing as he checked out the apartment. "Where are we?"

"That's what we need to talk about." She started toward Turney's prophecy-filled room, and Caius followed close behind.

Once inside, he looked around silently, approaching the closest wall to read the random thoughts. Snatching a sketch of her off the wall, he spun around in a fury. "Is someone stalking you?"

Rory's mouth fell open as the veins on Caius' chest crawled toward his neck, and his golden eyes darkened.

"Caius, stop," she pleaded. What was happening to him?

*Following her gaze, he glanced down at his chest and closed his eyes briefly, stopping the marks from spreading. **Not tattoos.***

The words scribbled on the adjacent wall jumped out at her, and she couldn't form a coherent sentence.

He was across the room in a flash, and his hands snaked around her neck to cup the sides of her jaw, rubbing tenderly to soothe her. "I'm fine." He grabbed her hand and placed it on his chest. The skin was hot, and it did nothing to calm her.

*"**He fills himself with poison**," she recited with a trembling lip. Fear slammed into her. **His darkness is poison.***

"Poison? What are you talking about?" His eyes searched hers.

She could only point at the wall behind her. Was she losing him? Her mother warned her, as did Turney. She didn't care that he might not save her, but she cared if he died. He couldn't go to the aether before her; she wouldn't survive losing him again.

"What are you doing to yourself?" She tried to regain

control of her emotions, reminding herself that he was here and whole. "Whatever it is you're doing, stop."

"A **Sibyl** lives here," Caius surmised as he read the prophecy Turney scribbled on the wall earlier that day.

"Yes, and he said you're filling yourself with poison, just like my mother did." She placed a hand on his shoulder and prompted him to look at her. "Please. You can't save me if you're dead." Being saved was the last thing on her mind. She could save herself, but appealing to his protective side was the only thing she could think to do. "You would risk destroying yourself and leaving me to fight Gedeon alone?"

The roots climbed up his neck and teased the bottom of his jaw. Whatever coursed through him was connected to his anger, and she made it worse. "Calm down. I'm fine," she said, repeating his words as she grabbed his hand and pressed it to her chest.

His eyes brightened, and he pressed his forehead to hers. "I know these scare you, but they prove I'm getting stronger. Every time they grow, I create a larger object than before."

The look of the veins didn't bother her, but the implications of what they meant did. Her eyes tracked over every inch of his torso. "Explain."

"The shadows I control created the realms," he explained. "Cat discovered the story in an old storybook, and Sam confirmed it."

"Okay." She wasn't following.

"I can control what **created** the realms. With practice, I have created boulders out of thin air using shadows." Her brows rose. "A real boulder, not shadows shaped like one."

"How?" She didn't know what to say. It was hard to believe without seeing it for herself, but he wouldn't lie.

"If I build my strength, I can create a way through the

magic barrier." His eyes implored her to believe him. "Did you think I would let anything keep you from me, knowing you're in danger?"

Something felt wrong. Glancing back at the prophecy on the wall, she chewed on the inside of her cheek as she processed what he'd said. Caius was filling himself with rage-fueled darkness, but Turney said the son would explode. Whatever that meant.

Twisting around to look at the other walls, she searched for something to help decipher his riddles.

"What are you thinking?" Caius asked curiously.

"I will die by the Lux King's hand if the son is not found in time," she said quietly and flipped around to look at Caius. His golden hair and eyes were the living embodiment of light. He might wield darkness, but he exuded light. "The light comes **from** the realm!" Caius looked thoroughly confused. "The son explodes!"

She wished Sam were here. He would understand what she discovered. The light coming from the realm was the son exploding. If Caius' strength was fueled by positive emotions, would it be golden instead of black?

"Listen to me," she commanded him, eating up the distance between them.

That signature smirk that drove her crazy made an appearance. "Yes, Miss Raven."

"I'm serious. I don't have time to fully explain, but I am telling you that you can only save me with light, not darkness."

All mirth dropped from his face. "I cannot control light like Gedeon."

"The prophecies aren't literal," she said. "Do these marks spread when you're upset?"

"Yes," he replied slowly. "If that's what it takes to get to you, I will welcome the pain with open arms."

"Stop talking like a poet. What if positive emotions had the same effect, but instead of blackening your insides, it brightened them?"

He wasn't the type to roll his eyes, but if he was, she imagined he would do it now.

"My mother said you were the one to save me. She also said only the golden child can save me." She waited for him to agree, but he didn't. "Don't poison your soul, or you'll never escape Vincula. Please, trust me."

His eyes bounced between hers, and the silence was deafening, but he finally blew out a breath and ran a hand through his already tousled hair. "I will try it your way," he conceded. "But if I don't progress, we go back to my way."

She threw her arms around him as relief filled her to the brim. "Thank you." Her lips pressed against his jaw. "I can't lose you."

Running his fingers through her hair, he gripped it tight, pulling her head back to kiss her gently. "I already lost you, and I'll damn myself to hell before I lose you again."

Every muscle in his body ceased movement, and his hand left her hair, trailing across the skin between her neck and shoulder. "You have a bite mark."

She'd forgotten to tell him. "It's from our last soulscape," she said excitedly. "I was going to tell you tonight, but we were sidetracked."

His eyes never left her neck. "It must be because it's how I last saw you."

"I woke up with it this morning," she said, pointing at the bruise. "Did you know that if we are physically altered here, it stays?"

When his eyes met hers, they were filled with a predatory gleam. "I would like to find out. Mark me, Miss Raven." His voice was husky, and it made heat pool between her thighs. "If I wake with it tomorrow, then we'll have a definite answer."

She traced his skin, wondering where she would leave her mark. Wait. "You have immortal healing. It won't work on you."

"I don't have any of my immortal abilities here." He lifted his arms wide. "Mark me."

"Will it not heal when you wake up?" she asked skeptically.

"It depends on what you do to me." He cocked his head to the side. "My body is yours, Miss Raven. Do with it as you please."

She made a show of running her hand up his chest and around his neck as seductively as she could. "Even if I want to carve my name into you?" she asked innocently.

A scoff or a teasing laugh–those were the reactions she expected, not his eyes growing darker. "Do you know what the thought of walking around with your mark carved into my skin does to me?"

Her lips parted at his words. Their stare down lasted less than a minute before he reached his arm out to the side and leaned forward with his lips hovering near her ear. "Make sure you go deep enough to pierce every layer of skin I have."

When he pulled back, he held a huge metal cookie cutter with an odd flat wooden handle that stuck out. The design looked more intricate than normal cutters, and she eyed it warily.

He dabbed his finger against the metal edge, yanked his hand back with a hiss, and stuck his finger in his mouth. "Perfect." The uncertainty must have been written on her face *because he wiggled the object in the air. "You're going to hold this here," he instructed, positioning the cutter over his heart. "Place your palm on the flat part, wrap your fingers under it, and push."*

She recoiled. "I'm not fucking stabbing you!" she yelled. "Are you crazy?"

He looked between her and the cutter in his hand. "Yes."

Gaping at him, she was too stunned to move or speak. He wouldn't dare.

"If you won't, I will," he warned her.

He would.

"Fine," she agreed reluctantly. She killed people as a hobby; stabbing her boyfriend shouldn't be an issue. "What is the picture?"

"You'll see," he replied and positioned the blade over his heart. "Grab the handle," Caius instructed.

With an exaggerated sigh, she stepped forward and grabbed the smooth wood. The organ in her chest was about to give out, and when she realized where she was about to stab him, she dropped the cutter like it was on fire. "You'll die."

*Keeping his eyes locked with hers, he picked up the cutter and placed it against his chest. "Don't!" she screamed, losing her composure. A **Royal** could only be killed one of two ways, and one of those was stabbing them in the heart.*

Caius hissed as he lodged the cutter into his skin, and Rory screamed as she grabbed his arm to yank it back. Blood dripped from the weaponized kitchen utensil, but it was nothing compared to her mate's chest.

"No," she cried as she yanked off her nightshirt to staunch the bleeding.

A warm hand engulfed hers. "I think I'll live."

The amusement in his voice brought her to a halt, and

when she saw him holding back a laugh, she wished she'd been the one to stab him. "It's not funny," she snapped. "What if you'd stabbed too deep?" She motioned wildly to the cutter on the ground. "Do you know how far into the chest a mystic's heart is or did you eyeball that monstrosity and hope for the best?"

"No," he admitted, "But I know ribs exist, and while this cuts like a scalpel," he said, grabbing the cutter to brandish the bloody blade. "It can't cut through bone."

The only thing worse than admitting you were wrong was having to admit you were wrong to your significant other. He afforded her the small mercy of not having to when he grabbed the shirt from her hand and cleaned himself off. "Come have a look."

When she studied his chest, she gasped. Caius looked at her with such tenderness that it was hard to turn away from his gaze.

But when she looked back at the sigil marking him as hers, she couldn't take her eyes off it.

It was cut with surgical precision, but the blood continued to flow, obscuring the design a bit. "I can't believe you did this." He was quiet as she stared, letting her assess his handiwork. It looked like an incomplete circle with a fancy 'A' in the center. "It's a really nice circle," she joked as she straightened.

He pulled his bottom lip between his teeth as he grinned at her. Oh shit, she knew that look. Looking back at the picture, she tried to figure out what the hell it was.

"It's a moon," he murmured, exuding raw sensuality; he always had, but the way he looked at her tonight was entirely different. "Do you remember the first Plenilune we spent together?" She shivered. It was impossible to forget. At her first Plenilune ball, he chased her through the garden.

*His smirk grew into a devious smile as his eyes moved to the bite mark on her neck. "It was the first time I heard you scream my name." He leaned forward and nipped at her skin, and she bit back a moan. "Now that I know what wearing your mark is like, I will never be without it. If it is gone when I wake, I will hire an **Alchemist** to curate a potion to keep it from healing when I do it again."*

No words came to her, only rapid breaths. It was the sexiest, sweetest, and stupidest thing she'd ever heard in her life.

He smoothed the hair back from her face with an affectionate smile. "Do you like it?"

"You're ridiculous," she breathed. **She loved it.**

He grinned and softly pecked her lips as the room shimmered. "Time to wake up."

CHAPTER 37

VINCULA

Caius ran his hand over his chest and felt slightly raised lines marring his skin.

He jumped out of bed and looked down at the scar with a disbelieving laugh. "It worked." *What did this mean?*

Once in the bathroom, he examined the scar, loving the scripted A in the center of the moon. It was true, when he thought of the Plenilune, he pictured Rory writhing on the ground, moaning his name, but it was more than that.

Everything changed that night for him. She might have still been plotting his death, but when Caius stepped into the garden, he knew nothing would be the same.

Last night when she mentioned carving her name into his skin, he could think of nothing better than his ruinous little mate filleting the area over his heart.

The strange object the soulscape provided for him was perfect. He'd been deciding if he'd rather have a moon or stick with something simple like an A, and when he willed a knife into his hand, the pre-designed cutter appeared instead.

A quick scan was all he needed to know how it worked. It was perfect.

The raised scar was white against his tan skin, and he couldn't stop touching it. Rory's neck was proof that what physically happened in the soulscape bled into reality, but he didn't think he'd scar. If anything, he should have woken up with a fresh wound that healed immediately.

Unless...

Old texts only told of the *Aeternum* bond and how it connects two mates, but there was nothing about the actual magic surrounding it. When Caius thought of the design and knife, it was with the hope whatever he did would stay with him forever. What if the blade was infused with something to make it happen?

They needed to test the boundaries of their soulscape to see how powerful the magic was. What if it could transport one of them to the other?

The morning flew by as he went through the movements, lost in thought. An idea bounced around in his head, but he needed more research before testing the theory.

After grabbing lunch, he pushed through the door of Vincula's library and raised a hand in greeting when Kit looked up from a book. "Hello, Your Grace."

"When no one else is around, please, call me Caius."

A mop of curly black hair popped out from behind a bookshelf. "What about me?" Cat asked him. Bellina and Lenora appeared moments later, and Caius forced his laugh down.

"It applies to all of you but no one else." Lenora bustled around Cat and Bellina and hugged him. Guilt made the moisture in his mouth turn to ash. "I'm sorry I wasn't the one to tell you about her memories."

She squeezed him once and released him. It'd been two days since Rory's memories returned, and when he saw Lenora in the kitchens, he was too caught up in his own problems to tell her.

Lauren told her that afternoon, but he felt awful for not telling her immediately. It was unlike him to be selfish in matters such as these.

"You need to worry about yourself and my daughter," Lenora told him, making him feel worse.

Bellina popped a hip and crossed her arms. "You didn't tell us either."

Caius looked to Kit for help, but she went back to reading. He saw her try not to smile. *Traitor.*

"I apologize," he said sincerely.

Bellina opened her mouth to respond, but Kit stopped her. "Leave him alone," she said from her desk without looking up.

The seamstress rolled her eyes and stepped forward. "To what do we owe this pleasure?"

It was good to see a bit of her old self peeking through after the attack. "I'm here to look for a book."

This caught Kit's attention. "You have an entire library of your favorite books."

He followed Lenora, Cat, and Bellina to a table covered with books and notepads.

Cat sat down and pointed at the chair next to her. "You can sit here." She jerked her thumb in Kit's direction. "She has the catalog."

Everyone else sat in their places and went back to reading. They devoted every day to researching ways to help his mate. Cat's furious scribbling caught his attention.

"Did you find something new?" he asked.

While still writing, she tapped the book with her other hand. "It's another story about Aemas and Lora."

Aemas and Lora?

Bellina leaned over the table and flipped the page to a picture of a gargantuan man with black hair, black eyes, and skin the color of snow. Next to him was a beautiful woman with long, light blonde hair, tan skin, and bright blue eyes.

It was the same couple from the other story, but different.

They stood in front of a fairytale castle, high on a hill, overlooking a sprawling city.

The castle looked to be carved out of a light, iridescent gemstone. He squinted his eyes as he leaned closer.

"It looks like opal," Cat said offhandedly. "I don't think that castle ever existed here."

"You don't know that," Kit argued.

Cat shot a miffed look at her friend. "Erdikoa has been charted meticulously. The detail they went through is impressive, even in the outer lands, and there is no record of a gemstone castle."

Kit snorted. "How would you know? The only copies are in The Crown library."

Bellina and Lenora's eyes volleyed between the other two women as they bickered back and forth. The former's lips were shut tight, and her brown skin pinked as she tried to hold in her laughter, causing his own to bubble to the surface.

"I've been there." Cat turned to Caius. "One good thing about coming to the prison realm is I get my memories back from my visits to The Capital. The magic in those walls is a bitch."

Bellina looked starstruck. "You've been to the Lux Palace?"

"No," both Kit and Cat answered before continuing their bickering.

Bellina's confusion was common when it came to the mysteries of The Capital. The Capital walls enclosed not only the Lux Palace but other Crown-sanctioned facilities, like The Crown library.

Caius knocked on the desk to draw their attention. When they both faced him, he pointed at the book again. "We can discuss the logistics of the magic jewelry castle later." Both women shot him a glare. "What is the story about?"

Cat sighed and picked up her notes to point at what Caius assumed were words. "This story is modern compared to the others from the early days. It might not be reliable."

He eyed the book in question. "They use potions to keep the books from deteriorating. Was there a publication date?"

Kit moved to stand next to Bellina and Lenora, who watched the exchange quietly. "Yes, the book is *old*. About four, maybe five-hundred years old, to be exact."

"How flattering," Caius deadpanned.

Bellina and Kit burst out laughing, Lenora tried her best not to, and Cat looked at them like they were crazy. "What?"

"Nothing." Caius pulled her attention back to the book. "You were saying?"

Flipping the page, she pointed to another picture. "The story is modern. Look at the layout of the city."

He pulled the book close and examined the page. She

was right. The biggest tell was the *Munin* compound. It wasn't built until Caius was a teenager.

"Then why take notes?" he asked, eyeing her paper.

The odds were someone who loved the creation story wrote their own using the same characters. As an avid reader since childhood, he'd come across several books like that.

Kit quickly jumped in to defend Cat. "Everything is relevant, especially when Rory's life is on the line."

That reminded Caius why he was here in the first place, but he owed it to the women and their hard work to listen to everything they had to say. "You're right."

Cat pointed at her notepad again. "Aemas and Lora lost their sun."

Leaning forward, he attempted to read what she'd written. It was the worst penmanship he'd ever seen. "May I?" he asked, picking up the notes.

Kit smirked when he tried reading them from different angles. Up close seemed to be the best. He read what he could and dropped the pad on the table. "Aemas and Lora lost their sun to the realms and sent the night to protect it?"

He and Cat stared at each other. She looked serious, and he waited for her to say it was a joke. *What did that even mean?*

"We don't know what it means, either," Lenora told him, seeing the question on his face.

Cat shrugged and grabbed her notes. "The story is long, but that's the gist of it. I don't think it means anything, but I took notes anyway."

"That's a good idea." He turned to Kit and stood. "Can you help me look up a few things?"

Her eyes brightened as she told him about the catalog and how it worked. He already knew, of course, but she was in her element, and the light-hearted rapport of the group raised his spirits if only a fraction.

Rory's pleas to focus on his happier emotions were fresh in his mind, and what better place to start than here?

~

The four women and Caius sat around a table at the bar with their shots held high. It was their second one, and Bellina stood. "To Caius fixing his stupid mistake so we can see our girl again."

"Here! Here!" they all shouted before throwing back the bourbon. It burned on the way down, and Caius licked his lips with a grin.

"For someone who rules an entire realm, I really am a dumbass," he agreed. The group reminded him of Rory, and he tried to envision her laughing with her Erdikoa friends. He discreetly slid his phone from his pocket and pushed the button. Her eyes glared back at him. Turning it off, he put it back in his pocket.

Yes, he saw her in the soulscape, but there was something different about being with her in reality.

Bellina tapped his forehead. "Get out of your head. We're having fun tonight, not sulking."

Lenora gestured to his drink. "She's right, dear. You can worry again tomorrow."

He found nothing at the library, and when his mood soured, the others dragged him here and shoved liquor down his throat. In the over five-hundred years he'd been alive, he hadn't had a group of friends since grade school, and even then, he had to leave them once he graduated.

He visited them periodically until he took the throne

when he was twenty-five, but since then, he'd only ever had acquaintances. Being the king of the prison realm had been a lonely life until the *Angels* arrived. Sam and Lauren appeared out of nowhere, and Caius took to them immediately.

But other than those two, Caius had no friends. He came with the women because they reminded him of his mate, but he stayed because he enjoyed their company. *Did they enjoy him too, or did they pity him?*

"Let's play a drinking game," Kit suggested, and Cat quickly agreed.

"Have you girls ever played crossfire?" Lenora asked.

They glanced at each other, and Caius couldn't stop himself from laughing. "You play drinking games?"

"Do you?" she returned. "You're much older than I am."

The group burst out laughing, Caius included. "I don't, actually. Not since I was in my early twenties."

"I didn't know liquor existed that long ago," Kit joked. At least he *thought* she was joking.

Bellina sipped her beer and asked Lenora, "How do you play?"

Rory's mother stopped a passing server. "Excuse me. Do you have plastic cups behind the bar?"

The waitress shook her head, quickly glancing at Caius. "We don't. I'm sorry."

"Don't apologize, dear," Lenora said with a motherly smile. "Thank you anyway."

"The home goods store is still open," Kit offered. "We can buy some there."

"Let's go," Cat said, jumping up.

"You all go outside, and I'll close out our tab," he told them as he left the table. He didn't have to pay, but he needed to inform the bartender the others' drinks were on him.

Once outside, they ventured to the home goods store and bought a few packages of cups. "We need beer, too," Lenora informed them.

After buying beer, they stood on the sidewalk outside. "Whose apartment are we using?" Bellina asked the group.

Caius didn't intend to join them, but he wanted to pay for their things. It didn't feel right to enjoy time with Rory's friends when she couldn't. "I'm going to turn in for the night. You ladies be careful."

"Where do you think you're going?" Lenora's sharp voice asked, stopping his retreat.

He lifted his mouth in a half-smile. "To bed. I am an old man, after all."

"You don't look tired," Cat accused. "Are we not important enough?"

Caius jerked back. "What? Of course not."

Lenora turned to the girls. "Give us a moment." She led him away until they were out of earshot. "Honey, Rory wouldn't want you punishing yourself every day."

He averted his gaze, unsure how to answer. "It doesn't feel right," he admitted. "I want to experience these things with her."

She rubbed his shirt sleeve and gave it an affectionate pat. "Do you want to be responsible for piling more guilt onto my daughter?"

His eyes snapped to hers. "How does me going home hurt Rory?"

Her brows rose. "If she finds out you intentionally avoided having fun, she'll blame herself."

"She won't find out," he argued.

Her eyes narrowed as she stepped closer. "Want to bet?"

His mouth fell open at her ruthlessness. "You wouldn't do that to her."

She harrumphed. "You don't know me very well, dear. I suggest you follow me back to the girls, or you won't like the outcome."

His lips twitched, and Lenora grinned widely. "Lead the way."

When they reached the others, Caius rubbed his jaw. "I have a room perfect for games," he offered.

"We get to party in the palace? I'm in," Cat announced and marched ahead, making Kit roll her eyes.

Lenora and Bellina linked arms as they followed the other two, with Caius trailing behind.

By the time they arrived at the palace, he was laughing at something Bellina said, and when Lenora looked at him and winked, his chest swelled with gratitude.

He led them into a banquet room undergoing construction. He had secretly started the remodel before Rory left as a surprise for her.

When they walked into the room, Cat spun around in awe. The bar was unfinished, but tables were set up across the wide room.

Kit looked at him quizzically. "You're building a bar in the palace?"

He nodded and removed a cover from one of the tables. "What else do we need?" he asked Lenora.

Scanning the room, her eyes landed on a table meant for larger groups. "A longer table."

From there, they worked to ready the game surface, and as he watched the women chatting and laughing amongst themselves, his heart longed for his mate. She would love this.

This carefree behavior was out of character for him, but he couldn't find it in himself to care. It was fun, and he would return to being the king tomorrow.

CHAPTER 38

ERDIKOA

When Kordie said their group would do fun things every day to enjoy their time together, she wasn't kidding. She forced them to go to an amusement park, and when Rory told Sam, he looked put out at the prospect. She was determined for him to have fun because she didn't think he'd had fun a day in his life.

"What are we doing first?" Kordie asked as she snagged a map from the ticket booth. "The crazy train ride is closest."

Sera looked over Kordie's shoulder to read the map. "I say we start at the train and make our way around like this." She moved her finger along the edge of the paper.

Keith dug around in Kordie's bag and pulled out a bottle of sun guard. "Everyone lotion up."

Dume looked up at the cloudless sky and nodded, reaching for the bottle after Keith finished rubbing Kordie and himself down.

Sera passed the bottle to Sam, who pushed it away. "I do not need any."

She pushed it back. "You think you're tougher than the sun?"

"I do not burn," he replied and passed the bottle back to Kordie.

Sera ignored him and turned to Dume. "You're riding with me. I don't want to be smashed between him and the side of the seat." She motioned to Sam as she spoke.

It didn't escape Rory's attention that Sera could have asked Rory to ride with her since she's smaller than both Sam and Dume. Sam's size had nothing to do with her asking Dume to be her seat buddy.

Sam frowned at Sera. "Dume is large as well."

"And yet you are twice his size," Sera said, looking him up and down.

Covering her mouth, Rory tried not to laugh. "I'll ride with you, Sammy."

He looked at the group and grunted. "You do not have a choice, and do not call me that."

"I would've picked you anyway," she told him, bumping his arm with her shoulder.

"I would like to get this over with and leave," he griped and stalked toward the ride.

Once everyone paired up, Rory made Sam ride on the inside. "I would rather ride on the outside," he said gruffly.

Her hair rustled as she shook her head vigorously. "You'll smash me into a pancake. Wait and see."

They loaded into the seats, and the ride started out slow. Sam side-eyed her. "You consider this fun?"

His thighs were large, and Rory nervously eyed the gap between her lap and the bar. "Yes." The ride picked up speed, slanting the seats, and she shrieked as her body flew into Sam's.

He made no sound, but his knuckles turned white around the bar. The ride spun even faster, and his face remained blank as the others screamed. She clung to his arm to keep from flying out, and looking over at her, he straightened his arm against her stomach to hold her in.

Everyone stumbled a little when they exited the ride, but not the *Angel*. Rory set her jaw. *Challenge accepted.*

Next, they did the gravity spin, a ride where you leaned against mats with no buckles, and the ride spun so fast you were glued to the wall. *Still nothing.*

After that, Rory pulled out her phone and handed it to Sam. "Will you take a picture of us?" She wanted to capture as many memories as she could.

He grabbed the phone, and before everyone smiled, he snapped the picture and held the phone out to her.

"Is he kidding?" Keith muttered.

"Wait until we're in place and smiling, then count to three and take the picture *after* you say three," Kordie instructed.

He sighed and held the camera up, and when the group was ready, he counted to three, snapped the picture, and handed it back.

Kordie shook her head and whispered to Rory, "Do we ask him to take a few more or leave it be?"

Dume snorted. "Leave it be."

Rory took her phone from Sam's outstretched hand. "Thank you." She lifted his arm, ducked under so it was draped across her shoulders, and leaned in while holding out her phone. "Smile!"

He scowled down at her, and she snapped a picture. "Try looking at the camera this time."

His mouth never moved as he glared at the camera. She sighed. "Good enough."

He pulled his phone from his pocket and pulled up the camera app. "One more."

Her heart leaped with affection. *He was having a good time,* she thought and leaned in with a big smile. Once the picture was taken, he hastily stuffed his phone in his pocket.

They rode a few more rides before Rory insisted on riding the biggest and fastest coaster in the park. He would be forced to show a reaction, and she couldn't wait.

When they piled into the seats, Sam pulled the padded safety bar over his shoulders and looked at her. "Is this a joke?"

The bar wouldn't close properly because he was so tall. "It's still holding you down," she said, pointing to his lap. "Plus, there's a seat belt." He grumbled under his breath, fastened the belt across his waist, and placed his hands on his thighs.

Rory screamed her head off during the entire ride as Sam stayed silent. His hair tie came loose, and his blonde hair whipped around his face. To her utter amazement, she saw the tiniest smile on his face when they unloaded from the car.

"How do these rides not affect you?" she asked him with wonder.

Looking down at her, he lifted a brow. "I can fly. These are nothing."

She stared after him as he followed the group, but her agitation melted away.

She couldn't wait to tell Caius she got him to smile at an amusement park. It was a miracle.

They spent the rest of the day playing games and stuffing themselves with fried foods from the vendors, and as Rory listened to her friends joke around, a deep sadness filled her heart.

Impossible decisions were always forced upon her, and just once, she wanted things to work out in her favor.

Rory, Sam, and her father sat at the dining table as the two men ate dinner. Rory's stomach hurt from the park food, and the thought of eating made her want to die.

"Any luck on finding a way back to Vincula?" her father asked between bites.

Sighing, she sipped her water. "I don't think it's possible. Caius has to find his way here." She glanced at Sam. "He thinks he found a way, but I'm worried about him."

The *Angel* said nothing at first. Setting his fork down and placing his napkin on his plate, he turned to her. "You have seen his marks."

"How could I not?" She scoffed. "They cover his entire upper body, and I saw them grow when he was angry."

His nostrils flared slightly. "They cover him?" She nodded, and he cursed under his breath. "He is going to kill himself."

"Turney and my mother both saw this happen," she whispered. "It's fueled by his anger, maybe more, but he won't stop."

"I will speak with him when I return," Sam assured her.

"He won't listen, but I made him promise to try another

way," Rory replied. "I asked him to call on overwhelmingly happy emotions." She grimaced. "I pulled it out of my ass, but I couldn't think of anything else."

"That was surprisingly good advice." Sam stood with his plate, and she glared at him.

Surprisingly? "Thanks for the vote of confidence," she snipped.

"You know nothing of the old magic, but you are correct," he returned. "It is controlled by emotion."

"Why didn't you tell him that?" She moved her chair back and grabbed her father's plate along with hers.

"I did not think he possessed the ability to use that much power," Sam admitted. "It was a fool's dream, yet he has done it."

"There's something I've been wondering." She placed the dishes in the washer. "You know a lot about the magic of the realms, but not all of it. How?"

He smirked. "It does not differ from knowledge of anything else. You know how to make drinks, serve them, where they come from, possibly even the ingredients in the liquor and mixers, but do you know precisely how that liquor is made?"

"Point taken." There was another thing she'd been wondering. "Are you a *Seraph*?"

He stepped into the dining room, and his wings shot out of his back, fluttering as he tucked them tightly against his body. "How many sets of wings do you see?"

She huffed. "You don't have to be a smartass. It was just a question." *Seraphim* had three sets of wings, but if Sam could shift his away, who's to say he wasn't keeping the others hidden? It was a logical question.

Rory's father eyed Sam's wings and shook his head. "I'll

never get used to that." Patrick kissed Rory goodbye and waved to Sam as he left for work.

Once he was gone, Rory and Sam settled in on the couch and watched an arrowball game. He surprised her by yelling at the ES when the red and gold team made an error. The game reminded her of the time she and Caius played, and she wished he were here. Would he and Sam root for the same team, or would they argue the entire time?

Yawning, she stretched and stood. "I'm heading to bed."

"Goodnight," he said distractedly, leaning around her to look at the game.

When she reached her room and started to undress, she felt something warm between her legs and paused before rushing to the bathroom. Much to her dismay, she'd started her period.

Tomorrow she would pick one up, but it wouldn't stop her current bleeding, only prevent it in the future. She searched the cabinets for something to absorb the blood, finding nothing.

"Great." After stuffing toilet paper into her panties, shuffling to her dresser to grab a fresh pair, and going back to switch them out, she begrudgingly went downstairs. "Can you take me to the store?" she asked as she entered the living room.

Sam never took his eyes off the ES. "We will go in the morning."

Moving her body between him and the game, she rested her hands on her hips. "I need period supplies."

She expected him to flinch or grow uncomfortable, but he did neither. Instead, he turned off the ES and rose to his feet. "List what products you need." He went to the door and pulled on his boots. "The brand, type, and size."

"What? I can run in to get them," she insisted.

He walked into the office, returning with a notepad and pen. "You have nothing on now?" he asked.

"I put toilet paper in my underwear to hold me over." She pulled on her shoes as well and waited by the door.

"That cannot be comfortable, nor is it secure," he informed her as though she wasn't the one with a wad of paper smashed in her underwear. "I will grab them while you stay in the vehicle," he continued. "Unless you want me to purchase the entire feminine aisle, I need you to write down your preferences."

Touched, she grabbed the pen and paper from him, writing quickly. "Thank you. I always knew you were a softy."

"Being a decent person does not make me soft," he replied and walked outside.

Sam held Rory's items in his left hand and approached the checkout line. The woman in front of him seemed familiar, and when she turned to the side, his entire body imploded with an unfamiliar emotion.

"Anastasia," he murmured before he could stop himself.

She glanced behind her with no recognition on her face. Something within him plummeted. Unless they were in The Capital, she would have no memory of him.

"Do I know you?" she asked in a polite tone.

He cleared his throat and placed Rory's items on the checkout conveyer belt. "We met once."

Twisting her mouth to the side, she scanned his face. "You would think I would remember someone like you."

Her neck turned red with her admission, and he couldn't help but smile.

"Why is that?" he asked, trying not to stare at the blush creeping into her face.

"Next!" the man behind the counter called out.

Flustered, Anastasia hurried forward without answering his question. She studiously ignored him as she checked out, and he wanted her to look at him. *Turn around, Anastasia.*

Gathering her two bags, she stepped away but stopped and turned back, making his heart thump harder. "I didn't get your name." The nervousness in her voice made it clear she didn't speak to strangers often.

He held out his hand for her to shake. "Sam."

She hesitantly stuck her hand in his, and his skin warmed where it touched hers. "It's nice to meet you."

"We've met," he reminded her, and her blush deepened. *Aether, he loved that.*

"Right. It was good to see you again." She left in a hurry, and he stared after her, wanting to call her back inside.

Glancing through the window, she looked at him, and he winked. Her eyes widened before she walked away, and laughing lightly to himself, he wondered where she was going. Her shift at the palace would have already started by now, and he assumed she was off tonight.

"Sir?" the clerk said loudly, drawing his attention.

Sam paid, grabbed his bag from the man, and left with nothing but Anastasia on his mind.

CHAPTER 39

VINCULA

Looking at his reflection in the mirror, Caius stared at his scar, tracing the raised skin with his finger for the millionth time. He had an idea, but everything had to be perfect.

Climbing into bed, he lay back and waited for sleep to drag him under.

~

The wildflowers were soft beneath Caius' feet, and he frowned at the ostentatious golden hues of the room. Why were they here?

"Did you paint your throne room?" Rory's voice echoed off the high ceilings.

*Twisting around, he drank in the sight of her as she walked toward him. **Fuck, she was gorgeous.***

"I would never," he assured her. "We're in the Lux Palace."

She froze in place. "Why?"

"I don't know," he replied, wanting their time together to be anywhere but here.

Turning in a slow circle, she surveyed the room once more. "It's identical to yours."

He nodded and closed the gap separating them. The wonder in her eyes was intoxicating. "The palaces have identical layouts."

Her eyes sparkled with something. Excitement maybe? "Then I know my way around the Lux Palace," she noted.

Protectiveness surged to the surface, and his voice hardened. "Do not go there."

"I'm not an idiot," she clipped. "It was just an observation."

***If she killed him in the soulscape, would he die in real life?** It was best he didn't find out. "What did you do today?" The need to know everything about her, even her day-to-day, was overwhelming.*

Her face split into the biggest smile he'd ever seen. "My friends and I went to an amusement park."

The happiness radiating from her soaked into him, and he pulled her to the ground to sit. "There's more," he said, noting the mischief in her words. "What did you do, Miss Raven? Terrorize the workers?"

She shot him a tiny glare, and he tried not to smile. "Sam went too," she revealed dramatically.

*Caius chuckled. "Did he hate it?" The **Angel** was allergic to anything fun.*

Her laughter died down, and she lifted a shoulder. "He pretended to, but I saw him smile."

"I never thought I'd see the day when the commander enjoyed anything," he commented.

"What'd you do today?" She lifted a brow. "Brood in your office? Destroy it and make an innocent bystander clean it up?"

"Mmm, I reserve that job for you and only you, Miss Raven."

She leaned over and pushed his shoulder. "Next time, I'll rip the pages out of your precious books."

"As long as you're bending over to do it, I don't care," he crooned, dragging his eyes up and down her body. She squirmed, and the action made him hungry to spread her thighs. He pushed the thought aside. "I went to the bar with your mother and friends."

She sat up and stared at him. "Truly?"

His face split into a wide grin. "Lenora taught us a drinking game." Rory's mouth hung open, making him laugh. "Cat and Bellina were quite the pair. Kit and I didn't stand a chance."

Something between a scoff and a laugh burst from her chest. "You were partners with Kit, and she didn't kill you?" She clapped as she laughed, throwing her head back, and Caius wished he had his phone to record her. "I would have given anything to see that."

His voice grew serious as he sat up and grabbed her chin. Her laughter petered out as he stared at her. "You will. I'll play again, and you'll be there to watch."

"I know," she whispered. "I know you'll find your way to me, and when you do, we'll kill Gedeon and return home."

Home. "We can't attack him without a plan. The most important thing is reuniting so we can marry." He ran his fingers over his scarred chest. "Once you're immortal, we can figure out what to do about him with the help of my sister and the **Angels**."

She nodded. "I'm glad to know your sister isn't on Gedeon's side, but what could she do to help? She has no power, only immortality. Can she at least fight to protect herself?"

Caius chewed on her question, hating that she had a point. "I don't know, but we'll discuss it later." He leaned forward and crawled over her, making her lay back. "For now, I want to make the most of the time we have left tonight."

Her pupils dilated as she bit her lower lip seductively. "And how will we do that, Your Grace?"

Nudging her knees apart with his own, he lowered himself over her, kissing her neck where his bite mark remained. "First, I'm going to fuck you with my fingers so I can suck them clean." He lifted his eyes to hers and licked his lips. "Then I'm going to bury my face in your cunt and fuck you with my tongue."

"That's a good way to start," she breathed, and his cock stiffened at the heady look in her eyes that quickly turned to a frown. Not a look he wanted to see before having sex. "We can't do anything for another few days," she lamented.

He pulled back and sat on his knees to tug down her shorts, needing to check that she was okay. "Why? Are you hurt?"

Slapping his hand away, she sat up. "I'm on my period."

Looking down at her shorts, he smirked. "Did you think your blood would deter me?" he asked her, and when she shrugged, he slipped his fingers under her waistband and tsked. "I have bathed in the blood of your enemies. What makes you think I would not paint myself with yours?"

She gasped and grabbed his wrist. "What makes you think I want you to?"

"Have you never had sex on your period, Miss Raven? I assure you, it's just as fun, if not more." He tugged on her shorts again. "Lift your hips for me, baby."

When he had her shorts off, he ran his thumb over the outside of her panties, but nothing was there. She must be wearing a tampon.

Leaning over her, he propped one arm by her head, and his other hand covered her panties as he stroked slowly, pressing down when he passed over her clit.

Her breathing picked up, and he lowered himself to kiss her, pulling on her bottom lip with his teeth. The panties beneath her fingers grew wet with every stroke, but that didn't make sense if she had a tampon in.

Sitting up, he pulled off her panties and looked at her wet pussy. There was no string nor blood, and he frowned. She leaned up and dove her hand between her legs, probing her own entrance.

His cock hardened more at the sight. "When I realized we couldn't have sex, I wished I wasn't on my period," she said sheepishly. "The soulscape must have taken it away."

*He let his disappointment show but said nothing. "Then our bloodbath will have to wait for another time. For now," he drawled, placing his hand over hers. "I've changed my mind." Her shoulders sagged. "I want to fuck you with **your** fingers."*

The grey in her eyes almost disappeared, and he groaned as she plunged her fingers deeper inside herself. The sight was magnificent, and he had to be inside her in some way.

As she fucked herself, he slid a finger in below hers and met her rhythm. She threw her head back when he used his other hand to work her clit, and he'd never been so turned on in his life as they both moved in and out, her arousal coating them both.

His palm faced the back of her hand, and he added another finger, making her moan. "I never thought I'd enjoy watching someone other than me fuck you, but I've changed my mind."

The feel of her walls dragging against the back of his fingers along with hers on the other side was euphoric, and his eyes were glued to the sight. He slowed their pace, and she moved her hips, riding them both.

He guided her fingers to rotate slowly as they moved in and out of her dripping cunt, and her moans grew louder while her hips jerked, needing more. Eventually, he gave her what she wanted and moved their hands faster, making her cry out.

Her breathing picked up as small sounds filled the air, and when he felt her muscles throb around them, he curled his fingers, pushing hers up to rub against the sweet spot inside her.

One of her legs jerked, and her back arched as she moaned. Their pace grew frantic, and when she released, he felt her cum coat their fingers. Their movements slowed, and when he extracted both their hands, he brought them to his mouth and licked them clean.

"Aether," she rasped, watching him. "You need to fuck me right now. If we run out of time and your cock hasn't been inside me, I'll buy one tomorrow and use it instead."

A deep sound rumbled in his chest as he covered her body with his. "Make sure you video it."

Her breath caught, and he slid his pants down, not bothering to take them off. Without warning, he slammed into her, and she yelled so loud that he dropped his head. "Do that again," he ordered as he thrust into her again.

He didn't move fast, but he drove hard and deep. "Squeeze your pussy around me." With his next stroke, she did, and he choked out a strangled sound. "**Seraphim**."

*Grabbing his neck, she yanked him down, bringing their lips close. "No **Seraphim** here. Just me."*

He lost control and fucked her harder than ever with her legs clamped around his waist. His dick throbbed, and he cursed, refusing to spill until she did.

Reaching between them, he pushed on her lower stomach, forcing her inner spot to rub against him as he moved in and out of her.

"Caius," she chanted like a prayer, and her muscles quivered around him.

"Come for me, baby. Let me hear you." He moved faster as he pulsed his hand over her lower abdomen, and when she released with a scream, he detonated.

Their breaths were loud as he slowed, but he didn't remove himself from her. He wanted to feel her warmth until he faded away. He kissed her, deep and slow. "I love you, Rory, and I can't wait to make you my wife."

He left a trail of kisses down her jaw until his mouth hovered above the fading bite mark. "You're mine."

Sinking his teeth into her neck, he bit her harder than last time, breaking the skin. She shrieked, and her arms wrapped around his back like a vise. Lifting his head, he licked the blood from his teeth.

The room shimmered, and he berated himself silently, having forgotten to ask her to do something for him, and his words came out in a rush. "Find information on the soulscape magic."

~

Caius jolted upright, breathing hard. "Fuck."

After dragging himself out of bed, he examined his

upper body in his bathroom mirror, twisting around to see his back. The black veins had receded. He noticed a small retreat when he woke up with his new scar, but this morning, they were gone from his chest completely and only covered his arms.

The only difference between now and two days ago was the overwhelming happiness he felt after waking from their soulscape, giving Rory's theory about positive emotions more weight. Today he would try it, and if it worked the same, he would focus on that instead of fueling the pit of anger inside him.

He had a new sense of hope with the discovery surrounding the soulscape. If his theory was correct, it would change everything, but first, he needed to see if Rory looked for the information he asked her to.

He dressed and slipped through the passage toward the pond, remembering every moment from last night. Reaching for every good memory he had with Rory, he stepped into the open area around the pond and closed his eyes to channel it.

The happiness and relief he would feel once he found a way to her was overwhelming, and when he opened his eyes, the shadows were already moving with impressive speed.

He imagined the way she would look at him when he found her in Erdikoa and how he would feel when she was in his arms. Shoving the swelling emotions outward, he watched an enormous boulder fall toward the water and quickly called on the other shadows to slow its descent.

The rock hovered, cradled by shadows, and his hands tingled with excitement. The object was larger than his throne, and he walked around the pond's edge for a better look. *Rory was right.*

His clever little mate.

Directing the shadows to carry the boulder to the far bank, he continued around the outside trail, and when he stood next to it, he placed his hand against the rough stone.

It was hot, and he yanked his hand back. When he examined his palm for burns, he couldn't believe his eyes. The veins were gone.

It wasn't just the veins disappearing. He felt different, too. Instead of the cool burn of the dark marks, his body tingled with warmth.

"I'll be damned." Still examining his arms, he backed away from the boulder and focused on what he wanted to do next.

He mastered creating an object, and now he needed to mold it into what he needed.

Using the same tactic as earlier, he watched in utter amazement and satisfaction as the rock carved itself into a replica of Rory. She looked seductive and wore nothing but a sheet surrounding her body like a dress.

She'd kill him when she saw this, but he didn't care. It was proof of his strength.

Now all he had to do was figure out how to translate his new skill into breaking through the barrier. When Sam returned, he'd ask his advice because how could the *Angel* refuse when his only reason for not helping Caius before was the darkness poisoning him?

CHAPTER 40

ERDIKOA

Rory's neck burned as she stepped out of the shower, and she promised Caius a slow death again for biting her like a rabid dog. Sure, the sentiment turned her on, but it hurt like a bitch.

She had an inkling he'd do it again once it healed, but she had an idea to put an end to it. The last thing he said before the soulscape ended plagued her. *"Find information on the soulscape magic."*

He looked desperate when he said it, so it must be important. She'd already asked her father to search for books about *Aeternums*, and if there was information on soulscape magic, it would have been there. She needed to think of something other than combing through books at the library.

Lost in thought, she floated down the stairs and into the kitchen for a cup of coffee, only to find Sam holding out a steaming cup.

"Thank you." She sighed and took a drink, hissing when

it singed her tongue. "How'd you know when to make this for me?"

He picked up a glass of raw eggs, and Rory had to look away. It was too early to throw up already. "You are loud when you move around."

She blew on her coffee and threw daggers with her eyes. "I am not. Do you have supermystic hearing?"

He ignored her and gulped down his *breakfast*. "Supermystics are not real."

She snorted, unable to help herself, and hoped he never changed. "Who was the woman you spoke to in the store last night?"

Sam had parked directly in front of the convenience store, and the front of the establishment was all windows. She watched him at the checkout, speaking to a woman who looked to be in her thirties, smiling at her like a love-struck teenager.

He ignored the question and left the kitchen, but she hurried after him, trying not to spill her coffee. "Who was she?"

"She was no one," he said dismissively.

"I don't need your powers to know you're lying." She planted herself in one of the oversized chairs across from him because he took up half the couch.

"I met her at the Lux Palace," he answered reluctantly. "She is a maid and agreed to report anything of value."

Rory watched his face for any clue about what he felt for the woman. The way his face looked when he spoke to her suggested she was more than an informant. "She's cute." His throat bobbed as he swallowed, but his face remained impassive.

The odds of him telling her were slim to none, so she

changed the subject. "You'll never believe what Caius told me last night."

This caught his attention. "He went out drinking with my mom, Kit, and..." Her voice trailed off as something occurred to her. *Why didn't she think of it before?* "Kit." She set her coffee down and jumped up. "Kit!"

Sam looked alarmed. "Did she die? Why is that a good thing?"

"No, she's not dead. What is wrong with you?" She ran into the office, looking for a computer. "Why is there an office but no computer?"

"Why are you yelling Kit's name?" he questioned as he watched her run around.

"Her parents are the best historians in the realm," she said, grabbing her phone to search their names on the essenet. "Do you know her parents' names?"

Sam tucked a piece of hair behind his ear. He usually had it pulled back halfway or in a low bun, but not today. *Maybe he hoped to run into that woman again.*

"Why do you need a historian?" he asked, clearly annoyed.

"The last thing Caius said last night was to find information on the soulscape magic," she explained as she searched for historians on her phone. *Did historians have netsites or did they work for companies?*

Sam stayed quiet as Rory typed away. "Dammit," she hissed. "I don't even know her last name."

He sat back down on the couch and said, "Her parents' names are Meena and Kellin Cooper."

She glowered at him. "Why didn't you tell me when I asked?"

"I am telling you," he deadpanned, and she wanted to ask to see his wings so she could pluck them bare.

Typing their names into her phone, she asked, "How do you know that?"

"She, your other friends, and your mother are researching ways to break the magic barrier." He dug a hair tie out of his pocket and pulled back the top half of his hair. "When Caius asked for her help, she told us to ask her parents, and I looked at her file for their names."

Rory's face was blank to hide her thirst for murder. "Why didn't you look them up?" she asked through clenched teeth.

"I had more pressing matters, and breaking the magic barrier is impossible," he replied. "It is a fool's errand."

A netsite popped up with their names, and she almost jumped up and down. It was an article about their contributions to one of the largest museums in the city where they worked. Rushing into the office, she jotted down the museum name and address and stuffed it in her sweatshirt pocket.

"The museum opens soon." She hopped on one foot as she struggled to put on her sneakers.

Sam sighed and grabbed his boots, tugging them on. "Any other pointless errands to run while we are out?"

She ignored his sour tone. "Yes. We'll go after talking to the Coopers."

~

Rory pulled her hat low before she and Sam walked through the revolving door of the museum and made a beeline to the information desk.

She couldn't enjoy the splendor of the place, but she made a note to come back later for a tour.

The young man at the desk looked up with an easy smile. "How can I help you today?"

"We need to speak with Meena and Kellin Cooper," Rory said, foregoing pleasantries.

The man typed something into his computer and clicked around before twisting back to them. "Did you have an appointment?"

"We do not," Sam said, his booming voice echoing around the large room, making the man behind the counter flinch.

"They don't see anyone without an appointment," he informed them, avoiding Sam's menacing glare.

"We are friends of their daughter, Kit, and it is important that we speak with them immediately," Rory insisted. She wasn't above tying this guy up if she had to.

He nodded meekly and picked up the desk phone, dialing quickly. "Hello, Mrs. Cooper. There are two people here to see you and Mr. Cooper." He paused, listening to the other person. "No, they do not have an appointment, but they said they are friends of Kit's, and it's important." Another pause. "I will bring them right away."

He stood and walked through the desk like air. An *Eidolon*. "Right this way."

Rory tried not to react to the absolute cluttered chaos when they entered the Cooper's massive office. Books littered the shelves, some thrown haphazardly on top of stacks of other books turned every which way.

Pillars of books, folders, and papers were on the floor, as well as a few tables. The only things clear were two desks on the back wall and a lighted glass case filled with relics and paintings.

"Please, come in," a woman said as she wove around stacks and tables. She was older and taller, like Kit.

A man pulled two empty chairs from a back room and set them in front of the desks before sticking his hand out when Sam and Rory approached. He was impossibly tall and a spitting image of his daughter. If Rory didn't know who she was meeting, she would still know this was Kit's father.

"Kellin Cooper," he said, shaking their hands. "This is my wife, Meena."

He was kind and soft, whereas she was suspicious and curt, just like Kit. Rory pressed her lips together when they tried to curl into a smile. "We appreciate you agreeing to see us. I'm Rory, and this is Sam."

"I understand you know our daughter," Meena said, getting to the point. "When did you meet? We know all of Kit's friends, and you are not one of them."

Rory looked at Sam, who nodded his head. At this point, she would either be killed by Gedeon or saved by Caius, and the only way to make the latter happen was with their help. Telling two more people her true identity wouldn't matter at this point.

She removed her hat and looked up, watching their faces pale. Meena stood firm, but Kellin stepped back. "Aurora Raven."

Nodding, she began talking, telling them her story. How she knew Kit, what Caius was to her, how she was back in Erdikoa, the threat Gedeon posed to not only her and Caius but the realms, and what Caius told her to find. When she was done, she held her breath.

The two wore matching blank expressions before Meena

burst out laughing. "You expect us to believe that?" She looked at her husband, who had shifted his gaze to Sam. Rory could practically see the wheels turning in his head, but he stayed silent. Meena, still laughing, turned back to the duo. "I admit, you look like The Butcher, and that was a convincing tale, but nothing you said is possible." Her laughter died down, and her face hardened. "And I do not appreciate you using my daughter's name for attention."

Sam stood and looked around before silently picking up entire stacks of books and moving them to clear a space.

"Don't touch our things," Meena admonished.

Kellin clasped her arm. "Meena," he cautioned. "Just wait."

Before she could reply, Sam turned to her, and his wings shot out. They were the widest Rory had ever seen them, and if she didn't know Sam, she would have pissed herself.

Kit's parents made sounds of surprise. Or fear. Rory wasn't sure.

Kellin stepped around the desk in a daze. "Samyaza."

"What?" Meena squawked. Her head snapped to Rory. "You're telling the truth."

She nodded. "We wouldn't be here if it wasn't important. When I was still in Vincula, Kit told me about you, and Sam said she's helping Caius research."

"Your daughter asked me to find you," Sam told them. "She thought you could help."

Meena smoothed her shirt down and pulled her shoulders back. "You cannot blame us for questioning the validity of your story. We are experts in our field, and according to the texts, what you've told us should be impossible."

"I understand," Rory rushed, not wanting Sam to piss them off. "But it's life or death, and if you could help us, we would be forever indebted to you." Getting an idea, she snapped and pointed at them. "I'll fund your research. Thanks to Caius, I have more money than I could use in multiple lifetimes."

"That won't be necessary," Kellin replied. "If what you say is true, and I believe it is, helping you will also help the realms."

"Thank you," Rory said, silently vowing to still fund their research.

"I would like one question answered," Meena added.

Rory and Sam exchanged a look. "What is it?"

She scurried around the stacks, stopped at one not far away, walked her fingers down the books and files, and yanked on a book. The stack wobbled, and she balanced it with her hand without looking.

The pages of the book flipped quickly as she picked through them. "Ah-ha!" She stood next to Sam and pointed to something on the page. "This is about you, isn't it?"

His eyes scanned the pages, and he scoffed. "I am not Aemas, nor am I Lora."

"Who are Aemas and Lota?" Rory asked, getting up to stand on Meena's other side to read the page over her shoulder.

"We know that," Kellin interjected. "But we have a theory." Sam shifted uncomfortably, and Rory knew whatever this man had to say was spot on. "The story tells of the two creators losing their sun to the realms and sending their night after it."

Rory's nose scrunched as she read the line herself. "What does that have to do with Sam?"

"It's no coincidence this was written not long after Samyaza arrived in the realms," Meena responded, turning the page. "We think the author of this story tried to mimic the old prose of earlier stories, using cryptic metaphors."

Rory tried to keep her voice polite. "That still doesn't answer my question."

Kellin moved to a blackboard behind his desk, picked up a piece of chalk, and wrote one sentence. *"Aemas and Lora lost their SON to the realms and sent their KNIGHT to protect it."*

Rory read the sentence multiple times. "You think Sam is a knight sent to watch over the creators' son?"

Sam had taken to not moving, maybe not even breathing. She resisted shaking him.

Kellin set the chalk down and dusted off his hands. "We think *he* is the son, and Jophiel is the knight."

Rory felt stupid in a room with the Coopers. "Who is Jophiel?" Glancing at Sam, she added, "That can't be true. I've never met a Jophiel, only Lauren, and she said they're the only two *Angels* in the realms."

Meena closed the book and set it on a random stack as she walked to another, counting the books before pulling one out. Picking through the pages, she muttered to herself before smiling. "Does she look anything like this?" she asked, holding out the book.

Rory scanned the page. "Holy aether." There was a picture of a large man with white wings, long blonde hair, and armor labeled *"Samyaza."* The face looked nothing like Sam's, but what almost made her faint was the woman next to him. Her likeness to Lauren was unmistakable. It was titled, *"Jophiel."*

"How many names does she have?" Rory demanded, turning to Sam. "Is this true? If you're their son, then you're a *Seraph*."

By some miracle, Sam finally addressed her. "We have been over this."

Rory blew a piece of rogue hair out of her face. "Yeah, I remember. You supposedly only have one set of wings, and they have three. That doesn't mean you can't shift them away."

Kit's parents exchanged a loaded look, and Kellin gave Sam the slightest nod. "Our mistake. You two have a seat, and let's discuss what you need from us."

They're dropping it just like that? "Is Lauren's name really Jophiel?" Rory asked Sam.

"Yes," he replied as he sat down, and she followed in a trance. Her friend was hiding something, but she knew when to push, and this was not it.

"You said the Umbra King needs information on your soulscape magic. Do you know why?" Kellin asked, all business.

Rory hadn't given that part much thought, but she had an inkling. "We recently discovered if something physically changes on our bodies in the soulscape, it happens in real life."

The fact was reinforced that morning, not only by her bite mark but also by the almost non-existent blood on the tampon she still wore. The soulscape didn't stop her period completely because she started to bleed again when she woke up, but for the night, her period was gone.

She guessed the tampon was still inside her because it wasn't part of her body, therefore, it didn't permanently change in the soulscape. *Why did her body change but nothing else?* Maybe the bond connecting them physically is what held the magic, not the actual soulscape itself.

"Changes how?" Meena asked, already moving around the room again. Did she ever sit down?

Rory had to show them the bite, and there was only one reason Caius would bite her. This wasn't something she wanted to discuss with her friend's parents, but she didn't have a choice.

Tugging her collar aside, she showed them the scabbed-over bite. It was deep and might leave a scar. She was going to kill him.

Kellin leaned forward. "Is that a bite mark?"

Sam coughed, and Rory glared at him. "Yes. He bit me in the soulscape, but that's not all. We tested it on him, too. The same thing happened. His cut was scarred the next morning. Healed, unlike mine, but the scar was there."

"Incredible," Kellin murmured and grabbed a pen to write something down.

Meena hummed as she meandered through the stacks back to her desk. "The funny thing about the realms," she said in a sing-song voice. "Is that there were no history books in the early days. Everything was told through tall tales, written in storybooks, or passed down by mouth.

"It's believed that Lora created the *Aeternum* bond," Meena went on. "She was obsessed with the idea of an undying love that tied souls together and thought everyone deserved loyal devotion, but Aemas wouldn't let her create fated mates for everyone. Their compromise was *Aeternums*."

"Why couldn't everyone have a mate?" Rory mused. "Why was he against it?"

Meena shook her head. "It doesn't say, but Aemas is told to be irrevocably in love with his wife. There must have been a good reason for him to deny her."

Leaning forward, Rory tried to get a glimpse of the page. "Then Lora is responsible for the soulscape magic?"

"If the story is true, then yes," Kellin confirmed. "While she is not as powerful as Aemas, she is a *Seraph* with the ability to *create*. If physical alterations transfer from the soulscape to reality, she made it that way intentionally."

Rory leaned on the arm of her chair, absorbing the information. "You're saying anything we physically change in the soulscape will change in real life, no matter what?"

"Theoretically, yes," Meena replied, closing the book. "I'm not sure if this information will be helpful to the king, but it is all we know about it."

"Thank you," Sam said, standing. "You have been accommodating."

He signaled for Rory to stand, and she could tell he was ready to leave. "We really appreciate it," she told Kit's parents as they crossed the room to leave.

"If there is anything you ever need, please ask," Kellin said, walking them to the door.

"Wait," Meena called after them. The woman looked nervous. "If you make it back to Vincula, will you tell our daughter we love her and miss her?"

Rory smiled empathetically at the historians. "Yes. She is proud of you two and the work you do."

The woman's eyes watered. "We're proud of her, too. Thank you. You two take care."

Sam didn't say a word, and as much as Rory wanted to ask him if he was okay, she didn't.

"I need to make one more stop before we head home," she told him as they exited the museum.

He nodded and waited as she searched for a shop on her

phone, plugged the address into her navigation app, and led them downtown.

That night, Rory, her friends, and Sam sat in a local pizza place, talking about nothing of importance. Mainly how their days went, what they were doing for the upcoming weekend, and whatever else they could think of.

Sam hadn't said much since leaving the museum, and it worried her, but she didn't press him. Unless he was like this tomorrow, then she'd bother him until he talked.

"Have you made any headway on finding a way back to Vincula?" Sera asked out of the blue.

Rory finished chewing her pizza and wiped her mouth with a napkin. "No. Sam and Lauren met—" Sam grabbed Rory's leg under the table and squeezed. She understood his message loud and clear. *Don't talk about their meeting with Adila.* She coughed to cover up her pause and took a drink of water. "With me, and we've decided I'll wait here."

She was suddenly nervous to mention Caius after Sam's behavior. *What was going on?* "Let's not talk about it," she added. "It's depressing."

The conversation carried on, but Rory felt apprehensive the rest of the night, even when she and Sam loaded into the SUV.

As soon as they pulled onto the road, she couldn't hold back any longer. "What was that about?"

Sam's jaw tensed as he stared straight ahead. "I am not sure, but Sera lied about her day."

Rory scoffed. "You acted like she killed a kitten. All she

said was work was boring. Maybe she had a terrible day and didn't want to bring the group down."

"Something is not right," Sam insisted. "I am not sure what, but there was something off about the little one tonight."

Rory sighed and leaned her head back. "Are you always in commander mode?"

He looked incredulous. "Are you always in danger?"

"Touché," she muttered and looked out the window, watching the city blocks turn into rural roads as they traveled toward their house.

"Are you okay?" She didn't expect him to answer, and he exceeded her expectations. Not only did they ride in an uncomfortable silence, but when Sam put the car in park, he jumped out and stalked inside before Rory even shut her door. Her stomach dropped. Today rattled her friend, and she didn't enjoy seeing him like this. She'd ask Caius about it tonight.

Something sounded behind her, and she whipped around, staring at the gravel road that doubled as their driveway. There were no headlights or other sounds, but she stayed still, listening.

She didn't know how long she stood there, but the door opened, making her scream. "Come inside," Sam said from the porch. "And stop screaming."

"You scared me," she griped, brushing past him with one last glimpse over her shoulder.

CHAPTER 41

Rory grinned at the wildflowers spread across the massive museum floor.

"Hello, Miss Raven," Caius' seductive voice said, and she turned to find him standing bare-chested in a pair of grey, low-slung sweatpants. He was different, and she hurried toward him when she realized what it was. "The veins are gone."

She examined his chest and arms, running her hand over the smooth skin. His chuckle drew her attention upward, and his smile made her panties melt. He was truly happy, and it was the best thing she'd seen since leaving Vincula.

"I took your advice." His biceps flexed when he ran his hand through his hair, and she tried not to drool. "Instead of focusing on my anger," he said in a husky voice as he closed the distance. "I thought about the way you came on my fingers."

Her nipples hardened, and she clutched the bottom of her nightie. "Lust? I told you to think happy thoughts, and you went with lust?"

He laughed, and she noticed the slightest indent on his chin. How had she never noticed that before?

"I thought of you laughing with your friends and glowering at me in the deli when I said you'd be my wife; the way you took my breath away when I saw your short, brown hair because just when I thought you couldn't get more stunning, you did." He trailed his hand down her arm, and a ball of emotion gathered in her chest. "I thought of every part of you because everything you do, everything you are, makes me happy. The strength to break free was never in me. It was always you."

She fought not to cry as she sniffled. "Are you trying to get laid?"

His chest vibrated against hers with his deep laugh, and his hand moved down to the bite mark on her neck.

"Don't even think about biting me again." She withdrew from his arms. "It hurt, and have you ever tried to explain why someone bit you without saying you fucked? I have, and it's not fun."

His smugness only agitated her more. "It's not funny."

"You're right," he said, and she braced for the catch to his compliance. "It's satisfying."

Moving the front of her nightie down to expose the area over her heart, she gave him a smug look of her own. "You don't have to mark me anymore. I took care of it."

Earlier that day, she and Sam stopped by a tattoo parlor where she drew the exact mark Caius had but with a C in place of an A.

He reached out to touch it, but she swatted his hand away. "It's still healing."

"I think I'd like to take you now," he said roughly.

"We have other things to discuss first," she informed him. "Then I'll ride you like a bicycle."

His hand slid to his sweats, where he cupped the obvious outline of his dick. "Talk fast."

Ignoring her growing need, she beckoned him toward the Coopers' office. As if he'd only now realized they weren't in a familiar place, he asked, "Where are we?"

"A museum in Erdikoa," she told him. "Sam and I came to see Kit's parents today."

When they stepped into the office, Caius skidded to a halt with a look of horror. "Did someone ransack this place?"

She waved a hand around and crossed the room. "No, but somehow Meena knew exactly where everything was amongst the chaos. It was impressive, really."

Hopefully, the last book Kit's mother grabbed was still on her desk, the one about Lora's power.

When they approached the two desks, Rory breathed a sigh of relief. The book was still open to the same story.

She and Caius leaned over the book, and he touched the page lightly. "Another story of Aemas and Lora?"

Rory glanced at him sideways. "Another?"

"Cat found a story about the two. Something about losing their sun," he said mindlessly as he flipped the page.

Rory stared at him in shock. "Meena and Kellin told us the same story."

He glimpsed at her before turning back to the book. "What are the odds?" he murmured.

"They think it's about Sam and Lauren," she said, feeling like she was telling him private information about their friends, and a bit of guilt trickled in.

"They think Sam and Lauren are Aemas and Lora?" His face said he thought they were crazy.

"No." *Remembering the blackboard, she pointed to the sentence still written there.* "They think it's a metaphor for that, and they think Sam is the son and Lauren is the knight. They also said her real name is Jophiel, and if that's true, I don't blame her for changing it."

With how hard he was staring, Caius could have burned a hole through the blackboard. "What did Sam say?"

Rory ran a hand through her short hair and sighed. "He denied it, but it changed something in him. He barely spoke all day, and when I tried to ask him about it, he ignored me."

"Good to know," *Caius noted and turned back to the book.* "What did they say about this story?"

Rory's excitement was palpable. "They said Lora created the **Aeternum** bonds and that she's a **Seraph** and really powerful."

Caius nodded along as she spoke. "What does that mean for the soulscape magic?"

"They said if the soulscape changes us physically in reality that she designed it that way on purpose. It's powerful magic."

The biggest smile spread across her mate's face, and she wanted to know his thoughts. Reaching for her hand, he led her back into the museum's main corridor, but before they made it, he stopped and backed her against the wall.

His hands were braced on either side of her head, and his eyes blazed a bright gold. "What are you doing?" *she asked, breathless.*

"What I should have done last night." *He moved his gaze down the length of her.* "And how lucky for me you dressed for the occasion."

Please let my period disappear tonight, *she thought as hard as she could. He dropped down quickly and ripped her underwear off, gazing up at her.* "Tell me. If I fuck you hard *enough to split you open, would you be able to walk tomorrow?"*

Aether, she hoped not. *"Why don't you try, and we'll find out."*

His smile turned feral as he grabbed both of her legs, slung them over his shoulders, and pushed her against the wall, standing slowly. The wall behind her was smooth and bare, and she slid easily as he stood.

Tilting his head back, he licked his lips. "You know I like sweets at night. Lift the hem."

She grabbed the bottom of her nightie and lifted it, exposing herself to him. He hummed, bending his head forward, and she gasped when his tongue licked the length of her core.

*"Fuck, I've missed doing this whenever I want," he said against her with another long lick. "And whenever **you** want."*

She gripped his hair as his head moved. He wasn't just licking; he was pressed into her hard enough for her to feel every bit of his face as he lapped up her arousal like a dog.

*The warmth of his tongue across her sensitive skin was heaven, and it glided smoothly through her pussy like it was made to be there. **Seraphim**, she wanted it to stay there.*

He sucked on the upstroke, teasing her clit just enough to leave her wanting more.

"Fuck," he groaned against her heat. "You smell so fucking good. I could stay buried down here forever."

"Shut up and eat."

Grinning against her, he continued with the sweetest torture. Not once did he flick his tongue fast like some men. No, he licked long and hard, and it drove her crazy. His hot tongue flattened against her as it drifted across her skin, and she begged him to go faster.

When her thighs clenched around his head, and she tried to move her hips, he pushed his tongue into her entrance. She made sounds only he would ever hear.

He moved to her clit and sucked so hard and fast that her stomach clenched as tingles spread out across her body. And when she orgasmed faster than should have been possible, white dots danced in her vision.

He slowed his strokes as she came down but still ate everything she gave him.

Kissing the inside of her thigh, he leaned his head back and smirked up at her, licking the shine from his lips as he lifted her off his shoulders.

She wrapped her arms around his neck on the way down, and he let her go, making her yelp. Before she hit the ground, he caught her with a devious smile.

"You could have warned me," she muttered.

"Then I wouldn't have gotten to hear you make that cute little noise," he said, slapping her ass.

After lowering her to the ground, he pulled her along, looking around the room until he led them to a giant marble replica of the Umbra throne, sitting next to a replica of the Lux throne.

In one swift movement, he slipped her nightie over her head, and the silk rubbing against her sensitive nipples made her shiver with need.

Her small, erect breasts begged to be licked, and he groaned, picking her up again to take one into his mouth. She whispered his name and rocked against him, needing the friction as he switched to the other side.

"I'll never get enough of you," he murmured against her. "Never."

Setting her on the cold, black throne, he stepped back to

stare at her with a wicked grin. "Turn around and raise to your knees."

Scrambling to turn around on the large seat, she faced the back of the throne on her hands and knees, dropping her head to see him under her arm. The throne's cushions were also made of marble, and it was freezing against her skin.

He grabbed her hair and pulled her straight. "I didn't say on all fours. I said on your knees."

Needing to be touched, she ran her hands over her breasts. "You always said you liked me on my knees."

"Don't touch what is mine," he ordered and grabbed her wrists. Pulling them gently behind her back, he secured them with one of his large hands. "Do you remember your safe word?"

She looked over her shoulder with a sly smile. "Yes, my **king**."

"Good girl," he praised in his deep voice that went straight to her core. Bending her forward slightly, he slid two fingers into her from behind and groaned. "Your cunt is always ready for me, isn't it?"

She pushed her hips back, but he removed his fingers and grabbed one of her hips with his free hand. "So eager," he teased and aligned his hips with hers. "The acoustics are nice in here. Use them well."

She expected a hard thrust, but he pushed into her slowly, and somehow it was pure torture. His hand on her hip kept her from moving, and the slow and steady pace he set was killing her. The slight ache as his cock slid in and out, paired with his heavy balls grazing her clit, was all she could concentrate on.

She was used to his hands all over her body, and when his strokes came faster, making their skin slap together, she needed him all over her.

Her attempts to free her wrists were futile, and she wanted to cry. "I need my hands," she begged, not caring if she sounded desperate. She was.

"Do you want to be touched, baby?" he breathed against her ear.

"Yes, please," she begged again.

He pulled out and released her hands. "Crawl forward and press yourself against the back of the throne."

What? She turned around to object, but he slapped her ass hard enough to leave a mark. "Do as I say, little mate."

He licked her from behind when she crawled forward, causing her to jerk. The throne was giant, and when she straightened against the back, Caius climbed in behind her.

His breath fanned against her cheek when his lips pressed to her ear. "Bend forward and press your chest against the marble, baby."

The cold against her skin made her breath hitch as she leaned forward, and he chuckled darkly. Her cheek and chest were secured against the stone, but her hips bent slightly. He grabbed her wrists again, holding them behind her, and his other hand moved around the front to cover her clit.

His fingers moved in a slow circle, and she hissed. "I want to hear you," he said before slamming into her, making her cry out.

With her body pressed against the stone and her hands behind her, she was completely at his mercy. His grunts and pants of pleasure made her feel like she was doing more than taking his cock. She felt powerful and helpless at the same time.

The slight burning as she stretched around him made her think he might actually split her open. Wanting to contribute more, she did the only thing she could think of and squeezed her pussy.

"**Fuck**," he yelled and thrust harder, moving his fingers faster.

The heat started in her stomach and moved to her arms, and the muscles in her legs tried to draw up right before she screamed his name as she pulsed around him. She drenched his cock with her cum.

"Beautiful," he said roughly as he continued to pound into her from behind.

His fingers and pace never slowed, and her sensitive skin lit up again. "Caius," she sobbed. "I can't."

He leaned against her, and she felt his smile. "You will." Releasing her arms, he moved off the throne and tugged her backward, flipping her around to lay her on her back. He entered her again, and within a few strokes, she felt him grow within her.

"Come for me," he commanded, but she was spent.

"I can't," she insisted weakly.

When he pulled out, her body sagged with relief, but it was short-lived when he leaned forward and took one of her breasts into his mouth as he pushed back into her. Making his way up her neck to her mouth, he kissed her deeply as his hips continued to move.

Withdrawing his lips from hers, he grabbed both of her thighs, pulled his dick out until only the tip remained inside, and yanked her hips toward him, impaling her. Her gasp bounced off the walls as she braced her arms on the stone seat.

His thumb returned to her swollen clit, making her legs draw up, and when he pushed on her lower stomach, she clawed at his arms as she came. Her entire body convulsed, and she no longer had control of her muscles.

He came seconds later with a long moan. They were panting, and her inner muscles were still twitching. Lifting his hand,

he stroked her hair, and it wasn't lust in his eyes. It was love.
"You did good, baby." He kissed her, and the room shimmered.

"Buy a new dress for tomorrow night," he whispered into
her ear as the soulscape faded away.

Rory stretched and yanked her arms down with a hiss,
rotating her shoulders. *Soreness does carry over,* she thought,
annoyed.

Jumping out of bed, she peeked through the window to
see the sun shining. She slept longer than usual this morning. At least she wouldn't have to wait long to go shopping.

Reaching for her phone on the nightstand, she walked to
the bathroom and texted Kordie and Sera to ask if they
wanted to join.

After showering, cleaning her new tattoo, and throwing
on a sundress that would be easy to take off for trying on
clothes, she meandered downstairs and kissed her dad on the
cheek.

"Good morning." She beamed at him and addressed
Sam. "I need to go shopping for a new dress today."

He set his fork down and leaned his arms on the table.
"Again? You bought a new dress recently."

"We're going," she replied with a saccharine smile. He
grumbled as he stood and took his dishes to the kitchen, and
Rory sat next to her father. "Can you take off tomorrow? I
want to spend the day together."

His eyes lit up, and she immediately regretted not asking
him sooner. "Of course, sport. I'll ask to leave early tonight
to get a few hours of shuteye before we start our day."

"Be thinking of things to do," she told him as she left to grab coffee.

Sam closed the washer and leaned against the counter with his arms crossed. "You are happy this morning."

She picked up the coffeepot and lifted a brow. "I'll try to sulk later if it makes you feel better."

When he said nothing, she glanced at him, and he pushed off the counter. "I dislike seeing you upset."

"I don't like seeing you upset, either," she replied. "You don't have to tell me why that story upset you yesterday, but don't shut me out. You're as important to me as Dume or any of my other friends."

The mug almost slipped from her hands when she saw him blink away what looked suspiciously like tears. "My reasons for being here are not ones I wish to discuss, but I am sorry for my behavior yesterday. I should not have treated you that way."

She nodded. "It's okay. I was upset and snapped at Lauren once. She almost killed me." Sam's mouth twitched, and she added, "Sometimes we take our pain out on those closest to us."

He shocked her further by hauling her in for a bear hug. "If you tell Lauren I hugged you, I will deny it."

"She can detect lies," Rory reminded him when he released her.

"Not mine," he replied as he brushed past her, leaving her to stare after him with a wide smile.

When Rory and Sam approached, Sera and Kordie were waiting outside of the boutique. Kordie wore a huge grin, and Sera clapped like a giddy schoolgirl.

"What's the occasion?" she asked when they reached the door.

Sam held it open as they filed inside, and Kordie gave him a once-over. "Wouldn't you rather wait outside?"

"You can sit on the bench like last time," Rory suggested. "This will be torture for you."

"I am staying," he replied, allowing no argument.

"Caius told me in the soulscape last night to buy a new dress for tonight," Rory whispered, answering Sera's question. A few other people were in the store, and she didn't want to be overheard.

Sera giggled. "What do you think he has planned?"

"I'm not sure." She glanced around the store. "I need a dress similar to the one I wore at the Vincula Plenilune ball."

Sera's face flashed with genuine surprise. "What's a Plenilune ball?"

Rory held up a dress and quickly put it back. "Caius throws the inmates a ball every Plenilune."

"Like the galas the rich people have?" Kordie asked, draping a dress over her arm.

Rory tilted her head from side to side. "Eh, kind of, but more relaxed."

"I wish someone here would throw a Plenilune ball for us lowly citizens," Sera whined, flipping through the clothes closest to her.

The racks rattled when Sam tried to squeeze between them with a frown. "You should have stayed outside," Rory said with a laugh, causing his frown to deepen.

"Is he always this grumpy?" Sera whispered.

"Yes," Rory replied, shaking her head with a chuckle. Remembering Sam telling her that Sera lied about her day at work, Rory asked, "Where do you work?" Other than being a *Visitant* and Bruce's daughter, she knew little about her new friend.

"I work in The Capital," Sera answered as she picked through a rack.

Rory and Kordie both turned. "Really?" they asked in unison. *That's why she lied*, Rory realized. She didn't know what her work was like and probably didn't want to get the third degree. Everyone was curious about The Capital.

Sera cracked a smile. "Yes." She offered nothing else, and Rory didn't pry, but Kordie studied her closely before shrugging and turning back to the racks.

After looking through every piece of clothing in the store, a clerk ushered them to a large changing room, and they piled inside with Sam standing as sentry near the door.

"Is he going to stay there the entire time?" Sera whispered.

Rory shot her a wry grin. "Yes." She plucked through the dresses, debating which to try on first.

"It doesn't matter which you pick," Kordie informed her. "You're trying them all on."

With a groan, Rory grabbed the first one and wished they hadn't chosen so many.

After what felt like hours, Rory stared at her reflection. The dress was bright red and floor-length with high slits up both legs. "This is the one."

"We'll put it in the yes pile," Sera said, reaching to unzip the garment.

"No," Rory objected as she wiggled out of the smooth fabric. "This is the one, and you won't change my mind."

Kordie sighed dramatically. "It's no use trying to sway her now. She's stubborn."

Sera shook her head and hung the dress on a hanger, poked her head outside, and signaled for the clerk to bag it up. "Do you have shoes?" she asked Rory.

Should she wear shoes in the soulscape? Better safe than sorry. Rory grabbed as many of the unwanted dresses as she could. "No." She stepped out and looked at Sam. "We have one more stop."

He grunted and grabbed the dresses from the ladies, returning them to the same clerk who helped them.

Before they checked out, she asked her friends if they wanted anything, but they declined. She had endless funds and wished they'd let her treat them to something, but they were as stubborn as she was.

After spending too long in a high-end shoe store, they left, and the sight of Sam carrying her shopping bags was too good to pass up. He'd insisted on holding them for her, and she snapped a picture to show Lauren.

Did Sam date? If so, whoever he ended up with was a lucky person.

They unloaded their bags in the car and met Keith and Dume at a nearby restaurant for an early dinner. When Keith saw Kordie, he stood with a love-struck smile and kissed her on the lips.

Rory beamed, happy for them and glad she didn't have to worry about her friends ending up with terrible people.

Dume slung his arm around Sera's shoulders and squeezed slightly. "How was shopping?"

"Exhausting but fun," she answered and ducked out of his embrace.

Once they were seated and placed their orders, Keith

leaned forward. "How are things with your dream boyfriend?" He wiggled his eyebrows.

Rory took a drink of water and sat back with a content smile. "Great, actually. I miss him, but seeing him every night helps soothe the ache."

Dume's demure smile didn't reach his eyes. "I wish Cora were here to see you this way. She would be planning your wedding."

A somber silence fell over the table. "We'd be planning them together." She played with the corner of her napkin. "I still can't believe Gedeon murdered his own mate."

"Didn't you try to kill Caius when you first met?" Keith asked, and Kordie slapped his chest. "*Ow!* What? She did. If the Lux King is as twisted as she says, imagine how easy it would have been for him to ignore the bond."

Rory couldn't refute his claim because it was true. Even after meeting Caius, she wanted his head on a spike. "What disgusts me most is that he trapped my sister's soul," she spat, her anger rising. "The least he could do was let her ascend into the aether. Lauren said there's no reincarnation here; he had to know that, yet he kept her soul, anyway."

"Did Caius know reincarnation didn't exist?" Sera asked. "If not, the Lux King might not either."

Rory recalled their conversation weeks ago when they figured out Cora was Gedeon's mate. Caius suggested his brother kept her soul in fear of reincarnation, but if the *Royal* children knew reincarnation wasn't possible, Caius wouldn't have thought that.

"No," she admitted with a long exhale.

"Maybe one of us can sneak into the palace and set her free," Keith offered. "The king can't always be in the palace, and Rory can pick locks."

"No," Sam boomed. "None of you will go to The Capital, let alone the palace. Gedeon would not hesitate to kill you on the spot, nor would his guards."

"I *have* to go to The Capital for work, but you're right," Dume agreed. "Sneaking around the palace is suicide." He glanced at Rory. "Especially for you."

"I wouldn't do it. If anyone knows how dangerous Gedeon is, it's me," Rory assured the table. "I've seen what he did to his mate, and I agree with Sam. None of you should go, either."

Keith adjusted in his seat, playing with the straw in his glass. "I only want to help."

Leaning across the table, she squeezed his forearm, loving the sight of his bright blue soul. "I know, and I love you for it, but I won't risk any of you."

Until then, she felt guilty for wanting to leave them, but now she felt guilty for staying. The people she loved would put themselves in danger time and again to help her, no matter what she said to stop them.

"I'd die before I let anything happen to you."

Keith once said those words to her, and she knew he meant it.

CHAPTER 42

VINCULA

Caius stared at himself in the mirror and straightened his suit jacket. He smoothed a hand over his perfectly styled hair and pictured Rory in a beautiful dress, walking toward him with a smile meant only for him.

It was time.

Sitting on top of his comforter, he leaned against the headboard and grabbed the sleeping potion he picked up from the pharmacy in town. Chugging it all, he wanted to stay asleep for as long as possible. This was a night he didn't want to rush.

Wildflowers covered the floor of Caius and Rory's bedroom, and candles scattered around the room to cast an iridescent glow. He didn't set those up before falling asleep, but the soulscape knew what he needed.

"Isn't this a fire hazard?" Rory's teasing voice asked as she stepped through the bathroom door.

He couldn't respond, too stunned to form coherent thoughts. His mate was gorgeous, and if he never woke from this dream, he would die happy.

Her hair fell in loose waves to her shoulders, her makeup accentuated her grey eyes, and her lips were the color of blood. The long red dress had slits to the top of her thighs, making him bite back a groan. Her look was reminiscent of their first Plenilune ball but in vivid color.

If he wasn't about to ask her the most important question of their lives, he would rip her dress to shreds right then and there.

She stood before him and ran her hand down the lapels of his jacket. "It's rude to stare."

He trailed a finger down the bare skin of her back, teasing the edge of her dress. "And yet, I can't stop. You look stunning."

"I've never seen you in a full suit before," she remarked. "Turns out, I love it."

His voice lowered as he brought his mouth to hers. "Then I shall wear one every day."

Their lips met, and while he wanted nothing more than to kiss her for hours, he withdrew from her arms. "I don't want to waste any time," he said quickly. "I want to do this properly without being rushed."

She tilted her head slightly. "Do what?"

"This," he murmured and dropped to his knee. She inhaled sharply with wide eyes as he removed a smokey grey box from his pants pocket and opened it to reveal the Umbra ring.

It was an antique, passed down from the early Umbra **Royals**, and comprised a large black diamond surrounded by *a halo of smaller black diamonds. Caius had thought it was obnoxious until he envisioned it on his mate's hand.*

"I have always been enamored with you," he murmured. "Even when I wished you would burn in hell for your crimes."

Her eyes watered as she laughed. "You are terrible at this."

Smiling, he grabbed her right hand to slide the ring onto her middle finger. "I would have followed you to hell and burned beside you for eternity, Aurora Raven. When I looked into your hate-filled eyes that fateful day in my throne room, my heart was no longer my own. I just didn't know it yet."

Her left hand swiped at her cheek as she stared at him lovingly.

"I should have kept my promise and married you that night in my office, but I am a fool, and that night is my biggest regret. I want to be with you always, whether it's at your feet or by your side." He released a shaky breath. "Will you marry me?"

Silence.

***"What if I don't want you to?"** she had asked him the day she regained her memories. The beating in his chest was so loud it could be heard in the aether.*

*"You are an arrogant fool," she said hoarsely. "But you're **my** arrogant fool. Yes."*

His head fell forward as happiness and relief thrummed below the surface of his skin, threatening to burst free. Rising to his feet, he grabbed her face gently and kissed her with everything he had.

He prayed to Lora, begging her to grant them a successful union in the soulscape. It was her magic, and he needed this to work.

***Please**, he begged the golden **Seraph** again. **Please**.*

"There's one last thing we have to do, and if this works,

you'll be safer until I can find my way to you," he said when he broke their kiss.

Her eyes moved between his before flaring slightly. "You think if we marry here, it will make me immortal?"

*"Yes." Releasing her, he walked to his dresser and removed a dagger from the top drawer. "The awareness will alert Gedeon of your transformation, but he'll find out about you anyway, and this will at least give you more protection when he does. Besides," he added, "it only tells him a new **Royal** exists. It doesn't tell him your location or identity."*

Her breathing picked up, and worry prickled Caius' spine when her panicked expression worsened. "You can't just spring immortality on someone with no warning." Her hand went to her throat. "I need water."

Rushing to the drink cart, she poured herself a glass and gulped it down. He followed her and took it from her hand, setting it on the cart. "You knew immortality was part of the deal when you agreed to marry me."

"I thought I'd have time to get used to the idea," she said, running a trembling hand through her hair. "I'm being dumb. I know that. I've always known this would happen." Closing her eyes, she took deep breaths and shook out her hands. "This is ridiculous."

*He cracked a smile. Even flustered, she was the cutest thing he'd ever seen. **Cute.** That was never a word he thought he'd use for The Butcher, but as he watched her flap her arms to calm down, he could think of no other word to describe her.*

Her demeanor calmed little by little, and when she finally turned to him, she looked embarrassed. "I don't know why I did that. It just took me by surprise."

He tugged her closer and bit back a smile. "Immortality is hard for any lesser mystic to fathom, and it's difficult to watch your loved ones die while you go on living, but I promise, we will meet them in the aether one day."

"I know," she replied softly. "The thought of marrying you makes me happier than I've ever been, but I'm still a normal person who had a tiny case of cold feet."

He ran his hands down her bare arms, his eyes never leaving hers. "I'll buy you warm socks, but first, I'd like to marry you."

The beautiful smile that spread across her face was all he needed. Stepping back, he picked up the dagger again.

"That's my dagger," she said in awe, taking it from him. It only seemed fitting to spit on Nina's grave by getting married with the very weapon that killed her.

"I'm going to cut our right palms, press them together, and then recite an incantation you'll need to repeat," he explained as excitement built in his chest.

"Can I do the cutting?" she asked as she inspected the handle and looked up.

He threw his head back and laughed before kissing her hand. "You can do whatever you want."

They held their hands palm side up, and Rory pressed the cold blade into each, drawing the smallest amount of blood before laying her palm on top of his.

Caius looked deep into her eyes and repeated the lines he'd memorized since childhood, and when she repeated them back, he felt their bond strengthen.

*Next came the **awareness**. It was a warm tingle in his chest, moving up his neck. His eyes closed as he relished in what it meant, and when he looked at their palms, the Umbra **Aeternum** sigil, a U surrounded by swirling shadows, was imprinted on their skin.*

She lifted her hand, staring at her palm. "If I'd known we were getting matching marks, I wouldn't have gotten a tattoo."

He narrowed his eyes. "I'd still have bitten you."

The laugh she released rang through the air like a melody. "What did it feel like?" she asked.

"I don't understand your question," he said, mindlessly rubbing the sigil on his palm.

"The awareness," she clarified. "Did it hurt?" She sounded worried.

"You didn't feel it?" She was a **Royal** now; why would she not?

"No. I didn't notice anything."

"It's a warm sensation that starts here," he said, pressing the bottom of her sternum. "It moves up like magic filling your body." As he spoke, he trailed his fingers up her chest until they skimmed her neck before dropping his arm to his side. "When it first happened, I didn't know what it meant because I'd never felt it before. The transfer of power to Gedeon wasn't immediate. It wasn't until Adila arrived to see Atarah's dead body that he glowed, and then I felt it. My siblings and I never mentioned it to one another, but I knew what it was."

He thought for a moment. "I assumed we all felt it, but it's possible Gedeon didn't since he was the one who transformed into a **Royal**."

She couldn't tell if he was joking or not. "He wasn't already a **Royal**?"

Caius shook his head slightly. "You aren't considered a **Royal** until you take one of the three **Royal** positions. As kids, they called us the **Royal** children or **Royal** heirs, but we weren't actually **Royals** yet."

She ran her hands up his chest, getting a bit of blood on his shirt. "I don't want to talk about him anymore."

*Caius didn't either. All he wanted to talk about, **think** about, was her. Tonight, he wouldn't ravish her; he would cherish her.*

Reading his mind, she stepped forward and pushed his jacket from his shoulders to kiss his neck. His arms slipped around her waist, lowering the zipper of her dress, and it slid down her body, pooling at her feet.

There were no undergarments in sight, and he licked his thumb to brush over one of her nipples. "You were bare for me?"

Nodding, she reached for him, removing his shirt before unbuttoning his pants. "Take off your shoes."

Soon they were both naked, and when she lifted her foot behind her to remove the sexiest shoes he'd ever seen, he stopped her. "The shoes stay on."

Once she was on the bed, he crawled over her, memorizing every inch of her. "I have waited for you my entire life," he whispered.

"I've been waiting for you too," she murmured. "I just didn't know it."

He sucked one of her breasts into his mouth and moved a hand down her stomach, feeling it quiver beneath his touch. Her hands went to his hair, and he smiled against her soft skin.

The arousal he found between her legs made him groan and bury his face in her soft chest. "Fuck, Rory, you're always so wet."

"Mmm," she hummed. "You would be too if someone who looked like you couldn't keep their hands off you."

He tugged her nipple between his teeth, making her squirm. "I'll keep that in mind."

His two middle fingers entered her with ease, and he

groaned again. "Oh," she breathed as he stroked in and out while lightly grinding his palm against her clit. "Caius."

"Tell me what you need," he commanded softly. "Tonight is about you."

She brought his face close to hers. "I only need you."

Her lips parted when he moved his hand in a circular motion, pleasuring her inside and out. When he added another finger, she squirmed, and his strokes came easier with each passing second as she drenched his skin.

He pressed his knee against the back of his hand to drive it deeper and watched as her head thrashed to the side.

When her pussy spasmed, he curled his digits and put more pressure on her clit with his palm. She cursed as her orgasm took over her body, and he let her ride his hand until her limbs went limp. After sucking his fingers clean, he moved between her legs, capturing her eyes with his to convey every ounce of love he had for her.

Reaching up to thread her fingers through his hair, she whispered, "I love you."

He pushed into her and hissed. The feeling of her warmth encompassing him would never get old. "I love you too, Umbra Queen."

Pinning her arms to the bed, he clasped his fingers through hers. Their bodies moved in perfect harmony because they were made for each other, and now that the bond was complete, the pleasure between them was unlike any other.

She tried to close her eyes, but he stopped. "Look at me." When her gaze met his, he rolled his hips into hers, and she lifted, meeting him halfway. Every stroke was ethereal, and the sounds they made were primal.

No thoughts ran through his mind other than his need for her. Taking her once wasn't enough, but for now, it was all he *had. They stared into each other's eyes, refusing to look away as their skin came together again and again.*

Releasing one of her hands, he moved his own to her neck, feeling her pulse beat wildly. "Never have I seen anything more beautiful," he murmured and pushed his cock as deep as possible, wanting to touch every inch of her.

She gasped, and the look in her eyes would have brought him to his knees had he been standing. "I love you," she whispered, lifting her hips faster.

"Fuck." He grunted between pants as his cock grew at her words.

Their movements grew frantic as they chased the high only the other could give. Squeezing his cock almost to the point of pain, she came, and he welcomed the ache, slamming into her harder. He finished, calling her name like a prayer.

Nothing would ever compare to making love to his mate, his **wife**. *The room shimmered, and she propped herself up on her elbow, tugging him to her. "I love you, husband."*

He sighed, happier than he'd ever been in his long existence because they were the sweetest words he'd ever heard.

"And I love you, wife."

~

The first thing Caius did when he opened his eyes was check the palm of his right hand. He stared disbelieving at the Umbra *Aeternum* sigil. *It worked.* If he was being honest with himself, he didn't think it would because they possessed none of their abilities in the soulscape.

His head tilted toward the aether, and he whispered, "Thank you, Lora."

He was a married man, and his wife had one more layer of protection against his brother.

The elation he felt made the marks on his arms recede. When Sam returned, they'd figure out what Caius needed to *create* to get through the barrier.

Sam's arrival couldn't come soon enough.

CHAPTER 43

ERDIKOA

Gedeon woke with a start, rubbing his chest at the burning there. It didn't hurt, per se, but it wasn't comfortable either, and unease prickled down his spine.

As a child, their nanny would complain about indigestion, and how she explained it made it sound similar to Gedeon's current ailment.

Sighing, he left his bed and padded to the bathroom to relieve himself, ignoring the cries coming from the woman on the floor. He finished his business and crouched down next to her.

"Why do you cry?" Tears streamed down her face, and he smirked. "It's not as though I've beaten you. I keep you fed, I give you water, and I even give your chains enough slack to reach the toilet when I leave," he crooned, reaching out to rub her face, but she yanked her head away. "Yet here you sit, an ungrateful little bitch." His voice was smooth, masking the pleasure he felt at the suffering little lamb in front of him.

"Fuck you," she spat as she lunged toward him.

He laughed, thoroughly enjoying the show. "You're lucky I haven't killed you, and if I didn't need you alive, you'd lose your head for your tone alone."

"If I could, I'd kill myself to stop you." Her chest heaved as she hurled her hate at him. "You're a fucking monster."

"And you're a means to an end." He left her and entered the bedroom to get dressed for the day. Grabbing the phone on the nightstand, he sent a quick text, setting up a meetup for later that afternoon.

He'd have Aurora Raven in his clutches soon. When he did, Caius would suffer as he watched every bit of the torture inflicted upon his mate. And when Gedeon killed her, his brother would follow. The anguish would leave him unable to live with himself for failing to protect her.

Two birds. One stone.

CHAPTER 44

Rory and her father pulled on their rented shoes at the rollerball alley while Sam stood in his socks. They didn't have shoes big enough to fit his feet, and when he said he wasn't playing, Rory wore him down until he reluctantly agreed.

He deserved more fun, and she was determined to give it to him. When she and Cora were younger, their father would bring them to the rollerball alley on the weekends he had off. Even though he owned his own veterinarian clinic, he and the other doctors that worked for him rotated out weekends to be on call.

It was the perfect activity for today.

Their names appeared on the screen after she typed them into the scoreboard and grabbed her ball. She wasn't great at rollerball, but she wasn't terrible either. Her first round knocked down a few pins, and her father, ever the athlete, made a strike.

"I still think you cheat," she accused when he walked back to the bench.

Patrick smiled at her and shook his head. "You always were a sore loser."

Leaning forward, she lowered her voice to sound threatening. "You haven't won yet, old man."

They both waited as Sam picked up the biggest ball on the carousel and stared at it. "My fingers will not fit."

Rory stood. "I know. I grabbed this one because it should be heavy enough for you, but you'll have to palm it." To demonstrate, she slapped her hand on the ball and gripped it. "Try it."

Sam snatched her wrist and examined her palm, staring at the Umbra *Aeternum* mark. His lips parted with a calculated stare. "How is this possible?"

He didn't look happy. She lowered her voice to a whisper and said, "In the soulscape. We didn't know if it would work, but it did."

He dropped her wrist, and a muscle feathered in his jaw. *Definitely mad.* "And now Gedeon knows you are here," he said, emphasizing each word.

"We don't know that he already didn't," she countered. "This way, at least I'm immortal."

"An immortal the Lux King knows how to kill." Sam wasn't just mad; he was furious.

"Why are you so upset?" she asked, throwing her hands up. "This is a good thing. You wanted him to marry me, did you not?"

"You did this without warning me," he replied, and she saw his anger for what it was. *Hurt.* "I need to know these things to better protect you."

"I'm sorry we didn't tell you," she apologized. "But I'm telling you now. Besides, Gedeon might not realize what's happened." She'd thought about it all morning. "He might not realize what the *awareness* is."

"Why would he not know?" Sam asked. She could tell he didn't believe her, but she had hope.

"I didn't feel the *awareness* when I turned, and the only reason Caius knew what it felt like was because he felt it at the exact moment Gedeon inherited the Lux power. Gedeon probably didn't feel it when he took the throne. How would he know what it is now?"

Sam looked thoughtful. "There is a chance you are correct."

It was as close to a '*Good job*' as she would get. She slapped her palm back on his ball. "Enough chit-chat. This is how you'll have to hold it."

She pulled back, and he mimicked her grip, walked to the lane, and threw it underhand. It arched high and landed with a loud thud, drawing the attention of those around them. The three of them watched the ball inch its way to the gutter and disappear through the back.

"You can't lob it like that," Rory said, managing not to laugh at the *Angel's* irritation.

"Here," Patrick offered as he got up and stood by Sam. "You're going to let it roll off your fingers, not throw it."

Sam looked determined, and Rory guessed he'd never been bad at anything in his life. She saw him observing other players as they rolled the ball down the lane, and when his ball returned, he picked it up, adjusted his grip, and released it with perfect form, knocking down all the pins.

She gaped at him. "Did you hustle us?"

Patrick laughed and clapped Sam on the back. "You're a fast learner, son."

Sam's lips curled into a crooked smile, and Rory

returned it tenfold. "I did not hurry you," he told Rory. "I merely watched and replicated. It is simple."

"No," she said, shaking her head. "I didn't mean literally. It's a—you know what? Nevermind. You're hopeless." She grabbed her own ball with a dramatic sigh.

Rory: two.

Sam's aversion to fun: zero.

Rory sat with her father and Sam at the kitchen table, rubbing her stomach. The empty pizza boxes on the table were mainly Sam's doing, but she put a pretty good dent in them, too.

"Sam, you don't say much," Patrick remarked as the *Angel* sat stoically across from him.

Sam was quiet, as always, before saying, "I have little to say."

"I would love to hear about your job as a commander," Patrick returned. "Have you always been over the Vincula legion?"

The *Angel* shifted uncomfortably, and Rory held her breath, hoping the question wouldn't send him back into the foul mood caused by the Coopers. "No. I once led an army of *Angels* in the aether."

Patrick awarded him with an impressed look. "That is nothing to sneeze at."

Sam's brow wrinkled, and Rory leaned over before he could say anything. "It's just an expression. He didn't mean to actually sneeze."

He shook his head. "Mystics are strange."

"Not here, we're not," she fired back playfully. "You're the outcast."

They prattled on, pulling Sam into conversations he probably didn't want to be a part of, until her father stood. "I'm heading to bed. I didn't sleep much this morning."

Rory got up and hugged him. "I love you, and I'll see you at breakfast."

"I love you, too," he said and turned to Sam. "Good-night, Sam."

Sam tipped his head and pushed back from the table. It was still daylight outside, but the sun would set soon. "Lauren and I change shifts tonight."

She nodded. "I know the drill. Stay here, or I'll die."

Sam pressed his lips together, but the corners lifted slightly. "Yes. I will see you later this week."

He left without another word, having never been one for goodbyes.

Rory's phone vibrated with a text from Sera, and after going back and forth, Sera decided to come hang out since Sam was gone and Patrick was asleep. Rory stood and stretched, running upstairs to change into a pair of leggings and a hooded sweatshirt.

When she passed by her mirror, she stopped and surveyed her clothes. It was her butcher outfit, but it no longer meant that to her. Funny how things changed.

Rory rolled the tension from her shoulders and ran downstairs to wait on the porch. Excited to have a girl's night, she reached for her phone, having forgotten to text Kordie about coming over. Neither of her girlfriends knew about her getting married, and she needed to tell them.

Earlier that day, she'd spoken with Dume on the phone and told him everything she'd learned, including Adila being on their side and why she couldn't send Rory to Vincula at will. She also told him she married Caius, and she could hear his heart attack through the phone.

Despite them seeing each other every day, she hadn't wanted to bring her friends down with more talk of her situation and held off on bringing it up. But Dume often took people accused of crimes before the Scales of Justice, and she didn't want him saying something terrible to Caius' sister. Dume might have a pure soul, but he was also protective to a fault.

He told her she needed to let the others know because they'd be hurt to learn she kept it from them.

If she survived Gedeon and reunited with Caius, Kordie and Sera would insist on throwing an outrageous wedding reception. She just had to tell them she was married first.

Before she could fire off a text to Kordie, a car pulled into the driveway, and Rory looked up with a wide smile. "Took you long enough!"

Sera parked and jumped out of her car with a grin. "I wouldn't miss tonight for anything."

CHAPTER 45

VINCULA

Caius fell to his knees as headlights and a small girl with bright red hair assaulted his mind. The girl was smiling and walking toward him like they were friends, and he didn't understand what was happening.

When his vision cleared, he stood on shaky legs, holding on to the bathroom sink. *What was that?*

He went over everything in his mind. There were trees behind the car, and the redhead climbed out of the driver's seat.

His blood turned to ice as fear blanketed him. The vision was in Erdikoa, and the only reason he'd have a nightmarish episode while awake was an *Aeternum* vision. Usually in his visions, he felt fear, pain, anxiety, or whatever Rory felt, but this time, he felt nothing but excitement. *She was oblivious to whatever danger awaited her.*

Unchecked emotions flooded him, circulating between fear, anguish, and pure, unadulterated rage.

His head swam, making him stumble. When he looked in the mirror, black veins branched over his jaw, and solid black eyes stared back at him.

They were the last thing he saw before everything faded to nothing.

CHAPTER 46

ERDIKOA

Rory fell to the ground, gasping for air as her body burned with an icy rage that wasn't her own. Her vision tunneled, and instead of seeing her surroundings, she saw Caius in a mirror, completely covered in black veins.

Soulless black eyes stared back at her, and it took everything she had to keep from screaming.

She watched those pits of nothingness roll back in his head as he fell, leaving her panting on the gravel driveway as Sera shook her with shock on her face.

"Rory!" she exclaimed, grabbing her by both shoulders.

A sob tore from Rory's chest as she tried to figure out what had happened. "I saw Caius." Her brain nagged at her, telling her she knew exactly what it meant.

When the fog cleared from her mind, she struggled to her feet, and her fear merged with panic. "He's dying," she croaked and pulled out her phone, fumbling it.

Sera gasped. "Who? Caius?"

"I need to call Sam. He has to get to him." Her hands shook so hard that she could barely press the buttons.

"I'll call him," Sera said, grabbing the phone from her. "You can't even talk. What's your code?"

Rory's hands tingled, and she tried to steady her breathing. "I don't have one. It swipes open."

Sera frowned at her. "That's not safe." Her fingers worked quickly, but the phone sparked, making her yelp and drop it. "What the hell?" She scooped the device off the ground, and Rory grew distraught. She didn't know Sam's or Lauren's number by heart, and Sera's next words confirmed her fear. "It's not working."

Rory fisted her hair. "I have to find them. Call Dume. Maybe he can get me into The Capital. Lauren and Sam switched shifts tonight. Sam left early, but maybe I can catch Lauren at the bunker when she arrives."

Sera perked up. "I can get you in. I work there, remember?"

"We need to leave now," Rory insisted, too frantic to thank her friend.

Sera nodded and ran to her car with Rory on her heels. "Don't worry," she soothed her. "We'll find them. I'm sure Caius is fine."

She sounded as unsure as Rory felt.

As they pulled onto the main road, it occurred to Rory that she could have woken up her father to see if he had Sam's number, but it was too late now. Her best bet was to catch one of the *Angel*s and beg them to save her husband.

It felt like hours before they neared The Capital, and once Sera parked in the far corner of the staff parking lot, Rory hopped out. *What if she couldn't find Sam or Lauren?*

She'd have to go to Adila. The *Royal* couldn't send her to Vincula, but Adila could go to check on him.

Rory turned toward the gates, but Sera grabbed her arm. "This way," she whispered and looked around to ensure no one was in the lot. "There's another entrance no one knows about. Only select staff members are allowed to use it." She held up a lanyard with a badge.

"What the hell do you do here that you get to use a secret entrance?" Rory whispered.

"There's no time for that." Sera slipped through the dense foliage surrounding the lot, beckoning Rory to follow her, and they crept around the outside wall.

"Are we going to the back?" Rory asked. They'd been walking for a while.

Sera abruptly stopped and turned to her. "We're here. When we go in, stay behind me, and don't talk to anyone. The less attention you draw to yourself, the better."

Rory nodded and watched as Sera touched the door, making it spark.

She didn't even use her badge.

Rory stepped back, remembering how her phone sparked when Sera held it.

Her eyes were trained on Sera as the door opened, and she failed to notice the two guards who stepped through. When they reached for her, it was too late to run.

Her training kicked in, and she fought, fending them off the best she could, but two-on-one was difficult. Sera stood with her arms crossed and a bored look on her face. Her betrayal ran deep.

How could she do this? She fooled them all.

Rory kicked one guard in the chin, and his head snapped back. She didn't have time to watch him fall to the ground as she fought the other. Her nose was bleeding, and one of her ribs was broken, but she fought through the pain. Hers and Caius' lives depended on her getting away.

She didn't notice the other guard get up; she thought she'd knocked him out, but her assumption was a fatal mistake.

He grabbed her arms from behind, pulling them behind her hard enough to rip something in her shoulder. She screamed, and the other guard punched her, hard. The pain shooting through her shoulder made it near impossible to break free.

Sera walked toward her with a satisfied smirk, and Rory glared at her with as much hatred as she could muster. "How could you?" her voice was weak from exhaustion and filled with hurt. "We trusted you! I saved your fucking life, and this is how you repay me?"

Sera threw her head back with a loud laugh, and Rory's stomach turned as Sera's body shifted into a spitting image of Caius. *Gedeon*.

The brothers were mirror images of each other, but there was no mistaking who he was. The way the Lux King carried himself and the pure malice in his eyes screamed evil.

She was stunned into silence, staring at the one she'd hated for the last eleven years, the one who put her mate away for a crime he didn't commit, and the one who tricked her like the fool she was.

She gasped, recalling her mother's prophecy. *"Don't let him fool you."*

"What's the matter?" Gedeon pouted. "Are you not happy to see me? We were to be brother and sister, were we not?"

He grabbed her chin, and she tried to yank it away, but

his grip was firm enough to bruise. "Twice over. Wouldn't that be something? Brothers marrying sisters." His face inched closer to hers, tracing her features with his golden eyes. "It seems I got the pretty twin. Too bad she couldn't stick around."

Rory thrashed against the guard's hold again, ignoring the pain, and Gedeon stepped back as he laughed.

"I will fucking rip your head from your body," she vowed.

His head cocked to the side mechanically. "No, you won't."

There was one small solace in seeing him before her. Sera hadn't betrayed them. *Sera.* "Where is Sera?" she demanded.

Grinning widely, he sauntered toward her again. "That girl is feistier than you are."

Numbness spread through Rory's body, and she could barely speak past the implication of his words. "Did you kill her?"

Gedeon sighed dramatically and waved her off. "Unfortunately, I couldn't. I cannot shift into someone unless they're still alive." When he saw Rory's face contort into shock, he winked. "As I'm sure you know by now, *Royals* take on a twisted version of their *Aeternum's* abilities."

Caius sensed black souls without touching them.

"As it turns out, the *Seraphim* blessed me with being able to shift into people instead of one animal." His body transformed into Rory's own, and she jerked back, horrified. Gedeon examined himself. "Unsettling, isn't it?"

It was her voice she heard, and another fear struck her. What if he went to Vincula disguised as her and hurt Caius? "No," she whispered before screaming, "*No!*"

He spun around slowly with his arms out, and when he faced her, he bowed. "Yes."

The smirk on his face was replaced with something akin to curiosity when he shifted back and moved closer to her. He ran a finger over her face, and she pulled away. "Don't fucking touch me."

"It's impossible," he murmured as he moved to the side and flipped over her right hand.

She had immortal healing now.

Rory realized her shoulder no longer hurt, nor did her ribs. She'd been so caught up in Gedeon's display that she never noticed her pain fading. The split skin on her face must have healed, too.

"You married him?" Gedeon's eyes blazed with anger, and his body sparked as bolts of light covered his skin. She tried to push away from him, but the guard held her steady.

The light faded as he calmed down, and a sinister smile slid into place. "This might be better. Do you know the things I can do to you that would kill a lesser mystic? But not you. You'll heal."

He clapped his hands together, pleased with his discovery. "Enough talking. Let's go inside, shall we?"

Sam perched his small bird body on a chandelier above the main door to Gedeon's office, waiting. In their past searches, he and Lauren had yet to come across anything useful, and it felt pointless to come at night anymore. The king was always either asleep or fucking someone.

Sam had come early tonight, but there was still no sign of Gedeon. The only place he could not access was Gedeon's office, and he had hoped to catch the Lux King leaving, but as dusk turned into night and no one left, he chuffed, frustrated with their lack of intel.

As he lifted his wings to leave, a familiar maid wheeled her cart toward the king's office and spoke with a guard, who smiled and let her into Gedeon's office.

Sam glared at the too-friendly man opening the door for her. The non-*Aatxe* guards, no matter how nice they seemed, could not be trusted, and he didn't like the way this one looked at Anastasia.

He knew he couldn't speak with her in Gedeon's office, where the guards could hear and would wait until she left. Sam wouldn't chance her getting hurt.

Sometime later, she exited the office, said goodbye to the guards, and pushed her cart down a different hallway. Sam took flight, following her until they were far enough away from prying eyes. There were no guards in this section of the hallway, and he flew in front of her, shifting mid-air.

She startled, and Sam clamped his hand over her mouth when she tried to scream. Her body trembled, and her skin looked sickly as she stared at him with wide eyes. Once she realized who he was, she relaxed and closed her eyes, still panting.

"Is there an empty room where we can talk?" he whispered.

Pushing his hand away, she nodded and looked behind her before leading him down another hallway and into a deserted banquet room.

Closing the door softly, she spun around and took measured steps toward him as though he would strike if she moved too fast. "What can I help you with, Commander?"

"Call me Sam," he replied as he prowled toward her. "You need to terminate your employment."

She stared at him with a blank expression that morphed into disbelief. "You're serious? I can't quit my job."

"Why would I say something if I was not serious?" he asked, perplexed. "It is not safe for you to work here."

She laughed in his face, and he curled his hands into fists. Did she not understand the gravity of the situation? "You are not listening," he barked, wincing at the tone he took with her.

Her laughter abruptly stopped, and he didn't think it was possible for her to pale further, but she did. "You're not kidding."

"I have already told you I was serious."

"Forgive me if I don't quit my job because a random *Angel* drops in periodically and tells me to," she whispered hotly.

He needed her to understand the severity of the situation, and with Rory now married to Caius, their time was running out. It was only a matter of time before everything came to a head.

The thought of Anastasia being hurt lit something within him. He couldn't explain it, but thinking about it threatened his control. If he had to carry her out of The Capital kicking and screaming, he would.

"Take a seat," he said, pointing to a chair. "I will tell you a story, and if, after I am done, you decide to continue working here, I will leave." *And come back when her shift was over to remove her from this place.*

She looked scared, like a mouse, and he didn't like that either. Once she lowered herself into a chair, he took a deep breath and told her everything from the beginning, starting with how Rory watched Gedeon murder Cora and ending with Rory's marriage to Caius.

It was a long story, and she listened patiently, calmer than he expected. The silence between them stretched on forever until she finally asked, "Her sister's soul is in a jar?"

Of everything he told her, that was her question? "Yes. It is presumed Gedeon still has Cora's soul somewhere."

"I think I know where it is." A look of determination crossed her face, and Sam's body tightened. "One night, I was late doing my chores, and he was in his office when I walked in. He was holding a jar that glowed a bright pink."

Only *Fey* could see souls with skin-to-skin contact or when they left dead bodies, but if a soul was trapped inside a jar by a *Merrow*, they're visible to everyone. There was no mistaking what Anastasia saw, but he couldn't let her try to retrieve it.

"Where in his office?" he asked her. The longer they talked, the more he felt the need to get her out of The Capital.

Her knee bounced as she thought. "In a cabinet. When you walk into his door, it's on this side," she said, waving her arm to the right.

Sam nodded. "Either my first in command or I will find it and free her."

She lifted her chin proudly. "I can do it."

"No," Sam snapped, making her flinch. "You are to leave the palace when your shift ends and never return."

She looked nervous, and he wanted to put her at ease, but he'd never done well at making people comfortable. "I won't remember why I quit when I leave," she murmured to herself.

He couldn't imagine what losing one's memory was like,

and he didn't want her agonizing over why she decided to leave her job. "Give me your phone number. I will be unreachable for a few days, but when I return, I will call you, and we can talk." She wouldn't remember him either, but at least he could put her mind at ease.

Anastasia took a deep breath. "Okay. I will inform the head night maid and return my badge to the gate guards."

Sam couldn't explain the elation he felt at hearing her words. The knowledge that she was safe cleared his mind.

"Thank you," he said sincerely, handing her his phone to program her number in. When she handed it back, he stuck it in his back pocket. "It is almost morning, and I must leave. I will call you when I return."

Standing, she stuck out her hand, and he clasped it in his. "Until next time," she said with a sweet smile.

He gave a curt nod, shifted into a bird, and slipped out when she opened the door. One less thing he had to worry about.

CHAPTER 47

Dume's phone rang early, *too* early, and he rolled over, blindly reaching for it. Bruce's number showed on the screen, and he bolted upright. "Hello?"

Bruce's voice was distraught and barely coherent. "Sera," he blubbered. "I-I came to check on her because she wasn't returning my calls." Dume heard Sera's voice say something in the background, and he relaxed slightly until Bruce spoke again. "We have to find Rory."

"What's happened to Sera and Rory?" Dume demanded, putting his phone on speaker while he pulled on a pair of jeans.

Bruce replied with more incoherent words, and there was rustling in the background before Sera's voice came through the speaker. "Dume, it's Gedeon," she yelled into the receiver. "H-he shifted into me days ago."

Dume's blood ran cold. "That's not possible."

She stopped crying enough that he could understand her, but barely. "He can shift into people. I don't understand how he does it. He chained me to the sink in my bathroom." Her sobs broke his heart, and if someone else didn't kill Gedeon, he would.

"He met with someone this afternoon," she hiccupped. "It might be Rory. You need to find her."

Dume grabbed his keys. "Put Bruce back on the phone."

"I'm sorry," Bruce said when he took the phone from his daughter.

"It's understandable," Dume assured him. "Call emergency services. Sera needs to see a doctor immediately, but do not tell them about the Lux King. Say it was an unknown intruder."

"I will." Bruce hung up, and Dume called Rory's phone.

It went straight to a recorded message. He tried Sam, and the *Angel* didn't answer either.

Lauren was his last hope. "Hello?"

His knees almost buckled at the sound of her voice. "Where's Rory?"

"She should be at the safe house," Lauren replied. "Why?"

Dume gave her a rundown of what happened, and she said every curse word he'd ever heard, along with some he hadn't. "Have you checked the house yet?"

"No. I'm headed there now." He cursed when he realized a cab couldn't drive him to the safe house. Holding his phone out, he texted Keith.

"I'll meet you there," she said and hung up.

Dume and Keith arrived at the safe house and jumped out of the truck. Kordie went to the hospital to check on Sera. Keith didn't want her coming with him in case something happened, and Dume agreed. Their friend had no skills to protect herself if they were to walk into an ambush.

Lauren's SUV pulled up shortly after, and once in the house, they called Rory's name, searching everywhere. Patrick walked out of his room with sleep-swollen eyes. "What's going on?"

"Did you see Rory when you got home this morning?" Lauren asked.

Patrick snapped out of his sleepy stupor. "I took off last night. I've been asleep, but she and Sam were here when I went to bed."

"Maybe she's with Sam," Keith suggested, with hope in his voice.

"Sam's phone is off. It's only off when he's back in Vincula," Lauren replied.

Violence radiated from the *Angel*, but her face betrayed nothing. "We can't take chances. We have to go to The Capital."

"How will we find her?" Dume asked. "The Capital is huge."

Lauren grabbed her hair and pulled it back into a tight ponytail. "Gedeon will keep her in the palace where he has control and his minion guards. I know I am risking your lives when I ask this of you, but I need your help searching the palace. It's too big for me to cover alone, and if I go to Vincula to find Sam, we might be too late."

"I'll go," Dume volunteered. "I've been to the palace before. I don't remember it now, but I will once inside The Capital gates."

"I'm going too," Keith added. "I can shift and try to find her scent."

"Head to the car while I throw on clothes," Patrick said,

rushing into his room. Dume knew that Patrick was thinking of Cora's death. They couldn't lose Rory too.

They ran outside and piled into Lauren's car, and once Patrick was ready, they left in a hurry.

As they drove, Lauren gave them instructions, sounding every bit the commander Sam was. Dume and Lauren were to search independently, and Keith was to sniff Rory out in wolf form with Patrick, who would help open doors for the *Shifter* or deter people when needed.

It was daytime, and there would be a full staff, but it wasn't completely unheard of for non-staff to be at the palace. It wasn't common, but it happened.

Lauren would go to Gedeon's quarters, and Dume would check the east wing near the judgment chambers since he was familiar with that area.

If any guards tried to stop them, they were to incapacitate them. Lauren told them to act like they needed help, and when they were close enough, hit a certain pressure point on their neck to knock them out.

They agreed to not kill any *Aatxe* guards because they were innocents and, worst case scenario, would take them to the judgment chambers to face Adila.

Non-*Aatxe* guards were a different story.

Dume's stomach flipped at the thought of hurting someone innocent, but he might not have a choice.

He and Lauren would have no issue taking down non-*Aatxe* guards, and Keith swore he could fight as a wolf. It would have to be enough. The one thing benefiting them was that no guns were allowed in The Capital, not even for the guards.

Assuming those rules still applied to the king's *special* guards.

Lauren kept barking out instructions as the others listened intently. If they found Rory and Gedeon was with her, they agreed to stay hidden and call Lauren. She was the only one powerful enough in their group to fight the Lux King.

Once at The Capital gates, Lauren spoke with the guards, and they permitted her to enter without inspection. After parking, she led them around the palace to the staff entrance.

With one last look at one another, they split up, praying to the *Seraphim* they'd find Rory in time.

CHAPTER 48

Rory's wrists were shackled and chained to the wall above her head in the sky room, or at least it was equivalent to the sky room, but here in the Lux Palace it had no essence screens on the ceiling.

She'd recognize the room anywhere, but even if she didn't, the way they arrived gave it away. The guards carried her through the secret passage near the gardens to Gedeon's room and then through the other passage leading to here.

She had gawked at her surroundings when they entered. Instead of a standard guest room, it was a torture chamber, and she shuddered at the horrors he had done to others here.

Gedeon dismissed the guards, who disappeared through the room's main entrance. She thought of the palace layout in her head, mapping an escape route, thankful that the palaces were the same.

Caius took up most of her thoughts. *Would she know if he died?* If visions alerted them to danger, surely something would alert them of the other's death. It was the only thread of hope she had.

"Do you like what I've done with the place?" Gedeon asked her and spread his arms wide with a hideous smile on his face.

"How many innocents have you hurt here?" she sneered.

His laugh grated on her nerves as he stepped closer and leaned down. She kicked at his knee, but he grabbed her ankle. Blinding light darted from the essence sconces on the walls and shot into her leg. The leg of her pants melted away as her skin burned, and she screamed from the unbearable pain.

He tutted and released her ankle. "I wouldn't do that if I were you."

Rory swallowed her whimper and pulled her leg back. She was smart enough to know she was no match for him. The only way to kill him would be from the back. Decapitation was a safer bet because the possibility of missing his heart from behind was too great.

"I'd love to sit and chat with you, but I think we should get to the fun part." He stood with a wink that made her skin crawl. "This is no supermystic movie where the villain gives a monologue to the hero about his hard life that led to his decisions."

Clasping his hands behind his back, he stared at a wall of knives. "My story is simple. My brother stole what was mine. I am returning the favor. The end."

This man was delusional. "Caius stole nothing from you. You stole your sister's life and her throne."

Gedeon looked unperturbed. "The Umbra throne should have been mine, but it went to him." He selected what looked to be an ice pick, and fear trickled down Rory's spine. "And then he shied away from me, acting as if he was better than I was our entire lives." Looking up, he shrugged. "And now I have his wife."

Anger would be better than the eerie calm he possessed.

She wanted to keep him talking to delay whatever he was going to do with the weapon in his hand. "I'm a *Fey*, and he inherited the ability to sense black souls without touching the mystic." She leaned forward with a taunting smile. "He was so powerful, he could even see the black soul of a *Royal*, and guess whose little black soul suffocated him the most?"

Gedeon pressed the ice pick under her chin. "Good. I hope he was tortured every night of our childhood when we slept in the same room." The prick of the cold steel made her heart race, and he smiled, pulling it back. "I wouldn't want to harm that sharp little tongue of yours. How else will you scream for help?"

The ice pick came down on her unburnt leg, and a howl of pain tore from her throat. She yanked against the chains as Gedeon laughed and withdrew his sadistic toy from her leg. Blood gushed, soaking into her leggings.

"*Seraphim*," she silently pleaded to the creators, begging them to hear her. "*Stop him.*"

The pain from the puncture wound slowly ebbed, as had the burns on her other leg, and Gedeon stood with a dramatic sigh. "No, not this one."

He strolled to the bathroom, and she heard the ice pick clatter as he tossed it into something and returned to the wall of knives. Choosing a smaller knife, he poked the end of the blade with his finger, seemingly satisfied as he returned to her.

As he kneeled, she resisted the urge to kick him again. Nothing she did would save her as long as he was here. Without warning, he sliced small cuts all over her face, and she forced herself to stay still so as not to stab herself in the eye. Salty tears mixed with the blood streaming down her face.

Shaking his head, he stood. "Not this one, either."

And the torture went on as he grabbed different tools, slicing and scraping the exposed skin on her arms, face, neck, and hands. She sobbed, hating herself for how she begged him to stop. He would just laugh and pick something else to try.

Rory called out for Caius, begging him to save her. In her moments of clarity, she hoped he didn't hear her because it would crush him, but in her delirious moments, she had no control of her mouth, her tears, her body, or her mind. All she knew was pain.

Gedeon particularly enjoyed stabbing her in the stomach. The first time, she screamed Caius' name, and Gedeon was beside himself with joy.

"I hope he's watching," Gedeon purred, running a knife down Rory's cheek. "Poor little brother, locked in Vincula with no way to get to you. Will he writhe on the ground as he experiences your pain and fear?"

"This is a great way to let off steam," Gedeon had told her at one point. *"Being king isn't easy, and sometimes you get the urge to destroy something."* Twirling his hand in the air, he'd said, *"This isn't the same, but it takes the edge off."*

Rory's vision had tunneled at his words. How many people did he torture over the last five-hundred years to curb his urges?

Thanks to her immortal healing, blood no longer poured from her body, but the sticky liquid coated everything. Her shirt was destroyed, as were the legs of her pants.

His eyes lit up as he stood. "I have just the thing for

you." After he walked away, she heard a door open, and the prospect of him leaving lit a fire under her. She had to get out.

"Don't move," he sang as the door closed.

CHAPTER 49

Stassi dragged her feet down the hallway, exhausted from her extended shift. Her talk with Sam put her behind on her duties *again*. The last time she ran late, the king choked her in his office, but today, one of the morning shift maids that usually delivered his food said the king was out for the day.

Stassi could have told the head maid she quit without finishing her duties, but that would leave them for someone else to do. Even though she wouldn't feel guilty once leaving The Capital, she couldn't do that to someone.

Eleven years as a palace maid, and she was quitting because a handsome *Angel* told her to. She would be lying if she said the man didn't consume her every thought while at work. Her memories of him didn't exist when at home, but here, she often walked with her head down to scan the floor for cats.

"I'm losing it," she muttered. *What would it be like to have someone like Sam interested in her?*

Not that she needed to worry about it. He looked like someone who liked his women young with perky bodies, and while she wasn't old, she was no spring chicken, nor was her body perky. Sighing, she put away her maid cart, lost in thought, as she meandered to the staff breakroom.

Stassi's parents would be overjoyed at the news of her quitting the palace. They were the best parents someone could ask for and were always supportive, but they hated the idea of her working in The Capital and losing her memories every day.

She understood their concern. It was strange at first, but she quickly adjusted to the sensation.

When she turned the corner, she crashed into someone and fell on her butt. A wolf stared back at her, and her first thought, because she was an idiot, was to say, "Sam?"

The wolf cocked his head, and the man she ran into helped her up. "Sam who?"

Realizing her mistake, she brushed off the back of her skirt. "No one."

"Excuse us," the man said. "We must be going."

She looked up then, recognizing him from somewhere. He and the wolf skirted around her as she searched her memory for the man's face, and when she remembered, she gasped. "Wait!"

The man and the wolf walked faster, and she jogged after them. He was The Butcher's father. Stassi saw him on the news after Aurora's arrest. If he was here, something was happening, and the way they were hurrying away from her only solidified her suspicions.

"I spoke with Samyaza!" she called out as she jogged toward them, cringing at how her voice bounced off the walls. Yelling his name wasn't her brightest moment.

The duo stopped and turned back to her, meeting her in the middle, and the man asked, "When?"

She tried not to look out of breath after such a short jog, but there was no way they missed her wheezing. "Today. Last night, I meant. He was here."

The man looked down at the wolf, and Stassi stepped back. "He told me about everything."

The man's wise eyes slid to her, assessing. "Why? Who are you?"

"My name is Stassi, and I've spoken with him a few times," she answered defensively. Her voice dropped to a whisper. "I was supposed to listen for anything important about the king, but I work nights, and the king wasn't around." The wolf chuffed, and she eyed him nervously. "I know where the stolen soul is, but that's it."

Both the man and wolf reacted to her words, and the man reached out to touch her shoulder. She side-stepped his grasp, and he held a hand up. "I'm sorry. I shouldn't have touched you. You said you know where Cora's soul is?"

She nodded. "It's in the king's office. He keeps it in a cabinet."

The two looked at each other, then back at her. "Do you know who Rory is?" the man asked.

Wasn't that what Sam called Aurora? "The Butcher?" she asked for clarification.

"Yes. Have you seen her here today?" His eyes looked hopeful, and Stassi felt terrible for telling him no.

"I haven't." She hesitated. "I heard another maid say the king is out today."

The man turned to the wolf and nodded. "Stassi, do you know if guards are near the king's office?"

"There are always two." The man nodded again, and she regretted what she was about to say, even before she said it. "I can take you there."

"I'm Patrick," the man said, tipping his head to the wolf. "This is Keith. He's a shifter. We would appreciate it if you took us most of the way. We will trail behind you, and when we get close, you leave. You don't need to get mixed up in this."

Stassi mapped out the way in her head. "When I adjust my bun and turn left, you stay straight and take the next right."

Patrick nodded, and the wolf looked side to side before shifting into a gorgeous man. Flustered, Stassi stepped back. "You should warn people before you do that."

"Next time, I'll growl," he replied with a charming grin. "Lead the way."

She considered stopping to grab her cleaning cart to look less conspicuous, but it was out of the way. Walking as nonchalant as possible, she made her way to the king's office, listening to the footsteps of the men who trailed far behind her in case they stopped.

When she approached the turnoff, she grabbed her bun and adjusted it, but before she could turn, Tag rounded the corner leading to the king's office. *Why was he still here?* He worked the night shift.

"Stassi," he said with a hint of surprise.

"Hey, Tag. What are you still doing here?" *Was her voice calm, or did she sound like someone gearing up to tell a lie?* She was terrible at lying and ended up saying something ridiculous if put on the spot.

"I could ask you the same thing," he said with an amiable smile.

Fiddling with her skirt, she considered pretending to faint because he would carry her to the infirmary and away from Patrick and Keith, but instead, she rambled, and that was never good.

"Last night was chilly, and I forgot my jacket at home," she said. *Shut up, Stassi. Just walk away.* "Luna let me borrow her jacket because she said it was hot. How can anyone be hot in this place? It's freezing." Why didn't she just say she was looking for another maid? She wanted to weep, but she was too far in now, and he was watching her with suspicion. Or maybe it was amusement.

Seraphim, *please let it be amusement.*

"Well," she laughed nervously, wondering where in the hell she was going with this story. "I was cleaning the king's office, and it was hot in there, so I took the jacket off and forgot to grab it before I left."

No. No. No. No. No. No. Why did she say that? He was going to take her exactly where Patrick and Keith told her not to go. She was never lying again. It never resulted in anything positive.

She held her breath, and when Tag laughed, she tried to release it without being obvious. "You are something else," he said, still laughing. "You can run in and get it. The king isn't here."

"Thank you," she said, marching to her death. Keith and Patrick must have hidden when Tag appeared. She glanced over her shoulder but didn't see them.

They saw where she was going to turn, meaning they could find the office and didn't need her help anymore. She would pretend to look for the jacket, say she must have forgotten it somewhere else, and leave without incident.

She hoped.

～

Dume headed for the stairs to search the second floor of the east wing after having no luck on the main floor. He poked his head into every room he passed but found nothing except a few maids cleaning empty rooms.

He grabbed the knob of the last door in the hallway but remembered it was the head guard's office. Before he could run up the stairs, the door swung open, and a young *Aatxe* guard stepped into the hall, closing the door behind her.

She caught sight of Dume walking away and called out to him. "I'm sorry, sir, but I need you to stop and show me your badge or pass. No civilians are allowed within The Capital without one."

Dammit. He pivoted on his heel with a flirtatious smile. "Hey. I don't recognize you. Have you worked at the palace long?" Women hit on him often, and while he never gave much thought to his looks, he hoped they got him out of the deep shit he'd stepped in.

The guard tossed her red braid over her shoulder with narrowed eyes. "Show me your badge or pass."

He was screwed.

Holding up a finger, he reached into his back pocket, feigned confusion, and checked his other ones. He pulled out his wallet and pretended to search through it. "I must have dropped it," he lied. "I'll run back to the gates and have them print a new one."

Before he could leave, she grabbed hold of his elbow. "I don't think so." People usually believed *Aatxe* because they're known for their honesty. Unfortunately, they're also loyal and thorough employees. "I will take your mystic card and call the gates myself, but until then, you're going into a holding cell."

Lauren told them to incapacitate the guards, but he

couldn't bring himself to hurt an innocent. Once in the cell, he would request to speak to Adila. If what Rory told him about the Scales of Justice was true, she was on their side. Maybe she'd even help him look.

When they stepped into the palace courtyard and turned toward the judgment chambers, Adila herself and another woman were walking in their direction.

Dume looked at the guard holding his arm. "I need to see the Scales of Justice."

She pushed him faster. "I don't know what you're playing at, but I can't let you near her."

Fine. "Adila!" he yelled, making the *Royal* turn, and the guard dragged him along faster. He was bigger than her, but all *Aatxe* were strong, no matter their gender. "I'm friends with Sam and Lauren," he shouted over his shoulder. "It's important that I speak to you."

"Please, stop and let him speak," Adila said to the guard holding him, who looked at Dume curiously.

She steered him over to the *Royal* and her companion. "You have a message for me from the commander?" Adila inquired regally.

Dume's eyes slid from the guard to the other woman standing beside Adila. "It's best we speak privately," he said carefully. "It concerns a newly released inmate."

Adila's lips tightened, and she nodded. "Heather," she addressed her friend before turning to the guard. "Jenessa. Please, excuse us."

Heather looked at Dume with narrowed eyes but nodded and walked to the palace with Jenessa.

"Follow me," Adila said and hurried into a back door of the judgment chambers. Once inside, she took him through a series of doors before they stepped into a dark hallway underground, lined with old, rusted cells, and pulled out her phone to use as a flashlight. Dume did the same.

"Is this a dungeon?" he asked incredulously.

"Yes," she replied as she continued down the hall. "It hasn't been used in a very long time." She took another few turns, pulled him into a small, dark room, and closed the door. "What's happened?"

Dume shined his light around the room and shuddered. "Gedeon has Rory," he explained. "We can't reach Sam because he's in Vincula, and a group of us came with Lauren to look for her. A guard caught me and was hauling me to a holding cell."

Adila listened intently and when he was finished, said, "We must find her. If Gedeon kills her, Caius won't survive it."

Dume felt the blood drain from his face. If one of them dies, does it kill the other?" *If Caius died, would it kill Rory?*

Adila was already opening the door to leave. "No, but the *Aeternum* bond is strong, and Caius won't want to live in a realm where she does not exist."

Dume hurried after her. "Do you know where he would keep her?"

Adila shook her head, making her golden waves sway over her back. "No, but his office and chambers are a good place to start."

"Lauren was going to Gedeon's chambers to look. Is there anywhere else you can think of?" he asked.

"Then we'll check his office," she replied. "They're next to each other, and we can make sure he hasn't hurt Lauren while we're at it."

Dume blew out a breath and took long strides to keep

up with her. "I don't think this is a good idea. I think we should split up."

"It doesn't matter what you think," she deadpanned. "I know my brother, and his rooms are probably the most secure locations in this palace. If he has her, she is there or in the area."

"Lauren said if we find him to lie low and call her. We can't just barge into his office."

"How stupid do you think I am?" Adila scoffed. "Gedeon's guards might tell him everything I do, but they're still required to follow my orders. If I tell them there is a problem somewhere and demand they follow me, they must do it." She shrugged. "They'll just report the incident to him later. We might not be the ones to fight Gedeon, but we can at least clear the way for Lauren."

She turned and walked away, leaving Dume no choice but to run after her.

CHAPTER 50

The shackles dug into Rory's wrists as she yanked on the chains. Half of the hair from her ponytail hung in her face, and she tried to shake it out of her eyes.

Her ponytail.

Since cutting her hair, the shorter front strands refused to stay up, and she had to use hairpins to keep them back.

Hairpins she could use to pick the locks.

Now to figure out how to remove them from her hair.

Craning her neck, she inspected the chains. They hung from a hook higher on the wall. In her current position, they stretched her arms to the point of pain, but if she stood, there would be slack.

Pressing her body against the wall, she dug her heels into the floor, but the blood made them slide around. "*Shit.*" There had to be a way.

The pools of blood were mostly isolated to the area under her body, with only droplets further out. When she spread her legs wide, her body dropped lower, and the weight ripped the crotch of her leggings. She was thankful

Gedeon hadn't touched her there, but she didn't want her exposure giving him ideas if she couldn't escape in time.

After wrapping her hands around the chains, she lifted herself enough to gain her footing. Her arms screamed as they took the brunt of her body weight, but she managed to stand and leaned over to find the pins in her hair.

Her fingers passed over one of the thin pieces of metal, and hot, happy tears pricked the backs of her eyes as she pulled it out and studied the cuff on her wrist. From this angle, her hands didn't come close enough to touch.

As she twisted to see her options, the door to Gedeon's room slammed open, and he stormed through, dragging a lifeless body by the leg. It didn't take Rory long to recognize Lauren, and she lunged forward on instinct. "*What did you do?*" she screamed in a panicked fury.

One of Gedeon's guards must have caught her when she and Sam were doing their rounds last night.

Lauren looked like a fresh corpse, but Rory caught the slight rise and fall of her friend's chest. She forced herself not to react in case Gedeon thought the *Angel* was dead. Lauren also had immortal healing, and if Rory could distract the Lux King long enough, Lauren could heal and escape.

Gedeon dropped Lauren's leg and crossed the room in seconds. Rory tried to back up when she saw the pure rage in his eyes, but he wrapped his hand around her neck, pushing her up the wall. The lack of airflow made her panic, but when he called on his searing light and pushed it into her, she wished for death.

Her throat was raw, but it didn't stop her screams as she convulsed under his hold.

"I'm done playing," he sneered, leaning closer. "I will enjoy carving my name into your dead body before having it delivered to Caius." He said her mate's name like it was vinegar on his tongue.

Another shot of light covered her entire body, and she felt it in her soul. "*Caius!*" she screamed over and over, sobbing. "Please, spare him," she begged the *Seraphim* in the aether. "Save him."

She couldn't hold on any longer. There was no time left for Caius to come and no golden child to save her.

"Caius," she whispered under her breath. "I'll meet you in the aether."

CHAPTER 51

THE VOID

*After seeing the redhead in a vision, nothing else existed for Caius except a darkness invading him like a sea of power. Was he moving? He couldn't tell, but he never wanted to leave. Here, he **was** darkness and power.*

__"Caius, help me,"__ a voice sobbed, crying out his name.

He wandered through the void, following the screams, unable to walk away. Whoever it was, their throat was raw but not enough to muffle their pain.

As her screams grew louder, the darkness faded, and clarity pushed at the recesses of his mind.

The woman cried out for him, and he broke into a run, needing to find her.

__"Caius,"__ she said in a broken whisper, ripping at his heart, but time stood still when her voice faded as she said, __"I'll meet you in the aether."__

__Rory.__

***

Vincula

Caius lay on his bathroom floor, staring at the ceiling.

Rory. Rory. Rory. Rory.

Her name echoed through his mind like a sacred chant.

He tried to understand what happened as he picked himself up off the floor. Remembering the vision of the redhead, he cursed.

A long whoosh escaped him when he stared at his reflection. The veins that had once vanished were back, covering everything but his face.

The time on his clock showed it was well into the morning. *Did he dream it all?*

If Rory was still in danger, he would have another vision, yet he couldn't shake the sense of *wrongness*.

After getting dressed, he grabbed a glass of water from the bar cart, but it shattered on the ground when he fell to his knees and screamed at the vision and pain assaulting him.

He couldn't breathe or move his arms, and white fire burned through him, causing more pain than Caius thought possible. Gedeon's face appeared in his line of sight. "I will enjoy carving my name into your dead body before having it delivered to Caius."

Caius was thrown back into his own body as a guttural sound unlike any he'd ever heard erupted from within him. His mate was dying.

The shadows from all corners of the realms rushed into him as he screamed her name.

Gedeon would not take her from him.

As fast as the shadows surged into him, they left, detonating his body until there was nothing left.

Sam stood in line at the cafe in Vincula, waiting on his coffee. The dark liquid coveted by so many was disgusting, but he'd been awake for over twenty-four hours, and even *Angels* needed sleep to function.

The inmates nearest the cafe windows had their attention on something outside, drawing his eyes to the street. Everyone stared in the same direction, and he sighed.

What now?

When he stepped onto the cobblestone sidewalk, he expected to see a fight or something of equal caliber. What he did not expect to see was Lenora running down the street, yelling his name.

Everything in him filled with a sense of doom as he ran to meet her.

"Sam!" Her eyes were wide with the beginnings of hysteria. "I was wrong! I was wrong!"

He grabbed her shoulders gently to calm her down. "Breathe." The woman wasn't easily rattled, and his hair stood on end. "What were you wrong about?"

"It's not her," she told him. "I couldn't see it before. I thought it was Rory, but it's not her."

He understood her words but not their meaning. "Who is not Rory?"

They were plunged into darkness as the realm shook beneath their feet.

He tucked Lenora into his chest and covered her head with his body, unsure of what was happening.

The dusky morning sky was gone, the candles illuminating the sidewalks and shops were snuffed out, and he couldn't see anything as if he were blindfolded.

Screams filled the air, and Sam barked orders at the legion members within hearing distance, telling them to collect who they could, seat them together to ensure their safety, and find their way to the nearest shops for candles and matches.

His legion spoke to the inmates, trying and failing to calm them down.

"Caius," Lenora whispered.

"You thought Caius was Rory in one of your visions?" he asked her, keeping his voice even. If his brother was in danger, he would drop everything to help him.

"No," she replied as her voice regained its strength. "Caius did this. He broke the barrier."

Sam pulled back, ready to take flight, but Lenora stopped him. "You must save her."

"Who?" He wouldn't ask again, not when Caius broke the sky and was going to Gedeon.

"The maid," she insisted, stopping his entire existence. "The maid holding my daughter's soul." Tears slid down Lenora's cheeks as she whispered, "Only the golden child can save her. *Only you* can save her."

Sam shot into the sky.

CHAPTER 52

ERDIKOA

Stassi pretended to look around the king's office for the alleged jacket, kicking herself for choking under pressure. She stood up and shrugged with a nervous laugh. "I must have left it somewhere else," she told Tag as she walked toward the door.

"I can help you find it," he offered.

Before she could respond, the guard outside yelled for Tag. "We got two wanderers out here."

"Stay here," Tag ordered and jogged across the room and into the hall, leaving the door open. The king's office was gigantic, and it was hard to hear from her current position. She dashed toward the door to find out what was going on.

"Our apologies, man. We're a little lost," Keith's voice said smoothly.

"What business do you have in the palace?" Tag asked, folding his arms across his chest.

As she was prone to do, Stassi made a stupid decision

and stuck her head through the door with a wide smile. "Hi, Dad! What are you two doing here?"

From the look on Patrick and Keith's faces, they didn't think she was still there. It shouldn't have taken as long as it did, but Tag kept asking her about trivial things, forcing her to stop and answer.

She stepped around the guards and gave Keith a hug. "You need to leave," he whispered against her ear, and she leaned back with a fake smile plastered across her face.

"Our interviews are today, honey," Patrick replied without missing a beat. "A guard told us where to go, but we must have taken a wrong turn somewhere."

The other guard shifted, glancing at Tag. "No one is permitted into the palace without a pass. We need to see yours."

Keith's eyes shifted to Stassi. "Hey, sis, why don't you walk us back out? Your shift should be over by now."

Oh, no. Stassi stared at Keith with wide eyes.

"You told me you were an only child," Tag said, shifting his attention to her. It was one of his many questions while she searched for the imaginary jacket. He turned back to the other guard. "Seize them."

Tag grabbed her arm in a bruising grip and slung her into the office. "What are you playing at?" he demanded. "Who are those men?"

She shook like a leaf and tried to loosen his grip with her other hand. A snarl sounded from the hall, and they both turned in time to see Keith clamping down on the other guard's neck, shaking him like a rag doll.

Fear paralyzed Stassi as she watched someone die for the first time in her life. She'd never even been to a funeral. Keith looked up with blood dripping from his muzzle and ran through the office door. In slow motion, Stassi watched Tag drop her arm, rip open his button-down shirt, and remove a gun from the holster on his chest. *Guns weren't allowed in The Capital.*

She screamed Keith's name, but it was too late. Stassi watched in horror as the bullet hit him in the chest. The wolf flew back, hitting the floor with a whimper, and his body slid across the marble, leaving a trail of blood in its wake.

Patrick ran through the office door and threw his arms wide, knocking Tag back with a gust of air. *A **Sylph**.*

The sounds of Stassi's terror filled the large office as she ran forward and hit her knees. She pressed her hand over the wound, unsure what to do. A choked sob was the only sound she could make as she watched the life leave Keith's body. His wolfish eyes stared straight ahead, unmoving, and when his chest fell under her hands, it didn't rise again.

Another gunshot went off, and she flattened herself on the ground, covering her ears.

She cried, fearing she would be next. Patrick approached her, holding the gun with blood spatter on his hands and shirt.

"He's dead," she cried, reaching for Keith as Patrick pulled her to her feet. The wolf's blood coated her hands and dress, and she could feel it on the sides of her head.

"I-I didn't see the gun in time," she said, going into shock. "*Keith!*"

She dropped to the floor again and shook him. He couldn't be dead. *But he was.* "I'm sorry. I'm so sorry."

Patrick hauled her up and held the sides of her face. "You need to leave," he said with tears lining his eyes. "I need to hide his body. If they find it, his family will be in danger."

"He's dead," she cried again. She wasn't made for this. Her day-to-day didn't include fighting guards and watching people die.

Patrick tried to soothe her. "I know. Stassi, I need you to leave. *Now*."

As she nodded, Patrick jogged into the hallway, picking up Keith's lifeless body. Stassi's eyes snagged on the cabinet where the pink soul was hidden.

She checked the hallway to ensure no one was coming before running across the room, and when she reached for the cabinet, the palace shook. Through the window, she saw the sky blacken. Terrified screams and shouts echoed through the hallways, sending chills down her spine.

She didn't know what was happening, but before leaving, she turned back toward the cabinet, refusing to let Keith's death be in vain.

CHAPTER 53

THE BARRIER

Summoned by Her broken cries, the King of Monsters fractured his gilded cage and emerged from the darkness, no longer a man but a beast forged in anguish and hate.

The realms trembled as he ripped them apart, and no man nor monster could keep him from getting to Her.

CHAPTER 54

ERDIKOA

Gedeon released Rory's neck, and she fought to drag air into her lungs as her feet slipped, causing the chains to yank on her arms. She fell with a silent scream, her throat no longer capable of producing sounds.

Pain encompassed her very being as she sat on her knees with her arms strung wide, watching the darkness take over, encasing them in a hellish coffin.

Was she dying? She hoped so.

The darkness parted, and there he was, a beautiful nightmare with black veins emerging from his blackened eyes. He looked like a monster, but she wasn't afraid; she felt safe.

At least her mind comforted her in her last moments, allowing her to see that which she loved the most.

Caius' rage was a tangible thing, even in her dreams, and he launched himself at Gedeon. The latter looked deranged, pawing at the air. *What was he doing?*

"You think I'd allow you access to the light after what

you've done to my mate?" Caius growled as if possessed by Orcus himself.

"What's wrong, dear brother?" Gedeon asked with a sickening smile. "She heals nicely. You can't even tell she was used."

A shadow slammed the Lux King to the ground, pinning him in place as Caius took measured steps toward him. When he stood over his brother, he crouched down and grabbed his chin, yanking it to look at him.

Shadows restrained Gedeon's body, and Caius' voice was lethal. "You will not fucking speak of her again." Gedeon laughed maniacally, and Rory flinched away from the noise. Caius punched him in the face, and his brother's head snapped to the side, spraying blood across the floor.

He continued to laugh in Caius' face. "Even now, you can't bring yourself to kill me." His laughter died down, and his face screwed up, but it was too dark for Rory to make out his expression. "You're *weak*. The *Seraphim* would never willingly give Vincula to someone like you. It belonged to *me*, and you stole it," he spat.

Caius' hands slid through the blood near his brother's mouth as he held his head still, and Rory could tell her husband's control was hanging on by a thread. "*You* have always been the weak one, but I didn't take you as the stupid one, too," Caius said and slammed Gedeon's head against the floor with a vicious smile. "If you think anyone in the realms can change fate, then you have bigger problems than not inheriting the Umbra throne."

Rory flattened her body against the wall, watching Caius play with his prey. He was devastating. A calm fury rolled off him, and the blackness in his eyes was something to behold.

She didn't know why her mind conjured him this way, but she was glad for it.

"Fuck you," Gedeon tried to say, but Caius' fingers didn't allow his jaw much movement.

Rory watched her husband stare at his brother, searching for a shred of decency. "Did you love us at all?" he asked, and Rory saw a hint of sorrow in his eyes.

Gedeon laughed loudly, and Caius slammed his head against the floor again. "Is this the part where we get to the root of my anger and repair our relationship?" he asked, mocking Caius with a dramatic frown. If Rory wasn't chained, she'd slit his throat for treating her mate that way, even in this false reality.

Gedeon's laughter faded, and his voice deadened. "Kill me and be done with it." She could barely see his eyes slide to look at her through the dark, and his white teeth flashed. "Do think of me and the fun we had together when you fuck my brother, won't you?"

Rory watched in slow motion as Caius' restraint snapped. He snatched Gedeon into the air by the neck. "You don't speak to her. You don't even think about her, or I won't grant you the solace of death. I'll keep you locked in a fucking iron box with no access to light and let you lay in your own shit for eternity." Caius leaned his head to the side slowly. "I wonder what it's like to live an immortal life without food or water, drowning in a coffin full of your own piss but never dying?"

Gedeon choked under his brother's hold, unable to move because the shadows still bound him. His face had a bluish hue, and his eyes were wide with fright. A sickening satisfaction filled Rory, and she let a smile of her own spread wide. He deserved to suffer for everything he'd done.

This felt real, and she let herself hope it was. Had Caius really made it in time? She paid closer attention to her surroundings, examining herself the best she could. Her mind wasn't as muddled anymore, and her body was healing.

If this was real, why wasn't Gedeon fighting back? Could Caius really cut off his access to the sun? She had to be dreaming.

But then Turney's words came back to her. *The day will disappear.*

Caius opened his hand, dropping Gedeon to the ground, and the latter inched around like a worm on his stomach with his body bound as he gasped for air. "How did it feel?" he rasped, looking at Caius.

Caius didn't answer, only watched as his brother coughed for air, but his silence didn't deter Gedeon from talking. "How did it feel when Atarah's blood coated your hands? How did it feel when you realized I would be the new king?"

Caius kicked his brother in the side, making him fly across the floor with a groan. "You don't deserve to utter our sister's name," he sneered and grabbed a fistful of Gedeon's hair, bending his head back. "You were never good enough to be one of us. We tried to include you, but you were vile, even as a child."

Rory jumped a little when her husband slammed Gedeon's face into the floor. With her head spinning, she couldn't tell if she was dreaming or awake. *The soulscapes felt real,* she reminded herself. Maybe this was a deathscape.

"I should have killed you in your fucking sleep," Gedeon said, rolling onto his back. "I had planned to when we were seven."

With every word Gedeon said, Caius' veins grew in number. The blackness in his irises bled into the whites of his eyes and spilled over, cracking his skin.

"Mother found out and moved me to a different room. Do you remember?" Gedeon sighed dramatically. "I was sloppy and left the kitchen knife under my pillow, and a maid found it." Shrugging, he smirked at Caius. "Had I succeeded, our sister might have lived."

Caius ignored him and walked to the knife wall, inspecting each tool, and Gedeon tried to inch toward Rory while her mate was distracted.

The chains held Rory in place, and she whimpered, feeling trapped.

Caius whipped around with a knife in his hand, shot across the room, and rammed a knee into Gedeon's spine. Fisting his brother's hair, Caius yanked the Lux King's head back, baring his neck.

Caius held the long blade to his brother's throat and leaned forward until his mouth was near his ear. "When you're alone in the pits of hell, wondering where you went wrong." He twisted Gedeon's head to look directly at Rory. "Her. *That's* where you went wrong. Touching my mate was your fatal mistake, and you will regret it every day as you burn for eternity."

As the ache in her arms became unbearable, Rory pushed to stand, forgetting about the slippery blood on the floor, and when her foot shot out from under her, she fell and screamed in pain as something in her shoulder ripped.

Caius turned to her, and his eyes widened with fear. Dropping the knife, he ran over and snapped Gedeon's neck to incapacitate him. The binding shadows dissolved when Caius threw Gedeon's body to the side to get to his wife.

Rory looked from her tormentor's lifeless body to Caius, whose body was covered in moving black lines. The veins were a living embodiment of his emotions, and the angrier he got, the more they grew.

Was she still dreaming? It felt real, and she whimpered, unsure of her reality.

"Rory, can you hear me?" Caius' soft voice warmed her, and he cupped her face gently. "Fuck. Hold on."

"I can't," she rasped, the sound barely audible. Other than her shoulder, her physical body was fine, but the Lux King had broken her mind, and at her admission, the shadows raged around them.

"Yes, you can," he said, inspecting the shackles on her wrists.

She didn't know how he did it, but they opened, and her body dropped like a bag of broken bones. Before she hit the ground, he caught her and held her to his chest, rocking back and forth.

His lips murmured against her hair, "I made it. I'm here. Please, come back to me."

She clutched his shirt and pressed her face into the crook of his neck. "Are you real?"

Smoothing her bloody hair away from her face, he gently lifted her chin to look at him. "Yes, baby. I'm real." His voice cracked, and her bottom lip trembled at the emotions raging between them.

She dropped her forehead and cried into his shoulder. "I thought I was dead," she rasped, anchoring herself to him.

Slowly, he moved back to look at her and met her watery eyes. "You think I would let you die and leave me here?" His lips pressed against her forehead. "The *Seraphim* couldn't stop me from getting to you. What makes you think death could?"

The black receded from his eyes, and when he leaned in to kiss her lips, they were back to a brilliant gold. This kiss wasn't chaste and fleeting. It was filled with love and longing. They desperately tried to make up for stolen time and the lives they almost lost. The soulscape didn't compare, and it never would. Pressing her body against his, she tried to reassure herself he wouldn't disappear.

"I love you," he murmured when he pulled back and rested his forehead against hers. "I can't believe I almost lost you."

She kissed the tear that trailed down his cheek. "I love you, too." Her fingers stroked the back of his neck, and she kissed him again, unable to stop touching him, afraid someone would take him from her.

When they separated again, she gained her bearings and looked around. It was still dark, despite him being calm. *Why were the shadows still surrounding them?* "What happened to the light?"

Caius withdrew the shadows that covered the essence lights, and Rory instinctively clutched him tighter when the light bounced off the wall of knives. She turned to where Gedeon lay and froze before searching the room frantically. "Where is he?" His body was gone.

Caius stood with her still in his arms and placed her gently on her feet. "His neck shouldn't have healed that fast," he said, perplexed. Shadows started bumping into things, and the sound of knives falling to the floor made her yelp. "He's probably hiding somewhere to finish healing," Caius guessed, furiously raking a hand through his hair.

"He has his power back," Rory said, shaking at the memory of the liquid fire scorching her skin.

Caius' face softened, and he engulfed her in his arms. "Hey," he soothed. "He doesn't have his power anymore. He won't hurt you."

After a few calming breaths, she met his intense gaze. "How do you know that?"

"There are no more suns." He looked guilty at the fact.

Rory stared at him, not comprehending. "What do you mean?"

Caius' bright eyes were in direct contrast with the dark lines covering his face, amplifying the emotion displayed there. "Exactly what I said. When I came through the barrier, the suns disappeared. Without access to them, he has no power, and he knows he can't win against me without it."

"We need to find him before he gets away," Rory urged as the ramifications of Gedeon walking around hit her.

Caius grabbed both sides of Rory's face gently. "You are my priority, and if you are terrified and shaking, I'm not leaving you. You come first, always."

A crash sounded, and they both spun around, prepared to fight, but the sight of Lauren stumbling toward them catapulted Rory into action. With everything that transpired, her mind hadn't fully caught up to reality yet, and she'd forgotten Gedeon dragged the *Angel* into the room.

Rory almost cried at the sight. "You healed." She moved her hands over Lauren to inspect for lingering injuries.

"I was in his room, and he walked in," Lauren told them, panting. "He electrocuted me, and I passed out." She looked around the room. "Where is he?"

"He got away," Caius said grimly, absentmindedly

rubbing a soothing hand down Rory's back. "Stay with her, and I'll finish him."

"I'm not staying here," Rory protested. *Like hell he would leave her again.* "My body healed. He has no power and is no more a threat to me than any other man." She steeled her spine and forced her body not to tremble. Caius glared at her but wisely said nothing.

Lauren pushed past them. "There's no time to argue. The others are here, and we need to find them before Gedeon does."

The others?

Rory stopped breathing when she understood. Swiping the knife Caius had thrown on the floor, she bolted toward the door closest to where Gedeon fell, not thinking about anything but getting to her friends.

Fear was a strange thing. Fear for her own well-being kept her subdued, but the second she realized her friends were in danger, a switch flipped.

No one would go through what she went through.

"*Rory!*" Caius yelled behind her as she sprinted down the stairs of the corridor.

Caius and Lauren's footsteps pounded after her, but the mortality of her friends raced through her mind, and she pushed harder.

She heard Gedeon's voice through the cracked doorway. "*Put her down!*"

The three of them burst through the door of Gedeon's office, and Rory looked around wildly. Across the room, a maid held a jar filled with a beautiful pink soul, and Rory stopped in her tracks.

Cora.

The maid's face paled as Gedeon closed in on her, but

instead of handing over the jar, she grabbed the lid with shaky fingers and ripped it off. The realm stood still, and Rory stared in awe as Cora's soul rose from the jar, twirled airily around the woman's arm, and caressed her cheek.

Months ago, when Rory released the trapped souls she found in the *Merrow's* apartment, that didn't happen. The souls went directly toward the aether.

Cora's soul finally left the woman's side and floated skyward, leaving everyone to stare.

"*She was mine!*" Gedeon thundered, his face filled with rage. "*And you took her from me!*"

What happened next took seconds, but it felt like a lifetime as Rory watched the horror unfold.

She didn't know how Gedeon got a knife, but he raised it high and stabbed the woman in the chest. Her screams of fear and pain set Rory in motion, but Caius grabbed her, pushed her toward Lauren, and ran at his brother. Shadows threw Gedeon back, and he slammed into a nearby table.

Before Lauren could touch her, Rory took off running, catching up to Caius with ease.

"You fucking bastard," Caius growled when they reached his brother. Rory careened around her husband and jumped on top of Gedeon, dropping the knife beside her.

Shadows bound his body, and Caius stayed back, giving Rory the kill. They both wanted to exact their vengeance, but after everything Rory suffered at Gedeon's hand, her mate gifted her the honor.

Gedeon's eyes were wide with unhinged delirium, and he bared his teeth. "She took my mate from me," he shouted.

Rory's fist hit his nose with a satisfying crunch. "*You* took my sister. She was only a child," she cried, delivering blow after blow. Despite wanting to, she couldn't beat him to death and picked up the knife, pressing the tip into the flesh over his heart. "This is for every person you took to that room." She pushed the tip of the knife into his chest.

He cried out in pain, throwing his badly beaten head back. Leaning forward, she used her body to put more pressure on the handle. "This is for Atarah and Cora." The knife cut deeper, and she delighted in his screams.

Sitting back, she tugged the knife from his chest, and his whimpers made her lip curl. He deserved more pain than that, but the others needed her.

Rory dreamed about this moment for eleven years, but it didn't feel right. Turning to Caius, she found him watching the Lux King with barely restrained anger raging in his eyes.

Because of Gedeon, Caius had lost everything: his sisters, his freedom, and his reputation. He even almost lost himself, and if anyone deserved to end the Lux King's life, it was him.

She beckoned him closer and held out the knife. He wrapped his hand around the handle and softly grabbed Rory's chin, kissing her deeply before turning his fury on the barely recognizable face of his twin brother.

"And this is for my wife," he snarled and slammed the blade deep into Gedeon's beating heart.

Rory refused to look away until the bastard was dead. Caius' hand still gripped the knife, and when Gedeon's pulse faded and his breathing stopped, he let go and helped her stand.

She buried her face in her husband's chest, and he kissed the side of her head, murmuring his appreciation and admiration for her.

Suddenly, the ground shook, and they stumbled as Sam appeared out of thin air and slammed onto the floor in a graceful crouch.

The *Angel's* eyes searched the room until they landed on Lauren crouching next to the maid on the floor. At the sight of the knife protruding from her chest, he released a roar so powerful that everyone fell to their knees, forced into submission.

Lauren scrambled out of the way as Sam crossed the room and scooped the woman into his arms. The maid turned her eyes to his, and her lips moved, speaking words only for him to hear.

Whatever she said, it *broke* him.

Three sets of golden wings flared from his back as he clutched the woman in his arms, and when he screamed to the aether, a golden light blasted from him, throwing the others back. As fast as it appeared, the light was snuffed out, smothered by what Rory could only describe as the night sky. A moving entity, black as night and filled with thousands of stars covered Sam, cutting him off from their view.

Rory felt the pressure holding her down dissolve, and Caius crushed her to his chest, but she couldn't take her eyes off the mysterious *thing*. "We need to help him."

Lauren grounded her, placing a firm hand on her shoulder. "He is safe. You will see."

She trusted Lauren, but it's not every day the sky fell on someone. "What is that?"

Lauren looked heart-stricken as she stared at the dark entity. "That is a selfless man losing the only thing he has ever allowed himself to want."

The woman was clearly important to Sam, and the *Seraphim* ripped her away from him. Rory's heart broke into tiny shards. Everything that happened over the last twenty-four hours was too much, and her body went limp.

Caius held her up, murmuring soothing words against her hair.

Could all of this have been prevented if she had never made her first kill? Would the pain and suffering have ended with Cora?

Adila and Dume ran into the room, and Rory turned slowly. Dume hurried toward her, and when he was close, Caius transferred her from his arms to Dume's. "You're okay," she whispered, not trusting herself to say more.

He nodded against her shoulder. "So are you."

Sam held Anastasia in his arms, watching the blood soak through her dress. He removed the knife and covered the wound with his hand.

He could save her. He had to.

"Son," his father's familiar voice said, and Sam looked up, staring at the man who had let this happen.

"She was innocent," he shouted, and when he felt her body take a last, shuddering breath, everything ceased to exist.

He watched her essence flicker out, and her sunflower-yellow soul ascended toward the aether. The sound that tore from his throat was not of these realms, and the very ground he kneeled on trembled with it.

Not caring about the consequences, he held his hand above the yellow orb and pushed it back into her body. Pressing down on Anastasia's chest, he forced his power into her, healing her wound and granting her a second life. It was forbidden, but he refused to watch her die.

He hung his head and cried with relief, his tears salting

the woman who deserved life more than most. She was *good*. The type of person who tried to sneak stray cats home and risked her life to free a soul she had no connection to. He didn't see her release Cora, but Lenora said as much, and the empty jar on the ground was proof enough.

His father observed silently, and Sam stared at Anastasia as her chest rose with the first signs of life.

"Thank you," he whispered, unable to look away from her sweet face. His father could have stopped him, *should* have stopped him, but he didn't.

"I have watched you move through life as a shell of the male you used to be. I know having to kill Michael destroyed you." His father's voice cracked, and Sam raised his head. "But I never imagined you could not put yourself back together." The king of Aravoth stared at Anastasia's sleeping form. "I cannot watch you go through that again, and your mother would never forgive me for allowing your mate to die."

Sam's wings flared wide at his father's words. "*Seraphim* do not have mates."

His father smiled sadly. "Every day, your mother visited the Hall of Fates to watch you, and every day her heart broke more and more. She knew a piece of your soul had died and petitioned Moira to grant you a mate. Her hope was that a mate would help you heal and give you a reason to live, not just exist."

Sam gazed down at his perfect match, and his heart soared, knowing she was his, but when his father covered his mouth and looked away, terror filled him.

"What else?" Sam demanded. "What are you not telling me?" Nothing came easy for him, and he should have known this would be no different.

"Son," his father said, clearing his throat. "You cannot stay in the realms. You agreed to the stipulations of coming here, and you put everyone in danger." His dark eyes trailed to Anastasia. "And you broke the cardinal rule. Moira will not allow you to stay."

Moira was the Fate of Aravoth. She controlled the destiny of every being in the kingdom and all realms under its jurisdiction.

Sam's heart shattered into a million pieces when he realized the implications. One had to petition their kingdom's Fate for permission to leave the aether. Moira granted him leave under two conditions: no one could know what he was, and he was never to use his true power. He did both on top of granting life to the dead.

When he saw Anastasia dying on the floor, he no longer had control of himself, and when she whispered her final words, he unleashed his power. If not for his father's arrival, trapping Sam's power with his own, the realms would no longer exist.

"May I say goodbye?" he asked in a broken voice, unable to look his father in the eye.

His father's power receded, and Sam stood with his mate in his arms to say goodbye to the only true friends he'd ever known.

CHAPTER 55

The darkness surrounding Sam disappeared, and Caius reached for Rory again, tucking her into his side. The threat against her died with Gedeon, but he needed her close after seeing her chained to a wall and tortured within an inch of her sanity.

Sam stood with the maid in his arms, and beside him was a man the same size as him, with jet-black wings covering his face, leaving only his mouth and black eyes exposed. Two large black wings protruded from his back, and another set of wings covered his legs. The skin on his arms and chin was white as snow, and Caius stared in awe.

"Aemas," he concluded with certainty.

The *Seraph* tipped his head. "Umbra King." He turned to Lauren and held out his arms with a fatherly smile. "Jophiel."

"Old man," she drawled, stepping into his embrace.

Aemas' laugh shook the room, startling the others. "Lora misses you."

Sadness flickered across Lauren's features as she stepped back. "Give her a hug for me."

Dume leaned over and whispered, "Who is Aemas, and why did he call her Jophiel?"

"I'll tell you later." Rory shrugged out of Caius' hold and trotted across the room toward Sam. "Is she alive?"

The others in the room watched with bated breaths. They all saw what she did for Rory and her family. This complete stranger freed Cora's soul, and if she died, Rory would mourn her like a loved one, and Caius ached at the thought.

The woman stirred in Sam's arms and looked at him with groggy eyes.

His mouth curled into a tender smile. "Anastasia."

Rory stared at the soft expression on the *Angel's* face with a look of awe. They'd never seen him act this way before.

"Commander," Anastasia replied with a wry smile of her own.

Caius saw something pass between them, and he knew something was wrong.

"I heard everything," she told Sam. "I couldn't wake up, but I could hear you."

Sam's eyes closed, and his agony hit them like a wave, almost knocking Caius to his knees again. Anastasia looked around, realizing they weren't alone, and gestured for Sam to put her down. He reluctantly lowered her to the ground, and she smoothed her bloody dress with a nervous smile.

It was then Caius noticed blood on the sides of her face, hands, and bottom of her dress. That blood couldn't be from her chest, and he dreaded to know whose it was.

"I'm Stassi."

Rory crashed into her, throwing her arms around her shoulders, whispering something in her ear. Stassi hugged her back, nodding at whatever she said.

One by one, the rest of the group approached her, introducing themselves and thanking her for her selfless act as Sam stood beside her like a watchdog.

Adila approached last, and when she reached for Stassi's hand, the *Royal* turned to pure light. Sam grabbed Stassi and pushed her behind him, and Caius clutched his burning chest as Rory did the same, staring wide-eyed at his sister. *The new Lux Queen.*

He turned to Aemas, who said nothing. "What's happening?" Caius knew the answer, but he didn't understand it.

Adila's light extinguished, and she stared slack-jawed at her hands, twisting to look at Caius.

Aemas clasped his hands behind his back and walked toward them. "Gedeon is dead, and the Lux power must be passed on." Before anyone could ask why it passed to a *Royal* who already possessed a title, the *Seraph* said, "Caius is next in line, but the shadows live within him now, and the Umbra King is all he can ever be."

Caius looked at his hands, remembering the black void that held him captive. "Why didn't I die?"

Aemas scrutinized him like a bug under a magnifying glass. "Your hatred for your brother almost consumed your soul and hand-delivered you to Orcus," he said finally, and Rory clutched Caius' arm. "But love has always been the more powerful emotion of the two, and when your mate was in danger, your soul did whatever it had to in order to save her. I believe it forged your hatred into a weapon, and quite impressively, might I add."

"Why did the Umbra power skip Gedeon to begin with?" Adila questioned their maker. "If he was good enough for the Lux power, why was he not given the Umbra power from the start?"

The *Seraph's* eyes slanted to Caius and back to Adila with a sigh. "Your brothers were two halves of a whole. Their souls were once one, and when they split within your mother's womb, the soul did not split evenly." His dark eyes filled with something akin to remorse. "There was nothing we could do to change the course of Fate. Caius received the goodness of their soul, and Gedeon received the opposite."

Caius took the words like a blow to the chest. Even if it wasn't his fault, he still felt guilty for the unfair hand dealt to his brother at birth.

"Because of this," Aemas went on. "Moira skipped him, but when Atarah perished, they had no choice but to grant Gedeon the power."

"What happens to the Scales of Justice power now?" Dume asked. "Does Adila hold two positions?" The *Aatxe* had yet to move closer, and Caius didn't blame him. Aemas and Sam side-by-side were intimidating at best.

Aemas glanced at Rory, who afforded him a mere nod in response. Caius was stunned into silence at the implication.

"The power belongs to me," his mate said evenly, showing little emotion. *Like the Scales of Justice during a trial.*

"You're taking the news well," Lauren observed, crossing her arms with an amused grin.

Rory glanced at her and quirked a brow. "I have been acting as judge and jury for years. Sending black souls to hell is a job I gladly accept."

"If the Lux power is passed down the line, even if a *Royal* already holds a position," Caius asked, not fully understanding how all of this worked. "Why did the Lux power not go to me and the Umbra title to Gedeon when Atarah died?"

Aemas' wings ruffled with annoyance, almost revealing the rest of his face. "We don't know, and Moira doesn't explain herself to anyone."

"Who is Moira?" Rory asked, but everyone ignored her. She opened her mouth to say something else, but Aemas cut her off.

"It's time," he told Sam grimly, who refused to look at him.

"Will I be able to tell my family goodbye?" Stassi asked the *Seraph*.

What? Caius looked to Lauren, who shrugged back.

"I am sorry, Anastasia," Sam responded with enough grief and agony that Caius knew they would bear witness to a tragedy.

Stassi's breath hitched, and she clutched the bloody fabric over her chest. "Do you mean to leave me?"

The way they looked at each other, you'd think they were... "She's your *Aeternum*," Caius guessed, appalled at the prospect of his friend leaving his mate behind.

Rory, Adila, and Lauren made various noises of surprise, and Stassi's eyes glittered with tears. "I don't know what that means, but he said I'm Sam's mate," she said, pointing at Aemas. "And I know what a soulmate is."

"In a sense, yes," Aemas replied. "It was his mother's doing."

"Mother?" Rory parroted, and when Aemas nodded, she pointed accusingly at Sam. "The Coopers were right. You're the son." Her eyes moved to Lauren, who smirked back. "And you're the knight."

Aemas looked between Rory, Lauren, and Sam. "I don't know what you're talking about, and unfortunately, we don't have time to discuss it."

Caius noticed Aemas did not speak as formally as his son, and he regarded his friend with intrigue.

"Wait," Stassi interjected. "Why can't I go?"

"Because Sam signed a contract before leaving Aravoth," Aemas replied with a look of regret. It was apparent he didn't like the situation any more than they did. "And it would be cruel to put you through that pain."

She faltered and looked at her mate. "What contract?"

Caius watched the heartbreak unfold when Sam stepped forward and spoke softly. "I agreed that if I ever returned to the aether, I would marry a royal heir from one of the other nine kingdoms and take my place on the Aravoth throne."

Stassi recoiled and staggered back.

"Then don't return," Rory said hotly. Her hostility surprised Caius, and he instinctively moved forward to position himself between her and Sam. "She is your mate. Do you know what leaving will do to her?"

"*Do you know what it will do to me?*" Sam shouted back as he took a step forward.

The power within Caius registered Sam as a threat, and he attacked, slamming him to the ground. Sam could decimate him, but the need to protect his wife was stronger than fear.

"Never yell at her again," he warned with a dangerous edge to his voice. "Be thankful she cares for your mate enough to risk the wrath of a fucking *Seraph*."

Sam's blue eyes dimmed, and Caius watched the light

drain out of him. He stood and grabbed Sam's hand to haul him up.

"Your mate isn't the only one who will miss you," Caius said quietly. "We all will, and Vincula won't be the same without you."

Sam nodded. "I will miss you, too, brother."

Rory pushed Caius aside and threw her arms around Sam's middle. "I'm sorry I yelled at you."

When she let go, he smirked. "No, you are not."

Smiling with tears in her eyes, she lifted her middle finger, laughing when he grabbed it. His smile faded. "Take care of Caius."

"Take care of yourself," she returned and lowered her voice, briefly glancing at Stassi. "I'll make sure she is taken care of."

"Thank you," he replied and hugged her again. Rory saw Lauren approach out of her peripheral, and her heart sank. They came to the realms together. "Are you leaving, too?"

Lauren waved her off. "Nice try. You can't get rid of me that easily."

Rory's shoulders sagged with relief, and she stepped back to give the two *Angels* privacy. Well, the *Angel* and the *Seraph*, though technically, *Seraphim* were a type of *Angel*.

They spoke low, their words for only them to hear, and when Lauren backed away, Rory swore she saw a tear trail down her cheek.

Adila stepped forward next. "You stayed by my brother's side when I could not and believed me when you had no reason to. For that, you have my undying gratitude."

Caius shifted next to Rory, and she grabbed his hand, giving it a squeeze.

"You do not need to thank me," Sam replied. "Do not abandon him again."

Rory bit her tongue to keep from laughing. Sam was right to hold her accountable for the way she treated Caius. Adila's reasons were sound, but they were also weak. She could have found a way to communicate with Caius without Gedeon finding out, but she was a coward. At the very least, she shouldn't have stopped trying.

Dume was next, shaking Sam's hand as he thanked him for helping Rory. They didn't know each other well, but Dume held Sam in high regard and respected the *Seraph* tremendously.

With one last goodbye to their friend, they stepped into the hallway, allowing Sam and Stassi to say goodbye without prying eyes.

Everyone's heart should be granted the solace of breaking in private.

Aemas walked into the hallway and asked the group to rejoin them in the office.

He was still speaking, but Rory ignored him, unable to take her eyes off Sam and Stassi. They stared at each other like two star-crossed lovers, and Rory's heart stuttered in her chest.

"My son has revealed his true form, as have I. By decree of the Fates, the memories of all lesser mystics in both realms will be wiped of having ever seen us," Aemas announced, snagging Rory's attention.

Her mouth fell open, and Anastasia looked around. "I already lose my memory when I leave," she protested.

Sam closed his eyes at her words, and Rory lost the battle with her emotions. Tears streaked through the crusted blood on her face.

"Dear girl, I am truly sorry," Aemas apologized, looking genuinely upset. "You will not remember us, even within The Capital walls."

The look on Stassi's face would break the heart of the blackest soul. Her panicked eyes pleaded with the two *Seraphim.* "No. Please, don't do this. Don't make me forget him. I won't say anything; I swear it!"

Rory stepped forward and gently curled her arm around Stassi, pulling her to her chest.

Aemas brought his fist to his mouth, giving himself a minute before speaking again. "It is not my decision. But fear not because when your memories are gone, so will be your hurt."

Rory watched Sam flinch and look away when Stassi's legs gave out while she begged Aemas to change his mind.

She leaned into Rory, and they cried together, but where Stassi's pain would soon be gone, Rory's would stay, remembering this day for the rest of her immortal life.

Caius moved to stand beside them, drawing Sam's attention. "We'll meet you in the aether one day," he promised him, and Rory's heart broke more as she watched her mate lose his best friend.

With a final nod, Sam and his father disappeared, leaving the others to pick up the pieces.

CHAPTER 56

Rory glanced down at the dazed woman in her arms. "Stassi?"

She looked up, breathing hard and shielding her eyes against the bright sunlight streaming in through the tall windows. When Sam and Aemas left, they cleared the darkness Caius released upon the realms. It turned out that he didn't destroy the suns; he covered them.

"What happened?" the maid croaked.

Rory looked nervously at Lauren. Did Aemas wipe all her memories from today, or did they only erase Sam? "What do you remember?"

Stassi clamored out of Rory's lap, and her hand went to her chest. She cried out, ripping at her dress. "He stabbed me." Her hand moved across her skin, and she looked at Rory, bewildered. "I remember him stabbing me. I died!" she shrieked.

They only erased Sam. Got it. "You didn't die," she lied. "We gave you a potion to close your wound before you lost too much blood."

Stassi's wide eyes landed on Gedeon's lifeless body, and she screamed before puking on the floor. "Normal people don't wake up to dead bodies lying around like piles of laundry," she cried.

Rory glared at Caius when he smothered a laugh. "Stassi," he said gently, avoiding the vomit on the floor. "We're taking you to the infirmary."

They helped her stand on shaky legs, but she stopped dead when Dume asked Lauren where Keith and Patrick were.

Rory dropped Stassi's arm and looked back at Dume. "My dad and Keith came with you?"

"We split up," he explained. "Keith's job was to shift and try to find your scent. Your dad went with him."

"*What?*" she yelled. "They're missing, and you're just now saying something? What the fuck is wrong with you?"

"They're probably lost," Lauren said. "If they were caught, we'd know by now because someone would have to alert Gedeon."

Stassi started sobbing, and Caius tried to calm her down, but she pushed him away, shaking her head frantically. "A guard shot Keith." Her sobs came harder, and Rory's world tilted on its axis. "H-he died. His chest s-stopped moving, and his eyes..." Stassi stopped, unable to finish her sentence as she buried her head in her hands.

Dume took Stassi from Caius, and Rory felt her husband's arms wrap around her as she slid to the ground.

Keith was dead?

"Are you sure?" Lauren asked. "Did you see Patrick?"

Stassi nodded. "I had my hand pressed to Keith's chest to stop the bleeding, and he stopped breathing," she cried. "He died right in front of me. Patrick said he needed to get

Keith's body out of here so they wouldn't find it and hurt his family." Her arm swiped across her nose. "Patrick wasn't hurt, but the guards," she whimpered, and her eyes trailed to a dead body lying near Gedeon's desk, making her skin turn a paler shade of green. "They were dead when he left."

Rory's eyes were unseeing as the room closed in on her.

Her father was safe.

Keith was dead.

Her eyes found Dume's, and her chest fractured down the middle. *Keith was dead.*

Caius held her as she screamed, wishing Aemas was still here so she could ask him why.

"I knew you were a supermystic."

She would never see his beautiful blue soul again. Never hear one of his stupid jokes or be talked into drinking too much on a weeknight.

What would she tell Kordie and his parents?

Lauren led Stassi out of the office, and Dume approached Rory, crouching down to check on her.

"May I help you?" Adila asked someone at the door.

"I'm looking for my daughter," Rory's father said, searching the room. His eyes landed on her, and she watched his shoulders sag with relief. He jogged across the office and bent down next to Dume.

"Are you hurt?" he asked frantically, lightly touching her face. "Why is there so much blood?"

"I'm fine," she hiccupped, unable to say anything else. Blood stained his clothes, but he didn't look hurt. *It was probably Keith's.*

"We need to tell Adila where Keith's body is. She can have someone transport it to the city," Dume said to Patrick. "I'll call his parents and Kordie."

Rory sat up and forced herself to stop crying. "I should be the one to call Kordie."

Dume tried to stand, but Patrick grabbed his arm. "What are you two talking about?"

They stared at him.

"Stassi said Keith was killed," Caius told Rory's father. "And that you moved his body."

Patrick's eyes flared. "Keith is alive."

Rory burst into more tears, unsure how she had any left to shed.

"Where is he?" Caius asked. "She needs to see him." He stood and scooped Rory into his arms, and she continued to cry into his chest.

Patrick rose to his feet. "He's in the infirmary. He was shot while in wolf form," he explained to them as they walked. "I thought he was dead, but he had a faint pulse when I got to him. His body had shut down, making him seem dead. I picked him up and ran back the way we came until I passed a maid.

"The infirmary doesn't have an operating room, but they had scalpels and sutures. The bullet nicked an artery, and he would've bled out without surgery. I had to work with what I had."

"You performed surgery on a wolf?" Caius asked in disbelief. "Successfully?"

Patrick grinned over his shoulder. "I'm one of the best vets in Erdikoa, son."

"That's impressive," Caius replied and kissed the side of Rory's head.

When they arrived at the infirmary, Caius set her down, and she and Dume rushed to Keith's side. He was still in his shifted form, and when he saw them, his tail thumped against the bed. The wolf tried lifting his head, but it dropped back onto the mattress.

"Why can't he shift back?" Rory asked, petting him softly.

He licked her hand, and she pulled it back with a glare.

"His anatomy is different in wolf form," Patrick explained. "The artery needs to heal before he can shift. He'll be like this for a few weeks."

Keith blew air out of his nose with a tiny bark. "We thought you were dead," Rory said, petting him again, and he whined. "Stassi said she saw you die."

"Is she okay?" her father asked. "We almost got that poor girl killed. I wouldn't be able to live with myself if something happened to her."

Rory forced herself to not react. No one in the room other than the *Royals* remembered Sam, and it would be impossible to explain what happened. "She's alive but shaken up."

Keith's tail whacked harder, and Patrick looked skyward. "Thank the *Seraphim*."

If only they knew.

"She freed Cora's soul," Dume said quietly. Patrick's breath hitched, and he turned away to swipe at his eyes while Keith whined.

"We'll make sure she's taken care of for the rest of her life," Caius promised them.

Patrick nodded. "I look forward to getting to know you, son."

CHAPTER 57

Caius watched Rory pull a suitcase from under her bed and throw clothes inside like a madwoman. They were packing her things to leave first thing in the morning.

"This place is quaint," he said, folding her clothes into neat piles.

She threw a shirt at his head. "That's something rich people say about poor people's houses."

"You are a rich person," he reminded her. "I like it here. If your dad moves back to the city, this can be our Erdikoa home." A heap of clothes landed on top of his folded piles, and he frowned. "Why do you have so many clothes?"

"Or we can stay at my place in the judgment chambers now that I'm the Scales of Justice." She looked around and waved her hand over the piles of clothes. "I don't have that many." She must have forgotten she had an entire closet and dresser full at home. "Why do you have ten million sets of the same thing?" she shot back, looking pointedly at his shirt.

He moved his eyes from his outfit to her and winked. "I

look good in black." Caius grabbed the bottom of his shirt and untucked it. "I look even better out of it."

A pair of balled-up socks hit him in the stomach. "We don't have time for that, but yes, you do."

"Stop throwing clothes at me," he warned and placed the neatly folded piles of clothes into her suitcase, arranging them methodically by clothing type. Rory stood still, watching him, and he stopped. "What?"

"What are you doing?" she asked, pointing at the clothes.

He waved a hand over the piles. "I'm helping you pack."

"You pack like a serial killer," she replied, folding a pair of pants and throwing them onto a pile.

He stared at the mess she called folded clothes. "Clearly, I do not." Her stunned silence made him grin widely. "What's the matter, Miss Raven?"

"Is that still my name?" she asked. Stopping, he looked at her in question. "Raven," she clarified. "Is that still my last name? Do you even have a last name?"

"You will always be Miss Raven to me." The suitcase cover fell closed with a thud. "And no, *Royals* don't have last names until they relinquish their positions."

"And then what is it?" she pressed.

His eyes lifted to hers as the corner of his mouth pulled into a smile. "Ours will be Raven."

Patrick knocked on the bedroom door. "You can come in, Dad," she called out.

He pushed his way in, looked at Rory's sloppy pile of clothes, and shook his head. "I have a meeting with Dr. Waddingham in an hour."

"Dr. Waddingham from your old clinic?" she asked as she plopped on the edge of her bed.

"Yes." Leaning on the door frame, he sighed. "I quit the library yesterday. I'll miss the slow pace, but I'm more useful at the clinic."

"I think that's a good idea," she agreed. "You saved Keith's life in the middle of a shit show. That's not a talent you want to waste."

Caius noticed Patrick tapping an envelope against his palm. Rory looked expectantly at her father, and Caius thought he seemed nervous.

Patrick held out the envelope. "Can you give this to your mother?" Rory nodded wordlessly and took the paper gently. "There's nothing about Erdikoa in it," he promised Caius. "I want to tell her a few things while she's clear of mind."

Rory's hand tightened on the envelope, and her voice came out a little hoarse. "I'll give it to her." She placed the envelope in her suitcase and moved around the bed to peck Caius on the cheek. "I'm going to walk Dad out."

"I'll fix this," he said, referring to Rory's heap of shoes in the closet. He watched her follow her father down the stairs with a smile, thanking the *Seraphim* for her safety.

It'd been two days since everything had happened. Caius and Rory had returned to the safe house and slept off and on for close to thirty-six hours.

A word doesn't exist to explain the bone-deep exhaustion they felt. But even sleep didn't come easy. Rory often woke up screaming from nightmares of Gedeon's torture chamber.

Lauren immediately disappeared to Vincula, claiming that she needed to check on the legion and update Lenora and the others. Caius knew that wasn't the only reason; she needed alone time to deal with the loss of Sam.

They all did.

The hospital released Sera yesterday, and Rory wanted to see her before they went back to Vincula the next day. She insisted on seeing her immediately, but Caius reminded her she was half dead on her feet, and she reluctantly agreed to rest first.

He kept his mind occupied with his wife and her friends, doing what he could to help them after all the trauma his brother caused. It distracted him from his own problems, like confronting his sister and losing his best friend.

Adila was busy putting the Lux Palace back in order, which would take weeks, if not months, as well as finding time to help Rory adjust to her new position while adjusting to her own.

She found him before they left the palace and asked if they could talk, but he wasn't ready to have that conversation yet.

One thing he told her she could do to earn his forgiveness was to have the Crown's lab begin research on modifying the *Merrow* elixir to work on *Sibyls*. Adila expressed great interest in the idea and said she would press to have it finished as soon as possible. It was shameless to use her need for his forgiveness to get the project rolling, but he wanted it finished before Lenora's release from Vincula in a year.

In truth, he already forgave his sister, but it would take time to repair their relationship.

If the roles were reversed, he wouldn't have stopped looking for a way to contact her, but Adila wasn't him. Not everyone would put forth the same energy given to them. It didn't always mean they loved any less, just differently. He understood that, but it was still a hard truth to accept.

Caius zipped the second suitcase filled with her shoes

and rolled both bags into the hall. Rory appeared and reached for one, but he lightly popped the back of her hand.

"I'll carry these," he said, lifting them to go around her.

He readied himself for her retort. "I can carry my own suitcase," she insisted as he carried them downstairs.

"I know you can," he drawled when he returned. "But I'd rather you use your strength to ride me, not carry your ridiculous amount of clothing up the stairs."

"There's only one suitcase of clothes," she argued.

"Did you forget the four other boxes that are already in the car?" he asked her, relishing in the look of her plump lips as she pouted. "Let's go, little mate. The sooner we get out of here, the sooner I'll have you on your back."

The car pulled into Bruce's house, and Caius unfolded his long body from the backseat before offering Rory a hand. She wiped her sweaty palms on her jeans, nervous to see the condition Sera was in.

Dume said Bruce was hysterical when he found Sera chained to the bathroom sink. He hadn't heard from her in a few days and went to her house to check on her. When he knocked on her front door, he heard her faint yelling and used his spare key to get inside.

Rory couldn't imagine finding a loved one like that. Eager to see her friend, she knocked on Bruce's door and waited impatiently for him to answer.

When he opened the door and stepped aside to let them in, he reached out and squeezed Rory's arm. "She's been asking about you. Dume told her you'd come."

Caius' hand landed on the small of Rory's back as a show of support she desperately needed.

"She's in the guest room," Bruce said, pointing to a door down the hall.

They thanked him and made their way over. When Rory stepped inside, she gasped. Sera looked perfect. No cuts, no swelling, no bruises, no anything. She was talking animatedly with Dume, and when she saw them enter, she jumped up and threw herself into Rory's arms.

"I'm sorry," she blubbered, stepping away. "I couldn't fight him off, and he changed into me. He even sounded like me." Sera's voice wobbled. "He took my phone."

Rory reared back like she'd been slapped. "None of this is your fault. It's Gedeon's. Don't apologize for something you had no control over." She tugged Sera back into a hug. "You need to get back in bed."

When they were seated, Rory's eyes roamed Sera's body. "I'm glad he didn't hurt you."

Sera and Dume glanced at each other, and Rory stiffened. "He didn't, right?" She motioned to Sera. "I don't see any injuries." Another possibility sucked the air from her lungs.

"No," Sera said sharply, guessing the direction of Rory's thoughts. "Nothing like that, but I had severe bruising and cuts around my neck, wrists, and ankles. I had a few torn ligaments and a broken wrist from trying to break free."

Rory tried to look around the house without being obvious. Potions to heal immediately were extremely expensive. She'd planned on paying for whatever Sera and Keith needed, but she didn't know what that was yet. Her father promised to get her a list for Keith today, and she had planned to take stock of Sera's injuries during this visit.

Her guilt over not arranging it immediately ate at her, but Caius assured her they were stable and insisted she rest before going anywhere. He was right, but it didn't make her feel any better.

Dume read her mind and nodded toward Caius. "He made arrangements for the potions."

Rory flipped around to look at her husband. "You did?"

Reaching out, he tucked a strand of hair behind her ear. "I'd do anything for them," he said, sticking his hands in his pockets. "Because they'd do anything for you."

"Keith?" she asked, and he smiled.

"Yes. We were going to surprise you tonight."

Dume chuckled. "She would have made the arrangements for his care before the end of the day. We would've had to tell her, anyway."

She shrugged sheepishly.

"How long did Gedeon masquerade as you?" Caius asked Sera.

"Three or four days, I think," she replied. "My bathroom doesn't have windows, and I had to guess."

Rory thought of the times she saw Sera over the last week, remembering Sam's unease around her. Her face twisted in disgust. "Did you go dress shopping with Kordie and me?" Sera shook her head sadly, and Rory clenched her jaw. "That bastard watched me change."

The shadows in the room moved around them, and she wrapped her arm around Caius' waist. "He's dead."

The muscle in his jaw feathered. "I'd raise him from the dead to kill him again if I could."

Rory patted his arm reassuringly and turned back to her friends. "Sera, do you work at The Capital?"

"No," Sera answered, sounding confused. "I'm a receptionist at a pediatric clinic downtown. Why?"

"Gedeon said you did when he wore your skin," Rory replied bitterly. He'd fooled them all for far longer than he should have.

"Rory," Dume said sharply. "Don't upset her."

Sera started to protest but stopped when her attention snagged on Caius. "Rory failed to mention you had tattoos," she commented, squinting at his forearm. "They make your blood look black." There was nothing judgmental in her tone. In fact, she sounded impressed.

Caius lifted a hand and wiggled his fingers with a wry grin. The dark marks had receded some, but not all the way. The remaining black veins covered his hands, arms, torso, and neck. A few crept over his jawline, but barely.

"They weren't there before," Rory answered, taking his hand to graze her thumb over his knuckles. "But he knows I like tattoos."

He lifted her palm to his lips and planted a soft kiss on her wedding mark. "I would tattoo my entire body for her if she asked."

Dume stood and fussed with Sera's blanket to cover her legs, and to Rory's surprise, she let him. "I know you haven't seen her in days, but Sera needs her rest," he said, turning to them. "I'll bring her to dinner tonight."

Rory's brows rose as she looked from Dume to Sera, who watched Dume with adoration.

"We understand," Caius replied and steered Rory into the hall. "We'll see you tonight."

"You didn't tell me your friends all dated each other," Caius said when they stepped outside, leading her to the car with a hand placed protectively on the small of her back. "I wouldn't have dreamed of killing the *Aatxe* if you had."

Her eyes crinkled at the seriousness in his tone. "They weren't until now." She jumped into the backseat of their car before the driver could open her door. "Besides, I like it when you're jealous."

Caius didn't know how to drive, having been locked away for so long, and instead of learning, he insisted on hiring a driver while in Erdikoa. She hated driving anyway.

The privacy screen closed, and Caius slid her across the seat, pulling her into his lap to face him. "How much do you like it, Miss Raven?" His fingers lifted the bottom of her sundress and ran along the edge of her panties. "Shall we see?"

"We don't have time," she reminded him. "The phone store isn't far from Sera's house."

After Gedeon fried hers, she insisted on getting a new one to use while in Erdikoa. Caius refused one, spouting a lie about owning a phone already.

He pulled her mouth to his and slipped his fingers beneath the thin fabric of her underwear, groaning against her lips. "Always wet for me, like a good little mate." She instinctively moved her hips when his fingers slipped through her arousal and caressed her sensitive skin. "Would you like to ride my hand, dear wife?"

"Yes, please."

He withdrew his hand and flipped her around with ease, pulling her back to his chest. "I need proper access," he murmured and slid her panties down. "Open your thighs."

She obeyed, leaning her head back on his shoulder as his fingers moved across her skin and into her center. Sucking in a sharp breath, she raised her hips, urging him to push deeper.

"We don't have time to play," he said. "Only time to come. Can you do that for me?"

When she nodded, he nipped at her ear. "Good girl."

While he moved his fingers in and out of her, he reached his other hand under the neckline of her dress. "Are you not wearing a bra?" His voice was husky, and she felt his dick harden beneath her ass.

"I don't need to with this dress," she replied with a coy smile.

He hummed against her neck and licked his thumb, ghosting it over her hardened nipple. She slid her hand under her dress, needing to touch her clit, but he removed his own from between her legs and clamped down on her wrist. "Tell me what you need."

She whimpered at the loss of his touch. "I need to touch my clit."

After placing her hand on the seat beside them, he returned to her pussy, pushing inside with two fingers. "Allow me." Another cool caress moved across her skin, and when shadows moved over the area she longed to touch, her hips bucked involuntarily.

"Fuck, Caius." Her words were a mix of cries and moans as the shadows picked up speed in direct contrast with the slow movements of his hand.

His laugh rumbled against her back. "I will later, but for now, come for me."

The vibrations on her clit, along with his fingers stroking in and out, made her body spark with intense pleasure. She twisted her head and pulled his mouth to hers, moving faster against his hand. "That's it, baby," he murmured against her lips.

The shadows started to vibrate in a pattern that made her body tighten. After a short burst of quick touches, they buzzed harder with added pressure, sending her over the edge.

Rory's mouth opened in a silent scream, and Caius trailed his lips down her neck, biting lightly. Her release moved through her in waves, and her pussy clamped around his fingers as she came.

When her body went limp, he kissed her neck and moved her to the seat beside him. She reached for her panties, but he snatched them from the floorboard and stuffed them in his pocket with a sly smile.

Before she could protest, the car stopped, and he winked. "Perfect timing."

That night, Rory ran around the kitchen, inspecting the food spread across the island. "They're not going to care what the food looks like," Caius assured her.

"I've never met Tammy before," she muttered as she straightened a dish. "What if she thinks it's terrible?"

Caius walked around the island and pinned her arms to her sides. "She is married to Max. There's no way she has a judgmental bone in her body, and if the food isn't to her taste, she can take it up with the caterer."

He was right, but she wanted everything to be perfect. It sounded like a herd of cattle walked in the door, and she stuck her head around the corner to see their friends piling inside.

When she hurried through the dining room to greet them, the sight of Keith made her chest squeeze. His sandy blonde hair was perfectly styled, and his blue eyes twinkled with his wide smile.

Stepping forward, he held out his arms. "Come here, supermystic."

Her arms wrapped around his neck, refusing to let him go. The way she felt when Stassi told her he died was no different from watching Gedeon kill Cora all those years ago.

"You're the supermystic," she mumbled against his shoulder.

Kordie pulled Keith back and shoved him away to throw her arms around Rory's middle. "We're making a safe word," she declared as she stepped back. "That way, we know it's really us."

"I agree," Sera said from next to Dume, whose hand was clasped tightly in hers.

Rory heard Caius enter the room behind her and said, "I vote for *king*."

"Nice try," Caius replied, holding her against his chest as he lowered his voice. "If anyone hears that word leave your lips again, I will slaughter them where they stand."

Sera raised a brow and looked between the two. "Is there something we should know?"

"No," they said at the same time.

"We will figure out a word later," Dume said. "I'm starving."

Rory redirected them to the living room. "Not yet. I invited Max and his wife, Tammy."

A knock at the door filled her with nervous excitement, and Caius moved around her. "I'll answer it."

He opened the door and smiled kindly at the older

couple on the porch. "It's good to see you again, Max. Please, come in."

"You as well, Your Grace," Max replied, and in true fashion, didn't give the veins on Caius' arms a second glance. "This is my wife, Tammy."

"Call me Caius. We're friends now, not warden and inmate." He turned to Tammy. "It's lovely to meet you. Let me introduce you to my wife."

Rory smiled at the couple, and Max's eyes wrinkled as he returned the gesture. "Wife? I guess queen *is* a more appropriate job for you than a gardener."

She laughed and hugged him before holding her hand out to his wife. "I'm Rory."

The old woman hauled her into a hug with surprising strength. "None of that, now. I'm Tammy. This old geezer told me all about you."

Rory tried not to laugh but failed. "I'm glad you two came," she said, sweeping her arm toward the living room. "I'd like to introduce you to my friends."

CHAPTER 58

VINCULA

Saying goodbye to her friends and father in Erdikoa wasn't an emotional experience this time because Rory and Caius could pass between realms as they wished.

She didn't understand how he broke himself out of Vincula without breaking the barrier's hold on everyone else in the realms. When she asked him about it, he said he *'became one'* with his power and that the immeasurable amount of power flowing through him broke the bonds placed by his sister.

Whatever that meant.

Her nerves were live wires when she and her mate returned from Erdikoa. It'd been months since seeing her mother and years since having more than a day with her mother clear-minded.

Someone barreled into Rory from behind, wrapping her in a hug. "I'm sorry your boyfriend is a dumbass," Cat said, releasing Rory from her death grip.

Rory spun around with a loud laugh. "I didn't take you as a hugger," she teased.

Cat waved her off and motioned up and down Rory's body. "I make an exception when someone narrowly escapes death. I like your hair," she commented, inspecting Rory from head to toe. "We tried asking the commander for details, but that didn't work."

Rory's heart stopped. *When did they see Sam?* "Commander?"

Cat shot her a strange look. "Did they wipe your memory again? Lauren arrived before you two but wouldn't tell us anything."

Rory's heart restarted long enough to plummet to the ground. "Right. My brain is mush after the last few days. I promise to tell you all the gory details."

Kit skirted around Cat and side-hugged Rory uncomfortably. "You should tell my parents, too," she suggested. "They'll record it for the history books."

"They're great," Rory replied. "Your mother is something else."

Kit grinned widely. "I know. I heard they helped you."

She nodded and wondered how the Coopers remembered their encounter with their memory wiped of Sam. Rory thought it was unnecessary to wipe every lesser mystic's memory of him. She understood people in The Capital, but *everyone* seemed excessive.

Kit stepped aside, and Bellina appeared. She and Rory stared at each other before throwing their arms around one another in a tight embrace. "I missed you," her friend said with a sniffle.

Rory nodded. "Me too." When they separated, she

pulled Bellina's note from her pocket. "You helped more than you know."

Bellina unfolded the note and read it, smiling. "You still have this?"

Cat plucked the paper from Bellina's hands, scanning the note with a snort. "If Lauren finds out you called her an overgrown buzzard, she'll kill you." She handed the note back to Rory. "Burn it if you value Bellina's life."

Rory squeezed the note. Sam didn't deserve to be erased, and she hated Aemas for doing so.

"I was mad," Bellina said defensively. "But maybe you should burn it. Just in case."

"Oh, I saw Max and met his wife," she told them excitedly. "She's hilarious and Max's polar opposite."

The three looked at each other and back at her. "He remembered you?"

Caius lightly pinched Rory's back, his message clear. *They can't know.* "No, but Lauren and I convinced him to help with my memories. She gave him a little power boost, and it worked." *Not a lie.* "We're friends now." Also, not a lie.

"Did you know your mom can drink like a fish?" Cat asked. "She might be more fun than you."

Rory held her chest in mock offense. "How dare you!"

"They're right, dear," Lenora said from behind Rory, and she spun around to face her mother with a racing heart. "You have your father's alcohol tolerance, I'm afraid."

Rory couldn't hold back the emotions welling inside her, and when her mother opened her arms, she lost it. "Shh," her mother soothed as she rubbed her back.

Rory extracted herself from her mother's embrace and

swiped her nose with her sleeve. "Gross," Cat mumbled. "*Ouch*."

"It's not the time," Bellina scolded, making Lenora laugh.

"I see why they're your friends," her mother remarked affectionately. "They remind me of you."

She turned to Caius, who stood back, letting Rory have her reunion. "You aren't going to greet your mother-in-law after almost dying? Shame on you."

He looked at Lenora with a vast fondness, and Rory felt her love for him grow.

Lenora opened her arms for him, and he walked into her embrace, resting his chin on her head. "I told you I would save her, no matter what."

Rory's mother patted his back. "I know you did, but losing a son hurts just as much as losing a daughter. Don't do that to an old woman."

Caius smirked. "I'm older than you."

"What did I tell you about using that tone with me?" she chided, swatting his arm.

Rory bit her tongue to keep from laughing, wishing she'd been able to watch their relationship grow.

"When is the wedding?" Kit asked.

Caius stuck his right hand in his pocket, and Rory tucked hers behind her back. They were going to lie, but Lenora beat them to it.

"I'm afraid we missed it," Rory's mother told the others. "But we'll celebrate at the next Plenilune ball."

Caius and Rory stared at her. "How did you know?"

She raised a brow at the two. "A mother always knows. Now, come, we have much to talk about."

"Yeah, you promised us the details," Cat piped up.

Caius stood at Rory's side and grabbed her hand, bringing it to his lips. "I'll let you four catch up. I need to find Lauren."

She stood on her toes for a quick kiss and let him go. "We'll see you at dinner," she promised.

"Ladies," he said to the others. "Always a pleasure."

Bellina linked her arm with Rory's. "I say we all have a drink."

The others agreed, and as they left the palace, Rory's heart was bursting with happiness. She would enjoy her time with her friends while she could, and when they left, forgetting her, she would endure it.

Caius found Lauren speaking with one of the *Aatxe* under her command, and when she saw him, she dismissed the guard and approached Caius with a half-hearted smile.

"Glad you made it back in one piece," she said, glancing at the marks on his hands.

"I could say the same," he volleyed. "Surviving Gedeon is no easy feat."

She nodded and looked away. "He's an idiot and thought he could kill me with his light."

How she survived was a mystery to Caius, and he couldn't help but press her for details. "How is that possible?"

"Lesser *Angels* can only be killed by the power of a *Seraph* or a blade forged by a *Seraph*," she explained, but her answer left him to wonder what it took to kill a *higher Angel*.

"Thank the *Seraphim* for that. I couldn't handle losing you and Sam both."

"About that." She sighed and asked Caius to follow her. "We need to talk."

He trailed after her with a sinking feeling. "What is this about?"

"Not here," she said and waited for him before she continued to walk. When they entered his office, she sat in a chair facing his desk, and he took his place across from her. "I'm leaving Vincula."

"Why?" he asked, incredulous. "Aemas said nothing of your departure, and everyone remembers you." *Did she not want to stay?* "Who will lead the Vincula legion?"

"I will train the most capable *Aatxe* to replace Sam and me," she assured him. "They led the legion just fine before we arrived."

"You don't have to do this," Caius tried again. "We all miss Sam, and I can't lose you, too."

"You're not losing me," she countered. He sat back, listening intently. "Sam asked me to look after Stassi."

"Ahh. I can't argue with that," he conceded.

"No, you can't, but I'll see you when you visit."

"How will you protect her if she doesn't remember you?" he asked.

Lauren grinned. "I always find a way."

"I know you do. Rory plans on becoming friends with Stassi, too. After what she did for Cora, she insists on paying for whatever the woman needs." Rory planned to stalk her and 'run into her' often. He chuckled at his wife's determination.

Lauren stood and strolled toward the door. "We'll figure it out," she promised. "As for now, I will train new commanders and check in on Stassi every few days until I can leave Vincula permanently."

He rounded his desk and stuck out his hand. "We'll miss you around here, but I understand. When Rory finds out, she will probably demand you leave and take care of Sam's mate as soon as possible."

"I can't think of a more fitting queen," Lauren admitted with an affectionate smile.

Caius couldn't agree more.

CHAPTER 59

ERDIKOA

Rory, Caius, and Adila sat in a booth in Erdikoa, and Rory rested her hand on Caius' thigh, reminding him she was there to support him. It'd been weeks since the showdown with Gedeon, and Adila called Caius every day, asking to see him.

She understood her mate's hurt, but she also understood fear, and fear kept Adila on a tight leash for five-hundred years.

Rory insisted they meet in the city to ensure there were no interruptions while they spoke. With the changes happening in both realms, someone always needed them.

As they waited on their drinks, Caius asked Adila if they'd made any progress hunting down Gedeon's spies.

The day Gedeon died, Caius rounded up a few *Aatxe* guards and barked orders like a commander. He had experience running a palace, whereas Adila looked like a frightened bunny.

The trusted guards rounded up the non-*Aatxe* guards hired by Gedeon, forced a truth potion down their throats, and learned about a large number of spies the late king had stationed around the city.

A guard named Titus had the most information, and when he showed Caius where to find the files on all of Gedeon's spies, Rory was hurt to learn Fiona was one of them, but the biggest surprise was learning she was Nina's mother.

Adila rattled off the latest updates as Rory half listened, lost in her morose thoughts, and after their server brought their drinks, Adila cleared her throat loudly. "Thank you for agreeing to hear me out."

Caius drummed his fingers on the table, avoiding eye contact. "I know what you're going to say. I understand you think you had no choice." His eyes met hers. "But I'll never understand why you gave up as easily as you did."

The Lux Queen's face filled with shame. "I'm not you or Atarah," she admonished. "I've never fought back a day in my life, and I hate myself for it. I hate myself for accepting things as they were. I am not excusing my actions," she assured him. "I am asking for another chance to be the sister I should have been."

"Five-hundred years is a long time," he replied quietly. "It will take me longer than a few weeks to get over it."

"I know." Her eyes looked hopeful. "And I'm not asking you to get over it. I'm asking for a chance to make it up to you."

"You'll get one." He threw back his drink and signaled for another. "Just not right now."

"Rory?" a man's voice asked, and they turned to see a

handsome guy in his twenties with shaggy hair gawking at her.

Where did she recognize him from?

"How are you here?" he asked, and her eyes bulged when she realized who he was.

Wyll the virgin. Shit. Rory still used her alias in Erdikoa, pretending to be Aurora Raven's cousin, but she'd answered when he called her name. *Double shit.*

"I think you have me confused with someone else," she replied politely.

Wyll's eyes flicked to Adila, widened, and rolled back in his head. Caius shot to his feet, catching the man before he hit the ground. "Who is this?" he asked Rory.

She grimaced. "I slept with him not long before I was arrested."

He scowled and dropped Wyll like a sack of potatoes.

"Caius," Adila hissed, looking around as she scooted out of the booth. People were staring, and she lifted a hand. "We're fine. He got a little excited." Some turned away, but a few still watched curiously.

Wyll's eyes opened in a daze. "I fucked The Butcher." He turned to Adila. "And you're…"

Caius' eyes flashed, and he lifted his foot above Wyll's head. Rory reached out and forced her husband into the booth before he could stomp the poor guy to death. "Don't you dare."

Adila held out her hand to help Wyll up, and when he grabbed it, they both gasped.

He pushed himself into a sitting position, and his eyes almost popped out of his head as they ate up their surroundings. "How is this possible?" he whispered, turning his wide eyes to Adila. "What did you do to me?"

He and Adila were lost in their own world, and Caius glanced at Rory.

"We need to get him out of here," Rory told him sternly. "Help him walk out, but if you hurt him, I won't touch you for a week."

"You slept with him," Caius replied through clenched teeth. "I am fighting the urge to disembowel him."

She tried to rub the tension from her forehead. "You can't kill anyone who touched me before we met."

His brows rose. "You did."

"That's not the same," she said hotly. "She tried to kill me. Pick him up."

Wyll drank in his surroundings, his handsome face filled with child-like wonder. Rory knew that look.

Caius roughly grabbed him by the arm and dragged him to his feet. "Walk, or I'll kill you."

Wyll straightened, nodding as he stumbled alongside Caius. A man grabbed Rory's arm when she passed his table. "Do we need to call emergency services?"

Caius shoved Wyll forward and caught the man's wrist. "If you touch my wife again, I will break every bone in your hand." *For fuck's sake.*

Rory had convinced him to wear casual clothes today, and while she loved him in a t-shirt and jeans, the black veins covering his arms made him look menacing. He was going to give this innocent bystander a heart attack.

"Wyll is fine," Rory told the man with a polite smile. "He needs air. Thank you."

She pushed her husband forward as he glared at the concerned patron, and when they were outside, she threw her hands up. "What the hell is wrong with you?"

He rubbed a hand over his jaw. "I don't like people

touching what is mine." His eyes slid to Wyll. "No matter when it happened."

"We'll talk about this later," she warned him and turned to Wyll and Adila, who stared at each other intently.

"Adila, is he what I think he is?" Rory asked her. She remembered Wyll was a *Sylph* and eyed the Lux Queen up and down. It was probably an inappropriate time to ask what twisted *Sylph* ability she inherited from her *Aeternum*, and Rory made a mental note to ask later.

"Did you have grey-scale sight?" Adila asked Wyll, who nodded in response, confirming their suspicions. "And can you see color now?"

He nodded again, and Caius muttered, "You have got to be kidding me."

"Call the car," Adila said without looking away from her *Aeternum*. "We need to take him to The Capital."

Wyll finally came to his senses and held up his hands. "What is going on?"

Adila looked both ways down the sidewalk, ensuring no one was close enough to hear her. "I'm going to show you something, and then you must come with me to the Lux Palace."

He ruffled his hair and exhaled loudly. "Okay."

She pulled him to the side of the building and motioned to Rory and Caius. "Can you two cover us?"

They both moved to hide the other two from prying eyes, and Adila held out her hand, calling light into her palm. It twined around Wyll's fingers, and he stared at it in awe. "It's beautiful," he murmured.

"I am the Lux Queen," she whispered to him. "There is much we need to discuss."

Wyll glanced at Rory, and she nodded. "She's telling the

truth. My husband is the Umbra King," she said, pointing to Caius. "Show him."

Caius glared at her, and she glared right back in a battle of wills. "Fine," he reluctantly agreed and held out his hand, showcasing his ability.

"Aether," Wyll muttered under his breath. "I don't know if I'm losing my mind or if you're telling the truth." His expression softened at the pleading look on Adila's face. "Fuck it. I'll go."

The three *Royals* breathed a sigh of relief, and Rory called Caius' driver to pick them up.

Caius pulled her into his side and leaned down to murmur in her ear, "If you ever threaten to withhold your body from me again, I will make you suffer when you give it back." He licked the point of her ear, sending tingles to the apex of her thighs. "The next time we meet one of your past lovers, I will fuck you in front of him to stake my claim."

"We can hear you," Adila snapped.

Caius smirked, never taking his eyes off his wife. "Good."

After dropping Wyll and Adila off at The Capital, Rory and Caius stayed the night in Erdikoa instead of returning to Vincula right away. As they walked hand in hand down the sidewalk toward one of Rory's favorite restaurants for dinner, she did a double take at the man across the street.

Could it be him? Tapping Caius on the shoulder, she discreetly pointed, trying to stay calm. "Is that who I think it is?"

He followed her line of sight and chuckled when he saw

the other man. "I believe it is." She pressed a hand over her pounding heart, and Caius gently tugged her forward. "We can say hi."

Her stomach did somersaults, and once they crossed the street, she jogged after the guy, leaving Caius behind as she called out to him. "Hey!"

He turned, and his messy hair and goofy grin made her heart stop. "Yeah?"

When she reached him, she ran a hand nervously through her hair. "I know you don't remember me, but we've met before, and you promised we'd hang out. You never gave me your number."

Turning to her fully, he crossed his arms with a smirk. "How do you know I don't remember you?"

"What's my name?" she challenged, mirroring his stance with a popped brow.

He narrowed his eyes at her and then laughed, shaking his head. "You got me."

She stuck out her hand with a smile so big her cheeks hurt. "I'm Lo, and that's my husband, Caius." She jerked her thumb over her shoulder toward Caius as he approached.

The man looked at her mate's bare arms and whistled. "Nice tats, man." His gaze slid back to Rory, and he shook her outstretched hand with a smile. "I'm Asher."

EPILOGUE

VINCULA

Caius thanked Lora for the gift he'd been given as he stared at Rory. She looked exquisite in a black dress, and her blood-red lips had him coming apart at the seams for a simple kiss. He slipped the Umbra ring on her right middle finger and succumbed to his desires, pressing his lips to hers.

Her palm pressed against his chest, and when he leaned back, she slid a simple obsidian band on his finger. The swelling in his chest overwhelmed him, and he grabbed both sides of her neck to kiss her again.

She was his everything, and if anyone tried to take her from him, the realms wouldn't survive him again.

"I have a gift for you," she informed him with a coy smile and signaled for Bellina to hand her a package.

"You didn't tell me we were exchanging gifts," he replied, carefully taking the box from her.

"It's nothing much. Just something that not even magic could make me forget."

He bit back a smile and dropped his voice for only her to hear. "Is it your dress from our first Plenilune?"

She smacked him on the shoulder, making him laugh, and when he removed the wrapping paper and lifted the lid, the simple object within the box made him love her even more.

Reaching inside, he pulled out a red bowl.

SAM AND STASSI'S STORY:
SILENCED FATE

Sam and Stassi's story is a standalone novel in the **Realms of the Aether** universe.

Below is a small excerpt from their book that takes place directly after the epilogue of *Aeternum*, followed by the official blurb.

~

Excerpt:

Stassi stared at the myriad of cookies adorning the shelves as she meandered down the aisle of Grab and Go, a little convenience store near her home.

"Back again?" a familiar voice asked.

Koda, a stock boy in his late teens, stood behind her with a cart full of cookies to be restocked.

She motioned to the shelves. "I forgot cookies."

The kid waved a package of vanilla wafers in front of her face. "Try these," he suggested. "They're my favorite."

She plucked them from his hand and tossed them into

her basket. "Thanks." Sighing, she scanned the shelves one more time.

Koda shoved more cookies onto the shelves with a long look in her direction. "Are you sure you're okay? You've come in at least three times a week for almost two months."

A pang of sadness hit her in the chest, and her vision blurred. She blindly reached for another bag of cookies and threw them into her basket. "I forget things," she lied.

She'd never been good at lying before, but now she was an expert.

He looked from her to the four packages of cookies in her basket. "Okay."

With a small wave, she turned on her heel and trudged toward the checkout lane. "See you in a few days," Koda called after her.

As she stood in line, she surveyed the impulse buy items stacked next to the conveyer belt, and when it was her turn, Verlon, the cashier, smiled. "Hey, Stassi."

She hoisted her basket onto the belt. "Hey. Busy night?"

"Not really," he replied. "You could have been out of here faster if you'd gone to Alani's line." He tipped his head toward the checkout counter next to his.

Her face dropped. She wanted to tell him to mind his business, but he didn't deserve that. Still, everyone knew she only used this checkout counter, no matter how long the line was.

After paying, she quickly grabbed her things. "Thanks."

Verlon smiled kindly, or maybe it was pity she saw. "See you soon."

The night air hit her when she pushed through the door, and she looked to the sky. She hated lying to Koda when he asked why she was back. What was she supposed to tell him?

No one would believe the truth, and no matter how hard she tried, she couldn't stay away from this place.

She no longer worked at the palace, and Grab and Go was the only place she had left that reminded her of the man they tried to make her forget.

With one last look at the sky, she whispered, "Be happy, Commander."

Because one of them had to be.

~

Blurb:

Sam

When Samyaza violates his agreement with the Fates, he must return to the Aether and face the consequences, leaving his mate, Anastasia, behind.

Upon his return, he is forced to choose a royal bride from another kingdom before taking his rightful place as the King of Aravoth, resigning himself to a life of loveless misery.

When a princess vying for the Aravoth throne notices Sam watching over his mate in the Hall of Fates, she knows he will never love another while pining after a mortal in another realm. After kidnapping and imprisoning Anastasia, the princess sets in motion her plans to secure her place as queen.

When Fate cuts off his access to watch Anastasia from afar, Sam distracts himself by courting bridal candidates from across the Aether. But when he stumbles upon a mysterious woman named Arielle imprisoned in a neighboring kingdom, he is inexplicably drawn to her.

After freeing Arielle, they form a friendship that transforms into something more. Unwilling to put her through the pain and degradation of becoming a mistress and ravaged by the guilt of wanting someone other than his mate, he ends their relationship, breaking both of their hearts.

Anastasia

Stolen from her home and forced to hide her identity by masquerading as a woman named Arielle, Anastasia is tormented by seeing Sam every day, knowing they can never be together.

When he finally chooses a bride that isn't her, she begs the Fates to send her to the final resting place to end her suffering. As she stands on the precipice of life and death, the Fates agree to grant her last wish: That Sam marries someone who will make him happy.

When Sam hears of her sacrifice, no entity in the universe can stop his wrath. Not even the Fates themselves.

A Little Mermaid retelling like you've never seen before, Silenced Fate is a steamy adult fantasy romance with humor, heartbreak, and a happily ever after.

EMPLOYEE OF THE MONTH

Get your own Erdikoa Meat Co. Employee of the Month shirt!

Order the hoodie below.

T-shirts available

ABOUT THE AUTHOR

"I regret nothing. The End."
-Ron Swanson

LET'S CONNECT!

TikTok

@jah.hdj.books

Instagram

@jah.hdj.books

Facebook Group

www.facebook.com/groups/jamieapplegatehunter.com

Website

www.jamieapplegatehunter.com

ACKNOWLEDGMENTS

I want everyone to know that my husband finally read The Umbra King and laughed at one point, proving that I am, in fact, funny.

A huge thank you to my beta readers. The amount of voice messages, text messages, and emails sent back and forth is enough to drive anyone insane, but somehow, y'all still talk to me. I stand by the statement that my books would not be readable without betas, and I appreciate y'all more than you know.

I'd also like to thank everyone at Brower Literary and Management for being patient and a pleasure to work with. I can't wait to do great things with you in the future.

As always, thank you to anyone who took a chance and read my work, even if you hated it.

CONTENT WARNINGS

Not suitable for those under 18. Contains mature language and situations.

Graphic violence and death; loss of a family member; a vigilante serial killer; explicit sex scenes, memory loss, torture

Brief mention of sexual assault, attempted rape, and child abuse in reference to why inmates are sentenced to hell and how the heroine saved someone from potential sexual assault.

Printed in the USA
CPSIA information can be obtained
at www.ICGtesting.com
LVHW05225308 0124
768489LV00035B/173